FIFTY SHADES DARKER

FIFTY SHADES DARKER

E L James

WINDSOR
PARAGON

First published in the UK 2012
by Arrow Books
This Large Print edition published 2012
by AudioGO Ltd
by arrangement with
The Random House Group Ltd

Hardcover   ISBN: 978 1 4713 0503 0
Softcover   ISBN: 978 1 4713 0504 7

The author published an earlier serialised version
of this story online with different characters as
Master of the Universe under the pseudonym
Snowqueen's Icedragon.

Printed and bound in Great Britain by the MPG Books Group

For Z and J
You have my unconditional love, always

ACKNOWLEDGMENTS

I owe a huge debt of gratitude to Sarah, Kay, and Jada. Thank you for all that you have done for me.

Also, HUGE thanks to Kathleen and Kristi, who stepped into the breach and sorted stuff out.

Thank you, too, to Niall, my husband, my lover, and my best friend (most of the time).

And a big shout-out to all the wonderful, wonderful women from all over the world whom I have had the pleasure of meeting since I started all this, and whom I now consider friends, including: Ale, Alex, Amy, Andrea, Angela, Azucena, Babs, Bee, Belinda, Betsy, Brandy, Britt, Caroline, Catherine, Dawn, Gwen, Hannah, Janet, Jen, Jenn, Jill, Kathy, Katie, Kellie, Kelly, Liz, Mandy, Margaret, Natalia, Nicole, Nora, Olga, Pam, Pauline, Raina, Raizie, Rajka, Rhian, Ruth, Steph, Susi, Tasha, Taylor, and Una. And also to the many talented, funny, warm women (and men) I have met online. You know who you are.

Thanks to Morgan and Jenn for all things Heathman.

And finally, thank you to Janine, my editor. You rock. That is all.

PROLOGUE

He's come back. Mommy's asleep or she's sick again.

I hide and curl up small under the table in the kitchen. Through my fingers I can see Mommy. She is asleep on the couch. Her hand is on the sticky green rug, and he's wearing his big boots with the shiny buckle and standing over Mommy shouting.

He hits Mommy with a belt. *Get up! Get up! You are one fucked-up bitch. You are one fucked-up bitch. You are one fucked-up bitch. You are one fucked-up bitch. You are one fucked-up bitch. You are one fucked-up bitch.*

Mommy makes a sobbing noise. *Stop. Please stop.* Mommy doesn't scream. Mommy curls up small.

I have my fingers in my ears, and I close my eyes. The sound stops.

He turns and I can see his boots as he stomps into the kitchen. He still has the belt. He is trying to find me.

He stoops down and grins. He smells nasty. Of cigarettes and drink. *There you are, you little shit.*

*   *   *

A chilling wail wakes him. *Christ!* He's drenched in sweat and his heart is pounding. *What the fuck?* He sits bolt upright in bed and puts his head in hands. *Fuck. They're back. The noise was me.* He takes a

ix

deep steadying breath, trying to rid his mind and nostrils of the smell of cheap bourbon and stale Camel cigarettes.

CHAPTER ONE

I have survived Day Three Post-Christian, and my first day at work. It has been a welcome distraction. The time has flown by in a haze of new faces, work to do, and Mr. Jack Hyde. Mr. Jack Hyde . . . he smiles down at me, his blue eyes twinkling, as he leans against my desk.

'Excellent work, Ana. I think we're going to make a great team.'

Somehow, I manage to curl my lips upward in a semblance of a smile.

'I'll be off, if that's okay with you,' I murmur.

'Of course, it's five thirty. I'll see you tomorrow.'

'Good night, Jack.'

'Good night, Ana.'

Collecting my bag, I shrug on my jacket and head for the door. Out in the early evening air of Seattle, I take a deep breath. It doesn't begin to fill the void in my chest, a void that's been present since Saturday morning, a painful hollow reminder of my loss. I walk toward the bus stop with my head down, staring at my feet and contemplating being without my beloved Wanda, my old Beetle . . . or the Audi.

I shut the door on that thought immediately. No. Don't think about him. Of course, I can afford a car—a nice, new car. I suspect he has been overgenerous in his payment, and the thought leaves a bitter taste in my mouth, but I dismiss it and try to keep my mind as numb and as blank as possible. I can't think about him. I don't want to start crying again—not out on the street.

The apartment is empty. I miss Kate, and I

imagine her lying on a beach in Barbados sipping a cool cocktail. I turn on the flat-screen television so there's noise to fill the vacuum and provide some semblance of company, but I don't listen or watch. I sit and stare blankly at the brick wall. I am numb. I feel nothing but the pain. How long must I endure this?

The door buzzer startles me from my anguish, and my heart skips a beat. Who could that be? I press the intercom.

'Delivery for Ms. Steele.' A bored, disembodied voice answers, and disappointment crashes through me. I listlessly make my way downstairs and find a young man noisily chewing gum, holding a large cardboard box, and leaning against the front door. I sign for the package and take it upstairs. The box is huge and surprisingly light. Inside are two dozen long-stemmed, white roses and a card.

> *Congratulations on your first day at work.*
> *I hope it went well.*
> *And thank you for the glider. That was very thoughtful.*
> *It has pride of place on my desk.*
> *Christian*

I stare at the typed card, the hollow in my chest expanding. No doubt, his assistant sent this. Christian probably had very little to do with it. It's too painful to think about. I examine the roses— they are beautiful, and I can't bring myself to throw them in the trash. Dutifully, I make my way into the kitchen to hunt down a vase.

*   *   *

2

And so a pattern develops: wake, work, cry, sleep. Well, try to sleep. I can't even escape him in my dreams. Gray burning eyes, his lost look, his hair burnished and bright all haunt me. And the music . . . so much music—I cannot bear to hear any music. I am careful to avoid it at all costs. Even the jingles in commercials make me shudder.

I have spoken to no one, not even my mother or Ray. I don't have the capacity for idle talk now. No, I want none of it. I have become my own island state. A ravaged, war-torn land where nothing grows and the horizons are bleak. Yes, that's me. I can interact impersonally at work, but that's it. If I talk to Mom, I know I will break even further—and I have nothing left to break.

*   *   *

I am finding it difficult to eat. By lunchtime on Wednesday, I manage a cup of yogurt, and it's the first thing I've eaten since Friday. I am surviving on a newfound tolerance for lattes and Diet Coke. It's the caffeine that keeps me going, but it's making me anxious.

Jack has started to hover over me, irritating me, asking me personal questions. What does he want? I'm polite, but I need to keep him at arm's length.

I sit and begin trawling through a pile of correspondence addressed to him, and I'm pleased with the distraction of menial work. My e-mail pings, and I quickly check to see who it's from.

Holy shit. An e-mail from Christian. *Oh no, not here . . . not at work.*

3

From: Christian Grey
Subject: Tomorrow
Date: June 8 2011 14:05
To: Anastasia Steele

Dear Anastasia

Forgive this intrusion at work. I hope that it's going well. Did you get my flowers?

I note that tomorrow is the gallery opening for your friend's show, and I'm sure you've not had time to purchase a car, and it's a long drive. I would be more than happy to take you—should you wish.

Let me know.

Christian Grey
CEO, Grey Enterprises Holdings, Inc.

Tears swim in my eyes. I hastily leave my desk and bolt to the restroom to escape into one of the stalls. José's show. I'd forgotten all about it, and I promised him I'd go. Shit, Christian is right; how am I going to get there?

I clutch my forehead. Why hasn't José phoned? Come to think of it—why hasn't anyone phoned? I've been so absentminded I haven't noticed that my cell phone has been silent.

Shit! I am such an idiot! I still have it set to forward calls to the BlackBerry. Holy hell. Christian's been getting my calls—unless he's just thrown the BlackBerry away. How did he get my e-mail address?

4

He knows my shoe size; an e-mail address is hardly going to present him with many problems.

Can I see him again? Could I bear it? Do I want to see him? I close my eyes and tilt my head back as grief and longing lance through me. Of course I do.

Perhaps—perhaps I can tell him I've changed my mind . . . No, no, no. I cannot be with someone who takes pleasure in inflicting pain on me, someone who can't love me.

Torturous memories flash through my mind— the gliding, holding hands, kissing, the bathtub, his gentleness, his humor, and his dark, brooding, sexy stare. I miss him. It's been five days, five days of agony that has felt like an eternity. I cry myself to sleep at night, wishing I hadn't walked out, wishing that he could be different, wishing that we were together. How long will this hideous overwhelming feeling last? I am in purgatory.

I wrap my arms around my body, hugging myself tightly, holding myself together. I miss him. I really miss him . . . I love him. Simple.

Anastasia Steele, you are at work! I must be strong, but I want to go to José's show, and deep down, the masochist in me wants to see Christian. Taking a deep breath, I head back to my desk.

From: Anastasia Steele
Subject: Tomorrow
Date: June 8 2011 14:25
To: Christian Grey

Hi Christian

Thank you for the flowers; they are lovely.

Yes, I would appreciate a lift.

Thank you.

Anastasia Steele
Assistant to Jack Hyde, Editor, SIP

Checking my phone, I find that it is still set to forward calls to the BlackBerry. Jack is in a meeting, so I quickly call José.

'Hi, José. It's Ana.'

'Hello, stranger.' His tone is so warm and welcoming it's almost enough to push me over the edge again.

'I can't talk long. What time should I be there tomorrow for your show?'

'You're still coming?' He sounds excited.

'Yes, of course.' I smile my first genuine smile in five days as I picture his broad grin.

'Seven thirty.'

'See you then. Good-bye, José.'

'Bye, Ana.'

From: Christian Grey
Subject: Tomorrow
Date: June 8 2011 14:27
To: Anastasia Steele

Dear Anastasia

What time shall I pick you up?

Christian Grey
CEO, Grey Enterprises Holdings, Inc.

From: Anastasia Steele
Subject: Tomorrow
Date: June 8 2011 14:32
To: Christian Grey

José's show starts at 7:30. What time would you suggest?

Anastasia Steele
Assistant to Jack Hyde, Editor, SIP

From: Christian Grey
Subject: Tomorrow
Date: June 8 2011 14:34
To: Anastasia Steele

Dear Anastasia

Portland is some distance away. I shall pick you up at 5:45.

I look forward to seeing you.

Christian Grey
CEO, Grey Enterprises Holdings, Inc.

From: Anastasia Steele
Subject: Tomorrow
Date: June 8 2011 14:38
To: Christian Grey

See you then.

Anastasia Steele
Assistant to Jack Hyde, Editor, SIP

Oh my. I'm going to see Christian, and for the first time in five days, my spirits lift a fraction and I allow myself to wonder how he's been.

Has he missed me? Probably not like I've missed him. Has he found a new submissive? The thought is so painful that I dismiss it immediately. I look at the pile of correspondence I need to sort for Jack and tackle it as I try to push Christian out of my mind once more.

That night in bed, I toss and turn, trying to sleep and it's the first time in a while I haven't cried myself to sleep.

In my mind's eye, I visualize Christian's face the last time I saw him as when I left. His tortured expression haunts me. I remember he didn't want me to go, which was odd. Why would I stay when things had reached such an impasse? We were each skirting around our own issues—my fear of punishment, his fear of . . . what? Love?

Turning on my side, I hug my pillow, filled with an overwhelming sadness. He thinks he doesn't deserve to be loved. Why does he feel that way? Does it have to do with his upbringing? His birth mom, the crack whore? My thoughts plague me into the early hours until eventually I fall into a fitful, exhausted sleep.

*   *   *

The day drags and drags and Jack is unusually attentive. I suspect it's due to Kate's plum dress and the black high-heeled boots I've stolen from her closet, but I don't dwell on the thought. I resolve to go clothes shopping with my first paycheck. The dress is looser on me than it was, but I pretend not to notice.

Finally it's five thirty, and I collect my jacket and purse, trying to quell my nerves. *I'm going to see him!*

'Do you have a date tonight?' Jack asks as he strolls past my desk on his way out.

'Yes. No. Not really.'

He raises an eyebrow, his interest clearly piqued. 'Boyfriend?'

I flush. 'No, a friend. An ex-boyfriend.'

'Maybe tomorrow you'd like to come for a drink after work. You've had a stellar first week, Ana. We should celebrate.' He smiles and an unknown, unsettling emotion flits across his face, making me uneasy.

Putting his hands in his pockets, he saunters through the double doors. I frown at his retreating back. Drinks with the boss, is that a good idea?

I shake my head. I have an evening of Christian Grey to get through first. How am I going to do this? I hurry into the restroom to make last-minute adjustments.

In the large mirror on the wall, I take a long, hard look at my face. I'm my usual pale self, dark circles around my too-large eyes. I look gaunt, haunted. I wish I knew how to use makeup. I apply some mascara and eyeliner and pinch my cheeks, hoping for some color. Tidying my hair so that it hangs artfully down my back, I take a deep breath. This will have to do.

Nervously I walk through the foyer with a smile and a wave to Claire at Reception. I think she and

I could become friends. Jack is talking to Elizabeth as I head for the doors. Smiling broadly, he hurries over to open them for me.

'After you, Ana,' he murmurs.

'Thank you.' I smile, embarrassed.

Outside on the curb, Taylor is waiting. He opens the rear door of the car. I glance hesitantly at Jack, who has followed me out. He's looking toward the Audi SUV in dismay.

I turn and climb into the back, and there he sits—Christian Grey—wearing his gray suit, no tie, white shirt open at the collar. His gray eyes are glowing.

My mouth dries. He looks glorious except he's scowling at me. *Why?*

'When did you last eat?' he snaps as Taylor closes the door behind me.

Crap. 'Hello, Christian. Yes, it's nice to see you, too.'

'I don't want your smart mouth now. Answer me.' His eyes blaze.

Holy shit. 'Um . . . I had a yogurt at lunchtime. Oh—and a banana.'

'When did you last have a real meal?' he asks acidly.

Taylor slips into the driver's seat, starts the car, and pulls out into the traffic.

I glance up and Jack is waving at me, though how he can see me through the dark glass, I don't know. I wave back.

'Who's that?' Christian snaps.

'My boss.' I peek up at the beautiful man beside me, and his mouth is pressed into a hard line.

'Well? Your last meal?'

'Christian, that really is none of your concern,' I

10

murmur, feeling extraordinarily brave.

'Whatever you do concerns me. Tell me.'

No, it doesn't. I groan in frustration, rolling my eyes heavenward, and Christian narrows his eyes. And for the first time in a long time, I want to laugh. I try hard to stifle the giggle that threatens to bubble up. Christian's face softens as I struggle to keep a straight face, and a trace of a smile kisses his lovely sculptured lips.

'Well?' he asks, his voice softer.

'Pasta *alla vongole,* last Friday,' I whisper.

He closes his eyes as fury, and possibly regret, sweeps across his face. 'I see,' he says, his voice expressionless. 'You look like you've lost at least five pounds, possibly more since then. Please eat, Anastasia,' he scolds.

I stare down at the knotted fingers in my lap. Why does he always make me feel like an errant child?

He shifts and turns toward me. 'How are you?' he asks, his voice still soft.

Well, I'm shit, really . . . I swallow. 'If I told you I was fine, I'd be lying.'

He inhales sharply. 'Me, too,' he murmurs and reaches over and clasps my hand. 'I miss you,' he adds.

Oh no. Skin against skin.

'Christian, I—'

'Ana, please. We need to talk.'

I'm going to cry. No. 'Christian, I . . . please . . . I've cried so much,' I whisper, trying to keep my emotions in check

'Oh, baby, no.' He tugs my hand, and before I know it I'm on his lap. He has his arms around me, and his nose is in my hair. 'I've missed you so much,

11

Anastasia,' he breathes.

I want to struggle out of his hold, to maintain some distance, but his arms are wrapped around me. He's pressing me to his chest. I melt. Oh, this is where I want to be.

I rest my head against him, and he kisses my hair repeatedly. This is home. He smells of linen, fabric softener, body wash, and my favorite smell— Christian. For a moment, I allow myself the illusion that all will be well, and it soothes my ravaged soul.

A few minutes later Taylor pulls to a stop at the curb, even though we're still in the city.

'Come'—Christian shifts me off his lap—'we're here.'

What?

'Helipad—on the top of this building.' Christian glances toward the building by way of explanation.

Of course. *Charlie Tango.* Taylor opens the door and I slide out. He gives me a warm, avuncular smile that makes me feel safe. I smile back.

'I should give you back your handkerchief.'

'Keep it, Miss Steele, with my best wishes.'

I blush as Christian comes around the car and takes my hand. He looks quizzically at Taylor, who stares impassively back at him, revealing nothing.

'Nine?' Christian says to him.

'Yes, sir.'

Christian nods as he turns and leads me through the double doors into the grandiose foyer. I revel in the feel of his hand and his long, skilled fingers curled around mine. The familiar pull is there—I'm drawn, Icarus to his sun. I've been burned already, and yet here I am again.

Reaching the elevators, he presses the 'call' button. I peek up at him, and he's wearing his enigmatic half smile. As the doors open, he releases my hand and ushers me in.

The doors close and I risk a second peek. He glances down at me, and it's there in the air between us, that electricity. It's palpable. I can almost taste it, pulsing between us, drawing us together.

'Oh my,' I gasp as I bask briefly in the intensity of this visceral, primal attraction.

'I feel it, too,' he says, his eyes clouded and intense.

Desire pools dark and deadly in my groin. He clasps my hand and grazes my knuckles with his thumb, and all my muscles clench tightly, deliciously, deep inside me.

How can he still do this to me?

'Please don't bite your lip, Anastasia,' he whispers.

I gaze up at him, releasing my lip. I want him. Here, now, in the elevator. How could I not?

'You know what it does to me,' he murmurs.

Oh, I still affect him. My inner goddess stirs from her five-day sulk.

Abruptly the doors open, breaking the spell, and we're on the roof. It's windy, and despite my black jacket, I'm cold. Christian puts his arm around me, pulling me into his side, and we hurry across to where *Charlie Tango* stands in the center of the helipad, with its rotor blades slowly spinning.

A tall, blond, square-jawed man in a dark suit leaps out and, ducking low, runs toward us. Shaking hands with Christian, he shouts above the noise of the rotors.

'Ready to go, sir. She's all yours!'

'All checks done?'

'Yes, sir.'

'You'll collect her around eight thirty?'

'Yes, sir.'

'Taylor's waiting for you out front.'

'Thank you, Mr. Grey. Safe flight to Portland. Ma'am.' He salutes me. Without releasing me, Christian nods, ducks down, and leads me to the helicopter door.

Once inside he buckles me firmly into my harness, cinching the straps tight. He gives me a knowing look and his secret smile.

'This should keep you in your place,' he murmurs. 'I must say I like this harness on you. Don't touch anything.'

I flush a deep crimson, and he runs his index finger down my cheek before handing me the headphones. *I'd like to touch you, too, but you won't let me.* I scowl. Besides, he's pulled the straps so tight I can barely move.

He sits in his seat and buckles himself in, then starts running through all his preflight checks. He's just so competent. It's very alluring. He puts on his headphones and flips a switch and the rotors speed up, deafening me.

Turning, he gazes at me. 'Ready, baby?' His voice echoes through the headphones.

'Yes.'

He grins his boyish grin. Wow—I've not seen it for so long.

'Sea-Tac tower, this is *Charlie Tango* Golf—Golf Echo Hotel, cleared for takeoff to Portland via PDX. Please confirm, over.'

The disembodied voice of the air traffic controller answers, issuing instructions.

'Roger, tower, *Charlie Tango* set, over and out.'

14

Christian flips two switches, grasps the stick, and the helicopter rises slowly and smoothly into the evening sky.

Seattle and my stomach drop away from us, and there's so much to see.

'We've chased the dawn, Anastasia, now the dusk,' his voice comes through on the headphones. I turn and gape at him in surprise.

What does this mean? How is it that he can say the most romantic things? He smiles, and I can't help my shy smile.

'As well as the evening sun, there's more to see this time,' he says.

The last time we flew to Seattle it was dark, but this evening the view is spectacular, literally out of this world. We're up among the tallest buildings, going higher and higher.

'Escala's over there.' He points toward the building. 'Boeing there, and you can just see the Space Needle.'

I crane my head. 'I've never been.'

'I'll take you—we can eat there.'

'Christian, we broke up.'

'I know. I can still take you there and feed you.' He glares at me.

I shake my head and decide not to antagonize him. 'It's very beautiful up here, thank you.'

'Impressive, isn't it?'

'Impressive that you can do this.'

'Flattery from you, Miss Steele? But I'm a man of many talents.'

'I'm fully aware of that, Mr. Grey.'

He turns and smirks at me, and for the first time in five days, I relax a little. Perhaps this won't be so bad.

'How's the new job?'

'Good, thank you. Interesting.'

'What's your boss like?'

'Oh, he's okay.' How can I tell Christian that Jack makes me uncomfortable? Christian glances at me.

'What's wrong?' he asks.

'Aside from the obvious, nothing.'

'The obvious?'

'Oh, Christian, you really are very obtuse sometimes.'

'Obtuse? Me? I'm not sure I appreciate your tone, Miss Steele.'

'Well, don't, then.'

His lips twitch into a smile. 'I have missed your smart mouth, Anastasia.'

I gasp and I want to shout, *I've missed you—all of you—not just your mouth*! But I keep quiet and gaze out the glass fishbowl that is *Charlie Tango's* windshield as we continue south. The dusk is to our right, the sun low on the horizon—large, blazing fiery orange—and I am Icarus again, flying far too close.

*　　　*　　　*

The dusk follows us from Seattle, and the sky is awash with opal, pinks, and aquamarines woven seamlessly together as only Mother Nature knows how. It's a clear, crisp evening, and the lights of Portland twinkle and wink, welcoming us as Christian sets the helicopter down on the helipad. We are on top of the strange brown brick building in Portland we left less than three weeks ago. It's been hardly any time at all. Yet I feel like

I've known Christian for a lifetime. He powers down *Charlie Tango*, flipping various switches so the rotors stop, and eventually all I hear is my own breathing through the headphones. Hmm. Briefly it reminds me of the Thomas Tallis experience. I blanch. I don't want to go there right now.

Christian unbuckles his harness and leans across to undo mine.

'Good trip, Miss Steele?' he asks, his voice mild, his eyes glowing.

'Yes, thank you, Mr. Grey,' I reply politely.

'Well, let's go see the boy's photos.' He holds his hand out to me and taking it, I climb out of *Charlie Tango*.

A gray-haired man with a beard walks over to meet us, grinning broadly, and I recognize him as the old-timer from the last time we were here.

'Joe.' Christian smiles and releases my hand to shake Joe's warmly.

'Keep her safe for Stephan. He'll be along around eight or nine.'

'Will do, Mr. Grey. Ma'am,' he says, nodding at me. 'Your car's waiting downstairs, sir. Oh, and the elevator's out of order; you'll need to use the stairs.'

'Thank you, Joe.'

Christian takes my hand, and we head to the emergency stairs.

'Good thing for you this is only three floors, in those heels,' he mutters in disapproval.

No kidding.

'Don't you like the boots?'

'I like them very much, Anastasia.' His gaze darkens and I think he might say something else, but he stops. 'Come. We'll take it slow. I don't want you falling and breaking your neck.'

17

We sit in silence as our driver takes us to the gallery. My anxiety has returned full force, and I realize that our time in *Charlie Tango* has been the eye of the storm. Christian is quiet and brooding . . . apprehensive even; our lighter mood from earlier has dissipated. There's so much I want to say, but this journey is too short. Christian stares pensively out the window.

'José is just a friend,' I murmur.

Christian turns and gazes at me, his eyes dark and guarded, giving nothing away. His mouth—oh, his mouth is distracting, and unbidden. I remember it on me—everywhere. My skin heats. He shifts in his seat and frowns.

'Those beautiful eyes look too large in your face, Anastasia. Please tell me you'll eat.'

'Yes, Christian, I'll eat,' I answer automatically, a platitude.

'I mean it.'

'Do you, now?' I cannot keep the disdain out of my voice. Honestly, the audacity of this man—this man who has put me through hell over the last few days. No, that's wrong. I've put myself through hell. No. It's him. I shake my head, confused.

'I don't want to fight with you, Anastasia. I want you back, and I want you healthy,' he says.

'But nothing's changed.' *You're still fifty shades.*

'Let's talk on the way back. We're here.'

The car pulls up in front of the gallery, and Christian climbs out, leaving me speechless. He opens the car door for me, and I clamber out.

'Why do you do that?' My voice is louder than I

18

expected.

'Do what?' Christian is taken aback.

'Say something like that and then just stop.'

'Anastasia, we're here. Where you want to be. Let's do this and then talk. I don't particularly want a scene in the street.'

I glance around. He's right. It's too public. I press my lips together as he glares down at me.

'Okay,' I mutter sulkily. Clasping my hand, he takes me into the building.

We are in a converted warehouse—brick walls, dark wood floors, white ceilings, and white pipe work. It's airy and modern, and there are several people wandering across the gallery floor, sipping wine and admiring José's work. For a moment, my troubles melt away as I grasp that José has realized his dream. *Way to go, José!*

'Good evening and welcome to José Rodriguez's show.' A young woman dressed in black with very short brown hair, bright red lipstick, and large hooped earrings greets us. She glances briefly at me, then much longer than is strictly necessary at Christian, then turns back to me, blinking as she blushes.

My brow creases. *He's mine*—or was. I try hard not to scowl at her. As her eyes regain their focus, she blinks again.

'Oh, it's you, Ana. We'll want your take on all this, too.' Grinning, she hands me a brochure and directs me to a table laden with drinks and snacks.

'You know her?' Christian frowns.

I shake my head, equally puzzled.

He shrugs, distracted. 'What would you like to drink?'

'I'll have a glass of white wine, thank you.'

19

His brow furrows, but he holds his tongue and heads for the open bar.

'Ana!'

José comes barreling through a throng of people.

Holy cow! He's wearing a suit. He looks good and he's beaming at me. He enfolds me in his arms, hugging me hard. And it's all I can do not to burst into tears. My friend, he's my only friend while Kate is away. Tears pool in my eyes.

'Ana, I'm so glad you made it,' he whispers in my ear. Abruptly he holds me at arm's length, examining me.

'What?'

'Hey are you okay? You look, well, odd. *Dios mío,* have you lost weight?'

I blink back my tears—*not him too.* 'José, I'm fine. I'm just so happy for you. Congratulations on the show.' My voice wavers as I see the concern etched on his oh-so-familiar face, but I have to hold myself together.

'How did you get here?' he asks.

'Christian brought me,' I say, suddenly apprehensive.

'Oh.' José's face falls and he releases me. 'Where is he?' His expression darkens.

'Over there, fetching drinks.' I nod in Christian's direction and notice that he's exchanging pleasantries with someone waiting in line. Christian glances up and our eyes lock. And in that brief moment, I'm paralyzed, staring at the impossibly handsome man who gazes at me with some unfathomable emotion. His gaze hot, burning into me, and we're lost for a moment staring at each other.

Holy cow . . . This beautiful man wants me back,

20

and deep down inside me sweet joy slowly unfurls like a morning glory in the early dawn.

'Ana!' José distracts me, and I'm dragged back to the here and now. 'I am so glad you came—listen, I should warn you—'

Suddenly, Miss Very Short Hair and Red Lipstick cuts him off. 'José, the journalist from the *Portland Printz* is here to see you. Come on.' She gives me a polite smile.

'How cool is this? The fame.' He grins, and I can't help but grin back—he's so happy. 'Catch you later, Ana.' He kisses my cheek, and I watch him stroll over to a young woman standing by a tall, lanky photographer.

José's photographs are everywhere, and in some cases, blown up onto huge canvases. There are both monochromes and colors. There's an ethereal beauty to many of the landscapes. In one taken near the lake at Vancouver, it's early evening and pink clouds are reflected in the stillness of the water. Briefly, I'm transported by the tranquility and the peace. It's stunning.

Christian joins me, and hands me my glass of white wine.

'Does it come up to scratch?' My voice sounds more normal.

He looks quizzically at me.

'The wine.'

'No. Rarely does at these kinds of events. The boy's quite talented, isn't he?' Christian is admiring the lake photo.

'Why else do you think I asked him to take your portrait?' The pride is obvious in my voice. His eyes glide impassively from the photograph to me.

'Christian Grey?' The photographer from the

Portland Printz approaches Christian. 'Can I have a picture, sir?'

'Sure.' Christian hides his scowl. I step back, but he grabs my hand and pulls me to his side. The photographer looks at both of us and can't hide his surprise.

'Mr. Grey, thank you.' He snaps a couple of photos. 'Miss . . .?' he asks.

'Ana Steele,' I reply.

'Thank you, Miss Steele.' He scurries off.

'I looked for pictures of you with dates on the Internet. There aren't any. That's why Kate thought you were gay.'

Christian's mouth twitches into a smile. 'That explains your inappropriate question. No, I don't do dates, Anastasia—only with you. But you know that.' His voice is quiet with sincerity.

'So you never took your'—I glance around nervously to check no one can overhear us—'subs out?'

'Sometimes. Not on dates. Shopping, you know.' He shrugs, his eyes not leaving mine.

Oh, so just in the playroom—his Red Room of Pain and his apartment. I don't know what to feel about that.

'Just you, Anastasia,' he whispers.

I blush and stare down at my fingers. In his own way, he does care about me.

'Your friend here seems more of a landscape man, not portraits. Let's look around.' I take his outstretched hand.

We wander past a few more prints, and I notice a couple nodding at me, smiling broadly as if they know me. It must be because I'm with Christian, but one young man is blatantly staring. *Odd.*

We turn the corner, and I see why I've been getting strange looks. Hanging on the far wall are seven huge portraits—of me.

I stare blankly at them, stupefied, the blood draining from my face. Me: pouting, laughing, scowling, serious, amused. All in super close up, all in black and white.

Holy shit! I remember José messing with the camera on a couple of occasions when he was visiting and when I'd been out with him as driver and photographer's assistant. He took snapshots, or so I thought. Not these invasive candid shots.

Christian is staring, transfixed, at each of the pictures in turn.

'Seems I'm not the only one,' he mutters cryptically, his mouth settling into a hard line.

I think he's angry.

'Excuse me,' he says, pinning me with his bright gaze for a moment. He heads to the reception desk.

What's his problem now? I watch mesmerized as he talks animatedly with Miss Very Short Hair and Red Lipstick. He fishes out his wallet and produces his credit card.

Shit. He must have bought one of them.

'Hey. You're the muse. These photographs are terrific.' A young man with a shock of bright blond hair startles me. I feel a hand at my elbow and Christian is back.

'You're a lucky guy.' Blond Shock says to Christian, who gives him a cold stare.

'That I am,' he mutters darkly, as he pulls me over to one side.

'Did you just buy one of these?'

'One of these?' he snorts, not taking his eyes off them.

23

'You bought more than one?'

He rolls his eyes. 'I bought them all, Anastasia. I don't want some stranger ogling you in the privacy of their home.'

My first inclination is to laugh. 'You'd rather it was you?' I scoff.

He glares down at me, caught off guard by my audacity, I think, but he's trying to hide his amusement.

'Frankly, yes.'

'Pervert,' I mouth at him and bite my lower lip to prevent my smile.

His mouth drops open, and now his amusement is obvious. He strokes his chin thoughtfully.

'Can't argue with that assessment, Anastasia.' He shakes his head, and his eyes soften with humor.

'I'd discuss it further with you, but I've signed an NDA.'

He sighs, gazing at me, and his eyes darken. 'What I'd like to do to your smart mouth,' he murmurs.

I gasp, knowing full well what he means. 'You're very rude.' I try to sound shocked and succeed. Has he no boundaries?

He smirks, amused then frowns.

'You look very relaxed in these photographs, Anastasia. I don't see you like that very often.'

What? Whoa! Change of subject—talk about non sequitur—from playful to serious.

I flush and glance down at my fingers. He tilts my head back, and I inhale sharply at the contact with his fingers.

'I want you that relaxed with me,' he whispers. All trace of humor has gone.

Deep inside me that joy stirs again. *But how can*

24

this be? We have issues.

'You have to stop intimidating me if you want that,' I snap.

'You have to learn to communicate and tell me how you feel,' he snaps back, eyes blazing.

I take a deep breath. 'Christian, you wanted me as a submissive. That's where the problem lies. It's in the definition of a submissive—you e-mailed it to me once.' I pause, trying to recall the wording. 'I think the synonyms were, and I quote, 'compliant, pliant, amenable, passive, tractable, resigned, patient, docile, tame, subdued.' I wasn't supposed to look at you. Not talk to you unless you gave me permission to do so. What do you expect?' I hiss at him.

His frown deepens as I continue.

'It's very confusing being with you. You don't want me to defy you, but then you like my 'smart mouth.' You want obedience, except when you don't, so you can punish me. I just don't know which way is up when I'm with you.'

He narrows his eyes. 'Good point well made, as usual, Miss Steele.' His voice is frigid. 'Come, let's go eat.'

'We've only been here for half an hour.'

'You've seen the photos; you've spoken to the boy.'

'His name is José.'

'You've spoken to José—the man who, the last time I met him, was trying to push his tongue into your reluctant mouth while you were drunk and sick,' he snarls.

'He's never hit me,' I spit at him.

Christian scowls, fury emanating from every pore. 'That's a low blow, Anastasia,' he whispers

25

menacingly.

I pale, and Christian runs his hands through his hair, bristling with barely contained anger. I glare back at him.

'I'm taking you for something to eat. You're fading away in front of me. Find the boy, say good-bye.'

'Please, can we stay longer?'

'No. Go. Now. Say good-bye.'

I glower at him, my blood boiling. Mr. Damned Control Freak. Angry is good. Angry is better than tearful.

I drag my gaze away from him and scan the room for José. He's talking to a group of young women. I stalk off toward him and away from Fifty. Just because he brought me here, I have to do as he says? Who the hell does he think he is?

The girls are hanging on José's every word. One of them gasps as I approach, no doubt recognizing me from the portraits.

'José.'

'Ana. Excuse me, girls.' José grins at them and puts his arm around me, and on some level I'm amused—José all smooth, impressing the ladies.

'You look mad,' he says.

'I have to go,' I mutter mulishly.

'You just got here.'

'I know but Christian needs to get back. The pictures are fantastic, José—you're very talented.'

He beams. 'It was so cool seeing you.'

Jose sweeps me into a big bear hug, spinning me so I can see Christian across the gallery. He's scowling, and I realize it's because I'm in José's arms. So in a very calculating move, I wrap my arms around José's neck. I think Christian is going

26

to expire. His glare darkens to something quite sinister, and slowly he makes his way toward us.

'Thanks for the warning about the portraits of me,' I mumble.

'Shit. Sorry, Ana. I should have told you. D'you like them?'

'Um . . . I don't know,' I answer truthfully, momentarily knocked off balance by his question.

'Well, they're all sold, so somebody likes them. How cool is that? You're a poster girl.' He hugs me tighter as Christian reaches us, glowering at me now, though fortunately José doesn't see.

José releases me. 'Don't be a stranger, Ana. Oh, Mr. Grey, good evening.'

'Mr. Rodriguez, very impressive.' Christian sounds icily polite. 'I'm sorry we can't stay longer, but we need to head back to Seattle. Anastasia?' He subtly stresses *we,* and takes my hand as he does so.

'Bye, José. Congratulations again.' I give him a quick kiss on the cheek, and before I know it Christian is dragging me out of the building. I know he's boiling with silent wrath, but so am I.

He looks quickly up and down the street then heads left and suddenly sweeps me into a side alley, abruptly pushing me up against a wall. He grabs my face between his hands, forcing me to look up into his ardent, determined eyes.

I gasp, and his mouth swoops down. He's kissing me, violently. Briefly our teeth clash, then his tongue is in my mouth.

Desire explodes like the Fourth of July throughout my body, and I'm kissing him back, matching his fervor, my hands knotting in his hair, pulling it, hard. He groans, a low sexy sound in the back of his throat that reverberates through me, and his hand moves down my body to the top of my thigh, his fingers digging into my flesh through the plum dress.

I pour all the angst and heartbreak of the last few days into our kiss, binding him to me, and it hits me—in this moment of blinding passion—he's doing the same, he feels the same.

He breaks off the kiss, panting. His eyes are luminous with desire, firing the already heated blood that is pounding through my body. My mouth is slack as I try to drag precious air into my lungs.

'You. Are. Mine,' he snarls, emphasizing each word. He pushes away from me and bends, hands on his knees as if he's run a marathon. 'For the love of God, Ana.'

I lean against the wall, panting, trying to control the riotous reaction in my body, trying to find my equilibrium.

'I'm sorry,' I whisper once my breath has returned.

'You should be. I know what you were doing. Do you want the photographer, Anastasia? He obviously has feelings for you.'

I shake my head, guiltily. 'No. He's just a friend.'

'I have spent all my adult life trying to avoid any extreme emotion. Yet you . . . you bring out feelings in me that are completely alien. It's very . . .' He frowns, grasping for the word. 'Unsettling.

'I like control, Ana, and around you that just'—he stands, his gaze intense—'evaporates.' He waves his hand vaguely, then runs it through his hair and takes a deep breath. He clasps my hand.

'Come, we need to talk, and you need to eat.'

CHAPTER TWO

He whisks me into a small, intimate restaurant.

'This place will have to do,' Christian grumbles. 'We don't have much time.'

The restaurant looks fine to me. Wooden chairs, linen tablecloths, and walls the same color as Christian's playroom—deep bloodred—with randomly placed small gilt mirrors, white candles, and small vases of white roses. Ella Fitzgerald croons softly in the background about this thing called love. It's very romantic.

The waiter leads us to a table for two in a small alcove, and I sit, apprehensive and wondering what he's going to say.

'We don't have long,' Christian says to the waiter as we sit. 'So we'll each have sirloin steak cooked medium, béarnaise sauce if you have it, fries, and green vegetables, whatever the chef has; and bring me the wine list.'

'Certainly, sir.' The waiter, taken aback by Christian's cool, calm efficiency, scuttles off. Christian places his BlackBerry on the table. Jeez, don't I get a choice?

'And if I don't like steak?'

He sighs. 'Don't start, Anastasia.'

'I am not a child, Christian.'

'Well, stop acting like one.'

It's as if he's slapped me. So this is how it will be, an agitated, fraught conversation, albeit in a very romantic setting, but certainly no hearts and flowers.

'I'm a child because I don't like steak?' I mutter,

29

trying to conceal my hurt.

'For deliberately making me jealous. It's a childish thing to do. Have you no regard for your friend's feelings, leading him on like that?' Christian presses his lips together in a thin line and scowls as the waiter returns with the wine list.

I blush—I hadn't thought of that. Poor José—I certainly don't want to encourage him. Suddenly I'm mortified. Christian has a point; it was a thoughtless thing to do. He glances at the wine list.

'Would you like to choose the wine?' he asks, raising his eyebrows at me expectantly, arrogance personified. He knows I know nothing about wine.

'You choose,' I answer, sullen but chastened.

'Two glasses of the Barossa Valley Shiraz, please.'

'Er . . . we only sell that wine by the bottle, sir.'

'A bottle, then,' Christian snaps.

'Sir.' He retreats, subdued, and I don't blame him. I frown at Fifty. What's eating him? Oh, myself probably, and somewhere in the depths of my psyche, my inner goddess rises sleepily, stretches, and smiles. She's been asleep for a while.

'You're very grumpy.'

He gazes at me impassively. 'I wonder why that is?'

'Well, it's good to set the right tone for an intimate and honest discussion about the future, wouldn't you say?' I smile at him sweetly.

His mouth presses into a hard line, but then, almost reluctantly, his lips lift, and I know he's trying to stifle his smile.

'I'm sorry,' he says.

'Apology accepted, and I'm pleased to inform you I haven't decided to become a vegetarian since

30

we last ate.'

'Since that was the last time you ate, I think that's a moot point.'

'There's that word again, "moot."'

'Moot,' he mouths and his eyes soften with humor. He runs his hand through his hair, and he's serious again. 'Ana, the last time we spoke, you left me. I'm a little nervous. I've told you I want you back, and you've said . . . nothing.' His gaze is intense and expectant while his candor is totally disarming. What the hell do I say to this?

'I've missed you . . . really missed you, Christian. The past few days have been . . . difficult.' I swallow, and a lump in my throat swells as I recall my desperate anguish since I left him.

This last week has been the worst in my life, the pain almost indescribable. Nothing has come close. But reality hits home, winding me.

'Nothing's changed. I can't be what you want me to be.' I squeeze the words out past the lump in my throat.

'You are what I want you to be,' he says, his voice emphatic.

'No, Christian, I'm not.'

'You're upset because of what happened last time. I behaved stupidly, and you . . . So did you. Why didn't you safe-word, Anastasia?' His tone changes, becomes accusatory.

What? Whoa—change of direction.

'Answer me.'

'I don't know. I was overwhelmed. I was trying to be what you wanted me to be, trying to deal with the pain, and it went out of my mind. You know . . . I forgot,' I whisper, ashamed, and I shrug apologetically.

31

Perhaps we could have avoided all this heartache.

'You forgot!' he gasps with horror, grabbing the sides of the table and glaring. I wither under his stare.

Shit! He's furious again. My inner goddess glares at me, too. *See, you brought all this on yourself!*

'How can I trust you?' His voice is low. 'Ever?'

The waiter arrives with our wine as we sit staring at each other, blue eyes to gray. Both of us filled with unspoken recriminations, while the waiter removes the cork with an unnecessary flourish and pours a little wine into Christian's glass. Automatically Christian reaches out and takes a sip.

'That's fine.' His voice is curt.

Gingerly the waiter fills our glasses, placing the bottle on the table before beating a hasty retreat. Christian has not taken his eyes off me the whole time. I am the first to crack, breaking eye contact, picking up my glass and taking a large gulp. I barely taste it.

'I'm sorry,' I whisper, suddenly feeling stupid. I left because I thought we were incompatible, but he's saying I could have stopped him?

'Sorry for what?' he says alarmed.

'Not using the safeword.'

He closes his eyes, as if in relief.

'We might have avoided all this suffering,' he mutters.

'You look fine.' More than fine. You look like you.

'Appearances can be deceptive,' he says quietly. 'I'm anything but fine. I feel like the sun has set and not risen for five days, Ana. I'm in perpetual night here.'

I'm winded by his admission. *Oh my, like me.*

'You said you'd never leave, yet the going gets tough and you're out the door.'

'When did I say I'd never leave?'

'In your sleep. It was the most comforting thing I'd heard in so long, Anastasia. It made me relax.'

My heart constricts and I reach for my wine.

'You said you loved me,' he whispers. 'Is that now in the past tense?' His voice is low, laced with anxiety.

'No, Christian, it's not.'

He looks so vulnerable as he exhales. 'Good,' he murmurs.

I'm shocked by his admission. He's had a change of heart. When I told him I loved him before, he was horrified. The waiter is back. Briskly he places our plates in front of us and scuttles away.

Holy hell. Food.

'Eat,' Christian commands.

Deep down I know I'm hungry, but right now, my stomach is in knots. Sitting across from the only man I have ever loved and debating our uncertain future does not promote a healthy appetite. I look dubiously at my food.

'So help me God, Anastasia, if you don't eat, I will take you across my knee here in this restaurant, and it will have nothing to do with my sexual gratification. Eat!'

Keep your hair on, Grey. My subconscious stares at me over her half-moon specs. She is wholeheartedly in agreement with Fifty Shades.

'Okay, I'll eat. Stow your twitching palm, please.'

He doesn't smile but continues to glare at me. Reluctantly I lift my knife and fork and slice into my steak. Oh, it's mouthwateringly good. I am hungry, really hungry. I chew and he visibly relaxes.

We eat our supper in silence. The music's changed. A soft-voiced woman sings in the background, her words echoing my thoughts. I'll never be the same since he came into my life.

I glance at Fifty. He's eating and watching me. Hunger, longing, anxiety combined in one hot look.

'Do you know who's singing?' I try for some normal conversation.

Christian pauses and listens. 'No . . . but she's good, whoever she is.'

'I like her, too.'

Finally he smiles his private enigmatic smile. What's he planning?

'What?' I ask.

He shakes his head. 'Eat up,' he says mildly.

I have eaten half the food on my plate. I cannot eat any more. How can I negotiate this?

'I can't manage any more. Have I eaten enough for Sir?'

He stares at me impassively, not answering, then glances at his watch.

'I'm really full,' I add, taking a sip of the delicious wine.

'We have to go shortly. Taylor's here, and you have to be up for work in the morning.'

'So do you.'

'I function on a lot less sleep than you do, Anastasia. At least you've eaten something.'

'Aren't we going back via *Charlie Tango*?'

'No, I thought I might have a drink. Taylor will pick us up. Besides, this way I have you in the car all to myself for a few hours, at least. What can we do but talk?'

Oh, that's his plan.

Christian summons the waiter to ask for the check, then picks up his BlackBerry and makes a call.

'We're at Le Picotin, Southwest Third Avenue.' He hangs up.

He's still curt over the phone.

'You're very brusque with Taylor, in fact, with most people.'

'I just get to the point quickly, Anastasia.'

'You haven't gotten to the point this evening. Nothing's changed, Christian.'

'I have a proposition for you.'

'This started with a proposition.'

'A different proposition.'

The waiter returns, and Christian hands over his credit card without checking the bill. He gazes at me speculatively while the waiter swipes his card. Christian's phone buzzes once, and he peers at it.

He has a proposition? What now? A couple of scenarios run through my mind: kidnapping, working for him. No, nothing makes sense. Christian finishes paying.

'Come. Taylor's outside.'

We stand and he takes my hand.

'I don't want to lose you, Anastasia.' He kisses my knuckles tenderly, and the touch of his lips on my skin resonates through my body.

Outside the Audi is waiting. Christian opens my door. Climbing in, I sink into the plush leather. He heads to the driver's side; Taylor steps out of the car and they talk briefly. This isn't their usual protocol. I'm curious. What are they talking about? Moments later, they are both back in the car, and I glance at Christian, who's wearing his impassive face as he stares ahead.

I allow myself a brief moment to examine his profile: straight nose, sculpted full lips, hair falling deliciously over his forehead. This divine man is surely not meant for me.

Soft music fills the rear of the car, a grand orchestral piece that I don't know, and Taylor pulls into the light traffic, heading for I-5 and Seattle.

Christian shifts to face me. 'As I was saying, Anastasia, I have a proposition for you.'

I glance nervously at Taylor.

'Taylor can't hear you,' Christian reassures me.

'How?'

'Taylor,' Christian calls. Taylor doesn't respond. He calls again, still no response. Christian leans over and taps his shoulder. Taylor removes an earbud I hadn't noticed.

'Yes, sir?'

'Thank you, Taylor. It's okay; resume your listening.'

'Sir.'

'Happy now? He's listening to his iPod. Puccini. Forget he's here. I do.'

'Did you deliberately ask him to do that?'

'Yes.'

Oh. 'Okay, your proposition?'

Christian looks suddenly determined and businesslike. *Holy shit.* We're negotiating a deal. I listen attentively.

'Let me ask you something first. Do you want a regular vanilla relationship with no kinky fuckery at all?'

My mouth drops open. 'Kinky fuckery?' I squeak.

'Kinky fuckery.'

'I can't believe you said that.'

'Well, I did. Answer me,' he says calmly.

I flush. My inner goddess is down on bended knee with her hands clasped in supplication, begging me.

'I like your kinky fuckery,' I whisper.

'That's what I thought. So what don't you like?'

Not being able to touch you. Your enjoying my pain, the bite of the belt . . .

'The threat of cruel and unusual punishment.'

'What does that mean?'

'Well, you have all those canes and whips and stuff in your playroom, and they frighten the living daylights out of me. I don't want you to use them on me.'

'Okay, so no whips or canes—or belts, for that matter,' he says sardonically.

I gaze at him puzzled. 'Are you attempting to redefine the hard limits?'

'Not as such, I'm just trying to understand you, get a clearer picture of what you do and don't like.'

'Fundamentally, Christian, it's your joy in inflicting pain on me that's difficult for me to handle. And the idea that you'll do it because I have crossed some arbitrary line.'

'But it's not arbitrary; the rules are written down.'

'I don't want a set of rules.'

'None at all?'

'No rules.' I shake my head, but my heart is in my mouth. Where is he going with this?

'But you don't mind if I spank you?'

'Spank me with what?'

'This.' He holds up his hand.

I squirm uncomfortably. 'No, not really. Especially with those silver balls . . .' Thank heavens it's dark; my face is burning and my voice trails off

37

as I recall that night. *Yeah . . . I'd do that again.*

He smirks. 'Yes, that was fun.'

'More than fun,' I mutter.

'So you can deal with some pain.'

I shrug. 'Yes, I suppose.' Oh, where is he going with this? My anxiety level has shot up several magnitudes on the Richter scale.

He strokes his chin, deep in thought. 'Anastasia, I want to start again. Do the vanilla thing and then maybe, once you trust me more and I trust you to be honest and to communicate with me, we could move on and do some of the things that I like to do.'

I stare at him, stunned, with no thoughts in my head at all—like a computer crash. I think he's anxious, but I can't see him clearly, as we're shrouded in the Oregon darkness. It occurs to me, finally, this is it.

He wants the light, but can I ask him to do this for me? And don't I like the dark? Some dark, sometimes. Memories of the Thomas Tallis night drift invitingly through my mind.

'But what about punishments?'

'No punishments.' He shakes his head. 'None.'

'And the rules?'

'No rules.'

'None at all? But you have needs.'

'I need you more, Anastasia. These last few days have been hell. All my instincts tell me to let you go, tell me I don't deserve you.

'Those photos the boy took . . . I can see how he sees you. You look untroubled and beautiful, not that you're not beautiful now, but here you sit. I see your pain. It's hard, knowing that I'm the one who has made you feel this way.

'But I'm a selfish man. I've wanted you since you fell into my office. You are exquisite, honest, warm, strong, witty, beguilingly innocent; the list is endless. I'm in awe of you. I want you, and the thought of anyone else having you is like a knife twisting in my dark soul.'

My mouth goes dry. *Holy shit.* If that isn't a declaration of love, I don't know what is. And the words tumble out of me—a dam breached.

'Christian, why do you think you have a dark soul? I would never say that. Sad maybe, but you're a good man. I can see that . . . you're generous, you're kind, and you've never lied to me. And I haven't tried very hard.

'Last Saturday was such a shock to my system. It was my wake-up call. I realized that you'd been easy on me and that I couldn't be the person you wanted me to be. Then, after I left, it dawned on me that the physical pain you inflicted was not as bad as the pain of losing you. I do want to please you, but it's hard.'

'You please me all the time,' he whispers. 'How often do I have to tell you that?'

'I never know what you're thinking. Sometimes you're so closed off . . . like an island state. You intimidate me. That's why I keep quiet. I don't know which way your mood is going to go. It swings from north to south and back again in a nanosecond. It's confusing and you won't let me touch you, and I want so much to show you how much I love you.'

He blinks in the darkness, warily I think, and I can resist him no longer. I unbuckle my seat belt and scramble into his lap, taking him by surprise, and take his head in my hands.

'I love you, Christian Grey. And you're prepared to do all this for me. I'm the one who is undeserving, and I'm just sorry that I can't do all those things for you. Maybe with time . . . I don't know

. . . but yes, I accept your proposition. Where do I sign?'

He snakes his arms around me and crushes me to him.

'Oh, Ana,' he breathes as he buries his nose in my hair.

We sit with our arms wrapped around each other, listening to the music—a soothing piano piece—mirroring the emotions in the car, the sweet tranquil calm after the storm. I snuggle into his arms, resting my head in the crook of his neck. He gently strokes my back.

'Touching is a hard limit for me, Anastasia,' he whispers.

'I know. I wish I understood why.'

After a while, he sighs, and in a soft voice he says, 'I had a horrific childhood. One of the crack whore's pimps . . .' His voice trails off, and his body tenses as he recalls some unimaginable horror. 'I can remember that,' he whispers, shuddering.

Abruptly, my heart constricts as I remember the burn scars marring his skin. *Oh, Christian.* I tighten my arms around his neck.

'Was she abusive? Your mother?' My voice is low and soft with unshed tears.

'Not that I remember. She was neglectful. She didn't protect me from her pimp.' He snorts. 'I think it was me who looked after her. When she finally killed herself, it took four days for someone to raise the alarm and find us . . . I remember that.'

I cannot contain my gasp of horror. Holy mother fuck. Bile rises in my throat.

'That's pretty fucked-up,' I whisper.

'Fifty shades,' he murmurs.

I press my lips against his neck, seeking and offering solace as I imagine a small, dirty, gray-eyed boy lost and lonely beside the body of his dead mother.

Oh, Christian. I breathe in his scent. He smells heavenly, my favorite fragrance in the entire world. He tightens his arms around me and kisses my hair, and I sit wrapped in his embrace as Taylor speeds into the night.

*   *   *

When I wake, we're driving through Seattle.

'Hey,' Christian says softly.

'Sorry,' I murmur as I sit up, blinking and stretching. I am still in his arms, on his lap.

'I could watch you sleep forever, Ana.'

'Did I say anything?'

'No. We're nearly at your place.'

Oh? 'We're not going to yours?'

'No.'

I sit up and gaze at him. 'Why not?'

'Because you have work tomorrow.'

'Oh.' I pout.

'Why, did you have something in mind?'

I squirm. 'Well, maybe.'

He chuckles. 'Anastasia, I am not going to touch you again, not until you beg me to.'

'What!'

'So that you'll start communicating with me. Next time we make love, you're going to have to tell

41

me exactly what you want in fine detail.'

'Oh.' He shifts me off his lap as Taylor pulls up outside my apartment. Christian climbs out and holds the car door open for me.

'I have something for you.' He moves to the back of the car, opens the trunk, and pulls out a large gift-wrapped box. What the hell is this?

'Open it when you get inside.'

'You're not coming in?'

'No, Anastasia.'

'So when will I see you?'

'Tomorrow.'

'My boss wants me to go for a drink with him tomorrow.'

Christian's face hardens. 'Does he, now?' His voice is laced with latent menace.

'To celebrate my first week,' I add quickly.

'Where?'

'I don't know.'

'I could pick you up from there.'

'Okay . . . I'll e-mail or text you.'

'Good.'

He walks me to the lobby door and waits while I dig my keys out of my purse. As I unlock the door, he leans forward and cups my chin, tilting my head back. His mouth hovers over mine, and closing his eyes, he runs a trail of kisses from the corner of my eye to the corner of my mouth.

A small moan escapes my mouth as my insides melt and unfurl.

'Until tomorrow,' he breathes.

'Good night, Christian.' I hear the need in my voice.

He smiles.

'In you go,' he orders, and I walk through the

42

lobby carrying my mysterious parcel.

'Laters, baby,' he calls, then turns and with his easy grace, heads back to the car.

Once in the apartment, I open the gift box and find my MacBook Pro laptop, the BlackBerry, and another rectangular box. What is this? I unwrap the silver paper. Inside is a black slim leather case.

Opening the case, I find an iPad. *Holy shit . . . an iPad.* A white card is resting on the screen with a message written in Christian's handwriting:

> *Anastasia—this is for you.*
> *I know what you want to hear.*
> *The music on here says it for me.*
> *Christian*

I have a Christian Grey mix tape in the guise of a high-end iPad. I shake my head in disapproval because of the expense, but deep down I love it. Jack has one at the office, so I know how they work.

I switch it on and gasp as the wallpaper image appears: a small model glider. *Oh my.* It's the Blanik L-23 I gave him, mounted on a glass stand and sitting on what I think is Christian's desk at his office. I gape at it.

He built it! He really did build it. I remember now he mentioned it in the note with the flowers. I'm reeling, and I know in that instant that he's put a great deal of thought into this gift.

I slide the arrow at the bottom of the screen to unlock it and gasp again. The background photograph is of Christian and me at my graduation in the tent. It's the one that appeared in the *Seattle Times*. Christian looks so handsome and I can't help my face-splitting grin—*Yes, and he's mine!*

With a swipe of my finger, the icons shift, and several new ones appear on the next screen. A Kindle app, iBooks, Words—whatever that is.

The British Library? I touch the icon and a menu appears: HISTORICAL COLLECTION. Scrolling down, I select NOVELS OF THE 18TH AND 19TH CENTURY. Another menu. I tap on a title: *The American* BY HENRY JAMES. A new window opens, offering me a scanned copy of the book to read. Holy crap—it's an early edition, published in 1879, and it's on my iPad! He's bought me the British Library at a touch of a button.

I exit quickly, knowing that I could be lost in this app for an eternity. I notice a 'good food' app that makes me roll my eyes and smile at the same time, a news app, a weather app, but his note mentioned music. I go back to the main screen, hit the iPod icon, and a playlist appears. I scroll through the songs, and the list makes me smile. Thomas Tallis— I'm not going to forget that in a hurry. I heard it twice, after all, while he flogged and fucked me.

'Witchcraft.' My grin gets wider—dancing around the great room. The Bach Marcello piece—*oh no, that's way too sad for my mood right now. Hmm.* Jeff Buckley—*yeah, I've heard of him.* Snow Patrol—my favorite band—and a song called 'Principles of Lust' by Enigma. How Christian. Another called 'Possession' . . . *oh yes, very Fifty Shades.* And a few more I have never heard.

Selecting a song that catches my eye, I press play. It's called 'Try' by Nelly Furtado. She starts to sing, and her voice is a silken scarf wrapping around me, enveloping me. I lie down on my bed.

Does this mean Christian's going to try? Try this new relationship? I drink in the lyrics, staring at the ceiling, trying to understand his turnaround. He missed me. I missed him. He must have some feelings for me. He must. This iPad, these songs, these apps—he cares. He really cares. My heart swells with hope.

The song ends and tears spring to my eyes. I quickly scroll to another—'The Scientist' by Coldplay—one of Kate's favorite bands. I know the track, but I've never really listened to the lyrics before. I close my eyes and let the words wash over and through me.

My tears start to flow. I can't stem them. If this isn't an apology, what is it? *Oh, Christian.*

Or is this an invitation? Will he answer my questions? *Am I reading too much into this? I am probably reading too much into this.*

I dash my tears away. I have to e-mail him to thank him. I leap off my bed to fetch the mean machine.

Coldplay continues as I sit cross-legged on my bed. The Mac powers up and I log in.

From: Anastasia Steele
Subject: IPAD
Date: June 9 2011 23:56
To: Christian Grey

You've made me cry again.

I love the iPad.

I love the songs.

I love the British Library App.

I love you.

45

Thank you.

Good night.

Ana xx

From: Christian Grey
Subject: iPad
Date: June 10 2011 00:03
To: Anastasia Steele

I'm glad you like it. I bought one for myself.

Now, if I were there, I would kiss away your tears.

But I'm not—so go to sleep.

Christian Grey
CEO, Grey Enterprises Holdings, Inc.

His response makes me smile—still so bossy, still so Christian. Will that change, too? And I realize in that moment that I hope not. I like him like this—commanding—as long as I can stand up to him without fear of punishment.

From: Anastasia Steele
Subject: Mr. Grumpy
Date: June 10 2011 00:07
To: Christian Grey

You sound your usual bossy and possibly

tense, possibly grumpy self, Mr. Grey.

I know something that could ease that. But then, you're not here—you wouldn't let me stay, and you expect me to beg . . .

Dream on, Sir.

Ana xx

PS: I also note that you included the Stalker's Anthem, 'Every Breath You Take.' I do enjoy your sense of humor, but does Dr. Flynn know?

From: Christian Grey
Subject: Zen-Like Calm
Date: June 10 2011 00:10
To: Anastasia Steele

My Dearest Miss Steele

Spanking occurs in vanilla relationships, too, you know. Usually consensually and in a sexual context . . . but I am more than happy to make an exception.

You'll be relieved to know that Dr. Flynn also enjoys my sense of humor.

Now, please go to sleep, as you won't get much tomorrow.

Incidentally—you will beg, trust me. And I look forward to it.

Christian Grey
Tense CEO, Grey Enterprises Holdings, Inc.

From: Anastasia Steele
Subject: Good Night, Sweet Dreams
Date: June 10 2011 00:12
To: Christian Grey

Well, since you ask so nicely, and I like your delicious threat, I shall curl up with the iPad that you have so kindly given me and fall asleep browsing in the British Library, listening to the music that says it for you.

A xxx

From: Christian Grey
Subject: One more request
Date: June 10 2011 00:15
To: Anastasia Steele

Dream of me.
x

Christian Grey
CEO, Grey Enterprises Holdings, Inc.

Dream of you, Christian Grey? Always.

I change quickly into my pajamas, brush my teeth, and slip into bed. Putting my earbuds in, I pull the flattened *Charlie Tango* balloon from underneath my pillow and hug it to me.

I am brimming with joy, a stupid, widemouthed grin on my face. What a difference a day can make. How am I ever going to sleep?

José Gonzalez starts to sing a soothing melody with a hypnotic guitar riff, and I drift slowly into sleep, marveling how the world has righted itself in one evening and wondering idly if I should make a playlist for Christian.

CHAPTER THREE

The one good thing about being carless is that on the bus on my way to work, I can plug my headphones into my iPad while it's safely in my purse and listen to all the wonderful tunes Christian has given me. By the time I arrive at the office, I have the most ludicrous grin on my face.

Jack glances up at me and does a double take.

'Good morning, Ana. You look . . . radiant.' His remark flusters me. *How inappropriate!*

'I slept well, thank you, Jack. Good morning.'

His brow crinkles.

'Can you read these for me and have reports on them by lunchtime, please?' He hands me four manuscripts. At my horrified expression, he adds, 'Just first chapters.'

'Sure.' I smile with relief, and he gives me a broad smile in return.

I switch on the computer to start work, finishing my latte and eating a banana. There's an e-mail from Christian.

From: Christian Grey
Subject: So Help Me . . .

Date: June 10 2011 08:05
To: Anastasia Steele

I do hope you've had breakfast.

I missed you last night.

Christian Grey
CEO, Grey Enterprises Holdings, Inc.

From: Anastasia Steele
Subject: Old books . . .
Date: June 10 2011 08:33
To: Christian Grey

I am eating a banana as I type. I have not had breakfast for several days, so it is a step forward. I love the British Library App—I started rereading Robinson Crusoe . . . and of course, I love you.

Now leave me alone—I am trying to work.

Anastasia Steele
Assistant to Jack Hyde, Editor, SIP

From: Christian Grey
Subject: Is that all you've eaten?
Date: June 10 2011 08:36
To: Anastasia Steele

You can do better than that. You're going to need your energy for begging.

50

Christian Grey
CEO, Grey Enterprises Holdings, Inc.

From: Anastasia Steele
Subject: Pest
Date: June 10 2011 08:39
To: Christian Grey

Mr. Grey—I am trying to work for a living—
and it's you that will be begging.

Anastasia Steele
Assistant to Jack Hyde, Editor, SIP

From: Christian Grey
Subject: Bring It On!
Date: June 10 2011 08:36
To: Anastasia Steele

Why, Miss Steele, I love a challenge . . .

Christian Grey
CEO, Grey Enterprises Holdings, Inc.

I sit grinning at the screen like an idiot. But I
need to read these chapters for Jack and write
reports on all of them. Placing the manuscripts on
my desk, I begin.

At lunchtime I head to the deli for a pastrami
sandwich and listen to the playlist on my iPad. First
up there's Nitin Sawhney, some world music called

51

'Homelands'—it's good. Mr. Grey has eclectic taste in music. I wander back listening to a classical piece, *Fantasia on a Theme by Thomas Tallis* by Ralph Vaughn Williams. Oh, Fifty has a sense of humor, and I love him for it. Will this stupid grin ever leave my face?

The afternoon drags. I decide, in an unguarded moment, to e-mail Christian.

From: Anastasia Steele
Subject: Bored . . .
Date: June 10 2011 16:05
To: Christian Grey

Twiddling my thumbs.

How are you?

What are you doing?

Anastasia Steele
Assistant to Jack Hyde, Editor, SIP

From: Christian Grey
Subject: Your thumbs
Date: June 10 2011 16:15
To: Anastasia Steele

You should have come to work for me.

You wouldn't be twiddling your thumbs.

I am sure I could put them to better use.

In fact I can think of a number of options . . .

I am doing the usual humdrum mergers and acquisitions.

It's all very dry.

Your e-mails at SIP are monitored.

Christian Grey
Distracted CEO, Grey Enterprises Holdings, Inc.

Oh, shit. I had no idea. How the hell does he know? I scowl at the screen and quickly check the e-mails we've sent, deleting them as I do.

Promptly at five thirty, Jack is at my desk. It is Casual Friday so he's wearing jeans and a black shirt..

'Drink, Ana? We usually like to go for a quick one at the bar across the street.'

'We?' I ask, hopeful.

'Yeah, most of us go . . . you coming?'

For some unknown reason, which I don't want to examine too closely, relief floods through me.

'I'd love to. What's the bar called?'

'Fifty's.'

'You're kidding.'

He looks at me oddly. 'No. Some significance for you?'

'No, sorry. I'll join you over there.'

'What would you like to drink?'

'A beer, please.'

'Cool.'

I make my way to the powder room and e-mail Christian from the BlackBerry.

From: Anastasia Steele
Subject: You'll Fit Right In
Date: June 10 2011 17:36
To: Christian Grey

We are going to a bar called Fifty's.

The rich seam of humor that I could mine from this is endless.

I look forward to seeing you there, Mr. Grey.

A. x

From: Christian Grey
Subject: Hazards
Date: June 10 2011 17:38
To: Anastasia Steele

Mining is a very, very dangerous occupation.

Christian Grey
CEO, Grey Enterprises Holdings, Inc.

From: Anastasia Steele
Subject: Hazards?
Date: June 10 2011 17:40
To: Christian Grey

And your point is?

From: Christian Grey
Subject: Merely . . .
Date: June 10 2011 17:42
To: Anastasia Steele

Making an observation, Miss Steele.

I'll see you shortly.

Sooners rather than laters, baby.

Christian Grey
CEO, Grey Enterprises Holdings, Inc.

I check myself in the mirror. What a difference a day can make. I have more color in my cheeks, and my eyes are shining. It's the Christian Grey effect. A little e-mail sparring with him will do that to a girl. I grin at the mirror and straighten my pale blue shirt—the one Taylor bought me. I am wearing my favorite jeans today, too. Most of the women in the office wear either jeans or floaty skirts. I will need to invest in a floaty skirt or two. Perhaps I'll do that this weekend and bank the check Christian gave me for Wanda, my Beetle.

As I head out of the building, I hear my name called.

'Miss Steele?'

I turn expectantly, and an ashen young woman approaches me cautiously. She looks like a ghost—so pale and strangely blank.

'Miss Anastasia Steele?' she repeats, and her features stay static even though she's speaking.

'Yes?'

She stops, staring at me from about three

feet away on the sidewalk, and I stare back, immobilized. Who is she? What does she want?

'Can I help you?' I ask. How does she know my name?

'No . . . I just wanted to look at you.' Her voice is eerily soft. Like me, she has dark hair that starkly contrasts with her fair skin. Her eyes are brown, like bourbon, but flat. There's no life in them at all. Her beautiful face is pale, and etched with sorrow.

'Sorry—you have me at a disadvantage,' I say, trying to ignore the warning tingle up my spine. On closer inspection, she looks odd, disheveled, and uncared for. Her clothes are two sizes too big, including her designer trench coat.

She laughs, a strange, discordant sound that only feeds my anxiety.

'What do you have that I don't?' she asks sadly.

My anxiety turns to fear. 'I'm sorry—who are you?'

'Me? I'm nobody.' She lifts her arm to drag her hand through her shoulder length hair, and as she does, the sleeve of her trench coat rides up, revealing a soiled bandage around her wrist.

Holy fuck.

'Good day, Miss Steele.' Turning, she walks up the street as I stand rooted to the spot. I watch as her slight frame disappears from view, lost among the workers pouring out of their various offices.

What was that about?

Confused, I cross the street to the bar, trying to assimilate what has just happened, while my subconscious rears her ugly head and hisses at me—*She has something to do with Christian.*

Fifty's is a cavernous, impersonal bar with baseball pennants and posters hanging on the wall.

Jack is at the bar with Elizabeth; Courtney, the other Editor; two guys from Finance; and Claire from Reception. She is wearing her trademark silver hoop earrings.

'Hi, Ana!' Jack hands me a bottle of Bud.

'Cheers . . . thank you,' I murmur, still shaken by my encounter with Ghost Girl.

'Cheers.' We clink bottles, and he continues his conversation with Elizabeth. Claire smiles sweetly at me.

'So, how has your first week been?' she asks.

'Good, thank you. Everyone seems very friendly.'

'You seem much happier today.'

'It's Friday,' I mutter quickly. 'So—do you have any plans this weekend?'

*   *   *

My patented distraction technique works and I'm saved. Claire turns out to be one of seven kids, and she's going to a big family get-together in Tacoma. She becomes quite animated, and I realize I haven't spoken to any women my own age since Kate left for Barbados.

Absently I wonder how Kate is . . . and Elliot. I must remember to ask Christian if he's heard from him. Oh, and Ethan, Kate's brother, will be back next Tuesday, and he'll be staying in our apartment. I can't imagine Christian is going to be happy about that. My earlier encounter with strange Ghost Girl slips further from my mind.

During my conversation with Claire, Elizabeth hands me another beer.

'Thanks.' I smile at her.

Claire is very easy to talk to—she likes to talk—

57

and before I know it, I am on my third beer, courtesy of one of the guys from Finance.

When Elizabeth and Courtney leave, Jack joins Claire and me. Where is Christian? One of the finance guys engages Claire in conversation.

'Ana, think you made the right decision coming here?' Jack's voice is soft, and he's standing a bit too close. But I've noticed that he has a tendency to do this with everyone, even at the office.

'I've enjoyed myself this week, thank you, Jack. Yes, I think I made the right decision.'

'You're a very bright girl, Ana. You'll go far.'

I blush. 'Thank you,' I mutter, because I don't know what else to say.

'Do you live far?'

'The Pike Market district.'

'Not far from me.' Smiling, he moves even closer and leans against the bar, effectively trapping me. 'Do you have any plans this weekend?'

'Well . . . um—'

I feel him before I see him. It's as if my whole body is highly attuned to his presence. It relaxes and ignites at the same time—a weird, internal duality—and I sense that strange pulsing electricity.

Christian drapes his arm around my shoulder in a seemingly casual display of affection—but I know differently. He is staking a claim, and on this occasion, it's very welcome. Softly he kisses my hair.

'Hello, baby,' he murmurs.

I feel relieved, safe, and excited with his arm around me. He draws me to his side, and I glance up at him while he stares at Jack, his expression impassive. Turning his attention to me, he gives me a brief crooked smile followed by a swift kiss. He's wearing his navy pinstriped jacket over jeans and an open white shirt. He looks edible.

Jack shuffles back uncomfortably.

'Jack, this is Christian,' I mumble apologetically. Why am I apologizing? 'Christian, Jack.'

'I'm the boyfriend,' Christian says with a small, cool smile that doesn't reach his eyes as he shakes Jack's hand. I glance up at Jack who is mentally assessing the fine specimen of manhood in front of him.

'I'm the boss,' Jack replies arrogantly. 'Ana did mention an ex-boyfriend.'

Oh, shit. You don't want to play this game with Fifty.

'Well, no-longer-ex,' Christian replies calmly. 'Come on, baby, time to go.'

'Please, stay and join us for a drink,' Jack says smoothly.

I don't think that's a good idea. Why is this so uncomfortable? I glance at Claire, who is, of course staring, openmouthed and with frankly carnal appreciation, at Christian. When will I stop caring about the effect he has on other women?

'We have plans,' Christian replies with his enigmatic smile.

We do? And a frisson of anticipation runs through my body.

'Another time, perhaps,' he adds. 'Come,' he says to me as he takes my hand.

'See you Monday.' I smile at Jack, Claire, and the guys from Finance, trying hard to ignore Jack's less-than-pleased expression, and follow Christian out of the door.

Taylor is at the wheel of the Audi waiting at the curb.

'Why did that feel like a pissing contest?' I ask

59

Christian as he opens the car door for me.

'Because it was,' he murmurs and gives me his enigmatic smile then shuts my door.

'Hello, Taylor,' I say and our eyes meet in the review mirror.

'Miss Steele,' Taylor acknowledges with a genial smile.

Christian slides in beside me, clasps my hand, and gently kisses my knuckles. 'Hi,' he says softly.

My cheeks turn pink, knowing that Taylor can hear us, grateful that he can't see the scorching, panty-combusting look that Christian is giving me. It takes all my self-restraint not to leap on him right here, in the backseat of the car.

Oh, the backseat of the car . . . hmm.

'Hi,' I breathe, my mouth dry.

'What would you like to do this evening?'

'I thought you said we had plans.'

'Oh, I know what I'd like to do, Anastasia. I'm asking you what you want to do.'

I beam at him.

'I see,' he says with a wickedly salacious grin. 'So . . . begging it is, then. Do you want to beg at my place or yours?' He tilts his head to one side and smiles his oh-so-sexy smile at me.

'I think you're being very presumptuous, Mr. Grey. But by way of a change, we could go to my apartment.' I bite my lip deliberately, and his expression darkens.

'Taylor, Miss Steele's, please.'

'Sir,' Taylor acknowledges and he heads off into the traffic.

'So how has your day been?' he asks.

'Good. Yours?'

'Good, thank you.'

His ridiculously broad grin reflects mine, and he kisses my hand again.

'You look lovely,' he says.

'As do you.'

'Your boss, Jack Hyde, is he good at his job?'

Whoa! That's a sudden change in direction. I frown. 'Why? This isn't about your pissing contest?'

Christian smirks. 'That man wants into your panties, Anastasia,' he says dryly.

I go crimson as my mouth drops open, and I glance nervously at Taylor.

'Well, he can want all he likes . . . why are we even having this conversation? You know I have no interest in him whatsoever. He's just my boss.'

'That's the point. He wants what's mine. I need to know if he's good at his job.'

I shrug. 'I think so.' Where is he going with this?

'Well, he'd better leave you alone, or he'll find himself on his ass on the sidewalk.'

'Oh, Christian, what are you talking about? He hasn't done anything wrong.' . . . *Yet*. He just stands too close.

'He makes one move, you tell me. It's called gross moral turpitude—or sexual harassment.'

'It was just a drink after work.'

'I mean it. One move and he's out.'

'You don't have that kind of power.' Honestly! And before I roll my eyes at him, the realization hits me with the force of a speeding freight truck. 'Do you, Christian?'

Christian gives me his enigmatic smile.

'You're buying the company,' I whisper in horror.

His smile slips in response to the panic in my voice. 'Not exactly,' he says.

61

'You've bought it. SIP. Already.'

He blinks at me, warily. 'Possibly.'

'You have or you haven't?'

'Have.'

What the hell? 'Why?' I gasp, appalled. Oh, this just is too much.

'Because I can, Anastasia. I need you safe.'

'But you said you wouldn't interfere in my career!'

'And I won't.'

I snatch my hand out of his. 'Christian . . .' Words fail me.

'Are you mad at me?'

'Yes. Of course I'm mad at you.' I seethe. 'I mean, what kind of responsible business executive makes decisions based on who he is currently fucking?' I blanch and glance nervously once more at Taylor, who is stoically ignoring us.

Shit. What a time to have a brain-to-mouth filter malfunction.

Christian opens his mouth then closes it again and scowls at me. I glare at him. The atmosphere in the car plunges from warm with sweet reunion to frigid with unspoken words and potential recriminations as we glower at each other.

Fortunately, our uncomfortable car journey doesn't last long, and Taylor pulls up outside my apartment.

I scramble out of the car quickly, not waiting for anyone to open the door.

I hear Christian mutter to Taylor, 'I think you'd better wait here.'

I sense him standing close behind me as I struggle to find the front door keys in my purse.

'Anastasia,' he says calmly as if I'm some

cornered wild animal.

I sigh and turn to face him. I am so mad at him, my anger is palpable—a dark entity threatening to choke me.

'First, I haven't fucked you for a while—a long while, it feels—and second, I wanted to get into publishing. Of the four companies in Seattle, SIP is the most profitable, but it's on the cusp and it's going to stagnate—it needs to branch out.'

I stare frigidly at him. His eyes are intense, threatening even, but sexy as hell. I could get lost in their steely depths.

'So you're my boss now,' I snap.

'Technically, I'm your boss's boss's boss.'

'And, technically, it's gross moral turpitude—the fact that I am fucking my boss's boss's boss.'

'At the moment, you're arguing with him.' Christian scowls.

'That's because he's such an ass,' I hiss.

Christian steps back in stunned surprise. *Oh, shit. Have I gone too far?*

'An ass?' he murmurs as his expression changes to one of amusement.

Goddamn it! I am mad at you, do not make me laugh!

'Yes.' I struggle to maintain my look of moral outrage.

'An ass?' Christian says again. This time his lips twitch with a repressed smile.

'Don't make me laugh when I am mad at you!' I shout.

And he smiles, a dazzling, full-toothed, all-American-boy smile, and I can't help it. I am grinning and laughing, too. How could I not be affected by the joy I see in his smile?

63

'Just because I have a stupid damn grin on my face doesn't mean I'm not mad as hell at you,' I mutter breathlessly, trying to suppress my high-school-cheerleader giggling. *Though I was never cheerleader*—the bitter thought crosses my mind.

He leans in, and I think he's going to kiss me but he doesn't. He nuzzles my hair and inhales deeply.

'As ever, Miss Steele, you are unexpected.' He leans back gazing at me, his eyes dancing with humor. 'So are you going to invite me in, or am I to be sent packing for exercising my democratic right as an American citizen, entrepreneur, and consumer to purchase whatever I damn well please?'

'Have you spoken to Dr. Flynn about this?'

He laughs. 'Are you going to let me in or not, Anastasia?'

I try for a grudging look—biting my lip helps—but I'm smiling as I open the door. Christian turns and waves to Taylor, and the Audi pulls away.

*　　　*　　　*

It's odd having Christian Grey in the apartment. The place feels too small for him.

I am still mad at him—his stalking knows no bounds, and it dawns on me that this is how he knew about the e-mail being monitored at SIP. He probably knows more about SIP than I do. The thought is unsavory.

What can I do? Why does he have this need to keep me safe? I am a grown-up—*sort of*—for heaven's sake. What can I do to reassure him?

I gaze at his face as he paces the room like a caged predator, and my anger subsides. Seeing

64

him here in my space when I thought we were over is heartwarming. More than heartwarming, I love him, and my heart swells with a nervous, heady elation. He glances around, assessing his surroundings.

'Nice place,' he says.

'Kate's parents bought it for her.'

He nods distractedly, and his bold gray eyes come to rest on mine, staring at me.

'Er . . . would you like a drink?' I mutter, flushing with nerves.

'No thank you, Anastasia.' His eyes darken.

Why am I so nervous?

'What would you like to do, Anastasia?' he asks softly as he walks toward me, all feral and hot. 'I know what I want to do,' he adds in a low voice.

I back up until I bump against the concrete kitchen island.

'I'm still mad at you.'

'I know.' He smiles a lopsided apologetic smile and I melt . . . Well, maybe not so mad.

'Would you like something to eat?' I ask.

He nods slowly. 'Yes. You,' he murmurs. Everything south of my waistline clenches. I'm seduced by his voice alone, but that look, that hungry I-want-you-now look—oh my.

He's standing in front of me, not quite touching, staring down into my eyes and bathing me in the heat that's radiating off his body. I'm stiflingly hot, flustered, and my legs are like jelly as dark desire courses through me. I want him.

'Have you eaten today?' he murmurs.

'I had a sandwich at lunch,' I whisper. I don't want to talk food.

He narrows his eyes. 'You need to eat.'

'I'm really not hungry right now . . . for food.'

'What are you hungry for, Miss Steele?'

'I think you know, Mr. Grey.'

He leans down, and again I think he's going to kiss me, but he doesn't.

'Do you want me to kiss you, Anastasia?' he whispers softly in my ear.

'Yes,' I breathe.

'Where?'

'Everywhere.'

'You're going to have to be a bit more specific than that. I told you I am not going to touch you until you beg me and tell me what to do.'

I am lost; he's not playing fair.

'Please,' I whisper.

'Please what?'

'Touch me.'

'Where, baby?'

He is so tantalizingly close, his scent intoxicating. I reach up, and immediately he steps back.

'No, no,' he chides, his eyes suddenly wide and alarmed.

'What?' *No . . . come back.*

'No.' He shakes his head.

'Not at all?' I can't keep the longing out of my voice.

He looks at me uncertainly, and I'm emboldened by his hesitation. I step toward him, and he steps back, holding up his hands in defense, but smiling.

'Look, Ana.' It's a warning, and he runs his hand through his hair, exasperated.

'Sometimes you don't mind,' I observe plaintively. 'Perhaps I should find a marker pen, and we could map out the no-go areas.'

He raises an eyebrow. 'That's not a bad idea.

Where's your bedroom?'

I nod in the direction. Is he deliberately changing the subject?

'Have you been taking your pill?'

Oh shit. My pill.

His face falls at my expression.

'No,' I squeak.

'I see,' he says, and his lips press into a thin line. 'Come, let's have something to eat.'

'I thought we were going to bed! I want to go to bed with you.'

'I know, baby.' He smiles, and suddenly darting toward me, he grabs my wrists and pulls me into his arms so that his body is pressed against mine.

'You need to eat and so do I,' he murmurs, burning eyes gazing down at me. 'Besides . . . anticipation is the key to seduction, and right now, I'm really into delayed gratification.'

Huh, since when?

'I'm seduced and I want my gratification now. I'll beg, please.' I sound whiny.

He smiles at me tenderly. 'Eat. You're too slender.' He kisses my forehead and releases me.

This is a game, part of some evil plan. I scowl at him.

'I'm still mad that you bought SIP, and now I am mad at you because you're making me wait.' I pout.

'You are one angry little madam, aren't you? You'll feel better after a good meal.'

'I know what I'll feel better after.'

'Anastasia Steele, I'm shocked.' His tone is gently mocking.

'Stop teasing me. You don't fight fair.'

He stifles his grin by biting his lower lip. He looks simply adorable . . . playful Christian toying with my libido. If only my seduction skills were better, I'd know what to do, but not being able to touch him does hamper me.

My inner goddess narrows her eyes and looks thoughtful. We need to work on this.

As Christian and I gaze at each other—me hot, bothered and yearning and him, relaxed and amused at my expense—I realize I have no food in the apartment.

'I could cook something—except we'll have to go shopping.'

'Shopping?'

'For groceries.'

'You have no food here?' His expression hardens.

I shake my head. Crap, he looks quite angry.

'Let's go shopping, then,' he says sternly as he turns on his heel and heads for the door, opening it wide for me.

* * *

'When was the last time you were in a supermarket?'

Christian looks out of place, but he follows me dutifully, holding a shopping basket.

'I can't remember.'

'Does Mrs. Jones do all the shopping?'

'I think Taylor helps her. I'm not sure.'

'Are you happy with a stir-fry? It's quick.'

'Stir-fry sounds good.' Christian grins, no doubt figuring out my ulterior motive for a speedy meal.

'Have they worked for you long?'

'Taylor, four years, I think. Mrs. Jones, about the same. Why didn't you have any food in the apartment?'

'You know why,' I murmur, flushing.

'It was you who left me,' he mutters disapprovingly.

'I know,' I reply in a small voice, not wanting that reminder.

We reach the checkout and silently stand in line.

If I hadn't left, would he have offered the vanilla alternative? I wonder idly.

'Do you have anything to drink?' He pulls me back to the present.

'Beer . . . I think.'

'I'll get some wine.'

Oh dear. I'm not sure what sort of wine is available in Ernie's Supermarket. Christian remerges empty-handed, grimacing with a look of disgust.

'There's a good liquor store next door,' I say quickly.

'I'll see what they have.'

Maybe we should just go to his place; then we wouldn't have all this hassle. I watch as he strolls purposefully and with easy grace out of the door. Two women coming in stop and stare. *Oh yes, eye my Fifty Shades,* I think despondently.

I want the memory of him in my bed, but he's playing hard to get. Maybe I should, too. My inner goddess nods frantically in agreement. And as I stand in line, we come up with a plan. Hmm . . .

*　　　*　　　*

Christian carries the grocery bags into the apartment. He's carried them as we've walked back to the apartment from the store. He looks odd. Not

69

his usual CEO demeanor at all.

'You look very—domestic.'

'No one has ever accused me of that before,' he says dryly. He places the bags on the kitchen island. As I start to unload them, he takes out a bottle of white wine and searches for a corkscrew.

'This place is still new to me. I think the opener is in that drawer there.' I point with my chin.

This feels so . . . normal. Two people, getting to know each other, having a meal. Yet it's so strange. The fear that I'd always felt in his presence has gone. We've already done so much together, I blush just thinking about it, and yet I hardly know him.

'What are you thinking about?' Christian interrupts my reverie as he shrugs out of his pinstripe jacket and places it on the couch.

'How little I know you.'

His eyes soften. 'You know me better than anyone.'

'I don't think that's true.' Mrs. Robinson comes unbidden, and very unwelcome, into my mind.

'It is, Anastasia. I'm a very, very private person.'

He hands me a glass of white wine.

'Cheers,' he says.

'Cheers,' I respond taking a sip as he puts the bottle in the fridge.

'Can I help you with that?' he asks.

'No, it's fine . . . sit.'

'I'd like to help.' His expression is sincere.

'You can chop the vegetables.'

'I don't cook,' he says, regarding the knife I hand him with suspicion.

'I imagine you don't need to.' I place a chopping board and some red peppers in front of him. He stares down at them in confusion.

70

'You've never chopped a vegetable?'

'No.'

I smirk at him.

'Are you smirking at me?'

'It appears this is something that I can do and you can't. Let's face it, Christian, I think this is a first. Here, I'll show you.'

I brush up against him and he steps back. My inner goddess sits up and takes notice.

'Like this.' I slice the red pepper, careful to remove the seeds.

'Looks simple enough.'

'You shouldn't have any trouble with it,' I mutter ironically.

He gazes at me impassively for a moment then sets about his task as I continue to prepare the diced chicken. He starts to slice, carefully, slowly. *Oh my, we'll be here all night.*

I wash my hands and hunt for the wok, the oil, and the other ingredients I need, repeatedly brushing against him—my hip, my arm, my back, my hands. Small, seemingly innocent touches. He stills each time I do.

'I know what you're doing, Anastasia,' he murmurs darkly, still preparing the first pepper.

'I think it's called cooking,' I say, fluttering my eyelashes. Grabbing another knife, I join him at the chopping board, peeling and slicing garlic, shallots, and French beans, continually bumping against him.

'You're quite good at this,' he mutters as he starts on his second red pepper.

'Chopping?' I bat my eyelashes at him. 'Years of practice.' I brush against him again, this time with my behind. He stills once more.

71

'If you do that again, Anastasia, I am going to take you on the kitchen floor.'

Oh wow. It's working. 'You'll have to beg me first.'

'Is that a challenge?'

'Maybe.'

He puts down his knife and saunters slowly over to me, his eyes burning. Leaning past me, he switches the gas off. The oil in the wok quiets almost immediately.

'I think we'll eat later,' he says. 'Put the chicken in the fridge.'

This is not a sentence I had ever expected to hear from Christian Grey, and only he can make it sound hot, really hot. I pick up the bowl of diced chicken, rather shakily place a plate on top of it, and stow it in the fridge. When I turn back, he's beside me.

'So you're going to beg?' I whisper, bravely gazing into his darkening eyes.

'No, Anastasia.' He shakes his head. 'No begging.' His voice is soft, seductive.

And we stand staring at each other, drinking each other in—the atmosphere charging between us, almost crackling, neither saying anything, just looking. I bite my lip as desire for this man seizes me with a vengeance, igniting my blood, shallowing my breath, pooling below my waist. I see my reactions reflected in his stance, in his eyes.

In a beat, he grabs me by my hips and pulls me to him as my hands reach for his hair and his mouth claims me. He pushes me against the fridge, and I hear the vague protesting rattle of bottles and jars from within as his tongue finds mine. I moan into his mouth and one of his hands moves into my hair, pulling my head back as we kiss savagely.

72

'What do you want, Anastasia?' he breathes.

'You,' I gasp.

'Where?'

'Bed.'

He breaks free, scoops me into his arms, and carries me quickly and seemingly without any strain into my bedroom. Setting me on my feet beside my bed, he leans down and switches on my bedside lamp. He glances quickly around the room and hastily closes the pale cream curtains.

'Now what?' he says softly.

'Make love to me.'

'How?'

Jeez.

'You have got to tell me, baby.'

Holy crap. 'Undress me.' I am panting already.

He smiles and hooks his index finger into my open shirt, pulling me toward him.

'Good girl,' he murmurs, and without taking his blazing eyes off mine, slowly starts to unbutton my shirt.

Tentatively I put my hands on his arms to steady myself. He doesn't complain. His arms are a safe area. When he's finished with the buttons, he pulls my shirt over my shoulders, and I let go of him to let the shirt fall to the floor. He reaches down to the waistband of my jeans, pops the button, and pulls down the zipper.

'Tell me what you want, Anastasia.' His eyes smolder and his lips part as he takes quick shallow breaths.

'Kiss me from here to here,' I whisper trailing my finger from the base of my ear, down my throat. He smoothes my hair out of the line of fire and bends, leaving sweet soft kisses along the path my finger took and then back again.

'My jeans and panties,' I murmur, and he smiles against my throat before he drops to his knees in front of me. Oh, I feel so powerful. Hooking his thumbs into my jeans, he gently pulls them and my panties down my legs. I step out of my flats and my clothes so that I'm left wearing only my bra. He stops and looks up at me expectantly, but he doesn't get up.

'What now, Anastasia?'

'Kiss me,' I whisper.

'Where?'

'You know where.'

'Where?'

Oh, he's taking no prisoners. Embarrassed, I quickly point at the apex of my thighs, and he grins wickedly. I close my eyes, mortified, but at the same time beyond aroused.

'Oh, with pleasure,' he chuckles. He kisses me and unleashes his tongue, his joy-inspiring expert tongue. I groan and fist my hands into his hair. He doesn't stop, his tongue circling my clitoris, driving me insane, on and on, around and around. *Ahhh . . . it's only been . . . how long . . . ? Oh . . .*

'Christian, please,' I beg. I don't want to come standing up. I don't have the strength.

'Please what, Anastasia?'

'Make love to me.'

'I am,' he murmurs, gently blowing against me.

'No. I want you inside me.'

'Are you sure?'

'Please.'

He doesn't stop his sweet, exquisite torture. I moan loudly.

'Christian . . . please.'

He stands and gazes down at me, and his lips glisten with the evidence of my arousal.

It's so hot . . .

'Well?' he asks.

'Well what?' I pant, staring up at him in frantic need.

'I'm still dressed.'

I gape at him in confusion.

Undress him? Yes, I can do this. I reach for his shirt and he steps back.

'Oh no,' he admonishes. Shit, he means his jeans.

Oh, and this gives me an idea. My inner goddess cheers loudly to the rafters, and I drop to my knees in front of him. Rather clumsily and with shaking fingers, I undo his waistband and fly, then yank down his jeans and boxers, and he springs free. *Wow.*

I peek up at him through my lashes, and he's gazing at me with . . . what? Trepidation? Awe? Surprise?

He steps out of his jeans and pulls off his socks, and I take hold of him in my hand and squeeze tightly, pushing my hand back like he's shown me before. He groans and tenses, and his breath hisses through clenched teeth. Very tentatively, I put him in my mouth and suck—hard. Mmm, he tastes good.

'Ahh. Ana . . . whoa, gently.'

He cups my head tenderly, and I push him deeper into my mouth, pressing my lips together as tightly as I can, sheathing my teeth, and sucking hard.

'Fuck,' he hisses.

Oh, that's a good, inspiring, sexy sound, so I do it again, pulling his length deeper, swirling my tongue

75

around the end. *Hmm* . . . I feel like Aphrodite.

'Ana, that's enough. No more.'

I do it again—*Beg, Grey, beg*—and again.

'Ana, you've made your point,' he grunts through gritted teeth. 'I do not want to come in your mouth.'

I do it once more, and he bends down, grasps me by my shoulders, hauls me to my feet, and tosses me on the bed. Dragging his shirt over his head, he then reaches down to his discarded jeans, and like a good Boy Scout, produces a foil packet. He's panting, like me.

'Take your bra off,' he orders.

I sit up and do as I'm told.

'Lie down. I want to look at you.'

I lie down, gazing up at him as he slowly rolls the condom on. I want him so badly. He stares down at me and licks his lips.

'You are a fine sight, Anastasia Steele.' He bends over the bed and slowly crawls up and over me, kissing me as he goes. He kisses each of my breasts and teases my nipples in turn, while I groan and writhe beneath him, and he doesn't stop.

No . . . Stop. I want you.

'Christian, please.'

'Please what?' he murmurs between my breasts.

'I want you inside me.'

'Do you now?'

'Please.'

Gazing at me, he pushes my legs apart with his and moves so that he's hovering above me. Without taking his eyes off mine, he sinks into me at a deliciously slow pace.

I close my eyes, relishing the fullness, the exquisite feeling of his possession, instinctively tilting my pelvis up to meet him, to join with him, groaning loudly. He eases back and very slowly fills me again. My fingers find their way into his silken unruly hair, and he oh-so-slowly moves in and out again.

'Faster, Christian, faster . . . please.'

He gazes down at me in triumph and kisses me hard, then really starts to move—*a punishing, relentless . . . oh fuck*—and I know it will not be long. He sets a pounding rhythm. I start to quicken, my legs tensing beneath him.

'Come on, baby,' he gasps. 'Give it to me.'

His words are my undoing, and I explode, magnificently, mind-numbingly, into a million pieces around him, and he follows, calling out my name.

'Ana! Oh fuck, Ana!' He collapses on top of me, his head buried in my neck.

CHAPTER FOUR

As sanity returns, I open my eyes and gaze up into the face of the man I love. Christian's expression is soft, tender. He strokes his nose against mine, bearing his weight on his elbows, his hands holding mine by the side of my head. Sadly, I suspect that's so I don't touch him. He plants a gentle kiss on my lips as he eases himself out of me.

'I've missed this,' he breathes.

'Me, too,' I whisper.

He takes hold of my chin and kisses me hard. A passionate, beseeching kiss, asking for what? I don't know. It leaves me breathless.

'Don't leave me again,' he implores, looking deep into my eyes, his face serious.

'Okay,' I whisper and smile at him. His answering smile is dazzling; relief, elation, and boyish delight combined into one enchanting look that would melt the coldest of hearts. 'Thank you for the iPad.'

'You are most welcome, Anastasia.'

'What's your favorite song on there?'

'Now, that would be telling.' He grins. 'Come cook me some food, wench. I'm famished,' he adds, sitting up suddenly and dragging me with him.

'Wench?' I giggle.

'Wench. Food, now, please.'

'Since you ask so nicely, sire, I'll get right on it.'

As I scramble out of bed, I dislodge my pillow, revealing the deflated helicopter balloon underneath. Christian reaches for it and gazes up at me, puzzled.

'That's my balloon,' I say, feeling proprietary as I reach for my robe and wrap it around myself. *Oh jeez . . . why did he have to find that?*

'In your bed?' he murmurs.

'Yes.' I flush. 'It's been keeping me company.'

'Lucky *Charlie Tango*,' he says, in surprise.

Yes, I'm sentimental, Grey, because I love you.

'My balloon,' I say again and turn on my heel and head out to the kitchen, leaving him grinning from ear to ear.

*   *   *

Christian and I sit on Kate's Persian rug, eating stir-fry chicken and noodles from white china bowls with chopsticks and sipping chilled white Pinot Grigio. Christian leans against the couch with his just-fucked hair, his long legs stretched out in front of him. He's wearing his jeans and his shirt, and that's all. The Buena Vista Social Club croons softly in the background from Christian's iPod.

'This is good,' he says appreciatively as he digs into his food.

I sit cross-legged beside him, eating greedily, beyond hungry, and admire his naked feet.

'I usually do all the cooking. Kate isn't a great cook.'

'Did your mother teach you?'

'Not really,' I scoff. 'By the time I was interested in learning how to, my mom was living with Husband Number Three in Mansfield, Texas. And Ray, well, he would've lived on toast and takeout if it weren't for me.'

Christian gazes down at me. 'Why didn't you stay in Texas with your mom?'

'Her husband, Steve, and I . . . we didn't get along. And I missed Ray. Her marriage to Steve didn't last long. She came to her senses, I think. She never talks about him,' I add quietly. I think that's a dark part of her life, which we've never discussed.

'So you stayed in Washington with your stepfather.'

'I lived very briefly in Texas. Then went back to Ray.'

'Sounds like you looked after him,' he says softly.

'I suppose.' I shrug.

'You're used to taking care of people.'

The edge in his voice attracts my attention, and I glance up at him.

'What is it?' I ask, startled by his wary expression.

'I want to take care of you.' His eyes glow with some unnamed emotion.

79

My heart rate spikes.

'I've noticed,' I whisper. 'You just go about it in a strange way.'

His brow creases. 'It's the only way I know how.'

'I'm still mad at you for buying SIP.'

He smiles. 'I know, but you being mad, baby, wouldn't stop me.'

'What am I going to say to my work colleagues, to Jack?'

He narrows his eyes. 'That fucker better watch himself.'

'Christian!' I admonish. 'He's my boss.'

Christian's mouth presses into a hard line. He looks like a recalcitrant schoolboy.

'Don't tell them,' he says.

'Don't tell them what?'

'That I own it. The heads of agreement was signed yesterday. The news is embargoed for four weeks while the management at SIP makes some changes.'

'Oh . . . will I be out of a job?' I ask, alarmed.

'I sincerely doubt it,' Christian says wryly, trying to stifle his smile.

I scowl. 'If I leave and find another job, will you buy that company, too?'

'You're not thinking of leaving, are you?' His expression alters, wary once more.

'Possibly. I'm not sure you've given me a great deal of choice.'

'Yes, I will buy that company, too.' He is adamant.

I scowl at him again. I am in a no-win situation here.

'Don't you think you're being a tad overprotective?'

'Yes. I am fully aware of how this looks.'

'Paging Dr. Flynn,' I murmur.

He puts down his empty bowl and gazes at me impassively. I sigh. I don't want to fight. Standing up, I reach for his bowl.

'Would you like dessert?'

'Now you're talking!' he says, giving me a lascivious grin.

'Not me.' *Why not me?* My inner goddess wakes from her doze and sits upright, all ears. 'We have ice cream. Vanilla.' I snicker.

'Really?' Christian's grin gets bigger. 'I think we could do something with that.'

What? I stare at him dumbfounded as he gracefully gets to his feet.

'Can I stay?' he asks.

'What do you mean?'

'The night.'

'I assumed that you would.'

'Good. Where's the ice cream?'

'In the oven.' I smile sweetly at him.

He cocks his head to one side, sighs, and shakes his head at me. 'Sarcasm is the lowest form of wit, Miss Steele.' His eyes glitter.

Oh, shit. What's he planning?

'I could still take you across my knee.'

I place the bowls in the sink. 'Do you have those silver ball things?'

He pats his hands down his chest, belly, and the pockets of his jeans. 'Funnily enough, I don't carry a spare set around with me. Not much call for them in the office.'

'I am very glad to hear it, Mr. Grey, and I thought you said that sarcasm was the lowest form of wit.'

'Well, Anastasia, my new motto is, "If you can't beat 'em, join 'em."'

I gape at him—*I can't believe he just said that*—and he looks sickeningly pleased with himself as he grins at me. Turning, he opens the freezer and takes out a pint of Ben & Jerry's finest vanilla.

'This will do just fine.' He looks up at me, eyes dark. 'Ben & Jerry's & Ana.' He says each word slowly, enunciating every syllable clearly.

Oh fucking my. I think my lower jaw is on the floor. He opens the cutlery drawer and grabs a spoon. When he looks up, his eyes hooded, and his tongue skims his top teeth. Oh, that tongue.

I feel winded. Desire, dark, sleek, and wanton runs hot through my veins. We're going to have fun, with food.

'I hope you're warm,' he whispers. 'I'm going to cool you down with this. Come.' He holds out his hand, and I place mine in his.

In my bedroom he places the ice cream on my bedside table, pulls the duvet off the bed, and removes both the pillows, placing them all in a pile on the floor.

'You have a change of sheets, don't you?'

I nod, watching him, fascinated. He holds up Charlie Tango.

'Don't mess with my balloon,' I warn.

His lips quirk upward in a half smile. 'Wouldn't dream of it, baby, but I do want to mess with you and these sheets.'

My body practically convulses.

'I want to tie you up.'

Oh. 'Okay,' I whisper.

'Just your hands. To the bed. I need you still.'

'Okay,' I whisper again, incapable of anything

more.

He strolls over to me, not taking his eyes off mine.

'We'll use this.' He takes hold of my robe sash and with delicious, teasing slowness, releases the bow, and gently pulls it free of the garment.

My robe falls open while I stand paralyzed under his heated gaze. After a moment, he pushes the robe off my shoulders. It falls and pools at my feet so that I'm standing naked before him. He strokes my face with the backs of his knuckles, and his touch resonates in the depths of my groin. Bending, he kisses my lips briefly.

'Lie on the bed, faceup,' he murmurs, his eyes darkening, burning into mine.

I do as I'm told. My room is shrouded in darkness except for the soft, insipid light from my lamp.

Normally I hate energy-saving bulbs—they are so dim—but being naked here, with Christian, I'm grateful for the muted light. He stands by the bed gazing down at me.

'I could look at you all day, Anastasia,' he says, and with that crawls on to the bed, up my body, and straddles me.

'Arms above your head,' he commands.

I comply and he fastens the end of my robe sash around my left wrist and threads the end through the metal bars at the head of my bed. He pulls it tight so my left arm is flexed above me. He then secures my right hand, tying the sash tightly.

When I'm tied up, staring at him, he visibly relaxes. He likes me tethered. I can't touch him this way. It occurs to me that none of his subs would have touched him either—and what's more, they would never have the opportunity to. He would have always been in control and at a distance. That's why he likes his rules.

He climbs off me and bends to give me a quick peck on the lips. Then he stands and lifts his shirt over his head. He undoes his jeans and drops them to the floor.

He is gloriously naked. My inner goddess is doing a triple axel dismount off the uneven bars, and abruptly my mouth is dry. He has a physique drawn on classical lines: broad muscular shoulders, narrow hips, the inverted triangle. He obviously works out. I could look at him all day. He moves to the end of the bed and grasps my ankles, pulling me swiftly and sharply downward so that my arms are stretched out and unable to move.

'That's better,' he mutters.

Picking up the pint of ice cream, he climbs smoothly back onto the bed to straddle me once more. Very slowly, he peels off the lid and dips the spoon in.

'Hmm . . . it's still quite hard,' he says with a raised brow. Scooping out a spoonful of the vanilla, he pops it into his mouth. 'Delicious,' he murmurs, licking his lips. 'Amazing how good plain old vanilla can taste.' He gazes down at me. 'Want some?' he teases.

He looks so freaking hot, young, and carefree— sitting on me and eating ice cream—eyes bright, face luminous. Oh, what the hell is he going to do to me? As if I can't tell. I nod, shyly.

He scoops out another spoonful and offers me the spoon, so I open my mouth; then he quickly pops it in his mouth again.

'This is too good to share,' he says, smiling

wickedly.

'Hey,' I start in protest.

'Why, Miss Steele, do you like your vanilla?'

'Yes,' I say more forcefully than I mean and try in vain to buck him off.

He laughs. 'Getting feisty, are we? I wouldn't do that if I were you.'

'Ice cream,' I plead.

'Well, as you've pleased me so much today, Miss Steele.' He relents and offers me another spoonful. This time he lets me eat it.

I want to giggle. He's really enjoying himself, and his good humor is infectious. He scoops another spoonful and feeds me some more; then he does it again. *Okay, enough.*

'Hmm, well, this is one way to ensure you eat—force-feed you. I could get used to this.'

Taking another spoonful, he offers me more. This time I keep my mouth shut and shake my head, and he lets it slowly melt on the spoon so that the melted ice cream drips onto my throat, onto my chest. He dips down and very slowly licks it off. My body lights up with longing.

'Mmm. Tastes even better off you, Miss Steele.'

I pull against my restraints and the bed creaks ominously, but I don't care—I'm burning with desire, it's consuming me. He takes another spoonful and lets the ice cream dribble onto my breasts. Then with the back of the spoon, he spreads it over each breast and nipple.

Oh . . . it's cold. Each nipple peaks and hardens beneath the cool of the vanilla.

'Cold?' Christian asks softly and bends to lick and suckle all the ice cream off me once more, his mouth hot compared to the cool of the ice.

85

It's torture. As it starts to melt, the ice cream runs off me in rivulets onto the bed. His lips continue their slow torture, sucking hard, nuzzling, softly—*Oh please!*—I'm panting.

'Want some?' And before I can confirm or deny his offer, his tongue is in my mouth, and it's cold and skilled and tastes of Christian and vanilla. Delicious.

And just as I am getting used to the sensation, he sits up again and trails a spoonful of ice cream down the center of my body, across my stomach, and into my navel where he deposits a large dollop of ice cream. *Oh, this is chillier than before, but weirdly it burns.*

'Now, you've done this before.' Christian's eyes shine. 'You're going to have to stay still, or there will be ice cream all over the bed.' He kisses each of my breasts and sucks each of my nipples hard, then follows the line of ice cream down my body, sucking and licking as he goes.

And I try; I try to stay still despite the heady combination of cold and his inflaming touch. But my hips start to move involuntarily, gyrating to their own rhythm, caught up in his cool vanilla spell. He shifts lower and starts eating the ice cream in my belly, swirling his tongue into and around my navel.

I moan. *Holy cow.* It's cold, it's hot, it's tantalizing, but he doesn't stop. He trails the ice cream farther down my body, into my pubic hair, on to my clitoris. I cry out, loudly.

'Hush now,' Christian says softly as his magical tongue sets to work lapping up the vanilla, and now I'm keening quietly.

'Oh . . . please . . . Christian.'

'I know, baby, I know,' he breathes as his tongue

works its magic. He doesn't stop, just doesn't stop, and my body is climbing—higher, higher. He slips one finger inside me, then another, and he moves them with agonizing slowness in and out.

'Just here,' he murmurs, and he rhythmically strokes the front wall of my vagina while he continues the exquisite, relentless licking and sucking.

I erupt unexpectedly into a mind-blowing orgasm that stuns all my senses, obliterating all that's happening outside my body as I writhe and groan. *Holy fucking cow,* that was so quick.

I am vaguely aware that he has stopped his ministrations. He's hovering over me, sliding on a condom, and then he's inside me, hard and fast.

'Oh yes!' he groans as he slams into me. He's sticky—the residual melted ice cream spreading between us. It's a strangely distracting sensation, but one I can't dwell on for more than a few seconds as Christian suddenly pulls out of me and flips me over.

'This way,' he murmurs and abruptly is inside me once more, but he doesn't start his usual punishing rhythm straight away. He leans over, releases my hands, and pulls me upright so I am practically sitting on him. His hands move up to my breasts, and he palms them both, tugging gently on my nipples. I groan, tossing my head back against his shoulder. He nuzzles my neck, biting down, as he flexes his hips, deliciously slowly, filling me again and again.

'Do you know how much you mean to me?' he breathes against my ear.

'No,' I gasp.

He smiles against my neck, and his fingers curl

around my jaw and throat, holding me fast for a moment.

'Yes, you do. I'm not going to let you go.'

I groan as he picks up speed.

'You are mine, Anastasia.'

'Yes, yours,' I pant.

'I take care of what's mine,' he hisses and bites my ear.

I cry out.

'That's right, baby, I want to hear you.' He snakes one hand around my waist while his other hand grasps my hip, and he pushes into me harder, making me cry out again. And the punishing rhythm starts. His breathing grows harsher and harsher, ragged, matching mine. I feel the familiar quickening deep inside. *Again!*

I am just sensation. This is what he does to me—takes my body and possesses it wholly so that I think of nothing but him. His magic is powerful, intoxicating. I'm a butterfly caught in his net, unable and unwilling to escape. *I'm his . . . totally his.*

'Come on, baby,' he growls through gritted teeth and on cue, like the sorcerer's apprentice I am, I let go, and we find our release together.

*   *   *

I am lying curled up in his arms on sticky sheets. His front is pressed to my back, his nose in my hair.

'What I feel for you frightens me,' I whisper.

He stills. 'Me too, baby,' he says quietly.

'What if you leave me?' The thought is horrific.

'I'm not going anywhere. I don't think I could ever have my fill of you, Anastasia.'

I turn and gaze at him. His expression is serious, sincere. I lean over and kiss him gently. He smiles and reaches up to tuck my hair behind my ear.

'I've never felt the way I felt when you left, Anastasia. I would move heaven and earth to avoid feeling like that again.' He sounds so sad, dazed even.

I kiss him again. I want to lighten our mood somehow, but Christian does it for me.

'Will you come with me to my father's summer party tomorrow? It's an annual charity thing. I said I'd go.'

I smile, feeling suddenly shy.

'Of course I'll come.' Oh, shit. I have nothing to wear.

'What?'

'Nothing.'

'Tell me,' he insists.

'I have nothing to wear.'

Christian looks momentarily uncomfortable.

'Don't be mad, but I still have all those clothes for you at home. I am sure there are a couple of dresses in there.'

I purse my lips. 'Do you, now?' I mutter, my voice sardonic. I don't want to fight with him tonight. I need a shower.

*   *   *

The girl who looks like me is standing outside SIP. Hang on—she is me. I am pale and unwashed, and all my clothes are too big; I'm staring at her, and she's wearing my clothes—happy, healthy.

'What do you have that I don't?' I ask her.

'Who are you?'

89

'I'm nobody . . . Who are you? Are you nobody, too . . .?'

'Then there's a pair of us—don't tell, they'd banish us, you know . . .' She smiles, a slow, evil grimace that spreads across her face, and it's so chilling that I start to scream.

*   *   *

'Jesus, Ana!' Christian is shaking me awake.

I am so disoriented. *I'm at home . . . in the dark . . . in bed with Christian.* I shake my head, trying to clear my mind.

'Baby, are you okay? You were having a bad dream.'

'Oh.'

He switches on the lamp so we're bathed in its dim light. He gazes down at me, his face etched with concern.

'The girl,' I whisper.

'What is it? What girl?' he asks soothingly.

'There was a girl outside SIP when I left this evening. She looked like me . . . but not really.'

Christian stills, and as the light from the bedside lamp warms up, I see his face is ashen.

'When was this?' he whispers, dismayed. He sits up, staring down at me.

'When I left work this evening,' I repeat. 'Do you know who she is?'

'Yes.' He runs a hand through his hair.

'Who?'

His mouth presses into a hard line, but he says nothing.

'Who?' I press.

'It's Leila.'

I swallow. The ex-sub! I remember Christian talking about her before we went gliding. Suddenly, he's radiating tension. Something is going on.

'The girl who put "Toxic" on your iPod?'

He glances at me anxiously.

'Yes,' he says. 'Did she say anything?'

'She said, 'What do you have that I don't have?' and when I asked who she was, she said, "Nobody."'

Christian closes his eyes as if in pain. What's happened? What does she mean to him?

My scalp prickles as adrenaline spikes through my body. *What if she means a lot to him? Perhaps he misses her? I know so little about his past . . . um, relationships.* She must have had a contract, and she would have done what he wanted, given him what he needed gladly.

Oh no—when I can't. The thought makes me nauseous.

Climbing out of bed, Christian drags on his jeans and heads into the main room. A glance at my alarm clock shows it's five in the morning. I roll out of bed, putting his white shirt on, and follow him.

Holy shit, he's on the phone.

'Yes, outside SIP, yesterday . . . early evening,' he says quietly. He turns to me as I move toward the kitchen and asks me directly, 'What time, exactly?'

'About ten to six?' I mumble. Who on earth is he calling at this hour? What's Leila done? He relays the information to whoever's on the line, not taking his eyes off me, his expression dark and earnest.

'Find out how . . . Yes . . . I wouldn't have said so, but then I wouldn't have thought she could do this.' He closes his eyes as if he's in pain. 'I don't know how that will go down . . . Yes, I'll talk to her . . . Yes . . . I know . . . Follow it up and let me

91

know. Just find her, Welch—she's in trouble. Find her.' He hangs up.

'Do you want some tea?' I ask. Tea, Ray's answer to every crisis and the only thing he does well in the kitchen. I fill the kettle with water.

'Actually, I'd like to go back to bed.' His look tells me that it's not to sleep.

'Well, I need some tea. Would you like to join me for a cup?' I want to know what's going on. I will not be sidetracked by sex.

He runs his hand through his hair in exasperation. 'Yes, please,' he says, but I can tell he's irritated.

I put the kettle on the stove and busy myself with teacups and the teapot. My anxiety level has shot to DEFCON 1. Is he going to tell me the problem? Or am I going to have to dig?

I sense his eyes on me—sense his uncertainty, and his anger is palpable. I glance up, and his eyes glitter with apprehension.

'What is it?' I ask softly.

He shakes his head.

'You're not going to tell me?'

He sighs and closes his eyes. 'No.'

'Why?'

'Because it shouldn't concern you. I don't want you tangled up in this.'

'It shouldn't concern me, but it does. She found me and accosted me outside my office. How does she know about me? How does she know where I work? I think I have a right to know what's going on.'

He runs a hand through his hair again, radiating frustration as if waging some internal battle.

'Please?' I ask softly.

His mouth sets into a hard line, and he rolls his eyes at me.

'Okay,' he says, resigned. 'I have no idea how she found you. Maybe the photograph of us in Portland, I don't know.' He sighs again, and I sense his frustration is directed at himself.

I wait patiently, pouring boiling water into the teapot as he paces back and forth. After a beat he continues.

'While I was with you in Georgia, Leila turned up at my apartment unannounced and made a scene in front of Gail.'

'Gail?'

'Mrs. Jones.'

'What do you mean, "made a scene"?'

He glares at me, appraising.

'Tell me. You're keeping something back.' My tone is more forceful than I feel.

He blinks at me, surprised. 'Ana, I—' he stops.

'Please?'

He sighs in defeat. 'She made a haphazard attempt to open a vein.'

'Oh no!' That explains the bandage on her wrist.

'Gail got her to hospital. But Leila discharged herself before I could get there.'

Crap. What does this mean? Suicidal? Why?

'The shrink who saw her called it a typical cry for help. He didn't believe her to be truly at risk—one step from suicidal ideation, he called it. But I'm not convinced. I've been trying to track her down since then to get her some help.'

'Did she say anything to Mrs. Jones?'

He gazes at me. He looks really uncomfortable.

'Not much,' he says eventually, but I know he's not telling me everything.

93

I distract myself with pouring tea into teacups. So Leila wants back into Christian's life and chooses a suicide attempt to attract his attention? *Whoa . . . scary.* But effective. Christian left Georgia to be at her side, but she disappears before he gets there? How odd.

'You can't find her? What about her family?'

'They don't know where she is. Neither does her husband.'

'Husband?'

'Yes,' he says distractedly, 'she's been married for about two years.'

What? 'So she was with you while she was married?' *Holy fuck.* He really has no boundaries.

'No! Good God, no. She was with me nearly three years ago. Then she left and married this guy shortly afterward.'

Oh. 'So why is she trying to get your attention now?'

He shakes his head sadly. 'I don't know. All we've managed to find out is that she ran out on her husband about four months ago.'

'Let me get this straight. She hasn't been your submissive for three years?'

'About two and a half years.'

'And she wanted more.'

'Yes.'

'But you didn't?'

'You know this.'

'So she left you.'

'Yes.'

'So why is she coming to you now?'

'I don't know.' And the tone of this voice tells me that he at least has a theory.

'But you suspect . . .'

94

His eyes narrow perceptibly with anger. 'I suspect it has something to do with you.'

Me? What would she want with me? *What do you have that I don't?'*

I stare at Fifty, magnificently naked from the waist up. I have him; he's mine. That's what I have, and yet she looked like me: same dark hair and pale skin. I frown at the thought. *Yes . . . what do I have that she doesn't?*

'Why didn't you tell me yesterday?' he asks softly.

'I forgot about her.' I shrug apologetically. 'You know, drinks after work, at the end of my first week. You turning up at the bar and your . . . testosterone rush with Jack, and then when we were here. It slipped my mind. You have a habit of making me forget things.'

'Testosterone rush?' His lips twitch.

'Yes. The pissing contest.'

'I'll show you a testosterone rush.'

'Wouldn't you rather have a cup of tea?'

'No, Anastasia, I wouldn't.'

His eyes burn into me, scorching me with his I-want-you-and-I-want-you-now look. *Fuck . . . it's so hot.*

'Forget about her. Come.' He holds out his hand.

My inner goddess does three back flips over the gym floor as I grasp his hand.

*　　　*　　　*

I wake, too warm, and I'm wrapped around a naked Christian Grey. Even though he's fast asleep, he's holding me close. Soft morning light filters through the curtains. My head is on his chest, my leg tangled with his, my arm across his stomach.

I raise my head, scared that I might wake him. He looks young and relaxed in sleep and he's mine.

Hmm . . . Reaching up, I tentatively stroke his chest, running my fingertips through the smattering of hair, and he doesn't stir. I can't quite believe it. He's really mine—for a few more precious moments. I lean over and tenderly kiss one of his scars. He moans softly but doesn't wake, and I smile. I kiss another and his eyes open.

'Hi.' I grin at him, guiltily.

'Hi,' he answers warily. 'What are you doing?'

'Looking at you.' I run my fingers down his happy trail. He captures my hand, narrows his eyes, then smiles a brilliant Christian-at-ease smile, and I relax. My secret touching stays secret.

Oh . . . why won't you let me touch you?

Suddenly he moves on top of me, pressing me into the mattress, his hands on mine, warning me. He strokes my nose with his.

'I think you're up to no good, Miss Steele,' he accuses, but his smile remains.

'I like being up to no good near you.'

'You do?' he asks and kisses me lightly on the lips. 'Sex or breakfast?' he asks, his eyes dark but full of humor. His erection is digging into me, and I tilt my pelvis up to meet him.

'Good choice,' he murmurs against my throat, as he trails kisses down to my breast.

*　　　*　　　*

I stand at my chest of drawers, staring at my mirror, trying to coax my hair into some semblance of style—really, it's just too long. I'm in jeans and a

T-shirt, and Christian, freshly showered, is dressing behind me. I gaze at his body hungrily.

'How often do you work out?' I ask.

'Every weekday,' he says, buttoning his fly.

'What do you do?'

'Run, weights, kickboxing.' He shrugs.

'Kickboxing?'

'Yes, I have a personal trainer, an ex-Olympic contender who teaches me. His name is Claude. He's very good. You'd like him.'

I turn to gaze at him as he starts to button up his white shirt.

'What do you mean, I'd like him?'

'You'd like him as a trainer.'

'Why would I need a personal trainer? I have you to keep me fit.'

He saunters over and wraps his arms around me, his darkening eyes meeting mine in the mirror.

'But I want you fit, baby, for what I have in mind. I'll need you to keep up.'

I flush as memories of the playroom flood my mind. Yes . . . the Red Room of Pain is exhausting. Is he going to let me back in there? Do I want to go back in?

Of course you do! My inner goddess screams.

I stare into his unfathomable, mesmerizing gray eyes.

'You know you want to,' he mouths at me.

I flush, and the undesirable thought that Leila could probably keep up slithers invidious and unwelcome into my mind. I press my lips together and Christian frowns at me.

'What?' he asks, concerned.

'Nothing.' I shake my head at him. 'Okay, I'll meet Claude.'

'You will?' Christian's face lights up in astounded disbelief. His expression makes me smile. He looks like he's won the lottery, though Christian's probably never even bought a ticket—he has no need.

'Yes, jeez—if it makes you that happy,' I scoff.

He tightens his arms around me and kisses my cheek. 'You have no idea,' he whispers. 'So—what would you like to do today?' He nuzzles me, sending delicious tingles through my body.

'I'd like to get my hair cut, and um . . . I need to bank a check and buy a car.'

'Ah,' he says knowingly and bites his lip. Taking one hand off me, he reaches into his jeans pocket and holds up the key to my little Audi.

'It's here,' he says quietly, his expression uncertain.

'What do you mean, it's here?' Boy. I sound angry. Crap. I *am* angry. *How dare he!*

'Taylor brought it back yesterday.'

I open my mouth then close it and repeat the process twice, but I have been rendered speechless. He's giving me back the car. Double crap. Why didn't I foresee this? Well, two can play at that game. I fish in the back pocket of my jeans and pull out the envelope with his check.

'Here, this is yours.'

Christian looks at me quizzically; then, recognizing the envelope, raises both his hands and steps away

'Oh no. That's your money.'

'No, it isn't. I'd like to buy the car from you.'

His expression changes completely. Fury—yes, fury—sweeps across his face.

'No, Anastasia. Your money, your car,' he snaps.

'No, Christian. My money, your car. I'll buy it from you.'

'I gave you that car for your graduation present.'

'If you'd given me a pen—that would be a suitable graduation present. You gave me an Audi.'

'Do you really want to argue about this?'

'No.'

'Good—here are the keys.' He puts them on the chest of drawers.

'That's not what I meant!'

'End of discussion, Anastasia. Don't push me.'

I scowl at him, then inspiration hits me. Taking the envelope, I rip it in two, then two again and drop the contents into my wastebasket. Oh, that feels good.

Christian gazes at me impassively, but I know I've just lit the fuse and should stand well back. He strokes his chin.

'You are, as ever, challenging, Miss Steele,' he says dryly. He turns on his heel and stalks into the other room. That is not the reaction I expected. I was anticipating full-scale Armageddon. I stare at myself in the mirror and shrug, deciding on a ponytail.

My curiosity is piqued. What is Fifty doing? I follow him into the room, and he's on the phone.

'Yes, twenty-four thousand dollars. Directly.'

He glances up at me, still impassive.

'Good . . . Monday? Excellent . . . No that's all, Andrea.'

He snaps the phone shut.

'Deposited in your bank account, Monday. Don't play games with me.' He's boiling mad, but I don't care.

'Twenty-four thousand dollars!' I'm almost

99

screaming. 'And how do you know my account number?'

My ire takes Christian by surprise.

'I know everything about you, Anastasia,' he says quietly.

'There's no way my car was worth twenty-four thousand dollars.'

'I would agree with you, but it's about knowing your market, whether you're buying or selling. Some lunatic out there wanted that death trap and was willing to pay that amount of money. Apparently it's a classic. Ask Taylor if you don't believe me.'

I glower at him and he glowers back, two angry stubborn fools glaring at each other.

And I feel it, the pull—the electricity between us—tangible, drawing us together. Suddenly he grabs me and pushes me up against the door, his mouth on mine, claiming me hungrily, one hand on my behind pressing me to his groin and the other in the nape of my hair, tugging my head back. My fingers are in his hair, twisting hard, holding him to me. He grinds his body into mine, imprisoning me, his breathing ragged. I feel him. He wants me, and I'm heady and reeling with excitement as I acknowledge his need for me.

'Why, why do you defy me?' he mumbles between his heated kisses.

My blood sings in my veins. Will he always have this effect on me? And I on him?

'Because I can.' I'm breathless. I feel rather than see his smile against my neck, and he presses his forehead to mine.

'Lord, I want to take you now, but I'm out of condoms. I can never get enough of you. You're a maddening, maddening woman.'

'And you make me mad,' I whisper. 'In every way.'

He shakes his head. 'Come. Let's go out for breakfast. And I know a place you can get your hair cut.'

'Okay,' I acquiesce and just like that, our fight is over.

*　　*　　*

'I'll get this.' I pick up the tab for breakfast before he does.

He scowls.

'You have to be quick around here, Grey.'

'You're right, I do,' he says sourly, though I think he's teasing.

'Don't look so cross. I'm twenty-four thousand dollars richer than I was this morning. I can afford'—I glance at the check—'twenty-two dollars and sixty-seven cents for breakfast.'

'Thank you,' he says grudgingly. Oh, the sulky schoolboy is back.

'Where to now?'

'You really want your hair cut?'

'Yes, look at it.'

'You look lovely to me. You always do.'

I blush and stare down at my fingers knotted in my lap. 'And there's your father's function this evening.'

'Remember, it's black tie.'

'Where is it?'

'At my parents' house. They have a tent. You know, the works.'

'What's the charity?'

Christian rubs his hands down his thighs, looking uncomfortable.

'It's a drug rehab program for parents with young kids called Coping Together.'

'Sounds like a good cause,' I say softly.

'Come, let's go.' He stands, effectively halting that topic of conversation and holds out his hand. As I take it, he tightens his fingers around mine.

It's strange. He's so demonstrative in some ways and yet so closed in others. He leads me out of the restaurant, and we walk down the street. It is a lovely, mild morning. The sun is shining, and the air smells of coffee and freshly baked bread.

'Where are we going?'

'Surprise.'

Oh, okay. I don't really like surprises.

We walk for two blocks, and the stores become decidedly more exclusive. I haven't yet had an opportunity to explore, but this really is just around the corner from where I live. Kate will be pleased. There are plenty of small boutiques to feed her fashion passion. Actually, I need to buy some floaty skirts for work.

Christian stops outside a large, slick-looking beauty salon and opens the door for me. It's called Esclava. The interior is all white and leather. At the stark white reception desk sits a young blonde woman in a crisp white uniform. She glances up as we enter.

'Good morning, Mr. Grey,' she says brightly, color rising in her cheeks as she bats her eyelashes at him. It's the Grey effect, but she knows him! How?

'Hello, Greta.'

And he knows her. What is this?

102

'Is this the usual, sir?' she asks politely. She's wearing very pink lipstick.

'No,' he says quickly, with a nervous glance at me.

The usual? What does that mean?

Holy fuck! It's Rule Number Six, the damned beauty salon. All the waxing nonsense . . . shit!

This is where he brought all his subs? Maybe Leila, too? What the hell am I supposed to make of this?

'Miss Steele will tell you what she wants.'

I glare at him. He's introducing the Rules by stealth. I've agreed to the personal trainer—and now this?

'Why here?' I hiss at him.

'I own this place, and three more like it.'

'You own it?' I gasp in surprise. Well, that's unexpected.

'Yes. It's a sideline. Anyway—whatever you want, you can have it here, on the house. All sorts of massage: Swedish, shiatsu; hot stones, reflexology, seaweed baths, facials, all that stuff that women like—everything. It's done here.' He waves his long-fingered hand dismissively.

'Waxing?'

He laughs. 'Yes waxing, too. Everywhere,' he whispers conspiratorially, enjoying my discomfort.

I blush and glance at Greta, who is looking at me expectantly.

'I'd like a haircut, please.'

'Certainly, Miss Steele.'

Greta is all pink lipstick and bustling Germanic efficiency as she checks her computer screen.

'Franco is free in five minutes.'

'Franco's fine,' says Christian reassuringly to me.

I am trying to wrap my head around this. Christian Grey, CEO, owns a chain of beauty salons.

I peek up at him, and suddenly he blanches— something, or someone, has caught his eye. I turn to see where he's looking, and right at the back of the salon a sleek platinum blonde has appeared, closing a door behind her and speaking to one of the hair stylists.

Platinum Blonde is tall, tanned, lovely, and in her late thirties or early forties—it's difficult to tell. She's wearing the same uniform as Greta, but in black. She looks stunning. Her hair shines like a halo, cut in a sharp bob. As she turns, she catches sight of Christian and smiles at him, a dazzling smile of warm recognition.

'Excuse me,' Christian mumbles hurriedly.

He strides quickly through the salon, past the hair stylists all in white, past the apprentices at the sinks, and over to her, too far away for me to hear their conversation. Platinum Blonde greets him with obvious affection, kissing both his cheeks, her hands resting on his upper arms, and they talk animatedly together.

'Miss Steele?'

Greta the receptionist is trying to get my attention.

'Hang on a moment, please.' I watch Christian, fascinated.

Platinum Blonde turns and looks at me, and gives me the same dazzling smile, as if she knows me. I smile politely back.

Christian looks upset about something. He's reasoning with her, and she's acquiescing, holding her hands up and smiling at him. He's smiling at her—clearly they know each other well. Perhaps they've worked together for a long time? Maybe she runs the place; after all, she has a certain look of authority.

Then it hits me like a wrecking ball, and I know, deep down in my gut on a visceral level, I know who it is. It's her. *Stunning, older, beautiful.*

It's Mrs. Robinson.

CHAPTER FIVE

'Greta, who is Mr. Grey talking to?' My scalp is trying to leave the building. It's prickling with apprehension, and my subconscious is screaming at me to follow it. But I sound nonchalant enough.

'Oh, that's Mrs. Lincoln. She owns the place with Mr. Grey.' Greta seems more than happy to share.

'Mrs. Lincoln?' I thought Mrs. Robinson was divorced. Perhaps she's remarried to some poor sap.

'Yes. She's not usually here, but one of our technicians is sick today so she's filling in.'

'Do you know Mrs. Lincoln's first name?'

Greta looks up at me, frowning, and purses her bright pink lips, questioning my curiosity. Shit, perhaps this is a step too far.

'Elena,' she says, almost reluctantly.

I'm swamped by a strange sense of relief that my spidey sense has not let me down.

Spidey sense? my subconscious snorts. *Pedo sense.*

They are still deep in discussion. Christian is talking rapidly to Elena, and she looks worried, nodding, grimacing, and shaking her head. Reaching out, she rubs his arm soothingly while biting her lip. Another nod, and she glances at me and offers me a small, reassuring smile.

I can only stare at her, stone-faced. I think I'm in shock. How could he bring me here?

She murmurs something to Christian; he looks my way briefly, then turns back to her and replies. She nods, and I think she's wishing him luck, but my lip-reading skills aren't highly developed.

Fifty strides back to me, anxiety etched on his face. *Damn right*. Mrs. Robinson returns to the back room, closing the door behind her.

Christian frowns. 'Are you okay?' he asks, but his voice is strained, cautious.

'Not really. You didn't want to introduce me?' My voice sounds cold, hard.

His mouth drops open, he looks as if I've pulled the rug from under his feet.

'But I thought—'

'For a bright man, sometimes . . .' Words fail me. 'I'd like to go, please.'

'Why?'

'You know why.' I roll my eyes.

He gazes down at me, his eyes burning.

'I'm sorry, Ana. I didn't know she'd be here. She's never here. She's opened a new branch at the Bravern Center, and that's where she's normally based. Someone was sick today.'

I turn on my heel and head for the door.

'We won't need Franco, Greta,' Christian snaps as we head out of the door. I have to suppress the impulse to run. I want to run fast and far away. I have an overwhelming urge to cry. I just need to get away from all this fucked-upness.

Christian walks wordlessly beside me as I try to mull all this over in my head. Wrapping my arms

106

protectively around myself, I keep my head down, avoiding the trees on Second Avenue. Wisely, he makes no move to touch me. My mind is boiling with unanswered questions. Will Mr. Evasive fess up?

'You used to take your subs there?' I snap.

'Some of them, yes,' he says quietly, his tone clipped.

'Leila?'

'Yes.'

'The place looks very new.'

'It's been refurbished recently.'

'I see. So Mrs. Robinson met all your subs.'

'Yes.'

'Did they know about her?'

'No. None of them did. Only you.'

'But I'm not your sub.'

'No, you most definitely are not.'

I stop and face him. His eyes are wide, fearful. His lips are pressed into a hard, uncompromising line.

'Can you see how fucked-up this is?' I glare up at him, my voice low.

'Yes. I'm sorry.' And he has the grace to look contrite.

'I want to get my hair cut, preferably somewhere where you haven't fucked either the staff or the clientele.'

He flinches.

'Now if you'll excuse me.'

'You're not running. Are you?' he asks.

'No, I just want a damn haircut. Somewhere I can close my eyes, have someone wash my hair, and forget about all this baggage that accompanies you.'

He runs his hand through his hair. 'I can have

Franco come to the apartment, or your place,' he says quietly.

'She's very attractive.'

He blinks. 'Yes, she is.'

'Is she still married?'

'No. She divorced about five years ago.'

'Why aren't you with her?'

'Because that's over between us. I've told you this.' His brow creases suddenly. Holding his finger up, he fishes his BlackBerry out of his jacket pocket. It must be vibrating because I don't hear it ring.

'Welch,' he snaps, then listens. We are standing on Second Avenue, and I gaze in the direction of the larch sapling in front of me, its leaves the newest green.

People bustle past us, lost in their Saturday morning chores, no doubt contemplating their own personal dramas. I wonder if they include stalker ex-submissives, stunning ex-Dommes, and a man who has no concept of privacy under US law.

'Killed in a car crash? When?' Christian interrupts my reverie.

Oh no. Who? I listen more closely.

'That's twice that bastard's not been forthcoming. He must know. Does he have no feelings for her whatsoever?' Christian shakes his head in disgust. 'This is beginning to make sense . . . no . . . explains why, but not where.' Christian glances around us as if searching for something, and I find myself mirroring his actions. Nothing catches my eye. There are just the shoppers, the traffic, and the trees.

'She's here,' Christian continues. 'She's watching us . . . Yes . . . No. Two or four, twenty-four seven . . .

I haven't broached that yet.' Christian looks at me directly.

Broached what? I frown and he regards me warily.

'What . . . ,' he whispers and pales, his eyes widening. 'I see. When? . . . That recently? But how? . . . No background checks? . . . I see. E-mail the name, address, and photos if you have them . . . twenty-four seven, from this afternoon. Establish liaison with Taylor.' Christian hangs up.

'Well?' I ask, exasperated. Is he going to tell me?

'That was Welch.'

'Who's Welch?'

'My security adviser.'

'Okay. So what's happened?'

'Leila left her husband about three months ago and ran off with a guy who was killed in a car accident four weeks ago.'

'Oh.'

'The asshole shrink should have found that out,' he says angrily. 'Grief, that's what this is. Come.' He holds out his hand, and I automatically place mine in his before I snatch it away again.

'Wait a minute. We were in the middle of a discussion about "us." About her, your Mrs. Robinson.'

Christian's face hardens. 'She's not my Mrs. Robinson. We can talk about it at my place.'

'I don't want to go to your place. I want to get my hair cut!' I shout. If I can just focus on this one thing . . .

He grabs his BlackBerry from his pocket again and dials a number. 'Greta, Christian Grey. I want Franco at my place in an hour. Ask Mrs. Lincoln . . . Good.' He puts his phone away. 'He's coming at one.'

'Christian . . . !' I splutter, exasperated.

'Anastasia, Leila is obviously suffering a psychotic break. I don't know if it's you or me she's after, or what lengths she's prepared to go to. We'll go to your place, pick up your things, and you can stay with me until we've tracked her down.'

'Why would I want to do that?'

'So I can keep you safe.'

'But—'

He glares at me. 'You are coming back to my apartment if I have to drag you there by your hair.'

I gape at him . . . this is beyond belief. Fifty Shades in Glorious Technicolor.

'I think you're overreacting.'

'I don't. We can continue our discussion back at my place. Come.'

I cross my arms and glare at him. This has gone too far.

'No,' I state stubbornly. I have to make a stand.

'You can walk or I can carry you. I don't mind either way, Anastasia.'

'You wouldn't dare.' I scowl at him. Surely he wouldn't make a scene on Second Avenue?

He half smiles at me, but the smile doesn't reach his eyes.

'Oh, baby, we both know that if you throw down the gauntlet, I'll be only too happy to pick it up.'

We glare at each other—and abruptly he sweeps down, clasps me around my thighs, and lifts me. Before I know it, I am over his shoulder.

'Put me down!' I scream. Oh, it feels good to scream.

He starts striding along Second Avenue, ignoring me. Clasping his arm firmly around my thighs, he swats my behind with his free hand.

'Christian!' I shout. People are staring. Could this be any more humiliating? 'I'll walk! I'll walk.'

He puts me down, and before he's even stood upright, I stomp off in the direction of my apartment, seething, ignoring him. Of course, he's by my side in moments, but I continue to ignore him. What am I going to do? I am so angry, but I'm not even sure what I am angry about—there's so much.

As I stalk back home, I make a mental list:

1. Over-the-shoulder carrying—unacceptable for anyone over the age of six.
2. Taking me to the salon that he owns with his ex-lover—how stupid can he be?
3. The same place he took his submissives—same stupidity at work here.
4. Not even realizing that this was a bad idea—and he's supposed to be a bright guy.
5. Having crazy ex-girlfriends. Can I blame him for that? I am so furious; yes, I can.
6. Knowing my bank account number—that's just too stalkery by half.
7. Buying SIP—he's got more money than sense.
8. Insisting I stay with him—the threat from Leila must be worse than he feared . . . he didn't mention that yesterday.

Realization dawns. Something's changed. What could that be? I halt, and Christian halts with me. 'What's happened?' I demand.

He knits his brow. 'What do you mean?'

'With Leila.'

'I've told you.'

'No, you haven't. There's something else. You didn't insist that I go to your place yesterday. So what's happened?'

He shifts uncomfortably.

'Christian! Tell me!' I snap.

'She managed to obtain a concealed weapons permit yesterday.'

Oh, shit. I gaze at him, blinking, and feel the blood drain from my face as I absorb this news. I may faint. Suppose she wants to kill him? *No!*

'That means she can just buy a gun,' I whisper.

'Ana,' he says, his voice full of concern. He places his hands on my shoulders, pulling me close to him. 'I don't think she'll do anything stupid, but—I just don't want to take that risk with you.'

'Not me . . . what about you?' I whisper.

He frowns down at me, and I wrap my arms around him and hug him hard, my face against his chest. He doesn't seem to mind.

'Let's get back,' he murmurs, and he reaches down and kisses my hair, and that's it. All my fury is gone, but not forgotten. Dissipated under the threat of some harm coming to Christian. The thought is unbearable.

*   *   *

Solemnly I pack a small case and place my Mac, the BlackBerry, my iPad, and the *Charlie Tango* balloon in my backpack.

'Charlie Tango's coming, too?' Christian asks.

I nod and he gives me a small, indulgent smile.

'Ethan is back Tuesday,' I mutter.

'Ethan?'

112

'Kate's brother. He's staying here until he finds a place in Seattle.'

Christian gazes at me blankly, but I notice the frostiness creep into his eyes.

'Well, it's good that you'll be staying with me. Give him more room,' he says quietly.

'I don't know that he's got keys. I'll need to be back then.'

Christian says nothing.

'That's everything.'

He grabs my case, and we head out the door. As we walk around to the back of the building to the parking lot, I'm aware that I am looking over my shoulder. I don't know if my paranoia has taken over or if someone really is watching me. Christian opens the passenger door of the Audi and looks at me expectantly.

'Are you getting in?' he asks.

'I thought I was driving.'

'No. I'll drive.'

'Something wrong with my driving? Don't tell me you know what I scored on my driving test . . . I wouldn't be surprised with your stalking tendencies.' Maybe he knows that I just scraped through the written test.

'Get in the car, Anastasia,' he snaps angrily.

'Okay.' I hastily climb in. *Honestly, chill, will you?*

Perhaps he has the same uneasy feeling, too. Some dark sentinel watching us—well, a pale brunette with brown eyes who has an uncanny resemblance to yours truly and, quite possibly, a concealed firearm.

Christian sets off into traffic.

'Were all your submissives brunettes?'

He frowns. 'Yes,' he mutters. He sounds

113

uncertain, and I imagine him thinking, *Where's she going with this?*

'I just wondered.'

'I told you. I prefer brunettes.'

'Mrs. Robinson isn't a brunette.'

'That's probably why,' he mutters. 'She put me off blondes forever.'

'You're kidding,' I gasp.

'Yes. I'm kidding,' he replies, exasperated.

I stare impassively out the window, spying brunettes everywhere, none of them Leila, though.

So, he only likes brunettes. I wonder why? Did Mrs. Extraordinarily Glamorous in Spite of Being Old Robinson really put him off blondes? I shake my head—Christian Mindfuck Grey.

'Tell me about her.'

'What do you want to know?' Christian's brow furrows, and his tone of voice tries to warn me off.

'Tell me about your business arrangement.'

He visibly relaxes, happy to talk about work. 'I am a silent partner. I'm not particularly interested in the beauty business, but she's built it into a successful venture. I just invested and helped get her started.'

'Why?'

'I owed it to her.'

'Oh?'

'When I dropped out of Harvard, she loaned me a hundred grand to start my business.'

Holy fuck . . . she's rich, too.

'You dropped out?'

'It wasn't my thing. I did two years. Unfortunately, my parents were not so understanding.'

I frown. Mr. Grey and Dr. Grace Trevelyan

114

disapproving; I can't picture it.

'You don't seem to have done too badly dropping out. What was your major?'

'Politics and Economics.'

Hmm . . . figures.

'So, she's rich?' I murmur.

'She was a bored trophy wife, Anastasia. Her husband was wealthy—big in timber.' He gives me a wolfish grin. 'He wouldn't let her work. You know, he was controlling. Some men are like that.' He gives me a quick sideways smile.

'Really? A controlling man, surely a mythical creature?' I don't think I can squeeze any more sarcasm into my response.

Christian's grin gets bigger.

'She lent you her husband's money?'

He nods and a small mischievous smile appears on his lips.

'That's terrible.'

'He got his own back,' Christian says darkly as he pulls into the underground garage at Escala.

Oh?

'How?'

Christian shakes his head, as if recalling a particularly sour memory, and parks beside the Audi Quattro SUV. 'Come—Franco will be here shortly.'

*　　　*　　　*

In the elevator Christian peers down at me. 'Still mad at me?' he asks matter-of-factly.

'Very.'

He nods. 'Okay,' he says, and stares straight ahead.

Taylor is waiting for us when we arrive in the foyer. How does he always know? He takes my case.

'Has Welch been in touch?' Christian asks.

'Yes, sir.'

'And?'

'Everything's arranged.'

'Excellent. How's your daughter?'

'She's fine, thank you, sir.'

'Good. We have a hairdresser arriving at one—Franco De Luca.'

'Miss Steele,' Taylor nods at me.

'Hi, Taylor. You have a daughter?'

'Yes ma'am.'

'How old is she?'

'She's seven.'

Christian gazes at me impatiently.

'She lives with her mother,' Taylor clarifies.

'Oh, I see.'

Taylor smiles. This is unexpected. Taylor's a father? I follow Christian into the great room, intrigued by this information.

I glance around. I haven't been here since I walked out.

'Are you hungry?'

I shake my head. Christian gazes at me for a beat and decides not to argue.

'I have to make a few calls. Make yourself at home.'

'Okay.'

Christian disappears into his study, leaving me standing in the huge art gallery he calls home and wondering what to do with myself.

Clothes! Picking up my backpack, I wander upstairs to my bedroom and check out the walk-in closet. It's still full of clothes—all brand-new with price tags still attached. Three long evening dresses, three cocktail dresses, and three more for everyday wear. All this must have cost a fortune.

I check the tag on one of the evening dresses: $2,998. *Holy fuck*. I sink to the floor.

This isn't me. I put my head in my hands and try to process the last few hours. It's exhausting. Why, oh why, have I fallen for someone who is plain crazy—beautiful, sexy as fuck, richer than Croesus, and crazy with a capital *K*?

I fish my BlackBerry out of my backpack and call my mom.

'Ana, honey! It's been so long. How are you, darling?'

'Oh, you know . . .'

'What's wrong? Still not worked it out with Christian?'

'Mom, it's complicated. I think he's nuts. That's the problem.'

'Tell me about it. Men, there's just no reading them sometimes. Bob's wondering if our move to Georgia was a good one.'

'What?'

'Yeah, he's talking about going back to Vegas.'

Oh, someone else has problems. I'm not the only one.

Christian appears in the doorway. 'There you are. I thought you'd run off.' His relief is obvious.

I hold my hand up to indicate that I'm on the phone. 'Sorry, Mom, I have to go. I'll call again soon.'

'Okay, honey—take care of yourself. Love you!'

'Love you, too, Mom.'

I hang up and gaze at Fifty. He frowns, looking

strangely awkward.

'Why are you hiding in here?' he asks.

'I'm not hiding. I'm despairing.'

'Despairing?'

'Of all this, Christian.' I wave my hand in the general direction of the clothes.

'Can I come in?'

'It's your closet.'

He frowns again and sits down, cross-legged, facing me.

'They're just clothes. If you don't like them, I'll send them back.'

'You're a lot to take on, you know?'

He scratches his chin . . . his stubbly chin. My fingers itch to touch him.

'I know. I'm trying,' he murmurs.

'You're very trying.'

'As are you, Miss Steele.'

'Why are you doing this?'

His eyes widen and his wary look returns. 'You know why.'

'No, I don't.'

He runs a hand through his hair. 'You are one frustrating female.'

'You could have a nice brunette submissive. One who'd say, "How high?" every time you said jump, provided of course she had permission to speak. So why me, Christian? I just don't get it.'

He gazes at me for a moment, and I have no idea what he's thinking.

'You make me look at the world differently, Anastasia. You don't want me for my money. You give me . . . hope,' he says softly.

What? Mr. Cryptic is back. 'Hope for what?'

He shrugs. 'More.' His voice is low and quiet.

'And you're right. I am used to women doing exactly what I say, when I say, doing exactly what I want. It gets old quickly. There's something about you, Anastasia, which calls to me on some deep level I don't understand. It's a siren's call. I can't resist you, and I don't want to lose you.' He reaches forward and takes my hand. 'Don't run, please— have a little faith in me and a little patience. Please.'

He looks so vulnerable . . . *It's disturbing.* Leaning up on my knees, I bend forward and kiss him gently on his lips.

'Okay. Faith and patience, I can live with that.'

'Good. Because Franco's here.'

*　　　*　　　*

Franco is small, dark, and gay. I love him.

'Such beautiful hair!' he gushes with an outrageous, probably fake Italian accent. I bet he's from Baltimore or somewhere, but his enthusiasm is infectious. Christian leads us both into his bathroom, exits hurriedly, and reenters carrying a chair from his room.

'I'll leave you two to it,' he mutters.

'*Grazie,* Mr. Grey.' Franco turns to me. '*Bene,* Anastasia, what shall we do with you?'

*　　　*　　　*

Christian is sitting on his couch, plowing through what look like spreadsheets. Soft, mellow, classical music drifts through the great room. A woman sings passionately, pouring her soul into the song. It's breathtaking. Christian glances up and smiles, distracting me from the music.

'See! I tell you he like it,' Franco enthuses.

'You look lovely, Ana,' Christian says appreciatively.

'My work 'ere is done,' Franco exclaims.

Christian rises and strolls toward us. 'Thank you, Franco.'

Franco turns, grasps me in an overwhelming bear hug, and kisses both my cheeks. 'Never let anyone else be cutting your hair, *bellissima* Ana!'

I laugh, embarrassed by his familiarity. Christian shows him to the foyer door and returns moments later.

'I'm glad you kept it long,' he says as he walks toward me, his eyes bright. He takes a strand between his fingers.

'So soft,' he murmurs, gazing down at me. 'Are you still mad at me?'

I nod and he smiles.

'What precisely are you mad at me about?'

I roll my eyes. 'You want the list?'

'There's a list?'

'A long one.'

'Can we discuss it in bed?'

'No.' I pout at him childishly.

'Over lunch, then. I'm hungry, and not just for food,' he gives me a salacious smile.

'I am not going to let you dazzle me with your sexpertise.'

He stifles a smile. 'What is bothering you specifically, Miss Steele? Spit it out.'

Okay.

'What's bothering me? Well, there's your gross invasion of my privacy, the fact that you took me to some place where your ex-mistress works and you

120

used to take all your lovers to have their bits waxed, you manhandled me in the street like I was six years old—and to cap it all, you let your Mrs. Robinson touch you!' My voice has risen to a crescendo.

He raises his eyebrows, and his good humor vanishes.

'That's quite a list. But just to clarify once more—she's not *my* Mrs. Robinson.'

'She can touch you,' I repeat.

He purses his lips. 'She knows where.'

'What does that mean?'

He runs both hands through his hair and closes his eyes briefly, as if he's seeking divine guidance of some kind. He swallows.

'You and I don't have any rules. I have never had a relationship without rules, and I never know where you're going to touch me. It makes me nervous. Your touch completely—' He stops, searching for the words. 'It just means more . . . so much more.'

More? His answer is completely unexpected, throwing me, and there's that little word with the big meaning hanging between us again.

My touch means . . . more. How am I supposed to resist when he says this stuff? Gray eyes search mine, watching, apprehensive.

Tentatively I reach out and apprehension shifts to alarm. Christian steps back and I drop my hand.

'Hard limit,' he whispers, a pained, panicked look on his face.

I can't help but feel a crushing disappointment. 'How would you feel if you couldn't touch me?'

'Devastated and deprived,' he says immediately.

Oh, my Fifty Shades. Shaking my head, I offer him a small, reassuring smile and he relaxes.

121

'You'll have to tell me exactly why this is a hard limit, one day, please.'

'One day,' he murmurs and seems to snap out of his vulnerability in a nanosecond.

How can he switch so quickly? He's the most capricious person I know.

'So, the rest of your list. Invading your privacy.' His mouth twists as he contemplates this. 'Because I know your bank account number?'

'Yes, that's outrageous.'

'I do background checks on all my submissives. I'll show you.' He turns and heads for his study.

I dutifully follow him, dazed. From a locked filing cabinet, he pulls a manila folder. Typed on the tab: ANASTASIA ROSE STEELE.

Holy fucking shit. I glare at him.

He shrugs apologetically. 'You can keep it,' he says quietly.

'Well, gee, thanks,' I snap. I flick through the contents. He has a copy of my birth certificate, for heaven's sake, my hard limits, the non-disclosure agreement, the contract—*Jeez*—my Social Security number, résumé, employment records.

'So, you knew I worked at Clayton's?'

'Yes.'

'It wasn't a coincidence. You didn't just drop by?'

'No.'

I don't know whether to be angry or flattered.

'This is fucked-up. You know that?'

'I don't see it that way. What I do, I have to be careful.'

'But this is private.'

'I don't misuse the information. Anyone can get hold of it if they have half a mind to, Anastasia.

To have control—I need information. It's how I've always operated.' He gazes at me, his expression guarded and unreadable.

'You do misuse the information. You deposited twenty-four thousand dollars that I didn't want into my account.'

His mouth presses in a hard line. 'I told you. That's what Taylor managed to get for your car. Unbelievable, I know, but there you go.'

'But the Audi . . .'

'Anastasia, do you have any idea how much money I make?'

I flush. 'Why should I? I don't need to know the bottom line of your bank account, Christian.'

His eyes soften. 'I know. That's one of the things I love about you.'

I gaze at him, shocked. *Love about me?*

'Anastasia, I earn roughly one hundred thousand dollars an hour.'

My mouth drops open. That is an obscene amount of money.

'Twenty-four thousand dollars is nothing. The car, the Tess books, the clothes, they're nothing.' His voice is soft.

I gaze at him. He really has no idea. Extraordinary.

'If you were me, how would you feel about all this . . . largesse coming your way?' I ask.

He stares at me blankly, and there it is, his problem in a nutshell—empathy or the lack thereof. The silence stretches between us.

Finally, he shrugs. 'I don't know,' he says, and he looks genuinely bemused.

My heart swells. This is it, the crux of his Fifty Shades, surely. He can't put himself in my shoes.

123

Well, now I know.

'It doesn't feel great. I mean, you're very generous, but it makes me uncomfortable. I have told you this enough times.'

He sighs. 'I want to give you the world, Anastasia.'

'I just want you, Christian. Not all the add-ons.'

'They're part of the deal. Part of what I am.'

Oh, this is going nowhere.

'Shall we eat?' I ask. This tension between us is draining.

He frowns. 'Sure.'

'I'll cook.'

'Good. Otherwise, there's food in the fridge.'

'Mrs. Jones is off on the weekends? So you eat cold cuts most weekends?'

'No.'

'Oh?'

He sighs. 'My submissives cook, Anastasia.'

'Oh, of course.' I flush. How could I be so stupid? I smile sweetly at him. 'What would Sir like to eat?'

'Whatever Madam can find,' he says darkly.

*　　　*　　　*

Inspecting the impressive contents of the fridge, I decide on a Spanish omelet. There are even cold potatoes—perfect. It's quick and easy. Christian is still in his study, no doubt invading some poor, unsuspecting fool's privacy and compiling information. The thought is unpleasant and leaves a bitter taste in my mouth. My mind is reeling. He really knows no bounds.

I need music if I'm going to cook, and I'm going

to cook nonsubmissively! I wander over to the iPod dock beside the fireplace and pick up Christian's iPod. I bet there are more of Leila's choices on here—I dread the very idea.

Where is she? I wonder. *What does she want?*

I shudder. What a legacy. I can't wrap my head around it.

I scroll through the extensive list. I want something upbeat. Hmm, Beyoncé—doesn't sound like Christian's taste. 'Crazy in Love.' Oh *yes*! How apt. I hit the 'repeat' button and put it on loud.

I sashay back to the kitchen and find a bowl, open the fridge, and take out the eggs. I crack them open and begin to whisk, dancing the whole time.

Raiding the fridge once more, I gather potatoes, ham, and—*yes!*—peas from the freezer. All of these will do. Finding a pan, I place it on the stove, put in a little olive oil, and go back to whisking.

No empathy, I muse. Is this unique to Christian? Maybe all men are like this, baffled by women. I just don't know. Perhaps it's not such a revelation.

I wish Kate were home; she would know. She's been in Barbados far too long. She should be back at the end of the week after her additional vacation with Elliot. I wonder if it's still lust at first sight for them.

One of the things I love about you.

I stop whisking. He said it. Does that mean there are other things? I smile for the first time since seeing Mrs. Robinson—a genuine, heartfelt, face-splitting smile.

Christian slips his arms around me, making me jump.

'Interesting choice of music,' he purrs as he kisses me below my ear. 'Your hair smells good.'

He nuzzles my hair and inhales deeply.

Desire uncurls in my belly. *No.* I shrug out of his embrace.

'I'm still mad at you.'

He frowns. 'How long are you going to keep this up?' he asks, dragging a hand through his hair.

I shrug. 'At least until I've eaten.'

His lips twitch with amusement. Turning, he picks up the remote control from the counter and switches off the music.

'Did you put that on your iPod?' I ask.

He shakes his head, his expression somber, and I know it was her—Ghost Girl.

'Don't you think she was trying to tell you something back then?'

'Well, with hindsight, probably,' he says quietly.

QED. No empathy. My subconscious crosses her arms and smacks her lips in disgust.

'Why's it still on there?'

'I quite like the song. But if it offends you, I'll remove it.'

'No, it's fine. I like to cook to music.'

'What would you like to hear?'

'Surprise me.'

He heads over to the iPod dock while I go back to my whisking.

Moments later the heavenly sweet, soulful voice of Nina Simone fills the room. It's one of Ray's favorites: 'I Put a Spell on You.'

I flush, turning to gape at Christian. What is he trying to tell me? He put a spell on me a long time ago. Oh my . . . his look has changed, the levity gone, his eyes darker, intense.

I watch him, enthralled as slowly, like the predator he is, he stalks me in time to the slow sultry beat of the music. He's barefoot, wearing just an untucked white shirt, jeans, and a smoldering look.

Nina sings 'you're mine' as Christian reaches me, his intention clear.

'Christian, please,' I whisper, the whisk redundant in my hand.

'Please what?'

'Don't do this.'

'Do what?'

'This.'

He's standing in front of me, gazing down at me.

'Are you sure?' he breathes and reaching over, he takes the whisk from my hand and places it back in the bowl with the eggs. My heart is in my mouth. I don't want this—I do want this—badly. He's so frustrating, so hot and desirable. I tear my gaze away from his spellbinding look.

'I want you, Anastasia,' he murmurs. 'I love and I hate, and I love arguing with you. It's very new. I need to know that we're okay. It's the only way I know how.'

'My feelings for you haven't changed,' I whisper.

His proximity is overwhelming, exhilarating. The familiar pull is there, all my synapses goading me toward him, my inner goddess at her most libidinous. Staring at the patch of hair in the V of his shirt, I bite my lip, helpless, driven by desire—I want to taste him there.

He's so close, but he doesn't touch me. His heat is warming my skin.

'I'm not going to touch you until you say yes,' he says softly. 'But right now, after a really shitty morning, I want to bury myself in you and just forget everything but us.'

Oh my . . . Us. A magical combination, a small, potent pronoun that clinches the deal. I raise my head to stare at his beautiful yet serious face.

'I'm going to touch your face,' I breathe, and see his surprise reflected briefly in his eyes before his acceptance registers.

Lifting my hand, I caress his cheek, and run my fingertips across his stubble. He closes his eyes and exhales, leaning his face into my touch.

He leans down slowly, and my lips automatically lift to meet his. He hovers over me.

'Yes or no, Anastasia?' he whispers.

'Yes.'

His mouth softly closes on mine, coaxing, coercing my lips apart as his arms enfold me, pulling me to him. His hand moves up my back, fingers tangling in the hair at the back of my head and tugging gently, while his other hand flattens on my behind, forcing me against him. I moan softly.

'Mr. Grey.' Taylor coughs, and Christian releases me immediately.

'Taylor,' he says, his voice frigid.

I whirl around to see an uncomfortable Taylor standing on the threshold of the great room. Christian and Taylor stare at each other, some unspoken communication passing between them.

'My study,' Christian snaps, and Taylor walks briskly across the room.

'Rain check,' Christian whispers to me before following Taylor out of the room.

I take a deep, steadying breath. Can I not resist him for one minute? I shake my head, disgusted at myself, grateful for Taylor's interruption, embarrassing though it is.

I wonder what Taylor has had to interrupt in

128

the past. What's he seen? I don't want to think about that. Lunch. I'll make lunch. I busy myself slicing potatoes. What does Taylor want? My mind races—is this about Leila?

Ten minutes later, they emerge, just as the omelet is ready. Christian looks preoccupied as he glances at me.

'I'll brief them in ten,' he says to Taylor.

'We'll be ready,' Taylor answers and leaves the great room.

I produce two warmed plates and place them on the kitchen island.

'Lunch?'

'Please,' Christian says as he perches on one of the barstools. Now he's watching me carefully.

'Problem?'

'No.'

I scowl. He's not telling me. I dish out lunch and sit down beside him, resigned to staying in the dark.

'This is good,' Christian murmurs appreciatively as he takes a bite. 'Would you like a glass of wine?'

'No, thank you.' *I need to keep a clear head around you, Grey.*

It does taste good, even though I'm not that hungry. But I eat, knowing Christian will nag if I don't. Eventually Christian disrupts our brooding silence and switches on the classical piece I heard earlier.

'What's this?' I ask.

'Canteloube, *Songs of the Auvergne*. This is called "Bailero."'

'It's lovely. What language is it?'

'It's in old French—Occitan, in fact.'

'You speak French; do you understand it?' Memories of the flawless French he spoke at his parents' dinner come to mind . . .

'Some words, yes.' Christian smiles, visibly relaxing. 'My mother had a mantra: "musical instrument, foreign language, martial art." Elliot speaks Spanish; Mia and I speak French. Elliot plays guitar, I play piano, and Mia the cello.'

'Wow. And the martial arts?'

'Elliot does Judo. Mia put her foot down at age twelve and refused.' He smiles at the memory.

'I wish my mother had been that organized.'

'Dr. Grace is formidable when it comes to the accomplishments of her children.'

'She must be very proud of you. I would be.'

A dark thought flashes across Christian's face, and he looks momentarily uncomfortable. He regards me warily, as if he's in uncharted territory.

'Have you decided what you'll wear this evening? Or do I need to come and pick something for you?' His tone is suddenly brusque.

Whoa! He sounds angry. *Why? What have I said?*

'Um . . . not yet. Did you choose all those clothes?'

'No, Anastasia, I didn't. I gave a list and your size to a personal shopper at Neiman Marcus. They should fit. Just so that you know, I have ordered additional security for this evening and the next few days. With Leila unpredictable and unaccounted for somewhere on the streets of Seattle, I think it's a wise precaution. I don't want you going out unaccompanied. Okay?'

I blink at him. 'Okay.' What happened to I-must-have-you-now Grey?

'Good. I'm going to brief them. I shouldn't be long.'

'They're here?'

'Yes.'

Where?

Collecting his plate, Christian places it in the sink and disappears from the room. What the hell was that about? He's like several different people in one body. Isn't that a symptom of schizophrenia? I must Google that.

I clear my plate, wash up quickly, and head back up to *my* bedroom carrying the ANASTASIA ROSE STEELE dossier. Back in the walk-in closet, I pull out the three long evening dresses. Now, which one?

*   *   *

Lying down on the bed, I gaze at my Mac, my iPad, and my BlackBerry. I am overwhelmed with technology. I set about transferring Christian's playlist from my iPad to the Mac, then fire up Google to surf the Net.

*   *   *

I'm lying across the bed looking at my Mac as Christian enters.

'What are you doing?' he inquires softly.

I panic briefly, wondering if I should let him see the Web site I'm on—Multiple Personality Disorder: The Symptoms.

Stretching out beside me, he eyes the Web page with amusement.

'On this site for a reason?' he asks nonchalantly.

Brusque Christian has gone—playful Christian is back. How the hell am I supposed to keep up with this?

'Research. Into a difficult personality.' I give him

131

my most deadpan look.

His lips twitch with a suppressed smile. 'A difficult personality?'

'My own pet project.'

'I'm a pet project now? A sideline. Science experiment maybe. When I thought I was everything. Miss Steele, you wound me.'

'How do you know it's you?'

'Wild guess.'

'It's true that you are the only fucked-up, mercurial, control freak that I know intimately.'

'I thought I was the only person you know intimately.' He arches a brow.

I flush. 'Yes. That, too.'

'Have you reached any conclusions yet?'

I turn and gaze at him. He's on his side stretched out beside me with his head resting on his elbow, his expression soft, amused.

'I think you're in need of intense therapy.'

He reaches up and gently tucks my hair behind my ears.

'I think I'm in need of you. Here.' He hands me a tube of lipstick.

I frown at him, perplexed. It's harlot red, not my color at all.

'You want me to wear this?' I squeak.

He laughs. 'No, Anastasia, not unless you want to. Not sure it's your color,' he finishes dryly.

He sits up on the bed cross-legged and drags his shirt off over his head. *Oh my.* 'I like your road map idea.'

I stare at him blankly. Road map?

'The no-go areas,' he says by way of explanation.

'Oh. I was kidding.'

'I'm not.'

132

'You want me to draw on you, with lipstick?'

'It washes off. Eventually.'

This means I could touch him freely. A small smile of wonder plays on my lips.

'What about something more permanent, like a Sharpie?'

'I could get a tattoo.' His eyes are alight with humor.

Christian Grey with a tat? Marring his lovely body, when it's marked in so many ways already? No way!

'No to the tattoo!' I laugh to hide my horror.

'Lipstick, then.' He grins.

Shutting the Mac, I push it to the side. This could be fun.

'Come.' He holds his hands out to me. 'Sit on me.'

I push my flats off my feet, scramble into a sitting position, and crawl over to him. He lies down on the bed but keeps his knees flexed.

'Lean against my legs.'

I clamber over him and sit astride as instructed. His eyes are wide and cautious. But he's amused, too.

'You seem—enthusiastic for this,' he comments wryly.

'I'm always eager for information, Mr. Grey, and it means you'll relax, because I'll know where the boundaries lie.'

He shakes his head, as if he can't quite believe that he's about to let me draw all over his body.

'Open the lipstick,' he orders.

Oh, he's in überbossy mode, but I don't care.

'Give me your hand.'

I give him my other hand.

'The one with the lipstick.' He rolls his eyes at me.

'Are you rolling your eyes at me?'

'Yep.'

'That's very rude, Mr. Grey. I know some people who get positively violent at eye-rolling.'

'Do you, now?' His tone is ironic.

I give him my hand with the lipstick, and suddenly he sits up so we are nose to nose.

'Ready?' he asks in a low, soft murmur that makes everything tighten and tense inside me. *Oh, wow*.

'Yes,' I whisper. His proximity is alluring, his toned flesh close, his Christian-smell mixed with my body wash. He guides my hand up to the curve of his shoulder.

'Press down,' he breathes, and my mouth goes dry as he directs my hand down, from the top of his shoulder, around his arm socket then down the side of his chest. The lipstick leaves a broad, livid red streak it in its wake. He stops at the bottom of his rib cage, and then directs me across his stomach. He tenses and stares, seemingly impassive, into my eyes, but beneath his careful blank look, I see his restraint.

His aversion is held in strict check, the line of his jaw is strained, and there's tension around his eyes. Midway across his stomach he murmurs, 'And up the other side.' He releases my hand.

I mirror the line I've drawn on his left side. The trust he's giving me is heady, but tempered by the fact that I can I count his pain. Seven small, round white scars dot his chest, and it's deep, dark purgatory to see this hideous, evil desecration of his beautiful body. Who would do this to a child?

'There, done,' I whisper, containing my emotion.

'No, you're not,' he replies and traces a line with his long index finger around the base of his neck. I follow the line of his finger with a scarlet streak. Finishing, I gaze into the gray depths of his eyes.

'Now my back,' he murmurs. He shifts so I have to climb off him, then he turns around on the bed and sits cross-legged with his back to me.

'Follow the line from my chest, all the way around to the other side.' His voice is low and husky.

I do as he says until a crimson line runs across the middle of his back, and as I do, I count more scars marring his beautiful body. Nine in all.

Holy fuck. I have to fight the overwhelming need to kiss each one and stop the tears pooling in my eyes. What kind of animal would do this? His head is down, and his body tense as I complete the circuit around his back.

'Around your neck, too?' I whisper.

He nods, and I draw another line joining the first around the base of his neck beneath his hair.

'Finished,' I murmur, and it looks like he's wearing a bizarre skin-colored vest with a harlot-red trim.

His shoulders slump as he relaxes, and he turns slowly to face me once again.

'Those are the boundaries,' he says quietly, his eyes dark and pupils dilated . . . from fear? From lust? I want to hurl myself at him, but I restrain myself and gaze at him in wonder.

'I can live with those. Right now I want to launch myself at you,' I whisper.

He gives me a wicked smile and holds out his hands, a silent gesture of consent.

'Well, Miss Steele, I'm all yours.'

I squeal with childish delight and catapult myself into his arms, knocking him flat. He twists, letting out a boyish laugh filled with relief that the ordeal is over. Somehow, I end up beneath him on the bed.

'Now, about that rain check,' he breathes and his mouth claims mine once more.

CHAPTER SIX

My hands fist in his hair while my mouth is feverish against Christian's, consuming him, relishing the feel of his tongue against mine. And he's the same, devouring me. It's heavenly.

Suddenly he drags me up and grasps the hem of my T-shirt, whipping it over my head and throwing it on the floor.

'I want to feel you,' he says greedily against my mouth as his hands move behind me to undo my bra. In one smooth move, it's off and he pitches it aside.

He pushes me back down onto the bed, pressing me into the mattress, and his mouth and hand move to my breasts. My fingers curl into his hair as he takes one of my nipples between his lips and tugs hard.

I cry out as the sensation sweeps through my body, spikes, and tightens all the muscles around my groin.

'Yes, baby, let me hear you,' he murmurs against my overheated skin.

Boy, I want him inside me now. With his mouth

he toys with my nipple, pulling at it, making me squirm and writhe and yearn for him. I sense his longing mixed with—what? Veneration. It's as if he's worshipping me.

He teases me with his fingers, my nipple growing hard and elongating under his skillful touch. His hand moves to my jeans, and he deftly undoes the button, tugs the zipper down, and slips his hand inside my panties, sliding his fingers against my sex.

His breath hisses out as his finger glides into me. I push my pelvis up into the heel of his hand, and he responds, rubbing against me.

'Oh, baby,' he breathes as he hovers over me, staring intently into my eyes. 'You're so wet.' His voice is filled with wonder.

'I want you,' I murmur.

His mouth joins with mine again, and I feel his hungry desperation, his need for me.

This is new—it's never been like this except perhaps when I came back from Georgia—and his words from earlier drift back to me . . . *I need to know we're okay. This is the only way I know how.*

The thought unravels me. To know that I have such an effect on him, that I can offer him solace, doing this . . . He sits up, grasps the hem of my jeans, and tugs them off, followed by my panties.

Keeping his eyes fixed on mine, he stands, takes a foil packet out of his pocket, and tosses it at me, then removes his jeans and boxers in one swift motion.

I rip the packet open greedily, and when he lies beside me again, I slowly roll the condom onto him. He grabs both my hands and rolls on to his back.

'You. On top,' he orders, pulling me astride him. 'I want to see you.'

137

Oh.

He guides me, and hesitantly I ease myself down onto him. He closes his eyes and flexes his hips to meet me, filling me, stretching me, his mouth forming a perfect *O* as he exhales.

Oh, that feels so good—possessing him, possessing me.

He holds my hands, and I don't know if it's to steady me or keep me from touching him, even though I have my road map.

'You feel so good,' he murmurs.

I rise again, heady with the power I have over him, watching Christian Grey slowly coming apart beneath me. He lets go of my hands and grabs my hips, and I place my hands on his arms. He thrusts into me sharply, causing me to cry out.

'That's right, baby, feel me,' he says, his voice strained.

I tip my head back and do exactly that. This is what he does so well.

I move—countering his rhythm in perfect symmetry—numbing all thought and reason. I am just sensation lost in this void of pleasure. *Up and down . . . again and again . . . Oh yes . . .* Opening my eyes, I stare down at him, my breathing ragged, and he's staring back at me, eyes blazing.

'My Ana,' he mouths.

'Yes,' I rasp. 'Always.'

He groans loudly, closing his eyes again, tipping his head back. Seeing Christian undone is enough to seal my fate, and I come audibly, exhaustingly, spinning down and around, collapsing on top of him.

'Oh, baby,' he groans as he finds his release, holding me still and letting go.

My head is on his chest in the no-go area, my cheek nestled against the springy hair on his sternum. I am panting, glowing, and I resist the urge to pucker my lips and kiss him.

I just lie on top of him, catching my breath. He smoothes my hair, and his hand runs down my back, caressing me as his breathing calms.

'You are so beautiful.'

I lift my head to gaze at him, my expression skeptical. He frowns in response and sits up quickly, taking me by surprise, his arm sweeping around to hold me in place. I clutch his biceps as we are nose to nose.

'You. Are. Beautiful,' he says again, his tone emphatic.

'And you're amazingly sweet sometimes.' I kiss him gently.

He lifts me and eases out of me. I wince as he does. Leaning forward, he kisses me softly.

'You have no idea how attractive you are, do you?'

I flush. Why's he going on about this?

'All those boys pursuing you—that isn't enough of a clue?'

'Boys? What boys?'

'You want the list?' Christian frowns. 'The photographer, he's crazy about you, that boy in the hardware store, your roommate's older brother. Your boss,' he adds bitterly.

'Oh, Christian, that's just not true.'

'Trust me. They want you. They want what's mine.' He pulls me against him, and I lift my arms to his shoulders, my hands in his hair, regarding him with amusement.

'Mine,' he repeats, his eyes glowing possessively.

'Yes, yours.' I reassure him, smiling. He looks mollified, and I feel perfectly comfortable naked in his lap on a bed in the full light of a Saturday afternoon. Who would have thought? The lipstick marks remain on his exquisite body. I note some smears on the duvet cover, though, and wonder briefly what Mrs. Jones will make of them.

'The line is still intact,' I murmur and bravely trace the mark on his shoulder with my index finger. He stiffens, blinking suddenly. 'I want to go exploring.'

He regards me skeptically.

'The apartment?'

'No. I was thinking of the treasure map that we've drawn on you.' My fingers itch to touch him.

His eyebrows lift in surprise, and he blinks with uncertainty. I rub my nose against his.

'And what would that entail exactly, Miss Steele?'

I lift my hand from his shoulder and run my fingertips down his face.

'I just want to touch you everywhere I'm allowed.'

Christian catches my index finger in his teeth, biting down gently.

'Ow,' I protest and he grins, a low growl coming from his throat.

'Okay,' he says, releasing my finger, but his voice is laced with apprehension. 'Wait.' He leans behind me, lifting me again, and removes his condom, dropping it unceremoniously on the floor beside the bed.

'I hate those things. I've a good mind to call Dr. Greene around to give you a shot.'

'You think the top ob-gyn in Seattle is going to come running?'

'I can be very persuasive,' he murmurs, hooking my hair behind my ear. 'Franco's done a great job on your hair. I like these layers.'

What?

'Stop changing the subject.'

He shifts me back so I'm straddling him, leaning on his propped-up knees, my feet on either side of his hips. He leans back on his arms.

'Touch away,' he says without humor. He looks nervous, but he's trying to hide it.

Keeping my eyes on his, I reach down and trace my finger underneath the lipstick line, across his finely sculptured abdominal muscles. He flinches and I stop.

'I don't have to,' I whisper.

'No, it's fine. Just takes some . . . readjustment on my part. No one's touched me for a long time,' he murmurs.

'Mrs. Robinson?' The words pop unbidden out of my mouth, and amazingly, I manage to keep all bitterness and rancor out of my voice.

He nods, his discomfort obvious. 'I don't want to talk about her. It will sour your good mood.'

'I can handle it.'

'No, you can't, Ana. You see red whenever I mention her. My past is my past. It's a fact. I can't change it. I'm lucky that you don't have one, because it would drive me crazy if you did.'

I frown at him, but I don't want to fight. 'Drive you crazy? More than you are already?' I smile, hoping to lighten the atmosphere between us.

141

His lips twitch. 'Crazy for you,' he whispers.

My heart swells with joy.

'Shall I call Dr. Flynn?'

'I don't think that will be necessary,' he says dryly.

Shifting back so he drops his legs, I place my fingers back on his stomach and let them drift across his skin. He stills once more.

'I like touching you.' My fingers skate down to his navel then southward along his happy, happy trail. His lips part as his breathing changes, his eyes darken, and his erection stirs and twitches beneath me. *Holy cow. Round two.*

'Again?' I murmur.

He smiles. 'Oh yes, Miss Steele, again.'

*   *   *

What a delicious way to spend a Saturday afternoon. I stand beneath the shower, absentmindedly washing myself, careful not to wet my tied-back hair, contemplating the last couple of hours. Christian and vanilla seem to be going well.

He's revealed so much today. It's staggering, trying to assimilate all the information and to reflect on what I've learned: his salary details—*whoa, he's stinking rich, and for someone so young, it's just extraordinary*—and the dossiers he has on me and on all his brunette submissives. I wonder if they are all in that filing cabinet?

My subconscious purses her lips at me and shakes her head—*Don't even go there*. I frown. *Just a quick peek?*

And there's Leila—with a gun, potentially, somewhere—and her crap taste in music still on his iPod. But even worse, Mrs. *Pedo* Robinson; I cannot wrap my head around her, and I don't want to. I don't want her to be a shimmering-haired specter in our relationship. He's right, I do go off the deep end when I think of her, so perhaps it's best if I don't.

I step out of the shower and dry myself, and I'm suddenly seized by unexpected anger.

But who wouldn't go off the deep end? What normal, sane person would do that to a fifteen-year-old boy? How much has she contributed to his fucked-upness? I don't understand her. And worse still, he says she helped him. How?

I think of his scars, the stark physical embodiment of a horrific childhood and a sickening reminder of what mental scars he must bear. My sweet, sad Fifty Shades. He's said such loving things today. *He's crazy for me.*

Staring at my reflection, I smile at the memory of his words, my heart brimming once more, and my face transforms with a ridiculous smile. Perhaps we can make this work. But how long will he want to do this without wanting to beat the crap out of me because I cross some arbitrary line?

My smile dissolves. This is what I don't know. This is the shadow that hangs over us. Kinky fuckery, yes, I can do that, but more?

My subconscious stares at me blankly, for once offering no snarky words of wisdom. I head back to my bedroom to dress.

Christian is downstairs getting ready, doing whatever he's doing, so I have the bedroom to myself. As well as all the dresses in the closet, I have drawers full of new underwear. I select a black bustier corset creation with a price tag of $540.

It has silver trim like filigree and the briefest of panties to match. Thigh-high stockings, too, in a natural color, so fine, pure silk. *Wow, they feel . . . slinky . . . and kind of hot . . .*

I am reaching for the dress when Christian enters unannounced. *Whoa, you could knock!* He stands immobilized, staring at me, eyes glimmering, hungrily. I blush crimson everywhere, it feels. He is wearing a white shirt and black suit pants; the neck of his shirt is open. I can see the lipstick line still in place, and he's still staring.

'Can I help you, Mr. Grey? I assume there is some purpose to your visit other than to gawk mindlessly at me.'

'I am rather enjoying my mindless gawk, thank you, Miss Steele,' he murmurs darkly, stepping farther into the room and drinking me in. 'Remind me to send a personal note of thanks to Caroline Acton.'

I frown. *Who the hell is she?*

'The personal shopper at Neiman's,' he says, spookily answering my unspoken question.

'Oh.'

'I'm quite distracted.'

'I can see that. What do you want, Christian?' I give him my no-nonsense stare.

He retaliates with his crooked smile and pulls the silver ball things from his pocket, stopping me in my tracks. Holy shit! He wants to spank me? Now? Why?

'It's not what you think,' he says quickly.

'Enlighten me,' I whisper.

'I thought you could wear these tonight.'

And the implications of that sentence hang between us as the idea sinks in.

144

'To this event?' I'm shocked.

He nods slowly, his eyes darkening.

Oh my.

'Will you spank me later?'

'No.'

For a moment, I feel a tiny fleeting stab of disappointment.

He chuckles. 'You want me to?'

I swallow. I just don't know.

'Well, rest assured I am not going to touch you like that, not even if you beg me.'

Oh! This is news.

'Do you want to play this game?' he continues, holding up the balls. 'You can always take them out if it's too much.'

I gaze at him. He looks so wickedly tempting— unkempt, recently fucked hair, dark eyes dancing with erotic thoughts, his lips raised in a sexy, amused smile.

'Okay,' I acquiesce softly. *Hell, yes!* My inner goddess has found her voice and is shouting from the rooftops.

'Good girl,' Christian grins. 'Come here, and I'll put them in, once you've put your shoes on.'

My shoes? I turn and glance at the dove gray suede stilettos that match the dress I've chosen to wear.

Humor him!

He holds out his hand to support me while I step into the Christian Louboutin shoes, a steal at $3,295. I must be at least five inches taller now.

He leads me to the bedside and doesn't sit, but walks over to the only chair in the room. Picking it up, he carries it over and places it in front of me.

'When I nod, you bend down and hold on to the

145

chair. Understand?' His voice is husky.

'Yes.'

'Good. Now open your mouth,' he orders, his voice still low.

I do as I'm told, thinking that he's going to put the balls in my mouth to lubricate them. No, he slips his index finger in.

Oh . . .

'Suck,' he says. I reach up and clasp his hand, holding him steady, and do as I'm told—see, I can be obedient, when I want.

He tastes of soap . . . hmm. I suck hard, and I'm rewarded when his eyes widen and his lips part as he inhales. I'm not going to need any lubricant at this rate. He puts the balls in his mouth as I fellate his finger, twirling my tongue around it. When he tries to withdraw it, I clamp my teeth down.

He grins then shakes his head, admonishing me, so I let go. He nods, and I bend down and grasp the sides of the chair. He moves my panties to one side and very slowly slides a finger into me, circling leisurely, so I feel him, on all sides. I can't help the moan that escapes from my lips.

He withdraws his finger briefly and with tender care, inserts the balls one at a time, pushing them deep inside me. Once they are in position, he smoothes my panties back into place and kisses my backside. Running his hands up each of my legs from ankle to thigh, he gently kisses the top of each thigh where my thigh-highs end.

'You have fine, fine legs, Miss Steele,' he murmurs.

Standing, he grasps my hips and pulls my behind against him so I feel his erection.

'Maybe I'll have you this way when we get home,

Anastasia. You can stand now.'

I feel giddy, beyond aroused as the weight of the balls push and pull inside me. Leaning down from behind me Christian kisses my shoulder.

'I bought these for you to wear to last Saturday's gala.' He puts his arm around me and holds out his hand. In his palm rests a small red box with *Cartier* inscribed on the lid. 'But you left me, so I never had the opportunity to give them to you.'

Oh!

'This is my second chance,' he murmurs, his voice stiff with some unnamed emotion. He's nervous.

Tentatively I reach for the box, and open it. Inside shines a pair of drop earrings. Each has four diamonds, one at the base, then a gap, then three perfectly spaced diamonds hanging one after the other. They're beautiful, simple, and classic. What I would choose myself, if I were ever given the opportunity to shop at Cartier.

'They're lovely,' I whisper, and because they are second-chance earrings, I love them. 'Thank you.'

He relaxes against me as the tension leaves his body, and he kisses my shoulder again.

'You're wearing the silver satin dress?' he asks.

'Yes. Is that okay?'

'Of course. I'll let you get ready.' He heads out the door without a backward glance.

*   *   *

I have entered an alternate universe. The young woman staring back at me looks worthy of a red carpet. Her strapless, floor-length, silver satin gown is simply stunning. Maybe I'll write to Caroline

147

Acton myself. It's fitted, and flatters what few curves I have.

My hair falls in soft waves around my face, spilling over my shoulders to my breasts. I tuck one side behind my ear, revealing my second-chance earrings. I have kept my makeup to a minimum, a natural look. Eyeliner, mascara, a little pink blush, and pale pink lipstick.

I don't really need the blush. I am a little flushed from the constant movement of the silver balls. Yes, they'll guarantee I have some color in my cheeks tonight. Shaking my head at the audacity of Christian's erotic ideas, I lean down to collect my satin wrap and silver clutch purse, and go in search of my Fifty Shades.

He is talking to Taylor and three other men in the hallway, his back to me. Their surprised, appreciative expressions alert Christian to my presence. He turns as I stand and wait awkwardly.

My mouth dries. He looks stunning . . . Black dinner suit, black bow tie, and his expression as he gazes at me is one of awe. He strolls toward me and kisses my hair.

'Anastasia. You look breathtaking.'

I flush at this compliment in front of Taylor and the other men.

'A glass of champagne before we go?'

'Please,' I murmur, far too quickly.

Christian nods to Taylor who heads into the foyer with his three cohorts.

In the great room, Christian retrieves a bottle of champagne from the fridge.

'Security team?' I ask.

'Close protection. They're under Taylor's control. He's trained in that, too.' Christian hands me a champagne flute.

'He's very versatile.'

'Yes, he is.' Christian smiles. 'You look lovely, Anastasia. Cheers.' He raises his glass, and I clink it with mine. The champagne is a pale rose color. It tastes deliciously crisp and light.

'How are you feeling?' he asks, his eyes heated.

'Fine, thank you.' I smile sweetly, giving nothing away, knowing full well he's referring to the silver balls.

He smirks.

'Here, you're going to need this.' He hands me a large velvet pouch that was resting on the kitchen island. 'Open it,' he says between sips of champagne. Intrigued, I reach into the bag and pull out an intricate silver masquerade mask with cobalt blue feathers in a plume crowning the top.

'It's a masked ball,' he states matter-of-factly.

'I see.' The mask is beautiful. A silver ribbon is threaded around the edges, and exquisite silver filigree is etched around the eyes.

'This will show off your beautiful eyes, Anastasia.'

I grin at him shyly.

'Are you wearing one?'

'Of course. They're very liberating in a way,' he adds, raising an eyebrow.

Oh. This is going to be fun.

'Come. I want to show you something.' Holding out his hand, he leads me out into the hallway and to a door beside the stairs. He opens it, revealing a large room roughly the same size as his playroom, which must be directly above us. This one is filled with books. *Wow,* a library, every wall crammed floor to ceiling. In the center is a full-sized billiard

149

table illuminated by a long, triangular-prism-shaped Tiffany lamp.

'You have a library!' I squeak in awe, overwhelmed with excitement.

'Yes, the balls room, as Elliot calls it. The apartment is quite spacious. I realized today, when you mentioned exploring, that I've never given you a tour. We don't have time now, but I thought I'd show you this room, and maybe challenge you to a game of billiards in the not-too-distant future.'

I grin.

'Bring it on.' I secretly hug myself with glee. José and I bonded over pool. We've been playing for the last three years. I am ace with a cue. José has been a good teacher.

'What?' Christian asks, amused.

Oh! I really must stop expressing every emotion I feel the instant I feel it, I scold myself.

'Nothing,' I say quickly.

Christian narrows his eyes.

'Well, maybe Dr. Flynn can uncover your secrets. You'll meet him this evening.'

'The expensive charlatan?' *Holy shit.*

'The very same. He's dying to meet you.'

*   *   *

Christian takes my hand and gently skims his thumb across my knuckles as we sit in the back of the Audi heading north. I squirm, and feel the sensation in my groin. I resist the urge to moan, as Taylor is in the front, not wearing his iPod, with one of the security guys whose name I think is Sawyer.

I am beginning to feel a dull, pleasurable ache deep in my belly, caused by the balls. Idly I wonder how long I will be able to manage without some, um . . . relief? I cross my legs. As I do, something that's been gnawing at me in the back of my mind suddenly surfaces.

'Where did you get the lipstick?' I ask Christian quietly.

He smirks at me and points toward the front. 'Taylor,' he mouths.

I burst out laughing. 'Oh.' And stop quickly—the balls.

I bite my lip. Christian smiles at me, his eyes gleaming wickedly. He knows exactly what he's doing, sexy beast that he is.

'Relax,' he breathes. 'If it's too much . . .' His voice trails off, and he gently kisses each knuckle in turn, then gently sucks the tip of my little finger.

Now I know he's doing this on purpose. I close my eyes as dark desire unfolds throughout my body. I surrender briefly to the sensation, my muscles clenching deep inside me.

When I open my eyes again, Christian is regarding me closely, a dark prince. It must be the dinner jacket and bow tie, but he looks older, sophisticated, a devastatingly handsome roué with licentious intent. He simply takes my breath away. I'm in his sexual thrall, and if I'm to believe him, he's in mine. The thought brings a smile to my face, and his answering grin is blinding.

'So what can we expect at this event?'

'Oh, the usual stuff,' Christian says breezily.

'Not usual for me,' I remind him.

Christian smiles fondly and kisses my hand again. 'Lots of people flashing their cash. Auction, raffle, dinner, dancing—my mother knows how to throw a party.' He smiles and for the first time all day, I allow myself to feel a little excited about this party.

There is a line of expensive cars heading up the driveway of the Grey mansion. Long, pale pink paper lanterns hang over the drive, and as we inch closer in the Audi, I can see they are everywhere. In the early evening light they look magical, as if we're entering an enchanted kingdom. I glance at Christian. How suitable for my prince—and my childish excitement blooms, eclipsing all other feelings.

'Masks on,' Christian grins, and as he dons his simple black mask, my prince becomes something darker, more sensual.

All I can see of his face is his beautiful mouth and strong *jaw*. My heartbeat lurches at the sight of him. I fasten my mask and ignore the hunger deep in my body.

Taylor pulls into the driveway, and a valet opens Christian's door. Sawyer leaps out to open mine.

'Ready?' Christian asks.

'As I'll ever be.'

'You look beautiful, Anastasia.' He kisses my hand and exits the car.

A dark green carpet runs along the lawn to one side of the house, leading to the impressive grounds at the rear. Christian has a protective arm around me, resting his hand on my waist, as we follow the green carpet with a steady stream of Seattle's elite dressed in their finery and wearing all manner of masks, the lanterns lighting the way. Two photographers marshal guests to pose for pictures against the backdrop of an ivy-strewn arbor.

'Mr. Grey!' one of the photographers calls. Christian nods in acknowledgment and pulls me close as we pose quickly for a photo. How do they know it's him? His trademark unruly copper hair, no doubt.

'Two photographers?' I ask Christian.

'One is from the *Seattle Times;* the other is for a souvenir. We'll be able to buy a copy later.'

Oh, my picture in the press again. Leila briefly enters my mind. This is how she found me, posing with Christian. The thought is unsettling, though it's comforting that I am unrecognizable beneath my mask.

At the end of the line, white-suited servers hold trays of glasses brimming with champagne, and I'm grateful when Christian passes me a glass— effectively distracting me from my dark thoughts.

We approach a large white pergola hung with smaller versions of the paper lanterns. Beneath it shines a black-and-white checkered dance floor surrounded by a low fence with entrances on three sides. Standing at each entrance are two elaborate ice sculptures of swans. The fourth side of the pergola is occupied by a stage where a string quartet is playing softly, a haunting, ethereal piece I don't recognize. The stage looks set for a big band but as there's no sign of the musicians, I figure this must be for later. Taking my hand, Christian leads me between swans onto the dance floor where the other guests are congregating, chatting over glasses of champagne.

Toward the shoreline stands an enormous tent, open on the side nearest to us so I can glimpse the formally arranged tables and chairs. *There are so many!*

'How many people are coming?' I ask Christian, thrown by the scale of the tent.

'I think about three hundred. You'll have to ask

153

my mother.' He smiles down at me.

'Christian!'

A young woman appears out of the throng and throws her arms around his neck, and immediately I know she's Mia. She's dressed in a sleek, pale pink, full-length chiffon gown with a stunning, delicately detailed Venetian mask to match. She looks amazing. And for a moment, I have never felt so grateful for the dress that Christian has given me.

'Ana! Oh, darling, you look gorgeous!' She gives me a quick hug. 'You must come and meet my friends. None of them can believe that Christian finally has a girlfriend.'

I shoot a quick panicked glance at Christian, who shrugs in a resigned, I-know-she's-impossible-I-had-to-live-with-her-for-years way, and let Mia lead me over to a group of four young women, all expensively attired and impeccably groomed.

Mia makes hasty introductions. Three of them are sweet and kind, but Lily, I think her name is, regards me sourly from beneath her red mask.

'Of course, we all thought Christian was gay,' she says snidely, concealing her rancor with a large, fake smile.

Mia pouts at her.

'Lily, behave yourself. It's obvious he has excellent taste in women. He was waiting for the right one to come along, and it wasn't you!'

Lily blushes the same color as her mask, as do I. Could this be any more uncomfortable?

'Ladies, if I could claim my date back, please?' Snaking his arm around my waist, Christian pulls me to his side. All four women flush, grin, and fidget, his dazzling smile doing what it always does.

Mia glances at me and rolls her eyes, and I have to laugh.

'Lovely to meet you,' I say as he drags me away.

'Thank you,' I mouth at Christian when we're some distance away.

'I saw that Lily was with Mia. She is one nasty piece of work.'

'She likes you,' I mutter dryly.

He shudders. 'Well, the feeling is not mutual. Come, let me introduce you to some people.'

I spend the next half hour in a whirlwind of introductions. I meet two Hollywood actors, two more CEOs, and several eminent physicians. *There is no way I am going to remember everyone's name.*

Christian keeps me close at his side, and I'm grateful. Frankly, the wealth, the glamour, and the sheer lavish scale of the event intimidate me. I have never been to anything like this in my life.

The white-suited servers move effortlessly through the growing crowd of guests with bottles of champagne, topping off my glass with worrying regularity. *I must not drink too much. I must not drink too much,* I repeat to myself, but I'm beginning to feel light-headed, and I don't know if it's the champagne, the charged atmosphere of mystery and excitement created by the masks, or the secret silver balls. The dull ache below my waist is becoming impossible to ignore.

'So you work at SIP?' asks a balding gentleman in a bear—or is it a dog?—half mask. 'Heard rumors of a hostile takeover.'

I flush. There *is* a hostile takeover, from a man who has more money than sense and is a stalker par excellence.

'I'm just a lowly assistant, Mr. Eccles. I wouldn't

155

know about these things.'

Christian says nothing and smiles blandly at Eccles.

'Ladies and gentlemen!' The master of ceremonies, wearing an impressive black-and-white harlequin mask, interrupts us. 'Please take your seats. Dinner is served.'

Christian takes my hand, and we follow the chattering crowd to the large tent.

The interior is stunning. Three enormous, shallow chandeliers throw rainbow-colored sparkles over the ivory silk lining of the ceiling and walls. There must be at least thirty tables, and they remind me of the private dining room at the Heathman Hotel—crystal glasses, crisp white linen covering the tables and chairs, and in the center an exquisite display of pale pink peonies gathered around a silver candelabra. Wrapped in gossamer silk beside it is a basket of goodies.

Christian consults the seating plan and leads me to a table in the center. Mia and Grace Trevelyan-Grey are already in situ, deep in conversation with a young man I don't know. Grace is wearing a shimmering mint green gown with a Venetian mask to match. She looks radiant, not stressed at all, and she greets me warmly.

'Ana, how delightful to see you again! And looking so beautiful, too.'

'Mother,' Christian greets her stiffly and kisses her on both cheeks.

'Oh, Christian, so formal!' she scolds him teasingly.

Grace's parents, Mr. and Mrs. Trevelyan, join us at our table. They seem exuberant and youthful, though it's difficult to tell beneath their matching

156

bronze masks. They are delighted to see Christian.

'Grandmother, Grandfather, may I introduce Anastasia Steele?'

Mrs. Trevelyan is all over me like a rash. 'Oh, he's finally found someone, how wonderful, and so pretty! Well, I do hope you make an honest man of him,' she gushes, shaking my hand.

Holy cow. I thank the heavens for my mask.

'Mother, don't embarrass Ana.' Grace comes to my rescue.

'Ignore the silly old coot, m'dear.' Mr. Trevelyan shakes my hand. 'She thinks because she's so old, she has a God-given right to say whatever nonsense pops into that woolly head of hers.'

'Ana, this is my date, Sean.' Mia shyly introduces her young man. He gives me a wicked grin, and his brown eyes dance with amusement as we shake hands.

'Pleased to meet you, Sean.'

Christian shakes Sean's hand as he regards him shrewdly. Don't tell me that poor Mia suffers from her overbearing brother, too. I smile at Mia in sympathy.

Lance and Janine, Grace's friends, are the last couple at our table, but there is still no sign of Mr. Carrick Grey.

Abruptly there's the hiss of a microphone, and Mr. Grey's voice booms over the PA system, causing the babble of voices to die down. Carrick stands on a small stage at one end of the tent, wearing an impressive gold Punchinello mask.

'Welcome, ladies and gentlemen, to our annual charity ball. I hope that you enjoy what we have laid out for you tonight and that you'll dig deep into your pockets to support the fantastic work that our team does with Coping Together. As you know, it's a cause that is very close to my wife's heart, and mine.'

I peek nervously at Christian, who is staring impassively, I think, at the stage. He glances at me and smirks.

'I'll hand you over now to our master of ceremonies. Please be seated, and enjoy,' Carrick finishes.

Polite applause follows; then the babble in the tent starts again. I am seated between Christian and his grandfather. I admire the small white place card with fine silver calligraphy that bears my name as a waiter lights the candelabra with a long taper. Carrick joins us, kissing me on both cheeks, surprising me.

'Good to see you again, Ana,' he murmurs. He really looks very striking in his extraordinary gold mask.

'Ladies and gentlemen: please nominate a table head,' the MC calls out.

'Oooh—me, me!' says Mia immediately, bouncing enthusiastically in her seat.

'In the center of the table you will find an envelope,' the MC continues. 'Would everyone find, beg, borrow, or steal a bill of the highest denomination you can manage, write your name on it, and place it inside the envelope? Table heads, please guard these envelopes carefully. We will need them later.'

Crap. I haven't brought any money with me. *How stupid—it's a charity event!*

Fishing out his wallet, Christian produces two $100 bills.

'Here,' he says.

158

What?

'I'll pay you back,' I whisper.

His mouth twists, and I know he's not happy, but he doesn't comment. I sign my name using his fountain pen—it's black, with a white flower motif on the cap—and Mia passes the envelope around.

In front of me I find another card inscribed with silver calligraphy—our menu.

A Masked Ball in Aid of Coping Together
Menu

Salmon Tartare with Crème Fraiche and
Cucumber on Toasted Brioche
Alban Estate Roussanne 2006

Roasted Muscovy Duck Breast
Creamy Jerusalem Artichoke Purée,
Thyme-Roasted Bing Cherries, Foie Gras
Châteauneuf-du-Pape Vieilles Vignes 2006
Domaine de la Janasse

Sugar-Crusted Walnut Chiffon
Candied Figs, Sabayon, Maple Ice Cream
Vin de Constance 2004 Klein Constantia

Selection of Local Cheeses and Breads
Alban Estate Grenache 2006

Coffee and Petits Fours

~ § ~

Well, that accounts for the number of crystal glasses in every size that crowd my place setting.

159

Our waiter is back, offering wine and water. Behind me, the sides of the tent through which we entered are being closed, while at the front, two servers pull back the canvas, revealing the sunset over Seattle and Meydenbauer Bay.

It's an absolutely breathtaking view, the twinkling lights of Seattle in the distance and the orange, dusky calm of the bay reflecting the opal sky. Wow. It's so calm and peaceful.

Ten servers, each holding a plate, come to stand between us. On a silent cue, they serve us our starters in complete synchronization, then vanish again. The salmon looks delicious, and I realize I am famished.

'Hungry?' Christian murmurs so only I can hear. I know he's not referring to the food, and the muscles deep in my belly respond.

'Very,' I whisper, boldly meeting his gaze, and Christian's lips part as he inhales.

Ha! See . . . two can play at this game.

Christian's grandfather engages me in conversation immediately. He's a wonderful old man, so proud of his daughter and three grandchildren.

It is weird to think of Christian as a child. The memory of his burn scars come unbidden to my mind, but quickly I quash it. I don't want to think about that now, though ironically it's the reason behind this party.

I wish Kate were here, with Elliot. She would fit in so well—the sheer number of forks and knives laid out before her wouldn't daunt Kate—and she would command the table. I imagine her duking it out with Mia over who should be table head. The thought makes me smile.

160

The conversation at the table ebbs and flows. Mia is entertaining, as usual, and quite eclipses poor Sean, who mostly stays quiet, like me. Christian's grandmother is the most vocal. She, too, has a biting sense of humor, usually at the expense of her husband. I begin to feel a little sorry for Mr. Trevelyan.

Christian and Lance talk animatedly about a device Christian's company is developing inspired by E. F. Schumacher's Small Is Beautiful principle. It's hard to keep up. Christian seems intent on empowering impoverished communities all over the world with windup technology—devices that need no electricity or batteries, and minimal maintenance.

Watching him in full flow is astonishing. He's passionate and committed to improving the lives of the less fortunate. Through his telecommunications company he's intent on being first to market with a windup mobile phone.

Whoa. I had no idea. I mean, I knew about his passion about feeding the world, but this . . .

Lance seems unable to comprehend Christian's plan to give the technology away and not patent it. I wonder vaguely how Christian made all his money if he's so willing to give it all away.

Throughout dinner a steady stream of men in smartly tailored dinner jackets and dark masks stop by the table, keen to meet Christian, shake his hand, and exchange pleasantries. He introduces me to some but not others. I'm intrigued to know how and why he makes the distinction.

During one such conversation, Mia leans across and smiles.

'Ana, will you help in the auction?'

161

'Of course,' I respond, only too willing.

By the time dessert is served, night has fallen, and I'm really uncomfortable. I need to get rid of the balls. Before I can excuse myself, the master of ceremonies appears at our table, and with him—if I'm not mistaken—is Miss European Pigtails.

What's her name? Hansel, Gretel . . . Gretchen.

She's masked, of course, but I know it's her when her gaze doesn't move beyond Christian. She blushes, and selfishly I'm beyond pleased that Christian doesn't acknowledge her at all.

The MC asks for our envelope and with a very practiced and eloquent flourish, asks Grace to pull out the winning bill. It's Sean's, and the silk-wrapped basket is awarded to him.

I applaud politely, but I'm finding it impossible to concentrate on any more of the proceedings.

'If you'll excuse me,' I murmur to Christian.

He looks at me intently.

'Do you need the powder room?'

I nod.

'I'll show you,' he says darkly.

When I stand, all the other men around the table stand with me. *Oh, such manners.*

'No, Christian! You're not taking Ana—I will.'

Mia is on her feet before Christian can protest. His jaw tenses; I know he's not pleased. Quite frankly, neither am I. *I have . . . needs.* I shrug apologetically at him, and he sits down quickly, resigned.

On our return, I feel a little better, though the relief of removing the balls has not been as instantaneous as I'd hoped. They're now stashed safely in my clutch purse.

Why did I think I could last the whole evening? I

162

am still yearning—perhaps I can persuade Christian to take me to the boathouse later. I flush at the thought and glance at him as I take my seat. He stares at me, the ghost of a smile crossing his lips.

Phew . . . he's no longer mad at a missed opportunity, though maybe I am. I feel frustrated—irritable even. Christian squeezes my hand, and we both listen attentively to Carrick, who is back on stage talking about Coping Together. Christian passes me another card—a list of the auction prizes. I scan them quickly.

AUCTION GIFTS AND GRACIOUS DONORS
FOR COPING TOGETHER

Signed Baseball Bat from the Mariners—
Dr. Emily Mainwaring

Gucci Purse, Wallet & Key Ring—Andrea
Washington

One-Day Voucher for Two at Esclava,
Bravern Center—
Elena Lincoln

Landscape and Garden Design—Gia Matteo

Coco De Mer Coffret & Perfume Beauty
Selection—
Elizabeth Austin

Venetian Mirror—Mr. and Mrs. J. Bailey

Two Cases of Wine of Your Choice from
Alban Estates—

163

Alban Estates

Two VIP Tickets for XTY in Concert—Mrs. L. Yesyov

Race Day at Daytona—EMC Britt Inc.

Pride and Prejudice *by Jane Austen, First Edition—Dr. A. F. M. Lace-Field*

Drive an Aston Martin DB7 for a Day— Mr. & Mrs. L. W. Nora

Oil Painting, Into the Blue *by J. Trouton— Kelly Trouton*

Gliding Lesson—Seattle Area Soaring Society

Weekend Break for Two at the Heathman Hotel, Portland—the Heathman Hotel

One-Weekend Stay in Aspen, Colorado (Sleeps Six)—Mr. C. Grey

One-Week Stay Aboard the SusieCue Yacht (Six Berths), Moored in St. Lucia—Dr. & Mrs. Larin

One Week at Lake Adriana, Montana (Sleeps Eight)—Mr. & Dr. Grey

~ § ~

Holy shit. I blink up at Christian.
'You own property in Aspen?' I hiss. The auction

is under way, and I have to keep my voice down.

He nods, surprised at my outburst and irritated, I think. He puts his finger to his lips to silence me.

'Do you have property elsewhere?' I whisper.

He nods again and inclines his head to one side in a warning.

The whole room erupts with cheering and applause; one of the prizes has gone for $12,000.

'I'll tell you later,' Christian says quietly. 'I wanted to come with you,' he adds rather sulkily.

Well, you didn't. I pout and I realize that I'm still querulous, and no doubt, it's the frustrating effect of the balls. My mood darkens after seeing Mrs. Robinson on the list of generous donors.

I glance around the tent to see if I can spot her, but I can't see her telltale hair. Surely Christian would have warned me if she was invited tonight. I sit and stew, applauding when necessary, as each lot is sold for astonishing amounts of money.

The bidding moves to Christian's place in Aspen and reaches $20,000.

'Going once, going twice,' the MC calls.

And I don't know what possesses me, but I suddenly hear my own voice ringing out clearly over the throng.

'Twenty-four thousand dollars!'

Every mask at the table turns to me in shocked amazement, the biggest reaction of all coming from beside me. I hear his sharp intake of breath and feel his wrath washing over me like a tidal wave.

'Twenty-four thousand dollars, to the lovely lady in silver, going once, going twice . . . Sold!'

CHAPTER SEVEN

Holy shit, did I really just do that? It must be the alcohol. I've had champagne plus four glasses of four different wines. I glance up at Christian, who's busy applauding.

Crap, he's going to be so angry, and we've been getting along so well. My subconscious has finally decided to make an appearance, and she's wearing her Edvard Munch *The Scream* face.

Christian leans over to me, a large, fake smile plastered across his face. He kisses my cheek and then moves closer to whisper in my ear in a very cold, controlled voice.

'I don't know whether to worship at your feet or spank the living shit out of you.'

Oh, I know what I want right now. I gaze up at him, blinking through my mask. I just wish I could read what's in his eyes.

'I'll take option two, please,' I whisper frantically as the applause dies down. His lips part as he inhales sharply. *Oh, that chiseled mouth—I want it on me, now*. I ache for him. He gives me a radiant sincere smile that leaves me breathless.

'Suffering, are you? We'll have to see what we can do about that,' he murmurs as he runs his fingers along my jaw.

His touch resonates deep, deep inside where that ache has spawned and grown. I want to jump him right here, right now, but we sit back to watch the auction of the next lot.

I can barely sit still. Christian drapes an arm around my shoulders, his thumb rhythmically stroking my back, sending delicious tingles down my spine. His free hand clasps mine, bringing it to his lips, then letting it rest on his lap.

Slowly and surreptitiously, so I don't realize his game until it's too late, he eases my hand up his leg and against his erection. I gasp, and my eyes dart in panic around the table, but all eyes are fixed on the stage. *Thank heavens for my mask.*

Taking full advantage, I slowly caress him, letting my fingers explore. Christian keeps his hand over mine, hiding my bold fingers, while his thumb skates softly over the nape of my neck. His mouth opens as he gasps softly, and it's the only reaction I can see to my inexperienced touch. But it means so much. He wants me. Everything south of my navel contracts. This is becoming unbearable.

A week by Lake Adriana in Montana is the final lot for auction. Of course Mr. and Dr. Grey have a house in Montana, and the bidding escalates rapidly, but I am barely aware of it. I feel him growing beneath my fingers, and it makes me feel so powerful.

'Sold, for one hundred ten thousand dollars!' the MC declares victoriously. The whole room bursts into applause, and reluctantly I follow as does Christian, ruining our fun.

He turns to me and his lips twitch. 'Ready?' he mouths over the rapturous cheering.

'Yes,' I mouth back.

'Ana!' Mia calls. 'It's time!'

What? No. Not again! 'Time for what?'

'The First Dance Auction. Come on!' She stands and holds out her hand.

I glance at Christian, who is, I think, scowling at Mia, and I don't know whether to laugh or cry, but it's laughter that wins. I succumb to a cathartic bubble of schoolgirl giggles, as we are thwarted once more by the tall, pink powerhouse that is Mia Grey. Christian peers at me, and after a beat, there's a ghost of a smile on his lips.

'The first dance will be with me, okay? And it won't be on the dance floor,' he murmurs lasciviously into my ear. My giggles subside as anticipation fans the flames of my need. *Oh yes!* My inner goddess performs a perfect triple Salchow in her ice skates.

'I look forward to it.' I lean over and plant a soft, chaste kiss on his mouth. Glancing around, I realize that our fellow guests at the table are astonished. Of course, they've never seen Christian with a date before.

He smiles broadly. And he looks . . . happy.

'Come on, Ana,' Mia nags. Taking her outstretched hand, I follow her onto the stage, where ten more young women have assembled, and I note with vague unease that Lily is one of them.

'Gentlemen, the highlight of the evening!' the MC booms over the babble of voices. 'The moment you've all been waiting for! These twelve lovely ladies have all agreed to auction their first dance to the highest bidder!'

Oh no. I blush from head to toe. I hadn't realized what this meant. How humiliating!

'It's for a good cause,' Mia hisses at me, sensing my discomfort. 'Besides, Christian will win.' She rolls her eyes. 'I can't imagine him letting anyone outbid him. He hasn't taken his eyes off you all evening.'

Yes, focus on the good cause, and Christian is bound to win. Let's face it, he's not short of a dime or two.

But it means spending more money on you! my subconscious snarls at me. But I don't want to dance with anyone else—I can't dance with anyone else—and it's not spending money on me, he's donating it to the charity. *Like the $24,000 he's already spent?* My subconscious narrows her eyes.

Shit. I seem to have gotten away with my impulsive bid. Why am I arguing with myself?

'Now, gentlemen, pray gather around, and take a good look at what could be yours for the first dance. Twelve comely and compliant wenches.'

Jeez! I feel like I'm in a meat market. I watch, horrified, as at least twenty men make their way to the stage area, Christian included, moving with easy grace between the tables and pausing to say a few hellos on the way. Once the bidders are assembled, the MC begins.

'Ladies and gentlemen, in the tradition of the masquerade we shall maintain the mystery behind the masks and stick to first names only. First up we have the lovely Jada.'

Jada is giggling like a schoolgirl, too. Maybe I won't be so out of place. She's dressed head to foot in navy taffeta with a matching mask. Two young men step forward expectantly. Lucky Jada.

'Jada speaks fluent Japanese, is a qualified fighter pilot, and an Olympic gymnast . . . hmm.' The MC winks. 'Gentlemen, what am I bid?'

Jada gapes, astounded at the MC; obviously, he's talking complete garbage. She grins shyly back at the two contenders.

'A thousand bucks!' one calls.

Very quickly the bidding escalates to $5,000.

'Going once . . . going twice . . . sold!' the MC

169

declares loudly, 'to the gentleman in the mask!' And of course, all the men are wearing masks so there are hoots of laughter, applause, and cheering. Jada beams at her purchaser and quickly exits the stage.

'See? This is fun!' whispers Mia. 'I hope Christian wins you, though . . . We don't want a brawl,' she adds.

'Brawl?' I answer horrified.

'Oh yes. He was very hotheaded when he was younger.' She shudders.

Christian brawling? Refined, sophisticated, likes-Tudor-choral-music Christian? I can't see it. The MC distracts me with his next introduction—a young woman in red, with long jet-black hair.

'Gentlemen, may I present the wonderful Mariah. What are we going to do about Mariah? She's an experienced matador, plays the cello to concert standard, and she's a champion pole-vaulter . . . how about that, gentlemen? What am I bid, please, for a dance with the delightful Mariah?'

Mariah glares at the MC and someone yells, very loudly, 'Three thousand dollars!' It's a masked man with blond hair and beard.

There is one counterbid, but Mariah sells for $4,000.

Christian is watching me like a hawk. Brawler Trevelyan-Grey—who would have known?

'How long ago?' I ask Mia.

She glances at me, nonplussed.

'How long ago was Christian brawling?'

'Early teens. Drove my parents crazy, coming home with cut lips and black eyes. He was expelled from two schools. He inflicted some serious damage on his opponents.'

170

I gape at her.

'Hasn't he told you?' She sighs. 'He got quite a bad rep among my friends. He was really persona non grata for a few years. But it stopped when he was about fifteen or sixteen.' She shrugs.

Holy fuck. Another piece of the jigsaw falls into place.

'So, what am I bid for the gorgeous Jill?'

'Four thousand dollars,' a deep voice calls from the left side. Jill squeals in delight.

I stop paying attention to the auction. So Christian was in that kind of trouble at school, fighting. I wonder why. I stare at him. Lily is watching us closely.

'And now, allow me to introduce the beautiful Ana.'

Oh, shit, that's me. I glance nervously at Mia, and she shoos me center stage. Fortunately I don't fall over, but stand embarrassed as hell on display for everyone. When I look at Christian, he's smirking at me. The bastard.

'Beautiful Ana plays six musical instruments, speaks fluent Mandarin, and is keen on yoga . . . well, gentlemen—' Before he can even finish his sentence Christian interrupts him, glaring at the MC through his mask.

'Ten thousand dollars.' I hear Lily's gasp of disbelief behind me.

Oh, fuck.

'Fifteen.'

What? We all turn as one to a tall, impeccably dressed man standing to the left of the stage. I blink at Fifty. Shit, what will he make of this? But he's scratching his chin and giving the stranger an ironic smile. It's obvious Christian knows him. The stranger nods politely at Christian.

'Well, gentlemen! We have high rollers in the house this evening.' The MC's excitement emanates through his harlequin mask as he turns to beam at Christian. This is a great show, but it's at my expense. I want to wail.

'Twenty,' counters Christian quietly.

The babble of the crowd has died. Everyone is staring at me, Christian, and Mr. Mysterious by the stage.

'Twenty-five,' the stranger says.

Could this be any more embarrassing?

Christian stares at him impassively, but he's amused. All eyes are on Christian. What's he going to do? My heart is in my mouth. I feel sick.

'One hundred thousand dollars,' he says, his voice ringing clear and loud through the tent.

'What the fuck?' Lily hisses audibly behind me, and a general gasp of dismay and amusement ripples through the crowd. The stranger holds his hands up in defeat, laughing, and Christian smirks at him. From the corner of my eye, I can see Mia bouncing up and down with glee.

'One hundred thousand dollars for the lovely Ana! Going once . . . going twice . . .' The MC stares at the stranger, who shakes his head with mock regret and bows chivalrously.

'Sold!' the MC cries out triumphantly.

In a deafening round of applause and cheering, Christian steps forward to take my hand and help me from the stage. He gazes at me with an amused grin as I make my way down, kisses the back of my hand then tucks it into the crook of his arm, and leads me toward the tent's exit.

'Who was that?' I ask.

He gazes down at me. 'Someone you can meet later. Right now, I want to show you something. We have about thirty minutes until the First Dance Auction finishes. Then we have to be back on the dance floor so that I can enjoy that dance I've paid for.'

'A very expensive dance,' I mutter disapprovingly.

'I'm sure it'll be worth every single cent.' He smiles down at me wickedly. Oh, he has a glorious smile, and the ache is back, blossoming in my body.

We're out on the lawn. I thought we would be heading to the boathouse, but disappointingly we seem to be heading for the dance floor where the big band is now setting up. There are at least twenty musicians, and a few guests are milling about, furtively smoking—but since most of the action is back in the tent, we don't attract too much attention.

Christian leads me to the rear of the house and opens a French window leading into a large comfortable sitting room that I've not seen before. He walks through the deserted hall toward the sweeping staircase with its elegant, polished wooden balustrade. Taking my hand from the crook of his arm, he leads me up to the second floor and up another flight of stairs to the third. Opening a white door, he ushers me into one of the bedrooms.

'This was my room,' he says quietly, standing by the door and locking it behind him.

It's large, stark, and sparsely furnished. The walls are white, as is the furniture; a double bed, a desk and chair, shelves crammed with books and lined with various trophies for kickboxing, by the look of them. The walls are hung with movie posters:

The Matrix, Fight Club, The Truman Show, and two framed posters featuring kickboxers. One is named Guiseppe DeNatale—I've never heard of him.

But what catches my eye is the white bulletin board above the desk, studded with myriad photographs, Mariners pennants, and ticket stubs. It's a slice of young Christian. My eyes come back to the magnificent man now standing in the center of the room. He looks at me darkly, brooding and sexy.

'I've never brought a girl in here,' he murmurs.

'Never?' I whisper.

He shakes his head.

I swallow convulsively, and the ache that has been bothering me for the last couple of hours is roaring now, raw and wanting. Seeing him standing there on the royal blue carpet in that mask . . . it's beyond erotic. I want him. Now. Any way I can get him. I have to resist launching myself at him and ripping his clothes off. He waltzes over to me slowly.

'We don't have long, Anastasia, and the way I'm feeling right this moment, we won't need long. Turn around. Let me get you out of that dress.'

I turn and stare at the door, grateful that he's locked it. Bending down he whispers softly in my ear, 'Keep the mask on.'

I groan as my body clenches in response. He's not even touched me yet.

He grasps the top of my dress, his fingers sliding against my skin, and the touch reverberates through my body. In one swift move, he opens the zipper. Holding my dress, he helps me to step out of it, then turns and drapes it artfully over the back of a chair. Removing his jacket, he places it over my dress. He pauses, and stares at me for a moment, drinking me in. I'm in the basque and matching panties, and I revel in his sensuous gaze.

'You know, Anastasia,' he says softly as he stalks toward me, undoing his bow tie so it hangs from either side of his neck, then undoing the top three buttons of his shirt. 'I was so mad when you bought my auction lot. All manner of ideas ran through my head. I had to remind myself that punishment is off the menu. But then you volunteered.' He gazes down at me through his mask. 'Why did you do that?' he whispers.

'Volunteer? I don't know. Frustration . . . too much alcohol . . . worthy cause,' I mutter meekly, shrugging. Maybe to get his attention?

I needed him then. I need him more now. The ache is worse, and I know he can soothe it, calm this roaring, salivating beast in me with the beast in him. His mouth presses into a line, and he slowly licks his upper lip. I want that tongue on me.

'I vowed to myself I would not spank you again, even if you begged me.'

'Please,' I beg.

'But then I realized you're probably very uncomfortable at the moment, and it's not something you're used to.' He smirks knowingly at me, arrogant bastard, but I don't care because he's absolutely right.

'Yes,' I breathe.

'So, there might be a certain . . . latitude. If I do this, you must promise me one thing.'

'Anything.'

'You will safe-word if you need to, and I will just make love to you, okay?'

'Yes.' I'm panting. I want his hands on me.

He swallows, then takes my hand, and moves toward the bed. Throwing the duvet aside, he sits down, grabs a pillow, and places it beside him. He gazes up at me standing beside him and suddenly tugs hard on my hand so that I fall across his lap. He shifts slightly so my body is resting on the bed, my chest on the pillow, my face to one side. Leaning over, he sweeps my hair over my shoulder and runs his fingers through the plume of feathers on my mask.

'Put your hands behind your back,' he murmurs.

Oh! He removes his bow tie and uses it to quickly bind my wrists so that my hands are tied behind me, resting in the small of my back.

'You really want this, Anastasia?'

I close my eyes. This is the first time since I met him that I really want this. I need it.

'Yes,' I whisper.

'Why?' he asks softly as he caresses my behind with his palm.

I groan as soon as his hand makes contact with my skin. *I don't know why . . . You tell me not to overthink. After a day like today—arguing about the money, Leila, Mrs. Robinson, the dossier on me, the road map, this lavish party, the masks, the alcohol, the silver balls, the auction . . . I want this.*

'Do I need a reason?'

'No, baby, you don't,' he says. 'I'm just trying to understand you.' His left hand curls around my waist, holding me in place as his palm leaves my behind and lands hard, just above the junction of my thighs. The pain connects directly with the ache in my belly

Oh, man . . . I moan loudly. He hits me again, in exactly the same place. I groan again.

176

'Two,' he murmurs. 'We'll go with twelve.'

Oh my! This feels different than the last time—so carnal, so . . . necessary. He caresses my behind with his long-fingered hands, and I'm helpless, trussed up and pressed into the mattress, at his mercy, and of my own free will. He hits me again, slightly to the side, and again, to the other side, then pauses as he slowly peels my panties down and pulls them off. He gently trails his palm across my behind again before continuing my spanking—each stinging smack taking the edge off my need—or fueling it—I don't know. I surrender myself to the rhythm of blows, absorbing each one, savoring each one.

'Twelve,' he murmurs his voice low and harsh. He caresses my behind again and trails his fingers down toward my sex and slowly sinks two fingers inside me, moving them in a circle, around and around and around, torturing me.

I moan loudly as my body takes over, and I come and come, convulsing around his fingers. It's so intense, unexpected, and quick.

'That's right, baby,' he murmurs appreciatively. He unties my wrists, keeping his fingers inside me as I lie panting and spent over him.

'I've not finished with you yet, Anastasia,' he says and shifts without removing his fingers. He eases my knees onto the floor so that now I'm leaning over the bed. He kneels on the floor behind me and undoes his zipper. He slides his fingers out of me, and I hear the familiar tear of a foil packet. 'Open your legs,' he growls, and I comply. He strokes my behind and eases into me.

'This is going to be quick, baby,' he murmurs and grabbing my hips, he eases out then slams into me.

'Ah!' I cry out, but the fullness is heavenly. He's hitting the bellyache square on, again and again, eradicating it with each sharp, sweet thrust. The feeling is mind-blowing, just what I need. I push back to meet him, thrust for thrust.

'Ana, no,' he grunts, trying to still me. But I want him too much, and I grind against him, matching him thrust for thrust.

'Ana, shit,' he hisses as he comes, and the tortured sound sets me off again, spiraling into a healing orgasm that goes on and on and wrings me out and leaves me spent and breathless.

Christian bends and kisses my shoulder, then pulls out of me. Placing his arms around me, he rests his head in the middle of my back, and we lie like this, both kneeling at the bedside, for what? Seconds? Minutes, even, as our breathing calms. My bellyache has disappeared, and all I feel is a soothing, satisfying serenity.

Christian stirs and kisses my back. 'I believe you owe me a dance, Miss Steele,' he murmurs.

'Hmm,' I respond, savoring the absence of achiness and basking in the afterglow.

He sits back on his heels and pulls me off the bed onto his lap. 'We don't have long. Come on.' He kisses my hair and forces me to stand.

I grumble but sit back down on the bed and collect my panties from the floor and scoop them on. Lazily I walk to the chair to retrieve my dress. I note with dispassionate interest that I did not remove my shoes during our illicit tryst. Christian is tying his bow tie, having finished straightening himself and the bed.

As I slip my dress back on, I check out the photographs on the bulletin board. Christian as a sullen teen was gorgeous even then: with Elliot and Mia on the ski slopes; on his own in Paris, the Arc de Triomphe serving as a giveaway to his location; in London; New York; the Grand Canyon; Sydney Opera House; even the Great Wall of China. Master Grey was well traveled at a young age.

There are ticket stubs to various concerts: U2, Metallica, the Verve, Sheryl Crow, the New York Philharmonic performing Prokofiev's *Romeo and Juliet*—what an eclectic mix! And in the corner, there's a passport-sized photograph of a young woman. It's in black and white. She looks familiar, but for the life of me, I can't place her. Not Mrs. Robinson, thank heavens.

'Who's this?' I ask.

'No one of consequence,' he mutters as he slips on his jacket and straightens his bow tie. 'Shall I zip you up?'

'Please. Then why is she on your bulletin board?'

'An oversight on my part. How's my tie?' He raises his chin like a small boy, and I grin and straighten it for him.

'Now it's perfect.'

'Like you,' he murmurs and grabs me, kissing me passionately. 'Feeling better?'

'Much, thank you, Mr. Grey.'

'The pleasure was all mine, Miss Steele.'

*　　　*　　　*

The guests are assembling on the dance floor. Christian grins at me—we've made it just in time—and he leads me onto the checkered floor.

'And now, ladies and gentlemen, it's time for the first dance. Mr. and Dr. Grey, are you ready?'

179

Carrick nods in agreement, his arms around Grace.

'Ladies and gentlemen of the First Dance Auction, are you ready?' We all nod in agreement. Mia is with someone I don't recognize. I wonder what happened to Sean?

'Then we shall begin. Take it away, Sam!'

A young man strolls onto the stage amid warm applause, turns to the band behind him, and snaps his fingers. The familiar strains of 'I've Got You Under My Skin' fill the air.

Christian smiles down at me, takes me in his arms, and starts to move. Oh, he dances so well, making it easy to follow. We grin at each other like idiots as he whirls me around the dance floor.

'I love this song,' Christian murmurs, gazing down at me. 'Seems very fitting.' He's no longer grinning, but serious.

'You're under my skin, too,' I respond. 'Or you were in your bedroom.'

He purses his lips but he's unable to hide his amusement.

'Miss Steele,' he admonishes me teasingly, 'I had no idea you could be so crude.'

'Mr. Grey, neither did I. I think it's all my recent experiences. They've been an education.'

'For both of us.' Christian is serious again, and it could just be the two of us and the band. We are in our own private bubble.

As the song finishes we both applaud. Sam the singer bows graciously and introduces his band.

'May I cut in?'

I recognize the man who bid on me at the auction. Christian grudgingly lets me go, but he's amused, too.

'Be my guest. Anastasia, this is John Flynn. John,

Anastasia.'

Shit!

Christian grins and wanders off to one side of the dance floor.

'How do you do, Anastasia?' Dr. Flynn says smoothly, and I realize he's British.

'Hello,' I stutter.

The band strikes up another song, and Dr. Flynn pulls me into his arms. He's much younger than I imagined, though I can't see his face. He's wearing a mask similar to Christian's. He's tall, but not as tall as Christian, and he doesn't move with Christian's easy grace.

What do I say to him? Why is Christian so fucked-up? Why did he bid on me? It's the only thing I want to ask him, but somehow that seems rude.

'I'm glad to finally meet you, Anastasia. Are you enjoying yourself?' he asks.

'I was,' I whisper.

'Oh. I hope I'm not responsible for your change of heart.' He gives me a brief, warm smile that puts me a little more at ease.

'Dr. Flynn, you're the shrink. You tell me.'

He grins. 'That's the problem, isn't it? The shrink bit?'

I giggle. 'I'm worried what I might reveal, so I'm a little self-conscious and intimidated. And really I only want to ask you about Christian.'

He smiles. 'First, this is a party so I'm not on duty,' he whispers conspiratorially. 'And second, I really can't talk to you about Christian. Besides,' he teases, 'we'd need until Christmas.'

I gasp in shock.

'That's a doctor's joke, Anastasia.'

I flush, embarrassed, and then feel slightly resentful. He's making a joke at Christian's expense. 'You've just confirmed what I've been saying to Christian . . . that you're an expensive charlatan,' I admonish him.

Dr. Flynn snorts with laughter. 'You could be on to something there.'

'You're British?'

'Yes. Originally from London.'

'How did you find yourself here?'

'Happy circumstance.'

'You don't give much away, do you?'

'There's not much to give away. I'm really a very dull person.'

'That's very self-deprecating.'

'It's a British trait. Part of our national character.'

'Oh.'

'And I could accuse you of the same, Anastasia.'

'That I'm a dull person, too, Dr. Flynn?'

He snorts. 'No, Anastasia. That you don't give much away.'

'There's not much to give away.' I smile.

'I sincerely doubt that.' He unexpectedly frowns.

I flush, but the music finishes and Christian is once more by my side. Dr. Flynn releases me.

'It's been a pleasure to meet you, Anastasia.' He gives me his warm smile again, and I feel that I've passed some kind of hidden test.

'John.' Christian nods at him.

'Christian.' Dr. Flynn returns his nod, turns on his heel, and disappears through the crowd.

Christian pulls me into his arms for the next dance.

'He's much younger than I expected,' I murmur

182

to him. 'And terribly indiscreet.'

Christian cocks his head to one side. 'Indiscreet?'

'Oh yes, he told me everything,' I tease.

Christian tenses. 'Well, in that case, I'll get your bag. I'm sure you want nothing more to do with me,' he says softly.

I stop. 'He didn't tell me anything!' My voice fills with panic.

Christian blinks before relief floods his face. He pulls me into his arms again. 'Then let's enjoy this dance.' He beams down at me, reassuring me, and then spins me around.

Why would he think that I'd want to leave? It makes no sense.

We dance for two more numbers, and I realize I need the restroom.

'I won't be long.'

As I make my way to the powder room, I remember I have left my purse on the dinner table, so I head down to the tent. When I enter, it's still lit but quite deserted, except for a couple at the other end, who really ought to get a room! I reach for my bag.

'Anastasia?'

A soft voice startles me, and I turn to see a woman dressed in a long, tight, black velvet gown. Her mask is unique. It covers her face to her nose but also covers her hair. It's stunning, with elaborate gold filigree.

'I'm so glad you're on your own,' she says softly. 'I've been wanting to talk to you all evening.'

'I'm sorry, I don't know who you are.'

She pulls the mask from her face and releases her hair.

Shit! It's Mrs. Robinson.

'I'm sorry, I startled you.'

I gape at her. *Holy cow—what the fuck does this woman want?*

I don't know what the social conventions are for meeting known molesters of children. She's smiling sweetly and gesturing for me to sit at the table. And because I am lacking any sphere of reference, I do as she asks out of stunned politeness, grateful that I am still wearing my mask.

'I'll be brief, Anastasia. I know what you think of me . . . Christian's told me.'

I gaze at her impassively, giving nothing away, but I'm pleased that she knows. It saves me telling her, and she's cutting to the chase. Part of me is beyond intrigued as to what she could have to say.

She pauses, glancing over my shoulder. 'Taylor's watching us.'

I peek around to see him scanning the tent by the doorway. Sawyer is with him. They are looking anywhere but at us.

'Look, we don't have long,' she says hurriedly. 'It must be obvious to you that Christian is in love with you. I have never seen him like this, *ever*.' She emphasizes the last word.

What? Loves me? No. Why is she telling me? To reassure me? I don't understand.

'He won't tell you because he probably doesn't realize it himself, notwithstanding what I've said to him, but that's Christian. He's not very attuned to any positive feelings and emotions he may have. He dwells far too much on the negative. But then, you've probably worked that out for yourself. He doesn't think he's worthy.'

I am reeling. *Christian loves me?* He hasn't said it, and this woman has told him that's how he feels?

184

How bizarre.

A hundred images dance through my head: the iPad, the gliding, flying to see me, all his actions, his possessiveness, $100,000 for a dance. Is this love?

And hearing it from this woman, having her confirm it for me is, frankly, unwelcome. I'd rather hear it from him.

My heart constricts. He feels unworthy? Why?

'I've never seen him so happy, and it's obvious that you have feelings for him, too.' A brief smile flits across her lips. 'That's great, and I wish you both the best of everything. But what I wanted to say is if you hurt him again, I will find you, lady, and it won't be pleasant when I do.'

She stares at me, ice-cold blue eyes boring into my skull, trying to get under my mask. Her threat is so astonishing, so off the wall, that an involuntary, disbelieving giggle escapes me. Of all the things she could say to me, this is the least expected.

'You think this is funny, Anastasia?' she splutters in dismay. 'You didn't see him last Saturday.'

My face falls and darkens. The thought of Christian unhappy is not a palatable one, and last Saturday I left him. He must have gone to her. The idea makes me queasy. Why am I sitting here, listening to this shit from her, of all people? I slowly rise, gazing at her intently.

'I'm laughing at your audacity, Mrs. Lincoln. Christian and I have nothing to do with you. And if I do leave him and you come looking for me, I'll be waiting—don't doubt it. And maybe I'll give you a taste of your own medicine on behalf of the fifteen-year-old child you molested and probably fucked up even more than he already was.'

Her mouth falls open.

185

'Now if you'll excuse me, I have better things to do than waste my time with you.' I turn on my heel, adrenaline and anger coursing through my body, and stalk toward the entrance of the tent where Taylor is standing just as Christian arrives, looking flustered and worried.

'There you are,' he mutters, then frowns when he sees Elena.

I stride past him, saying nothing, giving him the opportunity to choose—her or me. He makes the right choice.

'Ana,' he calls. I stop and face him as he catches up with me. 'What's wrong?' He gazes down at me, concern etched on his face.

'Why don't you ask your ex?' I hiss acidly.

His mouth twists and his eyes frost. 'I'm asking you,' he says, his voice soft but with an undertone of something far more menacing.

We glare at each other.

Okay, I can see this will end in a fight if I don't tell him. 'She's threatening to come after me if I hurt you again—probably with a whip,' I snap at him.

Relief flashes across his face, his mouth softening with humor. 'Surely the irony of that isn't lost on you?' he says, and I can tell he's trying hard to stifle his amusement.

'This isn't funny, Christian!'

'No, you're right. I'll talk to her.' He adopts his serious face, though he's still suppressing his amusement.

'You will do no such thing.' I cross my arms, my anger spiking again.

He blinks at me, surprised by my outburst.

'Look, I know you're tied up with her financially,

186

forgive the pun, but—' I stop. What am I asking him to do? Give her up? Stop seeing her? Can I do that? 'I need the restroom.' I glare up at him, my mouth set in a grim line.

He sighs and cocks his head to one side. Could he look any hotter? Is it the mask or just him?

'Please don't be mad. I didn't know she was here. She said she wasn't coming.' His tone is placating as if he's talking to a child. Reaching up he runs his thumb along my pouting bottom lip. 'Don't let Elena ruin our evening, please, Anastasia. She's really old news.'

'Old' being the operative word, I think uncharitably, as he tips my chin up and gently grazes his lips against mine. I sigh in agreement, blinking up at him. He straightens and takes my elbow.

'I'll accompany you to the powder room so you don't get interrupted again.'

He leads me across the lawn toward the luxurious temporary restrooms. Mia said they had been delivered for the occasion, but I had no idea they came in deluxe versions.

'I'll wait here for you, baby,' he murmurs.

When I come out, my mood has moderated. I have decided not to let Mrs. Robinson blight my evening because that's probably what she wants. Christian is on the phone some distance away and out of earshot of the few people laughing and chatting nearby. As I get closer, I can hear him. He's very terse.

'Why did you change your mind? I thought we'd agreed. Well, leave her alone . . . This is the first regular relationship I've ever had, and I don't want you jeopardizing it through some misplaced concern for me. Leave. Her. Alone. I mean it, Elena.' He pauses, listening. 'No, of course not.' He frowns deeply as he says this. Glancing up, he sees me regarding him. 'I have to go. Good night.' He presses the off button.

I cock my head to one side and raise an eyebrow at him. Why is he phoning her?

'How's the old news?'

'Cranky,' he replies sardonically. 'Do you want to dance some more? Or would you like to go?' He glances at his watch. 'The fireworks start in five minutes.'

'I love fireworks.'

'We'll stay and watch them, then.' He puts his arms around me and pulls me close. 'Don't let her come between us, please.'

'She cares about you,' I mutter.

'Yes, and I her . . . as a friend.'

'I think it's more than a friendship to her.'

His brow furrows. 'Anastasia, Elena and I . . . it's complicated. We have a shared history. But it is just that, history. As I've said to you time and time again, she's a good friend. That's all. Please, forget about her.' He kisses my hair, and in the interest of not ruining our evening, I let it go. I am just trying to understand.

We wander hand in hand back to the dance floor. The band is still in full swing.

'Anastasia.'

I turn to find Carrick standing behind us.

'I wondered if you'd do me the honor of the next dance.' Carrick holds his hand out to me. Christian shrugs and smiles, releasing my hand, and I let Carrick lead me onto the dance floor. Sam the bandleader launches into 'Come Fly with Me,' and

Carrick puts his arm around my waist and gently whirls me into the throng.

'I wanted to thank you for the generous contribution to our charity, Anastasia.'

From his tone, I suspect this is his roundabout way of asking whether I can afford it.

'Mr. Grey—'

'Call me Carrick, please, Ana.'

'I'm delighted to be able to contribute. I unexpectedly came into some money. I don't need it. And it's such a worthy cause.'

He smiles down at me, and I seize the opportunity for some innocent inquiries. *Carpe diem,* my subconscious hisses from behind her hand.

'Christian told me a little about his past, so I think it's appropriate to support your work,' I add, hoping that this might encourage Carrick to give me a small insight into the mystery that is his son.

Carrick is surprised. 'Did he? That's unusual. You certainly have had a very positive effect on him, Anastasia. I don't think I've ever seen him so, so . . . buoyant.'

I flush.

'Sorry, I didn't mean to embarrass you.'

'Well, in my limited experience, he's a very unusual man,' I murmur.

'He is,' Carrick agrees quietly.

'Christian's early childhood sounds hideously traumatic, from what he's told me.'

Carrick frowns, and I worry if I've overstepped the mark.

'My wife was the doctor on duty when the police brought him in. He was skin and bones, and badly dehydrated. He wouldn't speak.' Carrick frowns again, lost in the awful memory, despite the up-tempo music surrounding us. 'In fact, he didn't speak for nearly two years. It was playing the piano that eventually brought him out of himself. Oh, and Mia's arrival, of course.' He smiles down at me fondly.

'He plays beautifully. And he's accomplished so much, you must be very proud of him.' I sound distracted. *Holy Shit. Didn't speak for two years.*

'Immensely so. He's a very determined, very capable, very bright young man. But between you and me, Anastasia, it's seeing him like he is this evening—carefree, acting his age—that's the real thrill for his mother and me. We were both commenting on it today. I believe we have you to thank for that.'

I think I blush to my roots. What am I supposed to say to this?

'He's always been such a loner. We never thought we'd see him with anyone. Whatever you're doing, please don't stop. We'd like to see him happy.' He stops suddenly, as if *he's* overstepped the mark. 'I'm sorry, I don't mean to make you uncomfortable.'

I shake my head. 'I'd like to see him happy, too,' I mutter, unsure of what else to say.

'Well, I'm very glad you came this evening. It's been a real pleasure seeing the two of you together.'

As the final strains of 'Come Fly with Me' fade away, Carrick releases me and bows, and I curtsy, mirroring his civility.

'That's enough dancing with old men.' Christian is at my side again. Carrick laughs.

'Less of the "old," son. I've been known to have

my moments.' Carrick winks at me playfully and saunters into the crowd.

'I think my dad likes you,' Christian mutters as he watches his father mingle with the crowd.

'What's not to like?' I peek coquettishly up at him through my lashes.

'Good point well made, Miss Steele.' He pulls me into an embrace as the band starts to play 'It Had to Be You.'

'Dance with me,' he whispers seductively.

'With pleasure, Mr. Grey.' I smile in response, and he sweeps me across the dance floor once more.

*   *   *

At midnight we stroll down toward the shore between the tent and the boathouse where the other partygoers are gathered to watch the fireworks. The MC, back in charge, has permitted the removal of masks, the better to see the display. Christian has his arm around me, but I'm aware that Taylor and Sawyer are close by, probably because we're in the crowd now. They are looking anywhere but at the dockside where two technicians dressed in black are making their final preparations. Seeing Taylor reminds me of Leila. Perhaps she's here. *Shit*. The thought chills my blood, and I huddle closer to Christian. He gazes down at me as he pulls me closer.

'You okay, baby? Cold?'

'I'm fine.' I glance quickly behind us and see the other two security guys, whose names I forget, standing close by. Moving me in front of him, Christian puts both his arms around me over my shoulders.

Suddenly a stirring classical soundtrack booms over the dock and two rockets soar into the air, exploding with a deafening *bang* over the bay, lighting it all in a dazzling canopy of sparkling orange and white that's reflected in a glittering shower over the still calm water of the bay. My jaw drops as several more rockets fire into the air and explode in a kaleidoscope of color.

I can't recall ever seeing a display this impressive, except perhaps on television, and it never looks this good on TV. It's all in time to the music. Volley after volley, bang after bang, and light after light as the crowd answers with gasps and oohs and ahs. It is out of this world.

On the pontoon in the bay several silver fountains of light shoot up twenty feet in the air, changing color through blue, red, orange, and back to silver—and yet more rockets explode as the music reaches its crescendo.

My face is beginning to ache from the ridiculous grin of wonder plastered across it. I glance at Fifty, and he's the same, marveling like a child at the sensational show. For the finale a volley of six rockets shoot into the dark and explode simultaneously, bathing us in a glorious golden light as the crowd erupts into frantic, enthusiastic applause.

'Ladies and gentlemen,' the MC calls out as the cheers and whistles fade. 'Just one note to add at the end of this wonderful evening; your generosity has raised a total of one million eight hundred and fifty-three thousand dollars!'

Spontaneous applause erupts again, and out on the pontoon, a message lights up in silver streams of sparks forming the words 'Thank You from Coping Together,' sparkling and shimmering over the water.

'Oh, Christian . . . that was wonderful.' I grin up at him and he bends down to kiss me.

'Time to go,' he murmurs, a broad smile on his beautiful face, and his words hold so much promise.

Suddenly, I feel very tired.

He glances up again, and Taylor is close, the crowd dispersing around us. They don't speak but something passes between them.

'Stay with me a moment. Taylor wants us to wait while the crowd disperses.'

Oh.

'I think that fireworks display probably aged him a hundred years,' he adds.

'Doesn't he like fireworks?'

Christian gazes down at me fondly and shakes his head but doesn't elaborate.

'So, Aspen,' he says, and I know he's trying to distract me from something. It works.

'Oh . . . I haven't paid for my bid,' I gasp.

'You can send a check. I have the address.'

'You were really mad.'

'Yes, I was.'

I grin. 'I blame you and your toys.'

'You were quite overcome, Miss Steele. A most satisfactory outcome if I recall.' He smiles salaciously. 'Incidentally, where are they?'

'The silver balls? In my bag.'

'I'd like them back. They are far too potent a device to be left in your innocent hands.'

'Worried I might be quite overcome again, maybe with somebody else?'

His eyes glitter dangerously. 'I hope that's not

going to happen,' he says, a cool edge to his voice. 'But no, Ana. I want all your pleasure.'

Whoa. 'Don't you trust me?'

'Implicitly. Now, can I have them back?'

'I'll think about it.'

He narrows his eyes at me.

There's music once more from the dance floor but it's a DJ playing a thumping dance number, the bass pounding out a relentless beat.

'Do you want to dance?'

'I'm really tired, Christian. I'd like to go, if that's okay.'

Christian glances at Taylor, who nods, and we set off toward the house, following a couple of drunken guests. I'm grateful when Christian takes my hand—my feet are aching from the dizzying height and tight confinement of my shoes.

Mia comes bounding up to us. 'You're not going, are you? The real music's just beginning. Come on, Ana.' She grabs my hand.

'Mia,' Christian admonishes her. 'Anastasia's tired. We're going home. Besides, we have a big day tomorrow.'

We do?

Mia pouts but surprisingly doesn't push Christian.

'You must come by sometime next week. Maybe we can hit the mall?'

'Sure, Mia.' I grin, though in the back of my mind I'm wondering how since I have to work for a living.

She gives me a quick kiss then hugs Christian fiercely, taking us both by surprise. More astoundingly still, she places her hands directly on the lapels of his jacket, and he just gazes down at her, indulgently.

194

'I like seeing you this happy,' she says sweetly and kisses him on the cheek. 'Bye. You guys have fun.' She skips off toward her waiting friends—among them Lily, who looks even more sour-faced without her mask.

I wonder idly where Sean is.

'We'll say good night to my parents before we leave. Come.' Christian leads me through a gaggle of guests to Grace and Carrick, who wish us fond and warm farewells.

'Please do come again, Anastasia, it's been lovely having you here,' says Grace kindly.

I am a little overwhelmed by both her and Carrick's reaction. Fortunately, Grace's parents have retired for the evening, so at least I am spared their enthusiasm.

In a relaxed, weary silence, Christian and I walk hand in hand to the front of the house, where countless cars are lined up waiting to collect guests. I glance up at Fifty. He looks happy. It's a real pleasure to see him this way, though I suspect it's unusual after such an extraordinary day.

'Are you warm enough?' he asks.

'Yes, thank you.' I clasp my satin wrap.

'I really enjoyed this evening, Anastasia. Thank you.'

'Me too, some parts more than others.' I grin.

He grins and nods, then his brow creases. 'Don't bite your lip,' he warns in a way that makes my blood sing.

'What did you mean about a big day tomorrow?' I ask to distract myself.

'Dr. Greene is coming to sort you out. Plus, I have a surprise for you.'

'Dr. Greene!' I halt.

195

'Yes.'

'Why?'

'Because I hate condoms,' he says quietly. His eyes glint in the soft light from the paper lanterns, gauging my reaction.

'It's my body,' I mutter, annoyed that he hasn't asked me.

'It's mine, too,' he whispers.

I gaze up at him as various guests pass by, ignoring us. He looks so earnest. Yes, my body is his . . . he knows it better than I do.

I reach up, and he flinches ever so slightly but stays still. Grasping the corner of his bow tie, I pull so it unravels, revealing the top button of his shirt. Gently I undo it.

'You look hot like this,' I whisper. Actually he looks hot all the time, but really hot like this.

He smiles. 'I need to get you home. Come.'

At the car, Sawyer hands Christian an envelope. He frowns at it and glances at me as Taylor ushers me into the car. Taylor looks relieved for some reason. Christian climbs in and hands me the envelope, unopened, as Taylor and Sawyer take their seats in the front.

'It's addressed to you. One of the staff gave it to Sawyer. No doubt from yet another ensnared heart.' Christian's mouth twists. It's obvious this is an unpleasant concept to him.

I stare at the note. Who is this from? Ripping it open, I read it quickly in the dim light. Holy shit, it's from *her*! Why won't she leave me alone?

I may have misjudged you. And you
have definitely misjudged me. Call me
if you need to fill in any of the blanks—

we could have lunch. Christian doesn't want me talking to you, but I would be more than happy to help. Don't get me wrong, I approve, believe me—but so help me, if you hurt him . . . He's been hurt enough. Call me: (206) 279-6261
Mrs. Robinson

Fuck, she's signed it Mrs. Robinson! He told her. The bastard.

'You told her?'

'Told who, what?'

'That I call her Mrs. Robinson,' I snap.

'It's from Elena?' Christian is shocked. 'This is ridiculous,' he grumbles, running a hand through his hair, and I can tell he's irritated. 'I'll deal with her tomorrow. Or Monday,' he mutters bitterly.

And though I'm ashamed to admit it, a very small part of me is pleased. My subconscious nods sagely. Elena is pissing him off, and this can only be good—surely. I decide to say nothing for now but stash her note in my bag, and in a gesture guaranteed to lighten his mood, I hand him back the balls.

'Until next time,' I murmur.

He glances at me, and it's hard to see his face in the dark, but I think he's smirking. He reaches for my hand and squeezes it.

I gaze out of the window into the darkness, reflecting on this long day. I've learned so much about him, gleaned many missing details—the salons, the road map, his childhood—but there's still much more to discover. And what about Mrs. R? Yes, she cares for him, and deeply, it would appear. I can see that, and he cares for her—but not in the same way. I don't know what to think anymore. All this information is making my head hurt.

*   *   *

Christian wakes me just as we pull up outside Escala. 'Do I need to carry you in?' he asks gently.

I shake my head sleepily. No way.

As we stand in the elevator, I lean against him, putting my head against his shoulder. Sawyer stands in front of us, shifting uncomfortably.

'It's been a long day, eh, Anastasia?'

I nod.

'Tired?'

I nod.

'You're not very talkative.'

I nod and he grins.

'Come. I'll put you to bed.' He takes my hand as we exit the elevator, but we stop in the foyer when Sawyer holds up his hand. In that split second, I am instantly wide awake. Sawyer talks into his sleeve. I had no idea that he was wearing a radio.

'Will do, T,' he says and turns to face us. 'Mr. Grey, the tires on Ms. Steele's Audi have been slashed and paint thrown all over it.'

Holy shit. My car! Who would do that? And I know the answer as soon as the question materializes in my mind. Leila. I glance up at Christian, and he blanches.

'Taylor is concerned that the perp may have entered the apartment and may still be there. He wants to make sure.'

'I see,' Christian whispers. 'What's Taylor's plan?'

'He's coming up in the service elevator with Ryan and Reynolds. They'll do a sweep, then give us the all clear. I'm to wait with you, sir.'

'Thank you, Sawyer.' Christian tightens his arm around me. 'This day just gets better and better,' he sighs bitterly, nuzzling my hair. 'Listen, I can't stand here and wait. Sawyer, take care of Miss Steele. Don't let her in until you have the all clear. I am sure Taylor is overreacting. She can't get into the apartment.'

What? 'No, Christian—you have to stay with me,' I plead.

Christian releases me. 'Do as you're told, Anastasia. Wait here.'

No!

'Sawyer?' Christian says.

Sawyer opens the foyer door to let Christian enter the apartment then shuts the door behind him and stands in front of it, staring impassively down at me.

Holy shit. Christian! All manner of horrific outcomes run through my mind, but all I can do is stand and wait.

CHAPTER EIGHT

Sawyer talks into his sleeve again.

'Taylor, Mr. Grey has entered the apartment.' He flinches and grabs the earpiece, pulling it out of his ear, presumably receiving some powerful invective from Taylor.

Oh no—if Taylor is worried . . .

'Please let me go in,' I plead.

199

'Sorry, Miss Steele. This won't take long.' Sawyer holds both hands up in a defensive gesture. 'Taylor and the guys are just coming into the apartment now.'

Oh. I feel so impotent. Standing stock-still, I listen avidly for the slightest sound, but all I hear is my aggravated breathing. It's loud and shallow, my scalp prickles, my mouth is dry, and I feel faint. *Please, let Christian be okay,* I pray silently.

I have no idea how much time passes, and still we hear nothing. Surely no sound is good—there are no gunshots. I begin pacing around the table in the foyer and examine the paintings on the walls to distract myself.

I've never really looked at them before: all figurative paintings, all religious—the Madonna and child, all sixteen of them. *How odd.*

Christian isn't religious, is he? All of the paintings in the great room are abstracts—these are so different. They don't distract me for long. *Where is Christian?*

I stare at Sawyer and he watches me impassively.

'What's happening?'

'No news, Miss Steele.'

Abruptly, the doorknob moves. Sawyer spins like a top and draws a gun from his shoulder holster.

I freeze. Christian appears at the door.

'All clear,' he says, frowning at Sawyer, who puts his gun away immediately and steps back to let me in.

'Taylor is overreacting,' Christian grumbles as he holds out his hand to me. I stand gaping at him, unable to move, drinking in every little detail: his unruly hair, the tightness around his eyes, the tense jaw, the top two buttons of his shirt undone. I think

200

I must have aged ten years. Christian frowns at me in concern, his eyes dark.

'It's all right, baby.' He moves toward me, enveloping me in his arms, and kisses my hair. 'Come on, you're tired. Bed.'

'I was so worried,' I murmur, rejoicing in his embrace and inhaling his sweet, sweet scent with my head against his chest.

'I know. We're all jumpy.'

Sawyer has disappeared, presumably into the apartment.

'Honestly, your exes are proving to be very challenging, Mr. Grey,' I mutter wryly. Christian relaxes.

'Yes. They are.'

He releases me and, taking my hand, leads me across the hallway and into the great room.

'Taylor and his crew are checking all the closets and cupboards. I don't think she's here.'

'Why would she be here?' It makes no sense.

'Exactly.'

'Could she get in?'

'I don't see how. But Taylor is overcautious sometimes.'

'Have you searched your playroom?' I whisper.

Christian glances quickly at me, his brow creasing. 'Yes, it's locked—but Taylor and I checked.'

I take a deep, cleansing breath.

'Do you want a drink or anything?' Christian asks.

'No.' Fatigue sweeps through me—I just want to go to bed.

'Come. Let me put you to bed. You look exhausted.' Christian's expression softens.

I frown. Isn't he coming, too? Does he want to sleep alone?

I'm relieved when he leads me into his bedroom. I place my clutch bag on the chest of drawers and open it to empty the contents. I spy Mrs. Robinson's note.

'Here.' I pass it to Christian. 'I don't know if you want to read this. I want to ignore it.'

Christian scans it briefly and his jaw tenses.

'I'm not sure what blanks she can fill in,' he says dismissively. 'I need to talk to Taylor.' He gazes down at me. 'Let me unzip your dress.'

'Are you going to call the police about the car?' I ask as I turn around.

He sweeps my hair out of the way, his fingers softly grazing my naked back, and tugs down my zipper.

'No. I don't want the police involved. Leila needs help, not police intervention, and I don't want them here. We just have to double our efforts to find her.' He leans down and plants a gentle kiss on my shoulder.

'Go to bed,' he orders, and then he's gone.

*   *   *

I lie, staring at the ceiling, waiting for him to return. So much has happened today, so much to process. Where to start?

I wake with a jolt, disoriented. Have I been asleep? Blinking in the dim glow the hallway casts through the slightly open bedroom door, I notice that Christian is not with me. Where is he? I glance up. Standing at the end of the bed is a shadow. A woman, maybe? Dressed in black? It's difficult to tell.

In my befuddled state, I reach across and switch on the bedside light, then turn back to look but there's no one there. I shake my head. Did I imagine it? Dream it?

I sit up and look around the room, a vague, insidious unease gripping me—but I am quite alone.

I rub my face. What time is it? Where's Christian? The alarm clock shows that it's two fifteen in the morning.

Climbing groggily out of bed, I set off to hunt him down, disconcerted by my overactive imagination. I am seeing things now. It must be a reaction to the dramatic events of the evening.

The main room is empty, the only light emanating from the three pendulum lamps above the breakfast bar. But his study door is ajar, and I hear him on the phone.

'I don't know why you're calling at this hour. I have nothing to say to you . . . well, you can tell me now. You don't have to leave a message.'

I stand motionless by the door, eavesdropping guiltily. Who is he talking to?

'No, you listen. I asked you, and now I am telling you. Leave her alone. She has nothing to do with you. Do you understand?'

He sounds belligerent and angry. I hesitate to knock.

'I know you do. But I mean it, Elena. Leave her the fuck alone. Do I need to put it in triplicate for you? Are you hearing me? . . . Good. Good night.' He slams the phone down on the desk.

Oh, shit. I knock tentatively on the door.

'What?' he snarls, and I almost want to run and

203

hide.

He sits at his desk with his head in his hands. He glances up, his expression ferocious, but his face softens immediately when he sees me. His eyes are wide and cautious. Suddenly, he looks so tired and my heart constricts.

He blinks, and his eyes sweep down my legs and back again. I am wearing one of his T-shirts.

'You should be in satin or silk, Anastasia,' he breathes. 'But even in my T-shirt you look beautiful.'

Oh, an unexpected compliment. 'I missed you. Come to bed.'

He rises slowly out of the chair, still in his white shirt and black dress pants. But now his eyes are shining and full of promise . . . but there's a trace of sadness, too. He stands in front of me, staring intently but not touching me.

'Do you know what you mean to me?' he murmurs. 'If something happened to you, because of me . . .' His voice trails off, his brow creasing, and the pain that flashes across his face is almost palpable. He looks so vulnerable—his fear very much apparent.

'Nothing's going to happen to me,' I reassure him, my voice soothing. I reach up and stroke his face, running my fingers through the stubble on his cheek. It's unexpectedly soft. 'Your beard grows quickly,' I whisper, unable to hide the wonder in my voice at this beautiful, fucked-up man who stands before me.

I trace the line of his bottom lip then trail my fingers down his throat, to the faint smudge of lipstick at the base of his neck. He gazes down at me, still not touching me, his lips parted. I run my index finger along the line, and he closes his eyes. His soft breathing quickens. My fingers reach the edge of his shirt, and I run them down to the next fastened button.

'I'm not going to touch you. I just want to undo your shirt,' I whisper.

His eyes open wide, regarding me with alarm. But he doesn't move, and he doesn't stop me. Very slowly I unfasten the button, holding the material away from his skin, and move tentatively down to the next button, repeating the process—slowly, concentrating on what I am doing.

I don't want to touch him. *Well, I do . . . but I won't.* On the fourth button, the red line reappears, and I smile shyly up at him.

'Back on home territory.' I trace the line with my fingers before undoing the final button. I pull his shirt open and move to his cuffs, removing his black polished stone cufflinks one at a time.

'Can I take your shirt off?' I ask, my voice low.

He nods, eyes still wide, as I reach up and pull his shirt over his shoulders. He frees his hands so he's standing in front of me naked from the waist up. With his shirt off, he seems to recover his equilibrium. He smirks down at me.

'What about my pants, Miss Steele?' he asks, raising an eyebrow.

'In the bedroom. I want you in your bed.'

'Do you, now? Miss Steele, you are insatiable.'

'I can't think why.' I grab his hand, pull him from his study, and lead him to his bedroom. The room is chilly.

'You opened the balcony door?' he asks, frowning down at me as we arrive in his room.

'No.' I don't remember doing that. I recall

scanning the room when I woke. The door was definitely closed.

Oh shit . . . All the blood rushes from my face, and I stare at Christian as my mouth falls open.

'What?' he snaps, glaring at me.

'When I woke . . . there was someone in here,' I whisper. 'I thought it was my imagination.'

'What?' He looks horrified and dashes to the balcony door, peers out, then steps back into the room and locks the door behind him. 'Are you sure? Who?' he asks his voice tight.

'A woman, I think. It was dark. I'd only just woken up.'

'Get dressed,' he snarls at me on his way back in. 'Now!'

'My clothes are upstairs,' I whimper.

He pulls open one of the drawers in his chest of drawers and fishes out a pair of sweatpants.

'Put these on.' They are far too big, but he is not to be argued with.

He swipes a T-shirt, too, and quickly pulls it over his head. Grabbing the bedside phone, he presses two buttons.

'She's still fucking here,' he hisses down the phone.

Approximately three seconds later, Taylor and one of the other security guys burst into Christian's bedroom. Christian gives them a précis of what has happened.

'How long ago?' Taylor demands, staring at me all businesslike. He's still wearing his jacket. Does this man ever sleep?

'About ten minutes,' I mutter, for some reason feeling guilty.

'She knows the apartment like the back of her

hand,' says Christian. 'I am taking Anastasia away now. She's hiding here somewhere. Find her. When is Gail back?'

'Tomorrow evening, sir.'

'She's not to return until this place is secure. Understand?' Christian snaps.

'Yes, sir. Will you be going to Bellevue?'

'I'm not leading this problem to my parents. Book me somewhere.'

'Yes. I'll call you.'

'Aren't we all overreacting slightly?' I ask.

Christian glowers at me. 'She may have a gun,' he growls.

'Christian, she was standing at the end of the bed. She could have shot me then if that's what she wanted to do.'

Christian pauses for a moment to rein in his temper, I think. In a menacingly soft voice he says, 'I'm not prepared to take the risk. Taylor, Anastasia needs shoes.'

Christian disappears into his closet while the security guy watches me. I can't remember his name, Ryan maybe. He looks alternately down the hall and to the balcony windows. Christian emerges a couple of minutes later with a leather messenger bag, wearing jeans and his pinstriped blazer. He drapes a denim jacket around my shoulders.

'Come.' He clasps my hand tightly, and I have to practically run to keep up with his long strides into the great room.

'I can't believe she could hide somewhere in here,' I mutter, staring out the balcony doors.

'It's a big place. You haven't seen it all yet.'

'Why don't you just call her . . . tell her you want to talk to her?'

'Anastasia, she's unstable, and she may be armed,' he says irritably.

'So we just run?'

'For now—yes.'

'Supposing she tries to shoot Taylor?'

'Taylor knows and understands guns,' he says with distaste. 'He'll be quicker with a gun than she is.'

'Ray was in the army. He taught me to shoot.'

Christian raises his eyebrows and for a moment looks utterly bemused. 'You, with a gun?' he says incredulously.

'Yes.' I am affronted. 'I can shoot, Mr. Grey, so you'd better beware. It's not just crazy ex-subs you need to worry about.'

'I'll bear that in mind, Miss Steele,' he answers dryly, amused, and it feels good to know that even in this ridiculously tense situation, I can make him smile.

Taylor meets us in the foyer and hands me my small suitcase and my black Converse sneakers. I am stunned that he's packed me some clothes. I smile shyly at him with gratitude, and his returning smile is swift and reassuring. Before I can stop myself I hug him, hard. He's taken by surprise, and when I release him, he's pink in both cheeks.

'Be careful,' I murmur.

'Yes, Miss Steele,' he mutters, embarrassed.

Christian frowns at me and then looks questioningly at Taylor, who smiles very slightly and adjusts his tie.

'Let me know where I'm going.' Christian says.

Taylor reaches into his jacket, pulls out his wallet, and hands Christian a credit card.

'You might want to use this when you get there.'

Christian nods. 'Good thinking.'

Ryan joins us. 'Sawyer and Reynolds found nothing,' he says to Taylor.

'Accompany Mr. Grey and Miss Steele to the garage,' Taylor orders.

The garage is deserted. Well, it is nearly three in the morning. Christian ushers me into the passenger seat of the R8 and puts my case and his bag in the trunk at the front of the car. The Audi beside us is a complete mess—every tire slashed, white paint splattered all over it. It's chilling and makes me grateful that Christian is taking me somewhere else.

'A replacement will arrive on Monday,' Christian says bleakly when he's seated beside me.

'How could she have known it was my car?'

He glances anxiously at me and sighs. 'She had an Audi A3. I buy one for all my submissives—it's one of the safest cars in its class.'

Oh. 'So, not so much a graduation present, then.'

'Anastasia, despite what I hoped, you have never been my submissive, so technically it *is* a graduation present.' He pulls out of the parking space and speeds to the exit.

Despite what he hoped. Oh no . . . My subconscious shakes her head sadly. This is what we come back to all the time.

'Are you still hoping?' I whisper.

The in-car phone buzzes. 'Grey,' Christian snaps.

'Fairmont Olympic. In my name.'

'Thank you, Taylor. And, Taylor, be careful.'

Taylor pauses. 'Yes, sir,' he says quietly, and Christian hangs up.

The streets of Seattle are deserted, and Christian roars up Fifth Avenue toward I-5. Once on the interstate, he floors the gas pedal, heading north. He accelerates so quickly I'm momentarily thrown back in my seat.

I peek at him. He's deep in thought, radiating a deadly brooding silence. He hasn't answered my question. He glances frequently at the rearview mirror, and I realize he's checking that we're not being followed. Perhaps that's why we're on I-5. I thought the Fairmont was in Seattle.

I gaze out of the window, trying to rationalize my exhausted, overactive mind. If she'd wanted to hurt me, she had ample opportunity in the bedroom.

'No. It's not what I hope for, not anymore. I thought that was obvious.' Christian interrupts my introspection, his voice soft.

I blink at him, pulling his denim jacket tighter around me, and I don't know if the chill is emanating from within me or from outside.

'I worry that, you know . . . that I'm not enough.'

'You're more than enough. For the love of God, Anastasia, what do I have to do?'

Tell me about yourself. Tell me you love me.

'Why did you think I'd leave when I told you Dr. Flynn had told me all there was to know about you?'

He sighs heavily, closing his eyes for a moment, and for the longest time he doesn't answer. 'You cannot begin to understand the depths of my depravity, Anastasia. And it's not something I want to share with you.'

'And you really think I'd leave if I knew?' My voice is high, incredulous. Doesn't he understand that I love him? 'Do you think so little of me?'

'I know you'll leave,' he says sadly.

'Christian . . . I think that's very unlikely. I can't

210

imagine being without you.' *Ever . . .*

'You left me once—I don't want to go there again.'

'Elena said she saw you last Saturday,' I whisper quietly.

'She didn't.' He frowns.

'You didn't go to see her when I left?'

'No,' he snaps, irritated. 'I just told you I didn't— and I don't like to be doubted,' he scolds. 'I didn't go anywhere last weekend. I sat and made the glider you gave me. Took me forever,' he adds quietly.

My heart clenches again. Mrs. Robinson said she saw him.

Did she or didn't she? She's lying. Why?

'Contrary to what Elena thinks, I don't rush to her with all my problems, Anastasia. I don't rush to anybody. You may have noticed—I'm not much of a talker.' He tightens his hold on the steering wheel.

'Carrick told me you didn't talk for two years.'

'Did he, now?' Christian's mouth presses into a hard line.

'I kind of pumped him for information.' Embarrassed, I stare at my fingers.

'So what else did Daddy say?'

'He said your mom was the doctor who examined you when you were brought into the hospital. After you were discovered in your apartment.'

Christian's expression remains blank . . . careful.

'He said learning the piano helped. And Mia.'

His lips curl in a fond smile at the mention of her name. After a moment he says, 'She was about six months old when she arrived. I was thrilled, Elliot less so. He'd already had to contend with

211

my arrival. She was perfect.' The sweet, sad awe in his voice is affecting. 'Less so now, of course,' he mutters, and I recall her successful attempts at the ball to thwart our lascivious intentions. It makes me giggle.

Christian gives me a sideways glance. 'You find that amusing, Miss Steele?'

'She seemed determined to keep us apart.'

He laughs mirthlessly. 'Yes, she's quite accomplished.' He reaches across and squeezes my knee. 'But we got there in the end.' He smiles then glances in the rearview mirror once more. 'I don't think we've been followed.' He turns off I-5 and heads back to central Seattle.

'Can I ask you something about Elena?' We are stopped at some traffic lights.

He gazes at me warily. 'If you must,' he mutters sullenly, but I don't let his irritability deter me.

'You told me ages ago that she loved you in a way you found acceptable. What did that mean?'

'Isn't it obvious?' he asks.

'Not to me.'

'I was out of control. I couldn't bear to be touched. I can't bear it now. For a fourteen, fifteen-year-old adolescent boy with hormones raging, it was a difficult time. She showed me a way to let off steam.'

Oh. 'Mia said you were a brawler.'

'Christ, what is it with my loquacious family? Actually—it's you.' We've stopped at more lights, and he narrows his eyes at me. 'You inveigle information out of people.' He shakes his head in mock disgust.

'Mia volunteered that information. In fact, she was very forthcoming. She was worried you'd

212

start a brawl in the tent if you didn't win me at the auction,' I mutter indignantly.

'Oh, baby, there was no danger of that. There was no way I would let anyone else dance with you.'

'You let Dr. Flynn.'

'He's always the exception to the rule.'

Christian pulls into the impressive, leafy driveway of the Fairmont Olympic Hotel and parks near the front door, beside a quaint stone fountain.

'Come.' He climbs out of the car and retrieves our luggage. A valet rushes toward us, looking surprised—no doubt at our late arrival. Christian tosses him the car keys.

'Name of Taylor,' he says. The valet nods and can't contain his glee as he leaps into the R8 and drives off. Christian takes my hand and strides into the lobby.

As I stand beside him at the reception desk, I feel utterly ridiculous. Here I am, in Seattle's most prestigious hotel, dressed in an oversized denim jacket, oversized sweatpants, and an old T-shirt next to this elegant Greek god. No wonder the receptionist is looking from one to the other as if the equation doesn't add up. Of course, she's overawed by Christian. I roll my eyes as she flushes crimson and stutters. *Even her hands are shaking.*

'Do . . . you need a hand . . . with your bags, Mr. Taylor?' she asks, going scarlet again.

'No, Mrs. Taylor and I can manage.'

Mrs. Taylor! But I'm not wearing a ring. I put my hands behind my back.

'You're in the Cascade Suite, Mr. Taylor, eleventh floor. Our bellboy will help with your bags.'

'We're fine,' Christian says curtly. 'Where are the

213

elevators?'

Miss Flushing Crimson explains, and Christian grasps my hand once more. I glance briefly around the impressive, sumptuous lobby full of overstuffed chairs, deserted save for a dark-haired woman sitting on a cozy sofa, feeding tidbits to her Westie. She glances up and smiles at us as we make our way to the elevators. So, the hotel allows pets? Odd for a place so grand!

The suite has two bedrooms, a formal dining room, and comes complete with grand piano. A log fire blazes in the massive main room. This suite is bigger than my apartment.

'Well, Mrs. Taylor, I don't know about you, but I'd really like a drink,' Christian mutters, locking the front door securely.

In the bedroom, he puts my case and his satchel on the ottoman at the foot of the king-sized four-poster bed and leads me into the main room where the fire is burning brightly. It's a welcome sight. I stand and warm my hands while Christian fixes us both a drink.

'Armagnac?'

'Please.'

After a moment, he joins me by the fire and hands me a crystal brandy glass.

'It's been quite a day, huh?'

I nod and his gaze is searching, concerned.

'I'm okay,' I whisper reassuringly. 'How about you?'

'Well, right now I'd like to drink this and then, if you're not too tired, take you to bed and lose myself in you.'

'I think that can be arranged, Mr. Taylor.' I smile shyly at him as he shuffles out of his shoes and

214

peels off his socks.

'Mrs. Taylor, stop biting your lip,' he whispers.

I blush into my glass. The Armagnac is delicious, leaving a burning warmth in its wake as it glides silkily down my throat. When I glance up at Christian, he's sipping his brandy, watching me, his eyes dark—hungry.

'You never cease to amaze me, Anastasia. After a day like today—or yesterday, rather—you're not whining or running off into the hills screaming. I am in awe of you. You're very strong.'

'You're a very good reason to stay,' I murmur. 'I told you, Christian, I'm not going anywhere, no matter what you've done. You know how I feel about you.'

His mouth twists as if he doubts my words, and his brow creases as if what I'm saying is painful for him to hear. Oh, Christian, what do I have to do to make you realize how I feel?

Let him beat you, my subconscious sneers. I scowl inwardly at her.

'Where are you going to hang José's portraits of me?' I try to lighten the mood.

'That depends.' His lips twitch. This is obviously a much more palatable topic of conversation for him.

'On what?'

'Circumstances,' he says mysteriously. 'His show's not over yet, so I don't have to decide straightaway.'

I cock my head to one side and narrow my eyes.

'You can look as sternly as you like, Mrs. Taylor. I'm saying nothing,' he teases.

'I may torture the truth from you.'

He raises an eyebrow. 'Really, Anastasia, I don't

think you should make promises you can't fulfill.'

Oh my, is that what he thinks? I place my glass on the mantelpiece, reach over, and much to Christian's surprise, take his glass and place it beside mine.

'We'll just have to see about that,' I murmur. Very bravely—emboldened by the brandy, no doubt—I take Christian's hand and pull him toward the bedroom. At the foot of the bed I stop. Christian is trying to hide his amusement.

'Now that you have me in here, Anastasia, what are you going to do with me?' he teases, his voice low.

'I'm going to start by undressing you. I want to finish what I started earlier.' I reach for the lapels on his jacket, careful not to touch him, and he doesn't flinch but he's holding his breath.

Gently, I push his jacket over his shoulders, and his eyes stay on mine, all traces of humor gone, as they grow larger, burning into me, wary . . . and needful? There are so many interpretations of his look. *What is he thinking?* I place his jacket on the ottoman.

'Now your T-shirt,' I whisper and lift it by the hem. He cooperates, raising his arms and backing away, making it easier for me to pull it over his head. Once off, he gazes down at me, intently, wearing just his jeans that hang so provocatively from his hips. The band of his boxer briefs is visible.

My eyes move hungrily up across his taut stomach to the remains of the lipstick line, faded and smudged, then up to his chest. I want nothing more than to run my tongue through his chest hair to savor his taste.

'Now what?' he whispers, eyes blazing.

216

'I want to kiss you here.' I run my finger from hipbone to hipbone across his belly.

His lips part as he inhales sharply. 'I'm not stopping you,' he breathes.

I take his hand. 'You'd better lie down then,' I murmur and lead him to the side of the four-poster bed. He seems bewildered, and it occurs to me that perhaps no one has taken the lead with him since . . . her. *No, don't go there.*

Lifting the covers, he sits on the edge of the bed, gazing up at me, waiting, his expression wary and serious. I stand before him and slip off his denim jacket and let it drop to the floor, then I shuffle out of his sweatpants.

He rubs his thumb over the tips of his fingers. He's itching to touch me, I can tell, but he suppresses the urge. Taking a deep breath and beyond courageous, I reach for the hem of my T-shirt and lift it over my head so I am naked before him. His eyes don't leave mine, but he swallows and his lips part.

'You are Aphrodite, Anastasia,' he murmurs. I clasp his face in my hands, tip his head up, and bend to kiss him. He groans low in his throat.

As I place my mouth on his, he grabs my hips, and before I know it, I am pinned beneath him, his legs forcing mine apart so that he's cradled against my body between my legs. He's kissing me, ravaging my mouth, our tongues entwined. His hand trails from my thigh, over my hip, along my belly to my breast, squeezing, kneading, and pulling enticingly on my nipple.

I groan and tilt my pelvis involuntarily against him, finding a delicious friction against the seam of his fly and his growing erection. He stops kissing me and gazes down at me bemused and breathless. He flexes his hips so his erection pushes against me. . . . *Yes. Right there.*

I close my eyes and moan, and he does it again, but this time I push back, relishing his answering moan as he kisses me again. He continues the slow delicious torture—rubbing me, rubbing him. And he's right—getting lost in him—it's intoxicating to the exclusion of everything else. All my worries are obliterated. I am here in this moment with him—my blood singing in my veins, thrumming loudly through my ears, mixed with the sound of our panting breaths. I bury my hands in his hair, holding him to my mouth, consuming him, my tongue as avaricious as his. I trail my fingers down his arms, down his lower back to the waistband of his jeans, and push my intrepid, greedy hands inside, urging him on and on—forgetting everything, except us.

'You're going to unman me, Ana,' he whispers suddenly, breaking away from me and kneeling up. He briskly pulls down his jeans and hands me a foil packet.

'You want me, baby, and I sure as hell want you. You know what to do.'

With anxious, dexterous fingers, I rip open the foil and unroll the condom over him. He grins down at me, his mouth open, eyes misty gray and full of carnal promise. Leaning over me, he rubs his nose against mine, his eyes closed, and deliciously, slowly, he enters me.

I grasp his arms and tilt my chin up, reveling in the exquisitely full feeling of his possession. He runs his teeth along my chin, eases back, and then slides into me again—so slow, so sweet, so tender—

218

his body pressing down on me, his elbows and his hands on either side of my face.

'You make me forget everything. You are the best therapy,' he breathes, moving at an achingly leisurely pace, savoring every inch of me.

'Please, Christian—faster,' I murmur, wanting more, now.

'Oh no, baby. I need this slow.' He kisses me sweetly, gently biting my lower lip and absorbing my soft moans.

I move my hands into his hair and surrender myself to his rhythm as slowly and surely my body climbs higher and higher and plateaus, then falls hard and fast as I come around him.

'Oh, Ana,' he breathes as he lets go, my name a benediction on his lips as he finds his release.

*　　　*　　　*

His head rests on my belly, his arms wrapped around me. My fingers forage in his unruly hair, and we lie like this for I don't know how long. It's so late and I am so tired, but I just want to enjoy the quiet serene afterglow of making love with Christian Grey, because that's what we've done: gentle, sweet lovemaking.

He's come a long way, as have I, in such a short time. It's almost too much to absorb. With all the fucked-up stuff, I am losing sight of his simple, honest journey with me.

'I will never get enough of you. Don't leave me,' he murmurs and kisses my belly.

'I'm not going anywhere, Christian, and I seem to remember that I wanted to kiss your belly,' I grumble sleepily.

He grins against my skin. 'Nothing stopping you now, baby.'

'I don't think I can move . . . I'm so tired.'

Christian sighs and shifts reluctantly, coming to lie beside me with his head on his elbow and dragging the covers over us. He gazes down at me, his eyes glowing, warm, loving.

'Sleep now, baby.' He kisses my hair and wraps his arm around me and I drift.

*   *   *

When I open my eyes, light is filling the room, making me blink. My head is fuzzy from lack of sleep. *Where am I? Oh—the hotel . . .*

'Hi,' Christian murmurs, smiling fondly. He's lying beside me, fully dressed, on top of the bed. How long has he been here? Has he been studying me? Suddenly, I feel incredibly shy as my face heats under his steady gaze.

'Hi,' I murmur, grateful that I am lying on my front. 'How long have you been watching me?'

'I could watch you sleep for hours, Anastasia. But I've only been here about five minutes.' He leans over and kisses me gently. 'Dr. Greene will be here shortly.'

'Oh.' I'd forgotten about Christian's inappropriate intervention.

'Did you sleep well?' he inquires mildly. 'Certainly seemed like it to me, with all that snoring.'

Oh, playful teasing Fifty.

'I do not snore!' I pout petulantly.

'No. You don't.' He grins at me. The faint line of red lipstick is still visible around his neck.

220

'Did you shower?'

'No. Waiting for you.'

'Oh . . . okay.'

'What time is it?'

'Ten fifteen. I didn't have the heart to wake you earlier.'

'You told me you didn't have a heart at all.'

He smiles sadly, but doesn't answer. 'Breakfast is here—pancakes and bacon for you. Come, get up, I'm getting lonely out here.' He swats me sharply on my behind, making me jump, and rises from the bed.

Hmm . . . Christian's version of warm affection.

As I stretch, I'm aware I ache all over . . . no doubt a result of all the sex, dancing, and teetering in expensive high-heeled shoes. I stagger out of bed and make my way into the sumptuously appointed bathroom while going over the events of the previous day in my mind. When I come out, I don one of the overly fluffy bathrobes that hang on a brass peg in the bathroom.

Leila—the girl who looks like me—that's the most startling image my brain conjures for conjecture, that and her eerie presence in Christian's bedroom. What did she want? Me? Christian? To do what? And why the fuck has she wrecked my car?

Christian said I would have another Audi, like all his submissives. The thought is unwelcome. Since I was so generous with the money he gave me, there's not a lot I can do.

I wander into the main room of the suite—no sign of Christian. I finally locate him in the dining room. I take a seat, grateful for the impressive breakfast laid before me. Christian is reading the

Sunday papers and drinking coffee, his breakfast finished. He smiles at me.

'Eat up. You're going to need your strength today,' he teases.

'And why is that? You going to lock me in the bedroom?' My inner goddess jerks awake suddenly, all disheveled with a just-fucked look.

'Appealing as that idea is, I thought we'd go out today. Get some fresh air.'

'Is it safe?' I ask innocently, trying and failing to keep the irony from my voice.

Christian's face falls, and his mouth presses in a line. 'Where we're going, it is. And it's not a joking matter,' he adds sternly, narrowing his eyes.

I flush and stare down at my breakfast. I don't feel like being scolded after all the drama and such a late night. I eat my breakfast in silence, feeling petulant.

My subconscious is shaking her head at me. Fifty doesn't joke about my safety—I should know this by now. I want to roll my eyes at him, but I refrain.

Okay, I'm tired and testy. I had a long day yesterday and not enough sleep. Why, oh why does he get to look as fresh as a daisy? Life is not fair.

There's a knock at the door.

'That'll be the good doctor,' Christian grumbles, obviously still smarting from my irony. He stalks from the table.

Can't we just have a calm, normal morning? I sigh heavily, leaving half my breakfast, and get up to greet Dr. Depo-Provera.

*   *   *

We're in the bedroom, and Dr. Greene is staring at

222

me openmouthed. She's dressed more casually than last time, in a pale pink cashmere twin set and black pants, and her fine blonde hair is loose.

'And you just stopped taking it? Just like that?'

I flush, feeling beyond foolish.

'Yes.' Could my voice be any smaller?

'You could be pregnant,' she says matter-of-factly.

What! The world falls away at my feet. My subconscious collapses on the floor retching, and I think I'm going to be sick, too. *No!*

'Here, go pee in this.' She's all business today—taking no prisoners.

Meekly I accept the small plastic container she's offered and wander in a daze into the bathroom. No. No. *No.* No way . . . No way . . . Please no. No.

What will Fifty do? I go pale. He'll freak.

No, please! I whisper a silent prayer.

I hand Dr. Greene my sample, and she carefully places a small white stick in it.

'When did your period start?'

How am I supposed to think about such minutiae when all I can do is stare anxiously at the white stick?

'Er . . . Wednesday? Not the one just gone, the one before that. June first.'

'And when did you stop taking the pill?'

'Sunday. Last Sunday.'

She purses her lips.

'You should be okay,' she says sharply. 'I can tell by your expression that an unplanned pregnancy would not be welcome news. So medroxyprogesterone is a good idea if you can't remember to take the pill every day.' She gives me a stern look, and I quail under her authoritative

223

glare. Picking up the white stick, she peers at it.

'You're in the clear. You've not ovulated yet, so provided you've been taking proper precautions, you shouldn't be pregnant. Now, let me counsel you about this shot. We discounted it last time because of the side effects, but quite frankly, the side effects of a child are far-reaching and go on for years.' She smiles, pleased with herself and her little joke, but I can't begin to respond—I'm too stunned.

Dr. Greene launches into full disclosure mode about side effects, and I sit paralyzed with relief, not listening to a word. I think I'd tolerate any number of strange women standing at the end of my bed rather than confess to Christian that I might be pregnant.

'Ana!' Dr. Greene snaps. 'Let's do this thing.' She pulls me out of my reverie, and I willingly roll up my sleeve.

*   *   *

Christian closes the door behind her and gazes at me warily. 'Everything okay?' he asks.

I nod mutely, and he tilts his head to one side, his face tense with concern.

'Anastasia, what is it? What did Dr. Greene say?'

I shake my head. 'You're good to go in seven days,' I mutter.

'Seven days?'

'Yes.'

'Ana, what's wrong?'

I swallow. 'It's nothing to worry about. Please, Christian, just leave it.'

Christian looms in front of me. He grasps my chin, tipping my head back, and stares into my eyes,

224

trying to decipher my panic.

'Tell me,' he snaps.

'There's nothing to tell. I'd like to get dressed.' I pull my chin out of his reach.

He sighs and runs a hand through his hair, frowning at me. 'Let's shower,' he says eventually.

'Of course,' I mutter, distracted, and his mouth twists.

'Come,' he says sulkily, clasping my hand firmly. He stalks toward the bathroom as I trail behind him. I am not the only one in a bad mood, it seems. Firing up the shower, Christian quickly strips before turning to me.

'I don't know what's upset you, or if you're just bad-tempered through lack of sleep,' he says while unfastening my robe. 'But I want you to tell me. My imagination is running away with me, and I don't like it.'

I roll my eyes at him, and he glares at me, narrowing his eyes. *Shit! Okay . . . here goes.*

'Dr. Greene scolded me about missing the pill. She said I could be pregnant.'

'What?' He pales, and his hands freeze as he gazes at me, suddenly ashen.

'But I'm not. She did a test. It was a shock, that's all. I can't believe I was that stupid.'

He visibly relaxes. 'You're sure you're not?'

'Yes.'

He blows out a deep breath. 'Good. Yes, I can see that news like that would be very upsetting.'

I frown. . . . *upsetting*? 'I was more worried about your reaction.'

He furrows his brow at me, puzzled. 'My reaction? Well, naturally I'm relieved . . . it would be the height of carelessness and bad manners to

225

knock you up.'

'Then maybe we should abstain,' I hiss.

He gazes at me for a moment, bewildered, as if I'm some kind of science experiment. 'You are in a bad temper this morning.'

'It was just a shock, that's all,' I repeat petulantly.

Clasping the lapels of my robe, he pulls me into a warm embrace, kisses my hair, and presses my head against his chest. I'm distracted by his chest hair as it tickles my cheek. Oh, if I could just nuzzle him!

'Ana, I'm not used to this,' he murmurs. 'My natural inclination is to beat it out of you, but I seriously doubt you want that.'

Holy shit. 'No, I don't. This helps.' I hug Christian tighter, and we stand for an age in a strange embrace, Christian naked and I wrapped in a robe. I am once again floored by his honesty. He knows nothing about relationships, and neither do I, except what I've learned from him. Well, he's asked for faith and patience; maybe I should do the same.

'Come, let's shower,' Christian says eventually, releasing me.

Stepping back, he peels me out of my robe, and I follow him into the cascading water, holding my face up to the torrent. There's room for both of us under the gargantuan showerhead. Christian reaches for the shampoo and starts washing his hair. He hands it to me and I follow suit.

Oh, this feels good. Closing my eyes, I succumb to the cleansing, warming water. As I rinse off the shampoo, I feel his hands on me, soaping my body: my shoulders, my arms, under my arms, my breasts, my back. Gently he turns me around and pulls me against him as he continues down my body: my stomach, my belly, his skilled fingers between my legs—*hmm*—my behind. Oh, that feels good and so intimate. He turns me around to face him again.

'Here,' he says quietly, handing me the body wash. 'I want you to wash off the remains of the lipstick.'

My eyes open in a flurry and dart quickly to his. He's staring at me intently, soaking wet and beautiful, his glorious, bright gray eyes giving nothing away.

'Don't stray far from the line, please,' he mutters tightly.

'Okay,' I murmur, trying to absorb the enormity of what he's just asked me to do—to touch him on the edge of the forbidden zone.

I squeeze a small amount of soap on my hand, rub my hands together to create lather, then place them on his shoulders and gently wash away the line of lipstick on each side. He stills and closes his eyes, his face impassive, but he's breathing rapidly, and I know it's not lust but fear. It cuts me to the quick.

With trembling fingers, I carefully follow the line down the side of his chest, soaping and rubbing softly; he swallows, with his jaw tense as if his teeth are clenched. *Oh!* My heart constricts and my throat tightens. *Oh no, I'm going to cry.*

I stop to add more soap to my hand and feel him relax in front of me. I can't look up at him. I can't bear to see his pain—it's too much. It's my turn to swallow.

'Ready?' I murmur and the tension is loud and clear in my voice.

'Yes,' he whispers, his voice husky, laced with fear.

Gently, I place my hands on either side of his chest, and he freezes again.

It's too much. I am overwhelmed by his trust in me—overwhelmed by his fear, by the damage done to this beautiful, fallen, flawed man.

Tears pool in my eyes and spill down my face, lost in the water from the shower. *Oh, Christian! Who did this to you?*

His diaphragm moves rapidly with each shallow breath, his body is rigid, tension radiating off him in waves as my hands move along the line, erasing it. Oh, if I could just erase his pain, I would—I'd do anything—and I want nothing more than to kiss every single scar I see, to kiss away those hideous years of neglect. But I know I can't, and my tears fall unbidden down my cheeks.

'No. Please, don't cry,' he murmurs, his voice anguished as he wraps me tightly in his arms. 'Please don't cry for me.' And I burst into full-blown sobs, burying my face against his neck, as I think of a little boy lost in a sea of fear and pain, frightened, neglected, abused—hurt beyond all endurance.

Pulling away, he clasps my head with both hands, tilts it backward, and leans down to kiss me.

'Don't cry, Ana, please,' he murmurs against my mouth. 'It was long ago. I am aching for you to touch me, but I just can't bear it. It's too much. Please, please don't cry.'

'I want to touch you, too. More than you'll ever know. To see you like this . . . so hurt and afraid, Christian . . . it wounds me deeply. I love you so much.'

He runs his thumb across my bottom lip. 'I know. I know,' he whispers.

'You're very easy to love. Don't you see that?'

'No, baby, I don't.'

'You are. And I do and so does your family. So do Elena and Leila—they have a strange way of showing it—but they do. You are worthy.'

'Stop.' He puts his finger over my lips and shakes his head, an agonized expression on his face. 'I can't hear this. I'm nothing, Anastasia. I'm a husk of a man. I don't have a heart.'

'Yes, you do. And I want it, all of it. You're a good man, Christian, a really good man. Don't ever doubt that. Look at what you've done . . . what you've achieved,' I sob. 'Look what you've done for me . . . what you've turned your back on, for me,' I whisper. 'I know. I know how you feel about me.'

He gazes down at me, his eyes wide and panicked, and all we can hear is the steady stream of water as it flows over us in the shower.

'You love me,' I whisper.

His eyes widen further and his mouth opens. He takes a huge breath, as if winded. He looks tortured—vulnerable.

'Yes,' he whispers. 'I do.'

CHAPTER NINE

I cannot contain my jubilation. My subconscious gapes at me in stunned silence, and I wear a face-splitting grin as I gaze longingly up into Christian's tortured eyes.

His soft, sweet confession calls to me on some deep elemental level, as if he's seeking absolution; his three small words are my manna from heaven.

Tears prick my eyes once more. *Yes, you do. I know you do.*

It's such a liberating realization, as if a crushing millstone has been tossed aside. This beautiful, fucked-up man, whom I once thought of as my romantic hero—strong, solitary, mysterious—possesses all these traits, but he's also fragile and alienated and full of self-loathing. My heart swells with joy but also pain for his suffering. And I know in this moment that my heart is big enough for both of us. I *hope* it's big enough for both of us.

I reach up to clasp his dear, handsome face and kiss him gently, pouring all the love I feel into this one sweet connection. I want to devour him beneath the hot cascading water. Christian groans and encircles me in his arms, holding me as if I am the air he needs to breathe.

'Oh, Ana,' he whispers hoarsely, 'I want you, but not here.'

'Yes,' I murmur fervently into his mouth.

He switches off the shower and takes my hand, leading me out and enfolding me in my bathrobe. Grabbing a towel, he wraps it around his waist, then takes a smaller one and begins to gently dry my hair. When he's satisfied, he swathes the towel around my head so that in the large mirror over the sink I look like I'm wearing a veil. He's standing behind me and our eyes meet in the mirror, smoldering gray to bright blue, and it gives me an idea.

'Can I reciprocate?' I ask.

He nods, though his brow creases. I reach for another towel from the plethora of fluffy towels stacked beside the vanity, and standing before him on tiptoe, I start to dry his hair. He bends forward, making the process easier, and as I catch the occasional glimpse of his face beneath the towel, I see he's grinning like a small boy.

'It's a long time since anyone did this to me. A very long time,' he murmurs, but then frowns. 'In fact, I don't think anyone's ever dried my hair.'

'Surely Grace did? Dried your hair when you were young?'

He shakes his head, hampering my progress.

'No. She respected my boundaries from day one, even though it was painful for her. I was very self-sufficient as a child,' he says quietly.

I feel a swift kick in the ribs as I think of a small copper-haired child looking after himself because no one else cares. The thought is sickeningly sad. But I don't want my melancholy to hijack this blossoming intimacy.

'Well, I'm honored,' I gently tease him.

'That you are, Miss Steele. Or maybe it is I who am honored.'

'That goes without saying, Mr. Grey,' I respond tartly.

I finish with his hair, reach for another small towel, and move around to stand behind him. Our eyes meet again in the mirror, and his watchful, questioning look prompts me to speak.

'Can I try something?'

After a moment, he nods. Warily, and very gently, I run the soft cloth down his left arm, soaking up the water that has beaded on his skin. Glancing up, I check his expression in the mirror. He blinks at me, his eyes burning into mine.

I lean forward and kiss his bicep, and his lips part infinitesimally. I dry his other arm in a similar fashion, trailing kisses around his bicep, and a small smile plays on his lips. Carefully, I wipe his back beneath the faint lipstick line, which is still visible. I hadn't gotten around to washing his back.

'Whole back,' he says quietly, 'with the towel.' He takes a sharp breath and screws his eyes closed as I briskly dry him, careful to touch him only with the towel.

He has such an attractive back—broad, sculptured shoulders, all the small muscles clearly defined. He really looks after himself. The beautiful sight is marred only by his scars.

With difficulty I ignore them and suppress my overwhelming urge to kiss each and every one. When I finish he exhales, and I lean forward and reward him with a kiss on his shoulder. Putting my arms around him, I dry his stomach. Our eyes meet once more in the mirror, his expression amused but wary, too.

'Hold this.' I hand him a smaller face towel, and he gives me a bemused frown. 'Remember in Georgia? You made me touch myself using your hands,' I add.

His face darkens, but I ignore his reaction and put my arms around him. Gazing at us both in the mirror—his beauty, his nakedness, and me with my covered hair—we look almost biblical, as if from an Old Testament Baroque painting.

I reach for his hand, which he willingly entrusts to me, and guide that hand up to his chest to dry it, sweeping the towel slowly, awkwardly across his body. Once, twice—then again. He's completely immobilized, rigid with tension, except for his eyes, which follow my hand clasped around his.

My subconscious looks on with approval, her normally pursed mouth smiling, and I am the supreme puppet master. His anxiety ripples off his back in waves, but he maintains eye contact, though his eyes are darker, more deadly . . . showing their secrets, maybe.

Is this a place I want to go? Do I want to confront his demons?

'I think you're dry now,' I whisper as I drop my hand, gazing into the depths of his eyes in the mirror. His breathing is accelerated, lips parted.

'I need you, Anastasia,' he whispers.

'I need you, too.' And as I say the words, I am struck how true they are. I cannot imagine being without Christian, ever.

'Let me love you,' he says hoarsely.

'Yes,' I answer, and turning, he hauls me into his arms, his lips seeking mine, beseeching me, worshipping me, cherishing me . . . loving me.

*   *   *

He trails his fingers up and down my spine as we gaze at each other, basking in our postcoital bliss, replete. We lie together, me on my front hugging my pillow, he on his side, and I am treasuring his tender touch. I know that right now he needs to touch me. I am a balm for him, a source of solace, and how could I deny him that? I feel exactly the same about him.

'So you can be gentle,' I murmur.

'Hmm . . . so it would seem, Miss Steele.'

I grin. 'You weren't particularly the first time we . . . um, did this.'

'No?' He smirks. 'When I robbed you of your virtue.'

'I don't think you robbed me,' I mutter

233

haughtily—*I am not a helpless maiden.* 'I think my virtue was offered up pretty freely and willingly. I wanted you too, and if I remember correctly, I rather enjoyed myself.' I smile shyly at him, biting my lip.

'So did I if I recall, Miss Steele. We aim to please,' he drawls and his face softens, serious. 'And it means you're mine, completely.' All trace of humor has vanished as he gazes at me.

'Yes, I am,' I murmur back at him. 'I wanted to ask you something.'

'Go ahead.'

'Your biological father . . . do you know who he was?' This thought has been bugging me.

His brow creases, and then he shakes his head. 'I have no idea. Wasn't the savage who was her pimp, which is good.'

'How do you know?'

'Something my dad . . . something Carrick said to me.'

I gaze at my Fifty expectantly, waiting.

'So hungry for information, Anastasia,' he sighs, shaking his head. 'The pimp discovered the crack whore's body and phoned it in to the authorities. Took him four days to make the discovery, though. He shut the door when he left . . . left me with her . . . her body.' His eyes cloud at the memory.

I inhale sharply. Poor baby boy—the horror is too grim to contemplate.

'Police interviewed him later. He denied flat out I had anything to do with him, and Carrick said he looked nothing like me.'

'Do you remember what he did look like?'

'Anastasia, this isn't a part of my life I revisit very often. Yes, I remember what he looked like.

234

I'll never forget him.' Christian's face darkens and hardens, becoming more angular, his eyes frosting with anger. 'Can we talk about something else?'

'I'm sorry. I didn't mean to upset you.'

He shakes his head. 'It's old news, Ana. Not something I want to think about.'

'So what's this surprise, then?' I need to change the subject before he goes all Fifty on me. His expression lightens immediately.

'Can you face going out for some fresh air? I want to show you something.'

'Of course.'

I marvel how quickly he turns—mercurial as ever. He grins at me with his boyish, carefree, I'm-only-twenty-seven smile, and my heart lurches into my mouth. So it's something close to his heart, I can tell. He swats me playfully on my behind.

'Get dressed. Jeans will be good. I hope Taylor's packed some for you.'

He rises and pulls on his boxer briefs. Oh . . . I could sit here all day, watching him wander around the room.

'Up,' he scolds, bossy as ever. I gaze at him, grinning.

'Just admiring the view.'

He rolls his eyes at me.

As we dress, I notice that we move with the synchronization of two people who know each other well, each watchful and acutely aware of the other, exchanging the occasional shy smile and sweet touch. And it dawns on me that this is just as new for him as it is for me.

'Dry your hair,' Christian orders once we're dressed.

'Domineering as ever.' I smirk at him, and he

leans down to kiss my hair.

'That's never going to change, baby. I don't want you sick.'

I roll my eyes at him, and his mouth twists in amusement.

'My palms still twitch, you know, Miss Steele.'

'I am glad to hear it, Mr. Grey. I was beginning to think you were losing your edge.'

'I could easily demonstrate that is not the case, should you so wish.' Christian drags a large, cream, cable-knit sweater out of his bag and drapes it artfully over his shoulders. With his white T-shirt and jeans, his artfully rumpled hair, and now this, he looks as if he's stepped out of the pages of a high-end glossy magazine.

No one should look this good. And I don't know if it's the momentary distraction of his perfect looks or the knowledge that he loves me, but his threat no longer fills me with dread. This is my Fifty Shades; this is the way he is.

As I reach for the hair dryer, a tangible ray of hope blossoms. We will find a middle way. We just have to recognize each other's needs and accommodate them. *I can do that, surely?*

I gaze at myself in the dresser mirror. I'm wearing the pale blue shirt that Taylor bought and had packed for me. My hair is a mess, my face flushed, my lips swollen—I touch them, remembering Christian's searing kisses, and I can't help a small smile as I stare. *Yes, I do,* he said.

*   *   *

'Where are we going, exactly?' I ask as we wait in the lobby for the parking valet.

Christian taps the side of his nose and winks at me conspiratorially, looking like he's desperately trying to contain his glee. Frankly, it's very un-Fifty.

He was like this when we went gliding—perhaps that's what we're doing. I beam back at him. He stares down his nose at me in that superior way he has with his lopsided grin. Leaning down, he kisses me gently.

'Do you have any idea how happy you make me feel?' he murmurs.

'Yes . . . I know exactly. Because you do the same for me.'

The valet zooms up in Christian's car, wearing an enormous grin. Jeez, everyone is so happy today.

'Great car, sir,' he mumbles as he hands over the keys. Christian winks and gives him an obscenely large tip.

I frown at him. Honestly.

*   *   *

As we cruise through the traffic, Christian is deep in thought. A young woman's voice comes over the loudspeakers; it has a beautiful, rich, mellow timbre, and I lose myself in her sad, soulful voice.

'I need to make a detour. It shouldn't take long,' he says absentmindedly, distracting me from the song.

Oh, why? I'm intrigued to know the surprise. My inner goddess is bouncing about like a five-year-old.

'Sure,' I murmur. Something is amiss. Suddenly he looks grimly determined.

He pulls into the parking lot of a large car dealership, stops the car, and turns to face me, his expression wary.

'We need to get you a new car,' he says. I gape at him.

Now? On a Sunday? What the hell? And this is a Saab dealership.

'Not an Audi?' is, stupidly, the only thing I can think of to say, and bless him, he actually flushes.

Christian, embarrassed. This is a first!

'I thought you might like something else,' he mutters. He's almost squirming.

Oh, please . . . This is too valuable an opportunity not to tease him. I smirk. 'A Saab?'

'Yeah. A 9-3. Come.'

'What is it with you and foreign cars?'

'The Germans and the Swedes make the safest cars in the world, Anastasia.'

Do they? 'I thought you'd already ordered me another Audi A3?'

He gives me a darkly amused look. 'I can cancel that. Come.' Climbing out of the car, he strolls to my side and opens my door.

'I owe you a graduation present,' he says and holds his hand out for me.

'Christian, you really don't have to do this.'

'Yes, I do. Please. Come.' His tone says he's not to be trifled with.

I resign myself to my fate. A Saab? Do I want a Saab? I quite liked the Audi Submissive Special. It was very nifty.

Of course, now it's under a ton of white paint . . . I shudder. And she's still out there.

I take Christian's hand, and we wander into the showroom.

Troy Turniansky, the salesman, is all over Fifty like a cheap suit. He can smell a sale. His accent sounds oddly mid-Atlantic, maybe British? It's difficult to tell.

'A Saab, sir? Pre-owned?' He rubs his hands with glee.

'New.' Christian's lips set into a hard line.

New!

'Did you have a model in mind, sir?' And he's smarmy, too.

'9-3 2.0T Sport Sedan.'

'An excellent choice, sir.'

'What color, Anastasia?' Christian inclines his head.

'Er . . . black?' I shrug. 'You really don't need to do this.'

He frowns. 'Black's not easily seen at night.'

Oh, for heaven's sake. I resist the temptation to roll my eyes. 'You have a black car.'

He scowls at me.

'Canary yellow, then.' I shrug.

Christian makes a face—canary yellow is obviously not his thing.

'What color do you want me to have?' I ask as if he's a small child, which he is in many ways. The thought is unwelcome—sad and sobering at once.

'Silver or white.'

'Silver, then. You know I'll take the Audi,' I add, chastened by my thoughts.

Troy pales, sensing he's losing a sale. 'Perhaps you'd like the convertible, ma'am?' he asks, clapping his hands with enthusiasm.

My subconscious is cringing in disgust, mortified by the whole buying-a-car business, but my inner goddess tackles her to the floor. *Convertible? Drool!*

Christian frowns and peers at me. 'Convertible?' he asks, raising an eyebrow.

I flush. It's like he has a direct hotline to my

239

inner goddess, which, of course, he has. It's most inconvenient at times. I stare down at my hands.

Christian turns to Troy. 'What are the safety stats on the convertible?'

Troy, sensing Christian's vulnerability, heads in for the kill, reeling off all manner of statistics.

Naturally Christian wants me safe. It's a religion with him, and like the zealot he is, he listens intently to Troy's well-honed patter. Fifty really does care.

Yes. I do. I remember his whispered, choked words from this morning, and a melting glow spreads like warm honey through my veins. This man—God's gift to women—loves me.

I find myself grinning goofily at him, and when he glances down at me, he's amused yet puzzled by my expression. I want to hug myself, I am so happy.

'Whatever you're high on, I'd like some, Miss Steele,' he murmurs as Troy heads off to his computer.

'I'm high on you, Mr. Grey.'

'Really? Well you certainly look intoxicated.' He kisses me briefly. 'And thank you for accepting the car. That was easier than last time.'

'Well, it's not an Audi A3.'

He smirks. 'That's not the car for you.'

'I liked it.'

'Sir, the 9-3? I've located one at our Beverly Hills dealership. We can have it here for you in a couple of days.' Troy glows with triumph.

'Top of the range?'

'Yes, sir.'

'Excellent.' Christian produces his credit card, or is it Taylor's? The thought is unnerving. I wonder how Taylor is, and if he's located Leila in the apartment. I rub my forehead. Yes, there's all of Christian's baggage, too.

'If you'll come this way, Mr.'—Troy glances at the name on the card—'Grey.'

*   *   *

Christian opens my door, and I climb back into the passenger seat.

'Thank you,' I say when he's seated beside me.

He smiles.

'You're most welcome, Anastasia.'

The music starts again as Christian starts the engine.

'Who's this?' I ask.

'Eva Cassidy.'

'She has a lovely voice.'

'She does, she did.'

'Oh.'

'She died young.'

'Oh.'

'Are you hungry? You didn't finish all your breakfast.' He glances quickly at me, disapproval outlined on his face.

Uh-oh. 'Yes.'

'Lunch first, then.'

Christian drives toward the waterfront and then heads north along the Alaskan Way Viaduct. It's another beautiful day in Seattle; it's been uncharacteristically fine for the last few weeks.

Christian looks happy and relaxed as we sit back listening to Eva Cassidy's sweet, soulful voice and cruise down the highway. Have I ever felt this comfortable in his company before? I don't know.

I am less nervous of his moods, confident that he

241

won't punish me, and he seems more comfortable with me, too. He turns left, following the coast road, and eventually pulls up in a parking lot opposite a vast marina.

'We'll eat here. I'll open your door,' he says in such a way that I know it's not wise to move, and I watch him move around the car. Will this ever get old?

*   *   *

We stroll arm in arm to the waterfront, where the marina stretches out in front of us.

'So many boats,' I murmur in wonder. There are hundreds of them in all shapes and sizes, bobbing up and down on the calm, still waters of the marina. Out on Puget Sound there are dozens of sails in the wind, weaving to and fro. It's a wholesome, outdoorsy sight. The wind has picked up a little, so I pull my jacket around me.

'Cold?' he asks and pulls me tightly against him.

'No, just admiring the view.'

'I could stare at it all day. Come, this way.'

Christian leads me into a large seafront bar and makes his way to the counter. The decor is more New England than West Coast—white-limed walls, pale blue furnishings, and boating paraphernalia hanging everywhere. It's a bright, cheery place.

'Mr. Grey!' the barman greets Christian warmly. 'What can I get you this afternoon?'

'Dante, good afternoon.' Christian grins as we both slip onto barstools. 'This lovely lady is Anastasia Steele.'

'Welcome to SP's Place.' Dante gives me a friendly smile. He's black and beautiful, his dark

242

eyes assessing me and not finding me wanting, it seems. One large diamond stud winks at me from his ear. I like him immediately.

'What would you like to drink, Anastasia?'

I glance at Christian, who regards me expectantly. Oh, he's going to let me choose.

'Please, call me Ana, and I'll have whatever Christian's drinking.' I smile shyly at Dante. Fifty's so much better at wine than I am.

'I'm going to have a beer. This is the only bar in Seattle where you can get Adnams Explorer.'

'A beer?'

'Yes.' He grins at me. 'Two Explorers, please, Dante.'

Dante nods and sets up the beers on the bar.

'They do a delicious seafood chowder here,' Christian says.

He's asking me.

'Chowder and beer sound great.' I smile at him.

'Two chowders?' Dante asks.

'Please.' Christian grins at him.

We talk through our meal, as we never have before. Christian is relaxed and calm—he looks young, happy, and animated despite all that transpired yesterday. He recounts the history of Grey Enterprises Holdings, Inc., and the more he reveals, the more I sense his passion for fixing problem companies, his hopes for the technology he's developing, and his dreams of making land in the third world more productive. I listen, enraptured. He's funny, clever, philanthropic, and beautiful, and he loves me.

In turn he plagues me with questions about Ray and my mom, about growing up in the lush forests of Montesano, and my brief stints in Texas and

Vegas. He demands to know my favorite books and films, and I'm surprised by how much we have in common.

As we talk, it strikes me that he's turned from Hardy's Alec to Angel, debasement to high ideal in such a short space of time.

It's after two when we finish our meal. Christian settles the tab with Dante, who wishes us a fond farewell.

'This is a great place. Thank you for lunch,' I say as Christian takes my hand and we leave the bar.

'We'll come again,' he says, and we stroll along the waterfront. 'I wanted to show you something.'

'I know . . . and I can't wait to see it, whatever it is.'

*   *   *

We wander hand in hand along the marina. It is such a pleasant afternoon. People are out enjoying their Sunday—walking dogs, admiring the boats, watching their kids run along the promenade.

As we head down the marina, the boats grow progressively larger. Christian leads me onto the dock and stops in front of a huge catamaran.

'I thought we'd go sailing this afternoon. This is my boat.'

Holy cow. It must be at least forty, maybe fifty feet. Two sleek white hulls, a deck, a roomy cabin, and towering overhead an impressive mast. I know nothing about boats, but I can tell this one is special.

'Wow . . . ,' I murmur in wonder.

'Built by my company,' he says proudly, and my heart swells. 'She's been designed from the ground

244

up by the very best naval architects in the world and constructed here in Seattle at my yard. She has hybrid electric drives, asymmetric dagger boards, a square-topped mainsail—'

'Okay . . . you've lost me, Christian.'

He grins. 'She's a great boat.'

'She looks mighty fine, Mr. Grey.'

'That she does, Miss Steele.'

'What's her name?'

He pulls me to the side so I can see her name: *The Grace.* I'm surprised. 'You named her after your mom?'

'Yes.' He cocks his head to one side, quizzical. 'Why do you find that strange?'

I shrug. I'm surprised—he always seems ambivalent in her presence.

'I adore my mom, Anastasia. Why wouldn't I name a boat after her?'

I flush. 'No, it's not that . . . it's just . . .' Shit, how can I put this into words?

'Anastasia, Grace Trevelyan-Grey saved my life. I owe her everything.'

I gaze at him, and let the reverence in his softly spoken admission wash over me. It's obvious to me, for the first time, that he loves his mom. Why, then, his strange, strained ambivalence toward her?

'Do you want to come aboard?' he asks, his eyes bright, excited.

'Yes, please.' I smile.

He looks delighted and grasping my hand, he strides up the small gangplank taking me aboard. We stand on deck beneath a rigid canopy.

To one side there's a table and a U-shaped banquette covered in pale blue leather, which must seat at least eight people. I glance through the sliding doors to the interior of the cabin and jump, startled, when I spy someone there. The tall blond man opens the sliding doors and emerges— all tanned, curly-haired, and brown-eyed—wearing a faded pink short-sleeved polo shirt, shorts, and deck shoes. He must be in his early thirties.

'Mac.' Christian beams.

'Mr. Grey! Welcome back.' They shake hands.

'Anastasia, this is Liam McConnell. Liam, my girlfriend, Anastasia Steele.'

Girlfriend! My inner goddess performs a quick arabesque. She's still grinning over the convertible. I have to get used to this—it's not the first time he's said it, but hearing him say it is still a thrill.

'How do you do?' Liam and I shake hands.

'Call me Mac,' he says warmly, and I can't place his accent. 'Welcome aboard, Miss Steele.'

'Ana, please,' I mutter, flushing. He has deep brown eyes.

'How's she shaping up, Mac?' Christian interjects quickly, and for a moment, I think he's talking about me.

'She's ready to rock and roll, sir,' Mac beams. *Oh, the boat,* The Grace. *Silly me.*

'Let's get under way, then.'

'You going to take her out?'

'Yep.' Christian flashes Mac a wicked grin. 'Quick tour, Anastasia?'

'Yes, please.'

I follow him inside the cabin. An L-shaped cream leather sofa is directly in front of us, and above it, a massive curved window offers a panoramic view of the marina. To the left is the kitchen area—very well appointed, all pale wood.

'This is the main saloon. Galley beside,' Christian

says, waving his hand in the direction of the kitchen.

He takes my hand and leads me through the main cabin. It's surprisingly spacious. The floor is the same pale wood. It looks modern and sleek and has a light, airy feel, but it's all very functional, as if he doesn't spend much time here.

'Bathrooms on either side.' Christian points to two doors, then opens the small, oddly shaped door directly in front of us and steps in. We're in a plush bedroom. *Oh . . .*

It has a king-sized cabin bed and is all pale blue linen and pale wood like his bedroom at Escala. Christian obviously chooses a theme and sticks to it.

'This is the master cabin.' He gazes down at me, eyes glowing. 'You're the first girl in here, apart from family,' he says. 'They don't count.'

I flush under his heated stare, and my pulse quickens. *Really? Another first.* He pulls me into his arms, his fingers tangling in my hair, and kisses me, long and hard. We're both breathless when he pulls away.

'Might have to christen this bed,' he whispers against my mouth.

Oh, at sea!

'But not right now. Come, Mac will be casting off.' I ignore the stab of disappointment as he takes my hand and leads me back through the saloon. He indicates another door.

'Office in there, and at the front here, two more cabins.'

'So how many can sleep on board?'

'It's a six-berth cat. I've only ever had the family on board, though. I like to sail alone. But not when you're here. I need to keep an eye on you.'

He delves into a chest and pulls out a bright red

247

lifejacket.

'Here.' Putting it over my head, he tightens all the straps, a faint smile playing on his lips.

'You love strapping me in, don't you?'

'In any form,' he says, a salacious grin playing on his lips.

'You are a pervert.'

'I know.' He raises his eyebrows and his grin broadens.

'My pervert,' I whisper.

'Yes, yours.'

Once secured, he grabs the sides of the jacket and kisses me. 'Always,' he breathes, then releases me before I have a chance to respond.

Always! Holy shit.

'Come.' He grabs my hand and leads me outside, up some steps, and onto the upper deck to a small cockpit that houses a big steering wheel and a raised seat. At the prow of the boat Mac is doing something with ropes.

'Is this where you learned all your rope tricks?' I ask Christian innocently.

'Clove hitches have come in handy,' he says, looking at me appraisingly. 'Miss Steele, you sound curious. I like you curious. I'd be more than happy to demonstrate what I can do with a rope.' He smirks at me, and I gaze back impassively as if he's upset me. His face falls.

'Gotcha.' I grin.

His mouth twists and he narrows his eyes. 'I may have to deal with you later, but right now, I've got to drive my boat.' He sits at the controls, presses a button, and the engines roar into life.

Mac comes scooting back down the side of the boat, grinning at me, and jumps down to the deck below where he starts to unfasten a rope. Maybe he knows some rope tricks, too. The idea pops unwelcome into my head and I flush.

My subconscious glares at me. Mentally I shrug at her and glance at Christian—I blame Fifty. He picks up the receiver and radios the coast guard as Mac calls up that we are set to go.

Once more, I am dazzled by Christian's expertise. Is there nothing that this man can't do? Then I remember his earnest attempt to chop and dice a pepper in my apartment on Friday. The thought makes me smile.

Slowly Christian eases *The Grace* out of her berth and toward the marina entrance. Behind us, a small crowd has gathered on the dockside to watch our departure. Small children are waving, and I wave back.

Christian glances over his shoulder, then pulls me between his legs and points out various dials and gadgets in the cockpit. 'Grab the wheel,' he orders, bossy as ever, but I do as I'm told.

'Aye, aye, Captain!' I giggle.

Placing his hands snugly over mine, he continues to steer our course out of the marina, and within a few minutes we are out on the open sea, the cold blue waters of Puget Sound. Away from the shelter of the marina's protective wall, the wind is stronger, and the sea pitches and rolls beneath us.

I can't help but grin, feeling Christian's excitement—this is such fun. We make a large curve until we are heading west toward the Olympic Peninsula, the wind behind us.

'Sail time,' Christian says, excited. 'Here—you take her. Keep her on this course.'

What? He grins, reacting to the horror in my

face.

'Baby, it's really easy. Hold the wheel and keep your eye on the horizon over the bow. You'll do great; you always do. When the sails go up, you'll feel the drag. Just hold her steady. I'll signal like this'—he makes a slashing motion across his throat—'and you can cut the engines. This button here.' He points to a large black button. 'Understand?'

'Yes.' I nod frantically, feeling panicky. *Holy cow —I hadn't expected to do anything!*

He kisses me quickly, then steps off his captain's chair and bounds up to the front of the boat to join Mac, where he starts unfurling sails, untying ropes, and operating winches and pulleys. They work well together in a team, shouting various nautical terms to each other, and it's warming to see Fifty interacting with someone else in such a carefree manner.

Perhaps Mac is Fifty's friend. He doesn't seem to have many, as far as I can tell, but then, I don't have many, either. Well, not here in Seattle. The only friend I have is on vacation sunning herself in Saint James on the west coast of Barbados.

I feel a sudden pang for Kate. I miss my roommate more than I thought I would when she left. I hope she changes her mind and comes home with her brother, Ethan, rather than prolong her stay with Christian's brother, Elliot.

Christian and Mac hoist the mainsail. It fills and billows out as the wind seizes it hungrily, and the boat lurches suddenly, zipping forward. I feel it through the wheel. *Whoa!*

They get to work on the headsail, and I watch fascinated as it flies up the mast. The wind catches it, stretching it taut.

'Hold her steady, baby, and cut the engines!' Christian cries out to me over the wind, motioning me to switch off the engines. I can only just hear his voice, but I nod enthusiastically, gazing at the man I love all windswept, exhilarated, and bracing himself against the pitch and yaw of the boat.

I press the button, the roar of the engines ceases, and *The Grace* soars toward the Olympic Peninsula, skimming across the water as if she's flying. I want to yell and scream and cheer—this has to be one of the most exhilarating experiences of my life— except perhaps the glider, and maybe the Red Room of Pain.

Whoa. This boat can move! I stand firm, grasping the wheel, fighting the rudder, and Christian is behind me once more, his hands on mine.

'What do you think?' he shouts above the sound of the wind and the sea.

'Christian! This is fantastic.'

He beams, grinning from ear to ear. 'You wait until the spinney's up.' He points with his chin toward Mac, who is unfurling the spinnaker—a sail that's a dark, rich red. It reminds me of the walls in the playroom.

'Interesting color,' I shout.

He gives me a wolfish grin and winks. Oh, it's deliberate.

The spinney balloons out—a large, odd, elliptical shape—putting *The Grace* in overdrive. Finding her head, she speeds over the Sound.

'Asymmetrical sail. For speed.' Christian answers my unasked question.

'It's amazing.' I can think of nothing better to say. I have the most ridiculous grin on my face as

251

we whip through the water, heading for the majesty of the Olympic Mountains and Bainbridge Island. Glancing back, I see Seattle shrinking behind us, Mount Rainier in the far distance.

I had not really appreciated how beautiful and rugged Seattle's surrounding landscape is—verdant, lush, and temperate, tall evergreens and cliff faces jutting out here and there. It has a wild but serene beauty on this glorious sunny afternoon that takes my breath away. The stillness is stunning compared to our speed as we whip across the water.

'How fast are we going?'

'She's doing fifteen knots.'

'I have no idea what that means.'

'It's about seventeen miles an hour.'

'Is that all? It feels much faster.'

He squeezes my hands, smiling. 'You look lovely, Anastasia. It's good to see some color in your cheeks . . . and not from blushing. You look like you do in José's photos.'

I turn and kiss him.

'You know how to show a girl a good time, Mr. Grey.'

'We aim to please, Miss Steele.' He scoops my hair out of the way and kisses the back of my neck, sending delicious tingles down my spine. 'I like seeing you happy,' he murmurs and tightens his arms around me.

I gaze out over the wide blue water, wondering what I could possibly have done in the past to have fortune smile and deliver this man to me.

Yes, you're a lucky bitch, my subconscious snaps. *But you have your work cut out with him. He's not going to want this vanilla crap forever . . . you're going to have to compromise.* I glare mentally

252

at her snarky, insolent face and rest my head against Christian's chest. Deep down I know my subconscious is right, but I banish the thoughts. I don't want to spoil my day.

*   *   *

An hour later, we are anchored in a small, secluded cove off Bainbridge Island. Mac has gone ashore in the inflatable dinghy—for what, I don't know—but I have my suspicions because as soon as Mac starts the outboard engine, Christian grabs my hand and practically drags me into his cabin, a man with a mission.

Now he stands before me, exuding his intoxicating sensuality as his deft fingers make quick work of the straps on my lifejacket. He tosses it to one side and gazes intently down at me, eyes dark, dilated.

I'm already lost and he's barely touched me. He raises his hand to my face, and his fingers move down my chin, the column of my throat, my sternum, searing me with his touch, to the first button of my blue blouse.

'I want to see you,' he breathes and dexterously undoes the button. Bending, he plants a soft kiss on my parted lips. I am panting and eager, aroused by the potent combination of his captivating beauty, his raw sexuality in the confines of this cabin, and the gentle sway of the boat. He stands back.

'Strip for me,' he whispers, eyes burning.

Oh my. I'm only too happy to comply. Not taking my eyes off his, I slowly undo each button, savoring his scorching gaze. Oh, this is heady stuff. I see his desire—it's evident on his face . . . and elsewhere.

I let my shirt fall to the floor and reach for the button on my jeans.

'Stop,' he orders. 'Sit.'

I sit down on the edge of the bed, and in one fluid movement he's on his knees in front of me, undoing the laces of first one and then the other sneaker, pulling each off, followed by my socks. He picks up my left foot and raising it, plants a soft kiss on the pad of my big toe, then grazes his teeth against it.

'Ah!' I moan as I feel the effect in my groin. He stands in one smooth move, holds his hand out to me, and pulls me up off the bed.

'Continue,' he says and stands back to watch me.

I ease the zipper of my jeans down and hook my thumbs in the waistband as I sashay then slide the denim down my legs. A soft smile plays on his lips, but his eyes remain dark.

And I don't know if it's because he made love to me this morning, and I mean really made love to me, gently, sweetly, or if it was his impassioned declaration—*yes . . . I do*—but I don't feel embarrassed at all. I want to be sexy for this man. He deserves sexy—he makes me feel sexy. Okay, it's new to me, but I'm learning under his expert tutelage. And then again, so much is new to him, too. It balances the seesaw between us, a little, I think.

I am wearing some of my new underwear—a white lacy thong and matching bra—a designer brand with a price tag to match. I step out of my jeans and stand there for him in the lingerie he's paid for, but I no longer feel cheap. I feel his.

Reaching behind I unhook my bra, sliding the straps down my arms, and drop it on top of my blouse. Slowly, I slip my panties off, letting them fall to my ankles, and step out of them, surprised by my grace.

Standing before him, I am naked and unashamed, and I know it's because he loves me. I no longer have to hide. He says nothing, just gazes at me. All I see is his desire, his adoration even, and something else, the depth of his need—the depth of his love for me.

He reaches down, lifts the hem of his cream-colored sweater, and pulls it over his head, followed by his T-shirt, revealing his chest, never taking his bold gray eyes off mine. His shoes and socks follow before he grasps the button of his jeans.

Reaching over, I whisper, 'Let me.'

His lips purse briefly into an *ooh* shape, and he smiles. 'Be my guest.'

I step toward him, slip my fearless fingers inside the waistband of his jeans, and tug so he's forced to take a step closer to me. He gasps involuntarily at my unexpected audacity, then smiles down at me. I undo the button, but before I unzip him I let my fingers wander, tracing his erection through the soft denim. He flexes his hips into my palm and closes his eyes briefly, relishing my touch.

'You're getting so bold, Ana, so brave,' he whispers and clasps my face with both hands, bending to kiss me deeply.

I put my hands on his hips—half on his cool skin and half on the low-slung waistband of his jeans. 'So are you,' I murmur against his lips as my thumbs rub slow circles on his skin, and he smiles.

'Getting there.'

I move my hands to the front of his jeans and pull down the zipper. My intrepid fingers move through his pubic hair to his erection, and I grasp him tightly.

He makes a low sound in his throat, his sweet breath washing over me, and he kisses me again, lovingly. As my hand moves over him, around him, stroking him, squeezing him tightly, he puts his arms around me, his right hand flat against the middle of my back and his fingers spread. His left hand is in my hair, holding me to his mouth.

'Oh, I want you so much, baby,' he breathes, and steps back suddenly to remove his jeans and boxers in one swift, agile move. He is a fine, fine sight in or out of clothes, every single inch of him.

He is perfect. *His beauty is desecrated only by his scars,* I think sadly. And they run so much deeper than his skin.

'What's wrong, Ana?' he murmurs and gently strokes my cheek with his knuckles.

'Nothing. Love me, now.'

He pulls me into his arms, kissing me, twisting his hands into my hair. Our tongues entwined, he walks me backward to the bed and gently lowers me onto it, following me down so that he's lying by my side.

He runs his nose along my jawline as my hands move to his hair.

'Do you have any idea how exquisite your scent is, Ana? It's irresistible.'

His words do what they always do—flame my blood, quicken my pulse—and he trails his nose down my throat, across my breasts, kissing me reverentially as he does.

'You are so beautiful,' he murmurs, as he takes one of my nipples in his mouth and softly suckles.

I moan as my body bows off the bed.

'Let me hear you, baby.'

His hand trails down to my waist, and I glory in the feel of his touch, skin to skin—his hungry mouth at my breasts and his skilled long fingers caressing and stroking me, cherishing me. Moving over my hips, over my behind, and down my leg to my knee, and all this time he's kissing and sucking my breasts.

Grasping my knee, he suddenly hitches my leg up, curling it over his hips, making me gasp, and I feel rather than see his responding grin against my skin. He rolls over so that I am astride him and hands me a foil packet.

I shift back, taking him in my hands, and I just can't resist him in all his glory. I bend and kiss him, taking him in my mouth, swirling my tongue around him, then sucking hard. He groans and flexes his hips so that he's deeper in my mouth.

Mmm . . . he tastes good. I want him inside me. I sit up and gaze at him; he's breathless, mouth open, watching me intently.

Hurriedly I tear open the condom and unroll it over him. He holds out his hands for me. I take one and with my other hand, position myself over him, then slowly claim him as mine.

He groans low in his throat, closing his eyes.

The feel of him in me . . . stretching . . . filling me—I moan softly—*it's divine.* He places his hands on my hips and moves me up, down, and pushes into me. *Oh . . . it's so good.*

'Oh, baby,' he whispers, and suddenly he sits up so we're nose to nose, and the sensation is extraordinary—so full. I gasp, grabbing his upper arms as he clasps my head in his hands and gazes into my eyes—his intense and gray, burning with

257

desire.

'Oh, Ana. What you make me feel,' he murmurs and kisses me passionately with fervent ardor. I kiss him back, dizzy with the delicious feeling of him buried deep inside me.

'Oh, I love you,' I murmur. He groans as if pained to hear my whispered words and rolls over, taking me with him without breaking our precious contact, so that I'm lying beneath him. I wrap my legs around his waist.

He stares down at me with adoring wonder, and I am sure I mirror his expression as I reach up to caress his beautiful face. Very slowly, he starts to move, closing his eyes as he does and moaning softly.

The gentle sway of the boat and the peace and quiet tranquility of the cabin are broken only by our mingled breaths as he moves slowly in and out of me, so controlled and so good—it's heavenly. He puts his arm over my head, his hand on my hair, and he caresses my face with the other as he bends to kiss me.

I'm cocooned by him as he loves me, slowly moving in and out, savoring me. I touch him— sticking to the boundaries—his arms, his hair, his lower back, his beautiful behind—and my breathing accelerates as his steady rhythm pushes me higher and higher. He's kissing my mouth, my chin, my jaw, then nibbling my ear. I can hear his staccato breaths with each gentle thrust of his body.

My body starts to quiver. *Oh . . . This feeling that I now know so well . . . I am close . . . Oh . . .*

'That's right, baby . . . give it up for me . . . Please . . . Ana,' he murmurs and his words are my undoing.

'Christian,' I call out, and he groans as we both come together.

CHAPTER TEN

'Mac will be back soon,' he murmurs.

'Hmm.' My eyes flicker open to meet his soft gray gaze. Lord, his eyes are an amazing color—especially here, out on the sea—reflecting the light bouncing off the water through the small portholes into the cabin.

'As much as I'd like to lie here with you all afternoon, he'll need a hand with the dinghy.' Leaning over, Christian kisses me tenderly. 'Ana, you look so beautiful right now, all mussed up and sexy. Makes me want you more.' He smiles and rises from the bed. I lie on my stomach, admiring the view.

'You ain't so bad yourself, Captain.' I smack my lips in admiration and he grins.

I watch him move about the cabin as he dresses. This man who has just made such sweet love to me again. I can hardly believe my good fortune. I can't quite believe that he's mine. He sits down beside me to put on his shoes.

'Captain, eh?' he says dryly. 'Well, I am master of this vessel.'

I cock my head to one side. 'You are master of my heart, Mr. Grey.' *And my body . . . and my soul.*

He shakes his head incredulously and bends to kiss me. 'I'll be on deck. There's a shower in the bathroom if you want one. Do you need anything? A drink?' he asks solicitously, and all I can do is

259

grin at him. Is this the same man? Is this the same Fifty?

'What?' he says, reacting to my stupid grin.

'You.'

'What about me?'

'Who are you and what have you done with Christian?'

His lips twitch with a sad smile.

'He's not very far away, baby,' he says softly, and there's a touch of melancholy in his voice that makes me instantly regret asking the question. But he shakes it off. 'You'll see him soon enough'—he smirks at me—'especially if you don't get up.' Reaching over, he smacks me hard on my behind so I yelp and laugh at the same time.

'You had me worried.'

'Did I, now?' Christian's brow creases. 'You do give off some mixed signals, Anastasia. How's a man supposed to keep up?' He leans down and kisses me again. 'Laters, baby,' he adds, and with a dazzling smile, he gets up and leaves me to my scattered thoughts.

*   *   *

When I surface on deck, Mac is back on board, but he disappears onto the upper deck as I open the saloon doors. Christian is on his BlackBerry. *Talking to whom?* I wonder. He wanders over and pulls me close, kissing my hair.

'Great news . . . good. Yeah . . . Really? The fire escape stairwell? . . . I see . . . Yes, tonight.'

He hits the 'end' button, and the sound of the engines firing up startles me. Mac must be in the cockpit above.

'Time to head back,' Christian says, kissing me once more as he straps me into my lifejacket.

*　　　*　　　*

The sun is low in the sky behind us as we make our way back to the marina, and I reflect on a wonderful afternoon. Under Christian's careful, patient tuition, I have now stowed a mainsail, a headsail, and a spinnaker, as well as learned to tie a reef knot, clove hitch, and sheepshank. His lips were twitching throughout the lesson.

'I may tie you up one day,' I mutter crabbily.

His mouth twists with humor. 'You'll have to catch me first, Miss Steele.'

His words bring to mind him chasing me around the apartment, the thrill, and then the hideous aftermath. I frown and shudder. After that, I left him.

Would I leave him again now that he's admitted he loves me? I gaze up into his clear gray eyes. Could I ever leave him again—no matter what he did to me? Could I betray him like that? No. I don't think I could.

He's given me a more thorough tour of this beautiful boat, explaining all the innovative designs and techniques, and the high-quality materials used to build it. I remember the interview when I first met him; I picked up then on his passion for ships. I thought his love was only for the ocean-going freighters his company builds—not for super-sexy, sleek catamarans, too.

And, of course, he's made sweet, unhurried love to me. I shake my head, remembering my body bowed and wanting beneath his expert hands. He is

261

an exceptional lover, I'm sure—though, of course, I have no comparison. But Kate would have raved more if it was always like this; it's not like her to hold back on details.

But how long will this be enough for him? I just don't know, and the thought is unnerving.

Now he sits, and I stand in the safe circle of his arms for hours, it seems, in comfortable, companionable silence as *The Grace* glides closer and closer to Seattle. I have the wheel, Christian advising on adjustments every so often.

'There is poetry of sailing as old as the world,' he murmurs in my ear.

'That sounds like a quote.'

I sense his grin. 'It is. Antoine de Saint-Exupéry.'

'Oh . . . I adore *The Little Prince*.'

'Me, too.'

*   *   *

It is early evening as Christian, his hands still on mine, steers us into the marina. There are lights winking from the boats, reflecting off the dark water, but it is still light—a balmy, bright evening, an overture for what is sure to be a spectacular sunset.

A crowd gathers on the dockside as Christian slowly turns the boat around in a relatively small space. He does it with ease and reverses smoothly into the same berth we left earlier. Mac jumps on to the dock and ties *The Grace* securely to a bollard.

'Back again,' Christian murmurs.

'Thank you,' I murmur shyly. 'That was a perfect afternoon.'

Christian grins. 'I thought so, too. Perhaps we

262

can enroll you in sailing school, so we can go out for a few days, just the two of us.'

'I'd love that. We can christen the bedroom again and again.'

He leans forward and kisses me under my ear. 'Hmm . . . I look forward to it, Anastasia,' he whispers, making every single hair follicle on my body stand to attention.

How does he do that?

'Come, the apartment is clean. We can go back.'

'What about our things at the hotel?'

'Taylor has collected them already.'

Oh! When?

'Earlier today, after he did a sweep of *The Grace* with his team.' Christian answers my unspoken question.

'Does that poor man ever sleep?'

'He sleeps.' Christian quirks an eyebrow at me, puzzled. 'He's just doing his job, Anastasia, which he's very good at. Jason is a real find.'

'Jason?'

'Jason Taylor.'

I thought Taylor was his first name. Jason. It suits him—solid, reliable. For some reason it makes me smile.

'You're fond of Taylor,' Christian says, eyeing me with speculation.

'I suppose I am.' His question derails me. He frowns. 'I'm not attracted to him, if that's why you're frowning. Stop.'

Christian is almost pouting—sulky.

Jeez, he's such a child sometimes. 'I think Taylor looks after you very well. That's why I like him. He seems kind, reliable, and loyal. He has an avuncular appeal to me.'

'Avuncular?'

'Yes.'

'Okay, avuncular.' Christian is testing the word and meaning. I laugh.

'Oh, Christian, grow up, for heaven's sake.'

His mouth drops open, surprised by my outburst, but then he frowns as if considering my statement. 'I'm trying,' he says eventually.

'That you are. Very.' I answer softly but then roll my eyes at him.

'What memories you evoke when you roll your eyes at me, Anastasia.' He grins.

I smirk at him. 'Well, if you behave yourself, maybe we can relive some of those memories.'

His mouth twists with humor. 'Behave myself?' He raises his eyebrows. 'Really, Miss Steele—what makes you think I want to relive them?'

'Probably the way your eyes lit up like Christmas when I said that.'

'You know me so well already,' he says dryly.

'I'd like to know you better.'

He smiles softly. 'And I you, Anastasia.'

*   *   *

'Thanks, Mac.' Christian shakes McConnell's hand and steps on the dock.

'Always a pleasure, Mr. Grey, and good-bye. Ana, great to meet you.'

I shake his hand shyly. He must know what Christian and I were up to on the boat while he went ashore.

'Good day, Mac, and thank you.'

He grins at me and winks, making me flush. Christian takes my hand, and we walk up the dock

264

to the marina's promenade.

'Where's Mac from?' I ask, curious about his accent.

'Ireland . . . Northern Ireland,' Christian corrects himself.

'Is he your friend?'

'Mac? He works for me. Helped build *The Grace*.'

'Do you have many friends?'

He frowns. 'Not really. Doing what I do . . . I don't cultivate friendships. There's only—' He stops, his frown deepening, and I know he was going to mention Mrs. Robinson.

'Hungry?' he asks, trying to change the subject.

I nod. Actually, I'm famished.

'We'll eat where I left the car. Come.'

*   *   *

Next to SP's is a small Italian bistro called Bee's. It reminds me of the place in Portland—a few tables and booths, the decor very crisp and modern, with a large black-and-white photograph of a turn-of-the-century fiesta serving as a mural.

Christian and I are seated in a booth, poring over the menu and sipping a delicious light Frascati. When I glance up from the menu, having made my choice, Christian is gazing at me speculatively.

'What?' I ask.

'You look lovely, Anastasia. The outdoors agrees with you.'

I flush. 'I feel rather windburned, to tell the truth. But I had a lovely afternoon. A perfect afternoon. Thank you.'

He smiles, his eyes warm. 'My pleasure,' he

265

murmurs.

'Can I ask you something?' I decide on a fact-finding mission.

'Anything, Anastasia. You know that.' He cocks his head to one side, looking delicious.

'You don't seem to have many friends. Why is that?'

He shrugs and frowns. 'I told you, I don't really have time. I have business associates—though that's very different from friendships, I suppose. I have my family and that's it. Apart from Elena.'

I ignore the mention of the bitch-troll. 'No male friends your own age that you can go out with and let off steam?'

'You know how I like to let off steam, Anastasia.' Christian's mouth twists. 'And I've been working, building up the business.' He looks puzzled. 'That's all I do—except sail and fly occasionally.'

'Not even in college?'

'Not really.'

'Just Elena, then?'

He nods, his expression wary.

'Must be lonely.'

His lips curl in a small wistful smile. 'What would you like to eat?' he asks, changing the subject again.

'I'm going for the risotto.'

'Good choice.' Christian summons the waiter, putting an end to that conversation.

After we've placed our order, I shift uncomfortably in my seat, staring at my knotted fingers. If he's in a talking mood, I need to take advantage.

I have to talk to him about his expectations, about his, um . . . needs.

'Anastasia, what's wrong? Tell me.'

I glance up into his concerned face.

'Tell me,' he says more forcefully, and his concern evolves into what? Fear? Anger?

I take a deep breath. 'I'm just worried that this isn't enough for you. You know, to let off steam.'

His jaw tenses and his eyes harden. 'Have I given you any indication that this isn't enough?'

'No.'

'Then why do you think that?'

'I know what you're like. What you . . . um . . . need,' I stutter.

He closes his eyes and rubs his forehead with long fingers.

'What do I have to do?' His voice is ominously soft, as if he's angry, and my heart sinks.

'No, you misunderstand—you have been amazing, and I know it's just been a few days, but I hope I'm not forcing you to be someone you're not.'

'I'm still me, Anastasia—in all my fifty shades of fucked-upness. Yes, I have to fight the urge to be controlling . . . but that's my nature, how I've dealt with my life. Yes, I expect you to behave a certain way, and when you don't it's both challenging and refreshing. We still do what I like to do. You let me spank you after your outrageous bid yesterday.' He smiles fondly at the memory. 'I enjoy punishing you. I don't think the urge will ever go . . . but I'm trying, and it's not as hard as I thought it would be.'

I squirm and flush, remembering our illicit tryst in his childhood bedroom. 'I didn't mind that,' I whisper, smiling shyly.

'I know.' His lips curl in a reluctant smile. 'Neither did I. But let me tell you, Anastasia, this is all new to me and these last few days have been the

267

best in my life. I don't want to change anything.'

Oh!

'They've been the best in my life, too, without exception,' I murmur and his smile broadens. My inner goddess nods frantically in agreement—and nudges me hard. *Okay, okay.*

'So, you don't want to take me into your playroom?'

He swallows and pales, all trace of humor gone. 'No, I don't.'

'Why not?' I whisper. This is not the answer I expected.

And yes, there it is—that little pinch of disappointment. My inner goddess stomps off pouting, her arms crossed like an angry toddler's.

'The last time we were in there you left me,' he says quietly. 'I will shy away from anything that could make you leave me again. I was devastated when you left. I explained that. I never want to feel like that again. I've told you how I feel about you.' His gray eyes are wide and intense with his sincerity.

'But it hardly seems fair. It can't be very relaxing for you—to be constantly concerned about how I feel. You've made all these changes for me, and I . . . I think I should reciprocate in some way. I don't know—maybe . . . try . . . some role-playing games,' I stutter, my face as crimson as the walls of the playroom.

Why is this so hard to talk about? I have done all manner of kinky fuckery with this man, things I hadn't even heard of a few weeks ago, things that I would never have thought possible, yet the hardest of all is talking to him.

'Ana, you do reciprocate, more than you know.

Please, please don't feel like this.'

Gone is carefree Christian. His eyes are wider now with alarm, and it's gut-wrenching. 'Baby, it's only been one weekend,' he continues. 'Give us some time. I thought a great deal about us last week when you left. We need time. You need to trust me, and I you. Maybe in time we can indulge, but I like how you are now. I like seeing you this happy, this relaxed and carefree, knowing that I had something to do with it. I have never—' He stops and runs his hand through his hair. 'We have to walk before we can run.' Suddenly he smirks.

'What's so funny?'

'Flynn. He says that all the time. I never thought I'd be quoting him.'

'A Flynnism.'

Christian laughs. 'Exactly.'

The waiter arrives with our starters and bruschetta, and our conversation changes tack as Christian relaxes.

But when the unreasonably large plates are placed before us, I can't help think how I have thought of Christian today—relaxed, happy, and carefree. At least he's laughing now, at ease again.

I breathe an inward sigh of relief as he starts quizzing me about places I've been. This is a short discussion, since I have never been anywhere except the continental United States. Christian, on the other hand, has traveled the world. We slip into an easier, happier conversation, talking about all the places he's visited.

*   *   *

After our tasty and filling meal, Christian drives

269

back to Escala, with Eva Cassidy's gentle sweet voice singing over the speakers. It allows me a peaceful interlude in which to think. I have had a mind-blowing day: Dr. Greene; our shower; Christian's admission; making love at the hotel and on the boat; buying the car. Even Christian himself has been so different. It's as if he's letting go of something or rediscovering something—I don't know which.

Who knew he could be so sweet? Did he?

When I glance at him, he, too, looks lost in thought. It strikes me then that he never really had an adolescence—a normal one, anyway. I shake my head.

My mind drifts back to the ball and dancing with Dr. Flynn and Christian's fear that Flynn had told me all about him. Christian is still hiding something from me. How can we move on if he feels that way?

He thinks I might leave if I know him. He thinks that I might leave if he's himself. *Oh, this man is so complicated.*

As we get closer to his home, he starts radiating tension until it becomes palpable. He scans the sidewalks and side alleys, his eyes darting everywhere, and I know he's looking for Leila. I start looking, too. Every young brunette is a suspect, but we don't see her.

When he pulls into the garage, his mouth is set in a tense, grim line. I wonder why we've come back here if he's going to be so wary and uptight. Sawyer is in the garage, patrolling. The defiled Audi is gone. He comes to open my door as Christian pulls in beside the SUV.

'Hello, Sawyer,' I murmur my greeting.

'Miss Steele.' He nods. 'Mr. Grey.'

'No sign?' Christian asks.

'No, sir.'

Christian nods, grasps my hand, and heads for the elevator. I know his brain is working overtime—he's distracted. Once we're inside he turns to me.

'You are not allowed out of here alone. You understand?' he snaps.

'Okay.' *Jeez—keep your hair on.* But his attitude makes me smile. I want to hug myself—this man, all domineering and short with me, I know. I marvel that I would have found it so threatening only a week or so ago when he spoke to me this way. But now I understand him so much better. This is his coping mechanism. He's stressed about Leila, he loves me, and he wants to protect me.

'What's so funny?' he murmurs, a hint of amusement in his expression.

'You are.'

'Me? Miss Steele? Why am I funny?' he pouts.

Christian pouting is . . . hot.

'Don't pout.'

'Why?' He's even more amused.

'Because it has the same effect on me as I have on you when I do this.' I bite my lip deliberately.

He raises his eyebrows, surprised and pleased at the same time. 'Really?' He pouts again and leans down to give me a swift chaste kiss.

I raise my lips to meet his, and in the nanosecond when our lips touch, the nature of the kiss changes—wildfire spreading through my veins from this intimate point of contact, driving me to him.

Suddenly, my fingers are curling in his hair as he grabs me and pushes me against the elevator wall, his hands framing my face, holding me to his lips as our tongues thrash against each other. And I don't

271

know if it's the confines of the elevator making everything much more real, but I feel his need, his anxiety, his passion.

Holy shit. I want him, here, now.

The elevator pings to a halt, the doors slide open, and Christian drags his face from mine, his hips still pinning me to the wall, his erection digging into me.

'Whoa,' he murmurs panting.

'Whoa,' I mirror him, dragging a welcome breath into my lungs.

He gazes at me, eyes blazing. 'What you do to me, Ana.' He traces my lower lip with his thumb.

Out of the corner of my eye, Taylor steps backward so he's no longer in my line of sight. I reach up and kiss Christian at the corner of his beautifully sculptured mouth.

'What you do to me, Christian.'

He steps back and takes my hand, his eyes darker now, hooded. 'Come,' he orders.

Taylor is still in the foyer, waiting discreetly for us.

'Good evening, Taylor,' Christian says cordially.

'Mr. Grey, Miss Steele.'

'I was Mrs. Taylor yesterday.' I grin at Taylor, who flushes.

'That has a nice ring to it, Miss Steele,' Taylor says matter-of-factly.

'I thought so, too.'

Christian tightens his hold on my hand, scowling. 'If you two have quite finished, I'd like a debriefing.' He glares at Taylor, who now looks uncomfortable, and I cringe inwardly. I have overstepped the mark.

'Sorry,' I mouth at Taylor, who shrugs and smiles kindly before I turn to follow Christian.

'I'll be with you shortly. I just want a word with Miss Steele,' Christian says to Taylor, and I know I'm in trouble.

Christian leads me into his bedroom and closes the door.

'Don't flirt with the staff, Anastasia,' he scolds.

I open my mouth to defend myself—then close it again, then open it. 'I wasn't flirting. I was being friendly—there is a difference.'

'Don't be friendly with the staff or flirt with them. I don't like it.'

Oh. Good-bye, carefree Christian. 'I'm sorry,' I mutter and stare down at my fingers. He hasn't made me feel like a child all day. Reaching down he cups my chin, pulling my head up to meet his eyes.

'You know how jealous I am,' he whispers.

'You have no reason to be jealous, Christian. You own me body and soul.'

He blinks as if he's finding this fact hard to process. He leans down and kisses me quickly, but with none of the passion we experienced a moment ago in the elevator.

'I won't be long. Make yourself at home,' he says sulkily and turns, leaving me standing in his bedroom, dazed and confused.

Why on earth would he be jealous of Taylor? I shake my head in disbelief.

Glancing at the alarm clock, I notice it's just after eight. I decide to get my clothes ready for work tomorrow. I head upstairs to my room and open the walk-in closet. It's empty. All the clothes have gone. *Oh no!* Christian has taken me at my word and disposed of the clothes. *Shit.*

My subconscious glares at me. *Well, that would be you and your big mouth.*

273

Why did he take me at my word? My mother's advice comes back to haunt me: *'Men are so literal, darling.'* I pout, staring at the empty space. There were some lovely clothes, too, like the silver dress I wore to the ball.

I wander disconsolately into the bedroom. *Wait a minute—what is going on?* The iPad is gone. Where's my Mac? *Oh no.* My first uncharitable thought is that Leila may have stolen them.

I fly back downstairs and back into Christian's bedroom. On the bedside table are my Mac, my iPad, and my backpack. It's all here.

I open the walk-in closet door. My clothes are here—all of them—sharing space with Christian's clothes. When did this happen? Why does he never warn me before he does things like this?

I turn, and he's standing in the doorway.

'Oh, they managed the move,' he mutters, distracted.

'What's wrong?' I ask. His face is grim.

'Taylor thinks Leila was getting in through the emergency stairwell. She must have had a key. All the locks have been changed now. Taylor's team has done a sweep of every room in the apartment. She's not here.' He stops and runs a hand through his hair. 'I wish I knew where she was. She's evading all our attempts to find her when she needs help.' He frowns, and my earlier pique vanishes. I put my arms around him. Folding me into his embrace, he kisses my hair.

'What will you do when you find her?' I ask.

'Dr. Flynn has a place.'

'What about her husband?'

'He's washed his hands of her.' Christian's tone is bitter. 'Her family is in Connecticut. I think she's

274

very much on her own out there.'

'That's sad.'

'Are you okay with all your stuff being here? I want you to share my room,' he murmurs.

Whoa, quick change of direction.

'Yes.'

'I want you sleeping with me. I don't have nightmares when you're with me.'

'You have nightmares?'

'Yes.'

I tighten my hold around him. More baggage. My heart contracts for this man.

'I was just getting my clothes ready for work tomorrow,' I mutter.

'Work!' Christian exclaims as if it's a dirty word, and he releases me, glaring.

'Yes, work,' I reply, confused by his reaction.

He stares at me with complete incomprehension. 'But Leila—she's out there,' he pauses. 'I don't want you to go to work.'

What? 'That's ridiculous, Christian. I have to go to work.'

'No, you don't.'

'I have a new job, which I enjoy. Of course I have to go to work.' *What does he mean?*

'No, you don't,' he repeats, emphatically.

'Do you think I am going to stay here twiddling my thumbs while you're off being Master of the Universe?'

'Frankly . . . yes.'

Oh, Fifty, Fifty, Fifty . . . give me strength.

'Christian, I need to go to work.'

'No, you don't.'

'Yes. I. Do.' I say it slowly as if he's a child.

He scowls at me. 'It's not safe.'

'Christian . . . I need to work for a living, and I'll be fine.'

'No, you don't need to work for a living—and how do you know you'll be fine?' He's almost shouting.

What does he mean? He's going to support me? Oh, this is beyond ridiculous—I've known him for what—five weeks?

He's angry now, his eyes stormy and flashing, but I don't give a shit.

'For heaven's sake, Christian, Leila was standing at the end of your bed, and she didn't harm me, and yes, I do need to work. I don't want to be beholden to you. I have my student loans to pay.'

His mouth presses into a grim line, as I place my hands on my hips. I am not budging on this. Who the fuck does he think he is?

'I don't want you going to work.'

'It's not up to you, Christian. This is not your decision to make.'

He runs his hand through his hair as he stares at me. Seconds, minutes tick by as we glare at each other.

'Sawyer will come with you.'

'Christian, that's not necessary. You're being irrational.'

'Irrational?' he growls. 'Either he comes with you, or I will be really irrational and keep you here.'

He wouldn't, would he? 'How, exactly?'

'Oh, I'd find a way, Anastasia. Don't push me.'

'Okay!' I concede, holding up both my hands, placating him. *Holy fuck—Fifty is back with a vengeance.*

We stand, scowling at each other.

'Okay—Sawyer can come with me if it makes you

276

feel better.' I concede rolling my eyes. Christian narrows his and takes a menacing step in my direction. I immediately step back. He stops and takes a deep breath, closes his eyes, and runs both his hands through his hair. Oh no. Fifty is well and truly wound up.

'Shall I give you a tour?'

A tour? Are you kidding me? 'Okay,' I mutter warily. Another change of tack—Mr. Mercurial is back in town. He holds out his hand and when I take it, he squeezes mine softly.

'I didn't mean to frighten you.'

'You didn't. I was just getting ready to run,' I quip.

'Run?' Christian eyes widen.

'I'm joking!' *Oh, jeez.*

He leads me out of the closet, and I take a moment to calm down. Adrenaline is still coursing through my body. A fight with Fifty is not to be undertaken lightly.

He gives me a tour of the apartment, showing me the various rooms. Along with the playroom and three spare bedrooms upstairs, I'm intrigued to find that Taylor and Mrs. Jones have a wing to themselves—a kitchen, spacious living area, and a bedroom each. Mrs. Jones has not yet returned from visiting her sister who lives in Portland.

Downstairs, the room that catches my eye is opposite his study—a TV room with a too-large plasma screen and assorted games consoles. It's cozy.

'So, you do have an Xbox?' I smirk.

'Yes, but I'm crap at it. Elliot always beats me. That was funny, when you thought I meant this room was my playroom.' He grins down at me, his conniption forgotten. Thank heavens he's recovered his good mood.

'I'm glad you find me amusing, Mr. Grey,' I respond haughtily.

'That you are, Miss Steele—when you're not being exasperating, of course.'

'I'm usually exasperating when you're being unreasonable.'

'Me? Unreasonable?'

'Yes, Mr. Grey. Unreasonable could be your middle name.'

'I don't have a middle name.'

'Unreasonable would suit, then.'

'I think that's a matter of opinion, Miss Steele.'

'I would be interested in Dr. Flynn's professional opinion.'

Christian smirks.

'I thought Trevelyan was your middle name.'

'No. Surname. Trevelyan-Grey.'

'But you don't use it.'

'It's too long. Come,' he commands. I follow him out of the TV room through the great room to the main corridor past the utility room and an impressive wine cellar and into Taylor's own large, well-equipped office. Taylor stands when we enter. There's room in here for a meeting table that seats six. Above one desk is a bank of monitors. I had no idea the apartment had CCTV. It appears to monitor the balcony, stairwell, service elevator, and foyer.

'Hi, Taylor. I'm just giving Anastasia a tour.'

Taylor nods but doesn't smile. I wonder if he's been told off, too, and why is he still working? When I smile at him, he nods politely. Christian grabs my hand once more and leads me to the library.

'And, of course, you've been in here.' Christian opens the door. I spy the green baize of the billiard table.

'Shall we play?' I ask.

Christian smiles, surprised. 'Okay. Have you played before?'

'A few times,' I lie, and he narrows his eyes, cocking his head to one side.

'You're a hopeless liar, Anastasia. Either you've never played before or—'

I lick my lips. 'Frightened of a little competition?'

'Frightened of a little girl like you?' Christian scoffs good-naturedly.

'A wager, Mr. Grey.'

'You're that confident, Miss Steele?' He smirks, amused and incredulous at once. 'What would you like to wager?'

'If I win, you'll take me back into the playroom.'

He gazes at me as if he can't quite comprehend what I've said. 'And if I win?' he asks after several shell-shocked beats.

'Then it's your choice.'

His mouth twists as he contemplates his answer. 'Okay, deal.' He smirks. 'Do you want to play pool, English snooker, or carom billiards?'

'Pool, please. I don't know the others.'

From a cupboard beneath one of the bookshelves, Christian takes out a large leather case. Inside the pool balls are nested in velvet. Quickly and efficiently, he racks the balls on the baize. I don't think I've ever played pool on such a large table before. Christian hands me a cue and some chalk.

'Would you like to break?' He feigns politeness.

279

He's enjoying himself—he thinks he's going to win.

'Okay.' I chalk the end of my cue and blow the excess chalk off—staring up at Christian through my lashes. His eyes darken as I do.

I line up on the white ball and with a swift clean stroke, hit the center ball of the triangle square on with such force that a striped ball spins and plunges into the top right pocket. I've scattered the rest of the balls.

'I choose stripes,' I say innocently, smiling coyly at Christian. His mouth twists in amusement.

'Be my guest,' he says politely.

I proceed to pocket the next three balls in quick succession. Inside myself I'm dancing. At this moment I am so grateful to José for teaching me to play pool and play it well. Christian watches impassively, giving nothing away, but his amusement seems to ebb. I miss the green stripe by a hairbreadth.

'You know, Anastasia, I could stand here and watch you leaning and stretching across this billiard table all day,' he says appreciatively.

I flush. Thank heavens I am wearing my jeans. He smirks. He's trying to put me off my game, the bastard. He pulls his cream sweater over his head, tosses it onto the back of a chair, and grins at me, as he saunters over to take his first shot.

He bends low over the table. My mouth goes dry. *Oh, I see what he means.* Christian in tight jeans and white T-shirt, bending, like that . . . is something to behold. I quite lose my train of thought. He sinks four solids rapidly, then fouls by sinking the white.

'A very elementary mistake, Mr. Grey,' I tease.

He smirks. 'Ah, Miss Steele, I am but a foolish mortal. Your turn, I believe.' He waves at the table.

'You're not trying to lose, are you?'

'Oh no. For what I have in mind as the prize, I want to win, Anastasia.' He shrugs casually. 'But then, I always want to win.'

I narrow my eyes at him. *Right, then* . . . I'm so glad I'm wearing my blue blouse, which is pleasingly low-cut. I stalk around the table, bending low at every available opportunity—giving Christian an eyeful of my behind and my cleavage whenever I can. Two can play at that game. I glance at him.

'I know what you're doing,' he whispers, his eyes dark.

I tilt my head coquettishly to one side, gently fondling my cue, running my hand up and down it slowly. 'Oh. I am just deciding where to take my next shot,' I murmur distractedly.

Leaning across, I hit the orange stripe into a better position. I then stand directly in front of Christian and take the rest from underneath the table. I line up my next shot, leaning right over the table. I hear Christian's sharp intake of breath, and of course, I miss. *Shit.*

He comes to stand behind me while I am still bent over the table and places his hand on my backside. *Hmm* . . .

'Are you waving this around to taunt me, Miss Steele?' And he smacks me, hard.

I gasp. 'Yes,' I mutter, because it's true.

'Be careful what you wish for, baby.'

I rub my behind as he wanders to the other end of the table, leans over, and takes his shot. He hits the red ball, and it shoots into the left side pocket. He aims for the yellow, top right, and it just misses. I grin.

'Red Room, here we come,' I taunt him.

281

He merely raises an eyebrow and directs me to continue. I make quick work of the green stripe and by some fluke, manage to knock in the final orange stripe.

'Name your pocket,' Christian murmurs, and it's as if he's talking about something else, something dark and naughty.

'Top left-hand.' I take aim over the black, hit it, but miss. It skirts wide. *Damn*.

Christian smiles a wicked grin as he leans over the table and makes short work of the two remaining solids. I am practically panting, watching him, his lithe body stretching over the table. He stands and chalks his cue, his eyes burning into me.

'If I win . . .'

Oh yes?

'I am going to spank you, then fuck you over this billiard table.'

Holy shit. Every single muscle south of my navel clenches hard.

'Top right,' he murmurs, pointing to the black, and bends to take the shot.

CHAPTER ELEVEN

With easy grace, Christian taps the white ball so that it glides across the table, kisses the black, and oh-so-slowly the black rolls, teeters on the edge, and finally drops into the top right pocket of the billiard table.

Damn.

He stands, and his mouth twists in a triumphant I-so-own-you-Steele smile. Putting down his cue, he saunters casually toward me, all tousled hair, jeans, and white T-shirt. He doesn't look like a CEO—he looks like a bad boy from the wrong side of town. Holy cow, he's so fucking sexy.

'You're not going to be a sore loser, are you?' he murmurs, barely containing his grin.

'Depends how hard you spank me,' I whisper, holding on to my cue for support. He takes my cue and puts it to one side, hooks his finger into the top of my shirt, and pulls me toward him.

'Well, let's count your misdemeanors, Miss Steele.' He counts on his long fingers. 'One, making me jealous of my own staff. Two, arguing with me about working. And three, waving your delectable derriere at me for the last twenty minutes.'

His eyes glow a soft gray with excitement, and leaning down, he rubs his nose against mine. 'I want you to take your jeans and this very fetching shirt off. Now.' He plants a feather-soft kiss on my lips, wanders nonchalantly over to the door, and locks it.

When he turns and gazes at me, his eyes are burning. I stand paralyzed like a complete zombie, my heart pounding, my blood pumping, not actually able to move a muscle. In my mind, all I can think is—*this is for him*—the thought repeating like a mantra over and over again.

'Clothes, Anastasia. You appear to still be wearing them. Take them off—or I will do it for you.'

'You do it.' I finally find my voice, and it sounds low and heated. Christian grins.

'Oh, Miss Steele. It's a dirty job, but I think I can rise to the challenge.'

'You normally rise to most challenges, Mr. Grey.' I raise an eyebrow at him, and he smirks.

'Why, Miss Steele, whatever do you mean?' On his way over to me, he pauses at the small desk built into one of the bookshelves. Reaching over, he picks up a twelve-inch Perspex ruler. He holds each end and flexes it, his eyes not leaving mine.

Holy shit—his weapon of choice. My mouth goes dry.

Suddenly I'm hot and bothered and damp in all the right places. Only Christian could turn me on with just a look and the flex of a ruler. He slips it into the back pocket of his jeans and ambles toward me, eyes dark and full of promise. Without saying a word, he drops to his knees in front of me and starts to undo my laces, quickly and efficiently, dragging both my Converses and socks off. I lean on the side of the billiard table so I don't fall. Gazing down at him as he undoes my laces, I marvel at the depth of feeling that I have for this man. I love him.

He grabs my hips, slips his fingers into the waistband of my jeans, and undoes the button and zipper. He peers up through his long lashes, grinning his most salacious grin as he slowly peels my jeans off. I step out of them, glad that I'm wearing these pretty white lace panties, and he grasps the back of my legs and runs his nose along the apex of my thighs. I practically melt.

'I want to be quite rough with you, Ana. You'll have to tell me to stop if it's too much,' he breathes.

Oh my. He kisses me . . . there. I moan softly.

'Safeword?' I murmur.

'No, no safeword, just tell me to stop, and I'll stop. Understand?' He kisses me again, nuzzling me. *Oh, that feels good.* He stands up, his stare intense. 'Answer me,' he orders his voice velvet soft.

'Yes, yes, I understand.' I'm puzzled by his insistence.

'You've been dropping hints and giving me mixed signals all day, Anastasia,' he says. 'You said you were worried I'd lost my edge. I'm not sure what you meant by that, and I don't know how serious you were, but we are going to find out. I don't want to go back into the playroom yet, so we can try this now, but if you don't like it, you must promise to tell me.' A burning intensity born of his anxiety replaces his earlier cockiness.

Whoa, please don't be anxious, Christian. 'I'll tell you. No safeword,' I reiterate to reassure him.

'We're lovers, Anastasia. Lovers don't need safewords.' He frowns. 'Do they?'

'I guess not,' I murmur. *How do I know?* 'I promise.'

He searches my face for any clue that I might lack the courage of my convictions, and I'm nervous but excited, too. I'm much happier to do this, knowing that he loves me. It's very simple to me, and right now, I don't want to overthink it.

A slow smile stretches across his face, and he starts to unbutton my shirt, his deft fingers making short work of it, though he doesn't take it off. He leans over and picks up the cue.

Oh fuck, what's he going to do with that? A frisson of fear runs through me.

'You play well, Miss Steele. I must say I'm surprised. Why don't you sink the black?'

My fear forgotten, I pout, wondering why the hell he should be surprised—sexy, arrogant bastard. My inner goddess is limbering up in the background, doing her floor exercises—a great wide smile on her face.

I position the white ball. Christian strolls back around the table and stands right behind me as I lean over to take my shot. He places his hand on my right thigh and runs his fingers up and down my leg, up to my behind and back again, lightly stroking me.

'I am going to miss if you keep doing that,' I whisper, closing my eyes and relishing the feel of his hands on me.

'I don't care if you hit or miss, baby. I just wanted to see you like this—partially dressed, stretched out on my billiard table. Do you have any idea how hot you look at this moment?'

I flush, and my inner goddess grabs a rose between her teeth and starts to tango. Taking a deep breath, I try to ignore him and line up my shot. It's impossible. He caresses my behind, over and over again.

'Top left,' I murmur, then hit the white ball. He smacks me hard, squarely on my backside.

It's so unexpected, I yelp. The white hits the black, which bounces off the cushion wide of the pocket. Christian caresses my behind again.

'Oh, I think you need to try that again,' he whispers. 'You should concentrate, Anastasia.'

I'm panting now, excited by this game. He strolls to the end of the table, sets up the black ball again, then runs the white ball back down to me. He looks so carnal, dark-eyed with a lascivious smile. How could I ever resist him? I catch the ball and line it up, ready to strike again.

'Uh-uh,' he admonishes. 'Just wait.' Oh, he just loves prolonging the agony. He wanders back and stands behind me again. I close my eyes once more as he strokes my left thigh this time, then fondles

286

my backside again.

'Take aim,' he breathes.

I can't help my moan as desire twists and turns inside me. And I try, really try, to think about where I should hit the black with the white. I shift slightly to my right, and he follows me. I bend over the table once more. Using every last vestige of inner strength—which has diminished considerably since I know what will happen once I strike the white ball—I take aim and hit the white again. Christian smacks me once more, hard.

Ow! I miss again. 'Oh no!' I groan.

'Once more, baby. And if you miss this time, I'm really going to let you have it.'

What? Have what?

He sets up the black ball once more and walks, achingly slow, back to me until he's standing behind me, caressing my backside once more.

'You can do it,' he coaxes.

Oh—not when you're distracting me like this. I push my behind back against his hand, and he smacks me lightly.

'Eager, Miss Steele?' he murmurs.

Yes. I want you.

'Well, let's get rid of these.' He gently slides my panties down my thighs and off. I can't see what he does with them, but he leaves me feeling exposed as he plants a soft kiss on each cheek.

'Take the shot, baby.'

I want to whimper; this is so not going to happen. I know I am going to miss. I line up the white, hit it, and in my impatience, miss the black completely. I wait for the blow—but it doesn't come. Instead he leans right over me, flattening me against the table, takes the cue out of my hand and rolls it to the side cushion. I feel him, hard, against my backside.

'You missed,' he says softly in my ear. My cheek is pressed against the baize. 'Put your hands flat on the table.'

I do as he says.

'Good. I'm going to spank you now and next time, maybe you won't.' He shifts so he's standing to my left side, his erection against my hip.

I groan and my heart leaps into my mouth. My breath comes in short pants and a hot, heavy excitement courses through my veins. Gently, he caresses my behind and curls his other hand around the nape of my neck, his fingers tightening around my hair at the nape, his elbow at my back, holding me down. I am completely helpless.

'Open your legs,' he murmurs and for a moment, I hesitate. And he smacks me hard—with the ruler! The noise is harsher than the sting, and it takes me by surprise. I gasp, and he hits me again.

'Legs,' he orders. I open my legs, panting. The ruler strikes again. Ow—it stings, but its crack across my skin sounds worse than it feels.

I close my eyes and absorb the pain. It's not too bad, and Christian's breathing becomes harsher. He hits me again and again, and I moan. I am not sure how many more strokes I can bear—but hearing him, knowing how turned on he is, feeds my arousal and my willingness to continue. I am crossing to the dark side, a place in my psyche I don't know well but have visited before in the playroom—with the Tallis. The ruler strikes once more, and I moan loudly, and Christian groans in response. He hits me again—and again . . . and once more . . . harder this time—and I wince.

'Stop.' The word is out of my mouth before I'm

288

even aware that I've said it. Christian drops the ruler immediately and releases me.

'Enough?' he whispers.

'Yes.'

'I want to fuck you now,' he says, his voice strained.

'Yes,' I murmur with longing. He undoes his fly, as I lie panting on the table, knowing that he's going to be rough.

I marvel once more at how I have managed— and yes, enjoyed—what he's done to me up to this point. It's so dark but so him.

He eases two fingers inside me and moves them in a circular motion. The feeling is exquisite. Closing my eyes, I revel in the sensation. I hear the telltale rip of foil, then he's standing behind me, between my legs, pushing them wider.

Slowly he sinks into me, filling me. I hear his groan of pure pleasure, and it stirs my soul. He grasps my hips firmly, eases out of me again, and this time slams back into me, causing me to cry out. He stills for a moment.

'Again?' he asks softly.

'Yes . . . I'm fine. Lose yourself . . . take me with you,' I murmur breathlessly.

He moans low in his throat, eases out of me once more, then slams into me, and repeats this over and over slowly, deliberately—a punishing, brutal, heavenly rhythm.

Oh fucking my . . . My insides begin to quicken. He feels it, too, and increases the rhythm, pushing me, higher, harder, faster—and I surrender, exploding around him—a draining, soul-grabbing orgasm that leaves me spent and exhausted.

I'm vaguely aware that Christian, too, is letting

go, calling my name, his fingers digging into my hips, and then he stills and collapses on me. We sink to the floor, and he cradles me in his arms.

'Thank you, baby,' he breathes, covering my upturned face in soft feather-light kisses. I open my eyes and gaze up at him, and he wraps his arms tighter around me.

'Your cheek is pink from the baize,' he murmurs, rubbing my face tenderly. 'How was that?' His eyes are wide and cautious.

'Teeth-clenchingly good,' I mutter. 'I like it rough, Christian, and I like it gentle, too. I like that it's with you.'

He closes his eyes and hugs me even tighter.
Jeez, I'm tired.

'You never fail, Ana. You are beautiful, bright, challenging, fun, sexy, and I thank Divine Providence every day that it was you who came to interview me and not Katherine Kavanagh.' He kisses my hair. I smile and yawn against his chest. 'I'm wearing you out,' he continues. 'Come. Bath, then bed.'

*   *   *

We are both in Christian's bath, facing each other chin-deep in foam, the sweet scent of jasmine enveloping us. Christian is massaging my feet, one at a time. It feels so good it should be illegal.

'Can I ask you something?' I murmur.

'Of course. Anything, Ana, you know that.'

I take a deep breath and sit up, flinching only slightly.

'Tomorrow—when I go to work—can Sawyer just deliver me to the front door of the office, then

290

pick me up at the end of the day? Please, Christian. Please,' I plead.

His hands still as his brow creases. 'I thought we agreed,' he grumbles.

'Please,' I beg.

'What about lunchtime?'

'I'll make myself something to take from here so I don't have to go out, please.'

He kisses my instep. 'I find it very difficult to say no to you,' he mutters as if he senses this is a failing on his part. 'You won't go out?'

'No.'

'Okay.'

I beam at him. 'Thank you.' I lean up onto my knees, sloshing water everywhere, and kiss him.

'You're most welcome, Miss Steele. How's your behind?'

'Sore. But not too bad. The water is soothing.'

'I'm glad you told me to stop,' he says, gazing at me.

'So is my behind.'

He grins.

*　　　*　　　*

I stretch out in bed, so tired. It's only ten thirty, but it feels like three in the morning. This has to be one of the most exhausting weekends of my life.

'Didn't Ms. Acton provide any nightwear?' Christian asks, his voice laced with disapproval as he stares down at me.

'I have no idea. I like wearing your T-shirts,' I mumble sleepily.

His face softens, and he leans over and kisses my forehead.

'I need to work. But I don't want to leave you alone. Can I use your laptop to log in to the office? Will I disturb you if I work from here?'

'S'not my laptop.' I drift.

*   *   *

The alarm clicks on, startling me awake with the traffic news. Christian is still asleep beside me. Rubbing my eyes, I glance at the clock. Six thirty—too early.

It's raining outside for the first time in ages, and the light is muted and mellow. I'm cozy and comfortable in this vast modern monolith with Christian at my side. I stretch and turn to the delicious man beside me. His eyes spring open and he blinks sleepily.

'Good morning.' I smile and caress his face, leaning down to kiss him.

'Good morning, baby. I usually wake before the alarm goes off,' he murmurs in wonder.

'It's set so early.'

'That it is, Miss Steele.' Christian grins. 'I have to get up.' He kisses me, and then he's up and out of bed. I flop back against the pillows. Wow, waking up on a school day next to Christian Grey. How did this all happen? I close my eyes and doze.

'Come on, sleepyhead, get up.' Christian leans over me. He's shaved, clean, fresh—*hmm, he smells so good*—in a crisp white shirt and black suit, no tie—the CEO is back.

'What?' he asks.

'I wish you'd come back to bed.'

His lips part, surprised by my come-on, and he smiles almost shyly. 'You are insatiable, Miss

Steele. As much as that idea appeals, I have an eight thirty meeting, so I have to go shortly.'

Oh, I've slept for another hour or so. *Shit*. I leap out of bed, much to Christian's amusement.

*   *   *

I shower and dress quickly, wearing the clothes I set out yesterday: a fitted gray pencil skirt; pale gray silk shirt; and high-heeled black pumps, all care of my new wardrobe. I brush my hair and carefully put it up, then wander out to the great room, not really knowing what to expect. How am I going to get to work?

Christian is sipping coffee at the breakfast bar. Mrs. Jones is in the kitchen making pancakes and bacon.

'You look lovely,' Christian murmurs. Wrapping an arm around me, he kisses me under my ear. Out of the corner of my eye, I catch Mrs. Jones's smile. I flush.

'Good morning, Miss Steele,' she says as she places pancakes and bacon in front of me.

'Oh, thank you. Good morning,' I mumble. Jeez—I could get used to this.

'Mr. Grey says you'd like to take lunch with you to work. What would you like to eat?'

I glance at Christian, who is trying very hard not to smirk. I narrow my eyes at him.

'A sandwich . . . salad. I really don't mind.' I beam at Mrs. Jones.

'I'll rustle up a packed lunch for you, ma'am.'

'Please, Mrs. Jones, call me Ana.'

'Ana.' She smiles and turns to make me tea.

Wow . . . this is so cool.

I turn and cock my head at Christian, challenging him—go on, accuse me of flirting with Mrs. Jones.

'I have to go, baby. Taylor will come back and drop you at work with Sawyer.'

'Only to the door.'

'Yes. Only to the door.' Christian rolls his eyes. 'Be careful, though.'

I glance around and spy Taylor standing in the entranceway. Christian stands and kisses me, grasping my chin.

'Laters, baby.'

'Have a good day at the office, dear,' I call after him. He turns and flashes me his beautiful smile then he's gone. Mrs. Jones hands me a cup of tea, and suddenly I feel awkward with just the two of us here.

'How long have you worked for Christian?' I ask, thinking I ought to make some kind of conversation.

'Four years or so,' she says pleasantly, as she sets about making my packed lunch.

'You know, I can do that,' I mutter, embarrassed that she should be doing this for me.

'You eat your breakfast, Ana. This is what I do. I enjoy it. It's nice to look after someone other than Mr. Taylor and Mr. Grey.' She smiles very sweetly at me.

My cheeks flush with pleasure, and I want to bombard this woman with questions. She must know so much about Fifty, and although her manner is warm and friendly, it's also very professional. I know I'll only embarrass both of us if I start quizzing her, so I finish my breakfast in a reasonably comfortable silence, punctuated only by her questions on my general food preferences.

Twenty-five minutes later Sawyer appears at the entrance to the great room. I have brushed my teeth, and I'm waiting to go. Clutching my brown paper lunch bag—I can't even remember my mom doing this for me—Sawyer and I head to the first floor via the elevator. He's very taciturn, too, giving nothing away. Taylor is waiting in the Audi, and I climb into the rear passenger seat when Sawyer opens the door.

'Good morning, Taylor,' I say brightly.

'Miss Steele.' He smiles.

'Taylor, I'm sorry about yesterday and my inappropriate remarks. I hope I didn't get you into trouble.'

Taylor frowns in bemusement at me from the rearview mirror as he pulls out into the Seattle traffic.

'Miss Steele, I'm rarely in trouble,' he says reassuringly.

Oh, good. Maybe Christian didn't tell him off. Just me, then, I think sourly.

'I'm glad to hear it, Taylor.' I smile.

*　　　*　　　*

Jack gazes at me, assessing my appearance, as I make my way to my desk.

'Morning, Ana. Good weekend?'

'Yes, thanks. You?'

'It was good. Get settled in—I have work for you to do.'

I nod and sit down at my computer. It seems like years since I was at work. I switch on my computer and fire up my e-mail program—and of course there's an e-mail from Christian.

From: Christian Grey
Subject: Boss
Date: June 13 2011 08:24
To: Anastasia Steele

Good morning, Miss Steele

I just wanted to say thank you for a wonderful weekend in spite of all the drama.

I hope you never leave, ever.

And just to remind you that the news of SIP is embargoed for four weeks.

Delete this e-mail as soon as you've read it.

Yours

Christian Grey,
CEO, Grey Enterprises Holdings, Inc. & your boss's boss's boss.

Hope I never leave? Does he want me to move in? Holy Moses . . . I barely know the man. I press delete.

From: Anastasia Steele
Subject: Bossy
Date: June 13 2011: 09:03
To: Christian Grey

Dear Mr. Grey

Are you asking me to move in with you?
And of course, I remembered that the
evidence of your epic stalking capabilities
is embargoed for another four weeks. Do I
make a check out to Coping Together and
send to your dad? Please don't delete this
e-mail. Please respond to it.

ILY xxx

Anastasia Steele
Assistant to Jack Hyde, Editor, SIP

'Ana!' Jack makes me jump.
'Yes,' I flush, and Jack frowns at me.
'Everything okay?'
'Sure.' I scramble up and take my notebook into
his office.
'Good. As you probably remember, I'm going to
that Fiction Symposium in New York on Thursday.
I have tickets and reservations, but I'd like you to
come with me.'
'To New York?'
'Yes. We'll need to go Wednesday and stay
overnight. I think you'll find it a very educational
experience.' His eyes darken as he says this, but
his smile is polite. 'Would you make the necessary
travel arrangements? And book an additional room
at the hotel where I am staying? I think Sabrina, my
previous PA, left all the details handy somewhere.'
'Okay.' I smile wanly at Jack.
Crap. I wander back to my desk. This is not going
to go down well with Fifty—but the fact is, I want to
go. It sounds like a real opportunity, and I'm sure
I can keep Jack at arm's length if that's his ulterior

motive. Back at my desk there's a response from Christian.

From: Christian Grey
Subject: Me, Bossy?
Date: June 13 2011 09:07
To: Anastasia Steele

Yes. Please.

Christian Grey,
CEO, Grey Enterprises Holdings, Inc.

He does want me to move in. Oh, Christian—it's too soon. I put my head in my hands to try and recover my wits. This is all I need after my extraordinary weekend. I haven't had a moment to myself to think through and understand all that I have experienced and discovered these last two days.

From: Anastasia Steele
Subject: Flynnisms
Date: June 13 2011 09:20
To: Christian Grey

Christian

What happened to walking before we run?

Can we talk about this tonight, please?

I've been asked to go to a conference in

New York on Thursday.

It means an overnight stay on Wednesday.

Just thought you should know.

A x

Anastasia Steele
Assistant to Jack Hyde, Editor, SIP

From: Christian Grey
Subject: WHAT?
Date: June 13 2011 09:21
To: Anastasia Steele

Yes. Let's talk this evening.

Are you going on your own?

Christian Grey
CEO, Grey Enterprises Holdings, Inc.

From: Anastasia Steele
Subject: No Bold Shouty Capitals on a
Monday Morning!
Date: June 13 2011 09:30
To: Christian Grey

Can we talk about this tonight?

A x

Anastasia Steele
Assistant to Jack Hyde, Editor, SIP

From: Christian Grey
Subject: You Haven't Seen Shouty Yet.
Date: June 13 2011 09:35
To: Anastasia Steele

Tell me.

If it's with the sleazeball you work with, then the answer is no, over my dead body.

Christian Grey
CEO, Grey Enterprises Holdings, Inc.

My heart sinks. Shit—it's like he's my dad.

From: Anastasia Steele
Subject: No YOU haven't seen shouty yet.
Date: June 13 2011 09:46
To: Christian Grey

Yes. It is with Jack.

I want to go. It's an exciting opportunity for me.

And I have never been to New York.

Don't get your knickers in a twist.

Anastasia Steele
Assistant to Jack Hyde, Editor, SIP

From: Christian Grey
Subject: No YOU haven't seen shouty yet.
Date: June 13 2011 09:50
To: Anastasia Steele

Anastasia

It's not my fucking knickers I am worried about.

The answer is NO.

Christian Grey
CEO, Grey Enterprises Holdings, Inc.

'No!' I shout at my computer, causing the entire office to come to a standstill and stare at me. Jack peers out from his office.

'Everything all right, Ana?'

'Yes. Sorry,' I mutter. 'I er . . . just didn't save a document.' I am scarlet with embarrassment. He smiles at me, but with a puzzled expression. I take several deep breaths and quickly type a response. I am so mad.

From: Anastasia Steele
Subject: Fifty Shades
Date: June 13 2011 09:55
To: Christian Grey

Christian

You need to get a grip.

301

I am NOT going to sleep with Jack—not for all the tea in China.

I LOVE you. That's what happens when people love each other.

They TRUST each other.

I don't think you are going to SLEEP WITH, SPANK, FUCK, or WHIP anyone else. I have FAITH and TRUST in you.

Please extend the same COURTESY to me.

Ana

Anastasia Steele
Assistant to Jack Hyde, Editor, SIP

I sit waiting for his response. Nothing arrives. I call the airline and book a ticket for myself, ensuring I am on the same flight as Jack. I hear the *ping* of new mail.

From: Lincoln, Elena
Subject: Lunch Date
Date: June 13 2011 10:15
To: Anastasia Steele

Dear Anastasia

I would really like to have lunch with you. I think we got off on the wrong foot, and I'd like to make that right. Are you free sometime this week?

Elena Lincoln

Holy crap—not Mrs. Robinson! How the hell did she find out my e-mail address? I put my head in my hands. Can this day get any worse?

My phone rings and wearily I lift my head from my hands and answer, glancing at the clock. It is only ten twenty, and already I wish I hadn't left Christian's bed.

'Jack Hyde's office, Ana Steele speaking.'

An achingly familiar voice snarls at me, 'Will you please delete the last e-mail you sent me and try to be a little more circumspect in the language you use in your work e-mail? I told you, the system is monitored. I will endeavor to do some damage limitation from here.' He hangs up.

Holy fuck . . . I sit staring at the phone. Christian hung up on me. That man is stomping all over my fledgling career, and he hangs up on me? I glare at the receiver, and if it wasn't completely inanimate, I know it would shrivel in horror under my withering stare.

I open my e-mails and delete the one I sent him. It's not that bad. I just mention spanking and well, whipping. If he's so ashamed of it, he damn well shouldn't do it. I pick up my BlackBerry and call his mobile.

'What?' he snaps.

'I am going to New York whether you like it or not,' I hiss.

'Don't count—'

I hang up, cutting him off mid-sentence. Adrenaline is coursing through my body. There—that told him. I am so mad.

I take a deep breath, trying to compose myself. Closing my eyes, I imagine that I am in my happy place. *Hmm . . . a boat cabin with Christian.* I shake

303

the image off, as I am too mad at Fifty right now for him to be anywhere near my happy place.

Opening my eyes, I calmly reach for my notebook and carefully run through my to-do list. I take a long, deep breath, my equilibrium restored.

'Ana!' Jack shouts, startling me. 'Don't book that flight!'

'Oh, too late. I've done it,' I reply as he strides out of his office over to me. He looks mad.

'Look, there's something going on. For some reason, suddenly, all travel and hotel expenses for staff have to be approved by senior management. This has come right from the top. I am going up to see old Roach. Apparently, a moratorium on all spending has just been implemented. I don't understand it.' Jack pinches the bridge of his nose and closes his eyes.

Most of the blood drains from my face and knots form in my stomach. *Fifty!*

'Take my calls. I'll go see what Roach has to say.' He winks at me and strides off to see his boss—not the boss's boss.

Damn it. Christian Grey . . . My blood starts to boil again.

From: Anastasia Steele
Subject: What have you done?
Date: June 13 2011 10:43
To: Christian Grey

Please tell me you won't interfere with my work.

I really want to go to this conference.

304

I shouldn't have to ask you.

I have deleted the offending e-mail.

Anastasia Steele
Assistant to Jack Hyde, Editor, SIP

From: Christian Grey
Subject: What have you done?
Date: June 13 2011 10:46
To: Anastasia Steele

I am just protecting what is mine.

The e-mail that you so rashly sent is wiped from the SIP server now, as are my e-mails to you.

Incidentally, I trust you implicitly. It's him I don't trust.

Christian Grey
CEO, Grey Enterprises Holdings, Inc.

I check to see if I still have his e-mails, and they have disappeared. This man's influence knows no bounds. How does he do this? Who does he know that can stealthily delve into the depths of SIP's servers and remove e-mails? I am so out of my league here.

From: Anastasia Steele
Subject: Grown Up
Date: June 13 2011 10:48
To: Christian Grey

Christian

I don't need protecting from my own boss.

He may make a pass at me, but I would say no.

You cannot interfere. It's wrong and controlling on so many levels.

Anastasia Steele
Assistant to Jack Hyde, Editor, SIP

From: Christian Grey
Subject: The Answer is NO
Date: June 13 2011 10:50
To: Anastasia Steele

Ana

I have seen how 'effective' you are at fighting off unwanted attention. I remember that's how I had the pleasure of spending my first night with you. At least the photographer has feelings for you. The sleazeball, on the other hand, does not. He is a serial philanderer, and he will try to seduce you. Ask him what happened to his previous PA and the one before that.

I don't want to fight about this.

If you want to go to New York, I'll take you. We can go this weekend. I have an apartment there.

Christian Grey
CEO, Grey Enterprises Holdings, Inc.

Oh, Christian! That's not the point. He's so damn frustrating. And of course he has an apartment there. Where else does he own property? Trust him to bring up José. Will I ever live that down? I was drunk, for heaven's sake. I wouldn't get drunk with Jack.

I shake my head at the screen, but figure I cannot continue to argue with him over e-mail. I will have to bide my time until this evening. I check the clock. Jack is still not back from his meeting with Jerry, and I need to deal with Elena. I read her e-mail again and decide that the best way to handle it is to send it to Christian. Let him concentrate on her rather than me.

From: Anastasia Steele
Subject: FW Lunch date or Irritating Baggage
Date: June 13 2011 11:15
To: Christian Grey

Christian

While you have been busy interfering in my career and saving your ass from my

307

careless missives, I received the following e-mail from Mrs. Lincoln. I really don't want to meet with her—even if I did, I am not allowed to leave this building. How she got hold of my e-mail address, I don't know. What would you suggest I do? Her e-mail is below:

> *Dear Anastasia, I would really like to have lunch with you. I think we got off on the wrong foot, and I'd like to make that right. Are you free sometime this week?*
> *Elena Lincoln*

Anastasia Steele
Assistant to Jack Hyde, Editor, SIP

From: Christian Grey
Subject: Irritating Baggage
Date: June 13 2011 11:23
To: Anastasia Steele

Don't be mad at me. I have your best interests at heart.

If anything happened to you, I would never forgive myself.

I'll deal with Mrs. Lincoln.

Christian Grey
CEO, Grey Enterprises Holdings, Inc.

From: Anastasia Steele
Subject: Laters
Date: June 13 2011 11:32
To: Christian Grey

Can we please discuss this tonight?

I am trying to work, and your continued interference is very distracting.

Anastasia Steele
Assistant to Jack Hyde, Editor, SIP

Jack returns after midday and tells me that New York is off for me, though he is still going and there's nothing he can do to change senior management policy. He strides into his office, slamming the door, obviously furious. Why is he so angry?

Deep down, I know his intentions are less than honorable, but I am sure I can deal with him, and I wonder what Christian knows about Jack's previous PAs. I park these thoughts and continue with some work, but resolve to try to make Christian change his mind, though the prospects are bleak.

At one o'clock, Jack pokes his head out of the office door.

'Ana, please could you go and get me some lunch?'

'Sure. What would you like?'

'Pastrami on rye, hold the mustard. I'll give you the money when you're back.'

'Anything to drink?'

'Coke, please. Thanks, Ana.' He heads back into

309

his office as I reach for my purse.

Crap. I promised Christian I wouldn't go out. I sigh. He'll never know, and I'll be quick.

Claire from Reception offers me her umbrella since it is still pouring with rain. As I head out of the front doors, I pull my jacket around me and take a furtive glance in both directions from beneath the overlarge golf umbrella. Nothing seems amiss. There's no sign of Ghost Girl.

I march briskly, and I hope inconspicuously, down the block to the deli. However, the closer I get to the deli, the more I have a creepy sense that I am being watched, and I don't know if it's my heightened feeling of paranoia or a reality. Shit. I hope it's not Leila with a gun.

It's just your imagination, my subconscious snaps. *Who the hell would want to shoot you?*

Within fifteen minutes, I am back—safe and sound, but relieved. I think Christian's extreme paranoia and his overprotective vigilance is beginning to get to me.

As I take Jack's lunch in to him, he glances up from the phone.

'Ana, thanks. Since you're not coming with me, I'm going to need you to work late. We need to get these briefs ready. Hope you don't have plans.' He smiles up at me warmly, and I flush.

'No, that's fine,' I say with a bright smile and a sinking heart. This is not going to go down well. Christian will freak, I'm sure.

As I head back to my desk I decide not to tell him immediately; otherwise he might have time to interfere in some way. I sit and eat the chicken salad sandwich Mrs. Jones made for me. It's delicious. She makes a mean sandwich.

Of course, if I moved in with Christian, she would make lunch for me every weekday. The idea is unsettling. I have never had dreams of obscene wealth and all the trappings—only love. To find someone who loves me and doesn't try to control my every move. The phone rings.

'Jack Hyde's office—'

'You assured me you wouldn't go out,' Christian interrupts me, his voice cold and hard.

My heart sinks for the millionth time this day. Shit. How the hell does he know?

'Jack sent me out for some lunch. I couldn't say no. Are you having me watched?' My scalp prickles at the notion. No wonder I felt so paranoid—someone *was* watching me. The thought makes me angry.

'This is why I didn't want you going back to work,' Christian snaps.

'Christian, please. You're being'—*So Fifty*—'so suffocating.'

'Suffocating?' he whispers, surprised.

'Yes. You have to stop this. I'll talk to you this evening. Unfortunately I have to work late because I can't go to New York.'

'Anastasia, I don't want to suffocate you,' he says quietly, appalled.

'Well, you are. I have work to do. I'll talk to you later.' I hang up, feeling drained and vaguely depressed.

After our wonderful weekend, the reality is hitting home. I have never felt more like running. Running to some quiet retreat so I can think about this man, about how he is, and about how to deal with him. On one level, I know he's broken—I can see that clearly now—and it's both heartbreaking

311

and exhausting. From the small pieces of precious information that he's given me about his life, I understand why. An unloved child; a hideously abusive environment; a mother who couldn't protect him, whom he couldn't protect, and who died in front of him.

I shudder. My poor Fifty. I am his, but not to be kept in some gilded cage. How am I going to make him see this?

With a heavy heart, I drag one of the manuscripts Jack wants me to summarize into my lap and continue to read. I can think of no easy solution to Christian's fucked-up control issues. I will just have to talk to him later, face-to-face.

Half an hour later, Jack e-mails me a document that I need to tidy up, polish, and have ready to be printed in time for his conference. It will take me not just the rest of the afternoon but well into the evening, too. I set to work.

When I look up, it's after seven and the office is deserted, though the light in Jack's office is still on. I hadn't noticed everyone leaving, but I am nearly finished. I e-mail the document back to Jack for his approval and check my inbox. There's nothing new from Christian, so I quickly glance at my BlackBerry, and it startles me by buzzing—it's Christian.

'Hi,' I murmur.

'Hi, when will you be finished?'

'By seven thirty, I think.'

'I'll meet you outside.'

'Okay.'

He sounds quiet, nervous even. Why? Wary of my reaction?

'I'm still mad at you, but that's all,' I whisper.

'We have a lot to talk about.'

'I know. See you at seven thirty.'

Jack comes out of his office.

'I have to go. See you later.' I hang up.

I look up at Jack as he strolls casually toward me.

'I just need a couple of tweaks. I've e-mailed the brief back to you.'

He leans over me while I retrieve the document, rather close—uncomfortably close. His arm brushes mine. Accidentally? I flinch, but he pretends not to notice. His other arm rests on the back of my chair, touching my back. I sit up so I'm not leaning against the backrest.

'Pages sixteen and twenty-three, and that should be it,' he murmurs, his mouth inches from my ear.

My skin crawls at his proximity, but I choose to ignore it. Opening the document, I shakily start on the changes. He's still leaning over me, and all my senses are hyperaware. It's distracting and awkward, and inside I am screaming, *Back off!*

'Once this is done, it'll be good to go to print. You can organize that tomorrow. Thank you for staying late and doing this, Ana.' His voice is smooth, gentle, like he's talking to a wounded animal. My stomach twists.

'I think the least I could do is reward you with a quick drink. You deserve one.' He tucks a strand of my hair that's come loose from my hair tie behind my ear and gently caresses the lobe.

I cringe, gritting my teeth, and jerk my head away. *Shit!* Christian was right. *Don't touch me.*

'Actually, I can't this evening.' *Or any other evening, Jack.*

'Just a quick one?' he coaxes.

'No, I can't. But thank you.'

Jack sits on the end of my desk and frowns. Alarm bells sound loudly in my head. I am on my own in the office. I cannot leave. I glance nervously at the clock. Another five minutes before Christian is due.

'Ana, I think we make a great team. I'm sorry that I couldn't pull off this New York trip. It won't be the same without you.'

I'm sure it won't. I smile weakly up at him, because I can't think of what to say. And for the first time all day, I feel the tiniest hint of relief that I am not going.

'So, did you have a good weekend?' he asks smoothly.

'Yes, thanks.' Where is he going with this?

'See your boyfriend?'

'Yes.'

'What does he do?'

Owns your ass . . . 'He's in business.'

'That's interesting. What kind of business?'

'Oh, he has his fingers in all sorts of pies.'

Jack cocks his head to one side as he leans in toward me, invading my personal space—again.

'You're being very coy, Ana.'

'Well, he's in telecommunications, manufacturing, and agriculture.'

Jack raises his eyebrows. 'So many things. Who does he work for?'

'He works for himself. If you're happy with the document, I'd like to go, if that's okay?'

He leans back. My personal space is safe again.

'Of course. Sorry, I didn't mean to keep you,' he says disingenuously.

'What time does the building close?'

'Security is here until eleven.'

'Good.' I smile, and my subconscious flops down in her armchair, relieved to know that we are not alone in the building. Switching off my computer, I grab my purse and stand up, ready to leave.

'You like him then? Your boyfriend?'

'I love him,' I answer, looking Jack squarely in the eye.

'I see.' Jack frowns and he stands up from my desk. 'What's his surname?'

I flush.

'Grey. Christian Grey,' I mumble.

Jack's mouth drops open. 'Seattle's richest bachelor? That Christian Grey?'

'Yes. The same.' Yes, that Christian Grey, your future boss who will have you for breakfast if you invade my personal space again.

'I thought he looked familiar,' Jack says darkly and his brow creases again. 'Well, he's a lucky man.'

I blink at him. What do I say to that?

'Have a good evening, Ana.' Jack smiles, but the smile doesn't touch his eyes, and he walks stiffly back into his office without a backward glance.

I let out a long sigh of relief. Well, that problem might be solved. Fifty works his magic again. Just his name is my talisman, and it has this man retreating with his tail between his legs. I allow myself a small victorious smile. *You see, Christian? Even your name protects me—you didn't have to go to all that trouble of clamping down on expenses.* I tidy my desk and check my watch. Christian should be outside.

The Audi is parked by the sidewalk, and Taylor leaps out to open the rear passenger door. I have never been so pleased to see him, and I scramble into the car out of the rain.

315

Christian is in the rear seat, gazing at me, his eyes wide and wary. He's bracing himself for my anger, his jaw tight and tense.

'Hi,' I murmur.

'Hi,' he replies cautiously. He reaches over and grasps my hand, squeezing it tightly, and my heart thaws a little. I'm so confused. I haven't even worked out what I need to say to him.

'Are you still mad?' he asks.

'I don't know,' I murmur. He raises my hand and lightly grazes my knuckles with soft butterfly kisses.

'It's been a shitty day,' he says.

'Yes, it has.' But for the first time since he left for work this morning, I begin to relax. Just being in his company is a soothing balm; all the shit from Jack, and the snarky e-mails to and fro, and the nuisance that is Elena fade into the background. It's just me and my control freak in the back of the car.

'It's better now that you're here,' he murmurs. We sit in silence as Taylor weaves through the evening traffic, both of us brooding and contemplative; but I feel Christian slowly unwind beside me as he, too, relaxes, gently running his thumb across my knuckles in a soft, soothing rhythm.

Taylor drops us outside the apartment building, and we both duck inside, out of the rain. Christian clasps my hand as we wait for the elevator, his eyes scanning the front of the building.

'I take it you haven't found Leila yet.'

'No. Welch is still looking for her,' he mutters despondently.

The elevator arrives and in we step. Christian glances down at me, his eyes unreadable. Oh, he just looks glorious—tousled hair, white shirt, dark suit. And suddenly it's there, from nowhere, that feeling. *Oh my*—the longing, the lust, the electricity. If it were visible, it would be an intense blue aura around and between us; it's so strong. His lips part as he gazes at me.

'Do you feel it?' he breathes.

'Yes.'

'Oh, Ana.' He groans and he grabs me, his arms snaking around me, one hand at the nape of my neck, tipping my head back as his lips find mine. My fingers are in his hair and caressing his cheek as he pushes me back against the elevator wall.

'I hate arguing with you,' he breathes against my mouth, and there's a desperate, passionate quality to his kiss that mirrors mine. Desire explodes in my body, all the tension of the day seeking an outlet, straining against him, seeking more. We're all tongues and breathing and hands and touch and sweet, sweet sensation. His hand is on my hip, and abruptly he's pulling up my skirt, his fingers stroking my thighs.

'Sweet Jesus, you're wearing stockings.' He moans in appreciative awe as his thumb caresses the flesh above my stocking line. 'I want to see this,' he breathes, and he pulls my skirt right up, exposing the tops of my thighs.

Stepping back, he reaches over to press the 'stop' button, and the elevator coasts smoothly to a halt between the twenty-second and twenty-third floors. His eyes are dark, lips parted, and he's breathing as hard as am I. We gaze at each other, not touching. I am grateful for the wall against my back, holding me up while I bask in this beautiful man's sensual, carnal appraisal.

'Take your hair down,' he orders, his voice husky. I reach up and undo the tie, releasing my hair so it tumbles in a thick cloud around my shoulders to my breasts. 'Undo the top two buttons of your shirt,' he whispers, his eyes wilder now.

He makes me feel so wanton. I reach up and undo each button, achingly, slowly, so that the tops of my breasts are tantalizingly revealed.

He swallows. 'Do you have any idea how alluring you look right now?'

Very deliberately, I bite my lip and shake my head. He closes his eyes briefly, and when he opens them again, they are blazing. He steps forward and places his hands on the elevator walls on either side of my face. He's as close as he can be without touching me.

I tip my face up to meet his gaze, and he leans down and runs his nose against mine, so it's the only contact between us. I am so hot in the confines of this elevator with him. I want him—now.

'I think you do, Miss Steele. I think you like to drive me wild.'

'Do I drive you wild?' I whisper.

'In all things, Anastasia. You are a siren, a goddess.' And he reaches for me, grasping my leg above my knee and hitching it around his waist, so that I am standing on one leg, leaning into him. I feel him against me, feel him hard and wanting above the apex of my thighs as he runs his lips down my throat. I moan and wrap my arms around his neck.

'I'm going to take you now,' he breathes and I arch my back in response, pressing myself against him, eager for the friction. He groans deep and low in the back of his throat and boosts me higher as he

318

undoes his fly.

'Hold tight, baby,' he murmurs, and magically produces a foil packet that he holds in front of my mouth. I take it between my teeth, and he tugs, so that between us, we rip it open.

'Good girl.' He steps back a fraction as he slides on the condom. 'God, I can't wait for the next six days,' he growls and gazes down at me through hooded eyes. 'I do hope you're not overly fond of these panties.' He tears through them with his adept fingers, and they disintegrate in his hands. My blood is pounding through my veins. I am panting with need.

His words are intoxicating, all my angst from the day forgotten. It's just him and me, doing what we do best. Without taking his eyes off mine, he sinks slowly into me. My body bows and I tilt my head back, closing my eyes, relishing the feel of him inside me. He pulls back and then moves into me again, so slow, so sweet. I groan.

'You're mine, Anastasia,' he murmurs against my throat.

'Yes. Yours. When will you accept that?' I pant. He groans and starts to move, really move. And I surrender myself to his relentless rhythm, savoring each push and pull, his ragged breathing, his need for me, reflecting mine.

It makes me feel powerful, strong, desired, and loved—loved by this captivating, complicated man, whom I love in return with all my heart. He pushes harder and harder, his breathing ragged, losing himself in me as I lose myself in him.

'Oh, baby,' Christian moans, his teeth grazing my jaw, and I come hard around him. He stills, clutches me, and follows suit, whispering my name.

319

Now that Christian is spent, calm and kissing me gently, his breathing eases. He holds me upright against the elevator wall, our foreheads pressed together, and my body is like jelly, weak but gratifyingly sated from my climax.

'Oh, Ana,' he murmurs. 'I need you so much.' He kisses my forehead.

'And I you, Christian.'

Releasing me, he straightens my skirt and does up the two buttons on my shirt, then punches the combination into the keypad that starts the elevator again. It rises with a jolt so that I reach out and clasp his arms.

'Taylor will be wondering where we are.' He grins lasciviously at me.

Oh, crap. I drag my fingers through my hair in a vain attempt to combat the just-fucked look, then give up and fasten it in a ponytail.

'You'll do.' Christian smirks as he does up his fly and puts the condom in his pants pocket.

Once more he looks the embodiment of an American entrepreneur, and since his hair has the just-fucked look most of the time, there's very little difference. Except now he's smiling, relaxed, his eyes crinkling with boyish charm. Are all men this easily placated?

Taylor is waiting when the doors open.

'Problem with the elevator,' Christian murmurs as we both step out, and I cannot look either of them in the face. I scurry through the double doors to Christian's bedroom in search of some fresh underwear.

* * *

When I return, Christian has removed his jacket and is sitting at the breakfast bar chatting with Mrs. Jones. She smiles kindly at me as she puts out two plates of hot food for us. Mmm, it smells delicious—coq au vin if I am not mistaken. I am famished.

'Enjoy, Mr. Grey, Ana,' she says and leaves us to it.

Christian fetches a bottle of white wine from the fridge, and as we sit and eat, he tells me about how much nearer he's getting to perfecting a solar-powered mobile phone. He's animated and excited about the whole project, and I know then that he hasn't had an entirely shitty day.

I ask him about his properties. He smirks, and it turns out he only has apartments in New York, Aspen, and Escala. Nothing else. When we're done, I collect his plate and mine and take them to sink.

'Leave that. Gail will do it,' he says. I turn and gaze at him, and he's watching me intently. Will I ever get used to having someone clean up after me?

'Well, now that you are more docile, Miss Steele, shall we talk about today?'

'I think you're the one who's more docile. I think I'm doing a good job in taming you.'

'Taming me?' he snorts, amused. When I nod, he frowns as if reflecting on my words. 'Yes. Maybe you are, Anastasia.'

'You were right about Jack,' I murmur, serious now, and I lean across the kitchen island gauging his reaction. Christian's face falls and his eyes harden.

321

'Has he tried anything?' he whispers, his voice deathly cold.

I shake my head to reassure him. 'No, and he won't, Christian. I told him today that I'm your girlfriend, and he backed right off.'

'You're sure? I could fire the fucker.' Christian scowls.

I sigh, emboldened by my glass of wine. 'You really have to let me fight my own battles. You can't constantly second-guess me and try to protect me. It's stifling, Christian. I'll never flourish with your incessant interference. I need some freedom. I wouldn't dream of meddling in your affairs.'

He blinks at me. 'I only want you safe, Anastasia. If anything happened to you, I—' He stops.

'I know, and I understand why you feel so driven to protect me. And part of me loves it. I know that if I need you, you'll be there, as I am for you. But if we are to have any hope of a future together, you have to trust me and trust my judgment. Yes, I'll get it wrong sometimes—I'll make mistakes, but I have to learn.'

He stares at me, his expression anxious, spurring me to walk around to him so that I am standing between his legs while he sits on the barstool. Grabbing his hands, I put them around me and place my hands on his arms.

'You can't interfere in my job. It's wrong. I don't need you charging in like a white knight to save the day. I know you want to control everything, and I understand why, but you can't. It's an impossible goal . . . you have to learn to let go.' I reach up and stroke his face as he gazes at me, his eyes wide. 'And if you can do that—give me that—I'll move in with you,' I add softly.

He inhales sharply, surprised. 'You'd do that?' he whispers.

'Yes.'

'But you don't know me.' He frowns and sounds choked and panicky all of a sudden, very un-Fifty.

'I know you well enough, Christian. Nothing you tell me about yourself will frighten me away.' I gently run my knuckles across his cheek. His expression turns from anxious to dubious. 'But if you could just ease up on me,' I plead.

'I'm trying, Anastasia. I couldn't just stand by and let you go to New York with that . . . sleazeball. He has an alarming reputation. None of his assistants have lasted more than three months, and they're never retained by the company. I don't want that for you, baby.' He sighs. 'I don't want anything to happen to you. You being hurt . . . the thought fills me with dread. I can't promise not to interfere, not if I think you'll come to harm.' He pauses and takes a deep breath. 'I love you, Anastasia. I will do everything in my power to protect you. I cannot imagine my life without you.'

Holy cow. My inner goddess, my subconscious, and I all gape at Fifty in shock.

Three little words. My world stands still, tilts, then spins on a new axis; and I savor the moment, gazing into his sincere, beautiful gray eyes.

'I love you, too, Christian.' I lean over and kiss him, and the kiss deepens.

Entering unseen, Taylor clears his throat. Christian pulls back, gazing intently at me. He stands up, his arm around my waist.

'Yes?' he snaps at Taylor.

'Mrs. Lincoln is on her way up, sir.'

'What?'

Taylor shrugs apologetically. Christian sighs heavily and shakes his head.

'Well, this should be interesting,' he mutters and gives me a crooked grin of resignation.

Fuck! Why can't that damned woman leave us alone?

CHAPTER TWELVE

'Did you talk to her today?' I ask Christian as we wait for Mrs. Robinson's arrival.

'Yes.'

'What did you say?'

'I said that you didn't want to see her, and that I understood your reasons why. I also told her that I didn't appreciate her going behind my back.' His gaze is impassive, giving nothing away.

Oh, good. 'What did she say?'

'She brushed it off in a way that only Elena can.' His mouth flattens to a crooked line.

'Why do you think she's here?'

'I have no idea.' Christian shrugs.

Taylor enters the great room again. 'Mrs. Lincoln,' he announces.

And here she is . . . Why is she so damned attractive? She's dressed entirely in black: tight jeans, a shirt that emphasizes her perfect figure, and a halo of bright, glossy hair.

Christian pulls me close. 'Elena,' he says, his tone puzzled.

She gapes at me in shock, frozen to the spot. She blinks before finding her soft voice. 'I'm sorry. I didn't realize you had company, Christian. It's

Monday,' she says as if this explains why she's here.

'Girlfriend,' he says by way of explanation and tilts his head to one side and gives her a cool smile.

A slow, beaming smile directed entirely at him spreads across her face. It's unnerving.

'Of course. Hello, Anastasia. I didn't know you'd be here. I know you don't want to talk to me. I accept that.'

'Do you?' I assert quietly, gazing at her and taking all of us by surprise. With a slight frown, she moves farther into the room.

'Yes, I get the message. I'm not here to see you. Like I said, Christian rarely has company during the week.' She pauses. 'I have a problem, and I need to talk to Christian about it.'

'Oh?' Christian straightens up. 'Do you want a drink?'

'Yes, please,' she murmurs gratefully.

Christian fetches a glass while Elena and I stand awkwardly gazing at each other. She fidgets with a large silver ring on her middle finger, while I don't know where to look. Finally, she gives me a small tight smile and approaches the kitchen island and sits on the barstool at the end. She obviously knows the place well and feels comfortable moving around here.

Do I stay? Do I go? *Oh, this is so difficult.* My subconscious scowls at the woman with her most hostile harpy face.

There's so much I want to say to this woman, and none of it complimentary. But she's Christian's friend—his only friend—and for all my loathing of this woman, I am innately polite. Deciding to stay, I sit as gracefully as I can manage on the stool Christian's vacated. Christian pours wine into each of our glasses and sits between us at the breakfast bar. Can't he feel how weird this is?

'What's up?' he asks her.

Elena looks nervously at me, and Christian reaches over and clasps my hand.

'Anastasia's with me now,' he says to her silent query and squeezes my hand. I flush, and my subconscious beams at him, harpy face forgotten.

Elena's face softens as if she's pleased for him. *Really* pleased for him. Oh, I don't understand this woman at all, and I'm uncomfortable and edgy in her presence.

She takes a deep breath and shifts, perching on the edge of her barstool and looking agitated. She glances nervously down at her hands and starts manically twisting the large silver ring around and around on her middle finger.

What's wrong with her? Is it my presence? Do I have that effect on her? Because I feel the same way—I don't want her here. She raises her head and looks Christian squarely in the eye.

'I'm being blackmailed.'

Holy shit. Not what I expected out of her mouth. Christian stiffens. Has someone found out about her penchant for beating and fucking underage boys? I suppress my revulsion, and a fleeting thought about chickens coming home to roost crosses my mind. My subconscious rubs her hands together with ill-disguised glee. *Good.*

'How?' Christian asks, his horror clear in his voice.

She reaches into her oversized patent-leather designer purse, pulls out a note, and hands it to him.

'Put it down, lay it out.' Christian points to the

breakfast bar counter with his chin.

'You don't want to touch it?'

'No. Fingerprints.'

'Christian, you know I can't go to the police with this.'

Why am I listening to this? Is she fucking some other poor boy?

She lays the note out for him, and he bends to read it.

'They're only asking for five thousand dollars,' he says almost absentmindedly. 'Any idea who it might be? Someone in the community?'

'No,' she says in her soft sweet voice.

'Linc?'

Linc? Who's that?

'What—after all this time? I don't think so,' she grumbles.

'Does Isaac know?'

'I haven't told him.'

Who's Isaac?

'I think he needs to know,' Christian says. She shakes her head, and now I feel I'm intruding. I want none of this. I try to retrieve my hand from Christian's grasp, but he just tightens his hold and turns to gaze at me.

'What?' he asks.

'I'm tired. I think I'll go to bed.'

His eyes search mine, looking for what? Censure? Acceptance? Hostility? I keep my expression as bland as possible.

'Okay,' he says. 'I won't be long.'

He releases me and I stand. Elena watches me warily. I stay tight-lipped and return her gaze, giving nothing away.

'Good night, Anastasia.' She gives me a small

327

smile.

'Good night,' I mutter, my voice sounds cold. I turn to leave. The tension is too much for me to bear. As I exit the room they continue their conversation.

'I don't think there's a great deal I can do, Elena,' Christian says to her. 'If it's a question of money . . .' His voice trails off. 'I could ask Welch to investigate.'

'No, Christian, I just wanted to share,' she says.

When I am out of the room, I hear her say, 'You look very happy.'

'I am,' Christian responds.

'You deserve to be.'

'I wish that were true.'

'Christian,' she scolds.

I freeze, listening intently. I can't help it.

'Does she know how negative you are about yourself? About all your issues.'

'She knows me better than anyone.'

'Ouch! That hurts.'

'It's the truth, Elena. I don't have to play games with her. And I mean it, leave her alone.'

'What is her problem?'

'You . . . What we were. What we did. She doesn't understand.'

'Make her understand.'

'It's in the past, Elena, and why would I want to taint her with our fucked-up relationship? She's good and sweet and innocent, and by some miracle she loves me.'

'It's no miracle, Christian,' Elena scoffs good-naturedly. 'Have a little faith in yourself. You really are quite a catch. I've told you often enough. And she seems lovely, too. Strong. Someone to stand up to you.'

I can't hear Christian's response. So I'm strong, am I? I certainly don't feel that way.

'Don't you miss it?' Elena continues.

'What?'

'Your playroom.'

I stop breathing.

'That really is none of your fucking business,' Christian snaps.

Oh.

'I'm sorry.' Elena snorts insincerely.

'I think you'd better go. And please, call before you come again.'

'Christian, I am sorry,' she says, and from her tone, this time she means it. 'Since when are you so sensitive?' She's scolding him again.

'Elena, we have a business relationship that has profited us both immensely. Let's keep it that way. What was between us is part of the past. Anastasia is my future, and I won't jeopardize it in any way, so cut the fucking crap.'

His future!

'I see.'

'Look, I'm sorry for your trouble. Perhaps you should ride it out and call their bluff.' His tone is softer.

'I don't want to lose you, Christian.'

'I'm not yours to lose, Elena,' he snaps again.

'That's not what I meant.'

'What did you mean?' He's brusque, angry.

'Look, I don't want to argue with you. Your friendship means a lot to me. I'll back off from Anastasia. But I'm here if you need me. I always will be.'

'Anastasia thinks that you saw me last Saturday.

You called, that's all. Why did you tell her otherwise?'

'I wanted her to know how upset you were when she left. I don't want her to hurt you.'

'She knows. I've told her. Stop interfering. Honestly, you're like a mother hen.' Christian sounds more resigned, and Elena laughs, but there's a sad tone to her laugh.

'I know. I'm sorry. You know I care about you. I never thought you'd end up falling in love, Christian. It's very gratifying to see. But I couldn't bear it if she hurt you.'

'I'll take my chances,' he says dryly. 'Now, are you sure you don't want Welch to sniff around?'

She sighs heavily. 'I suppose it wouldn't do any harm.'

'Okay. I'll call him in the morning.'

I listen to them bickering, trying to figure this out. They do sound like old friends, as Christian says. Just friends. And she cares about him—maybe too much. Well, would anybody who knew him not care?

'Thank you, Christian. And I am sorry. I didn't mean to intrude. I'll go. Next time I'll call.'

'Good.'

She's going! Shit! I scamper up the hallway to Christian's bedroom and sit down on the bed. Christian enters a few moments later.

'She's gone,' he says warily, gauging my reaction.

I gaze up at him, trying to frame my question. 'Will you tell me all about her? I am trying to understand why you think she helped you.' I pause, thinking carefully about my next sentence. 'I loathe her, Christian. I think she did you untold damage. You have no friends. Did she keep them away from

330

you?'

He sighs and runs his hand through his hair.

'Why the fuck do you want to know about her? We had a very long-standing affair, she beat the shit out of me often, and I fucked her in all sorts of ways you can't even imagine, end of story.'

I pale. Shit, he's angry—with me. I blink at him. 'Why are you so angry?'

'Because all of that shit is *over*!' he shouts, glowering at me. He sighs in exasperation and shakes his head.

I blanch. *Shit.* I look down at my hands, knotted in my lap. I just want to understand.

He sits down beside me. 'What do you want to know?' he asks wearily.

'You don't have to tell me. I don't mean to intrude.'

'Anastasia, it's not that. I don't like talking about this shit. I've lived in a bubble for years with nothing affecting me and not having to justify myself to anyone. She's always been there as a confidante. And now my past and my future are colliding in a way I never thought possible.'

I glance at him and he's staring at me, his eyes wide.

'I never thought I had a future with anyone, Anastasia. You give me hope and have me thinking about all sorts of possibilities.' He drifts off.

'I was listening,' I whisper and stare back down at my hands.

'What? To our conversation?'

'Yes.'

'Well?' He sounds resigned.

'She cares for you.'

'Yes, she does. And I for her in my own way, but

it doesn't come close to how I feel about you. If that's what this is about.'

'I'm not jealous.' I'm wounded that he would think that—or am I? Shit. Maybe that's what this is. 'You don't love her,' I murmur.

He sighs again. He really is pissed. 'A long time ago, I thought I loved her,' he says through gritted teeth.

Oh. 'When we were in Georgia . . . you said you didn't love her.'

'That's right.'

I frown.

'I loved you then, Anastasia,' he whispers. 'You're the only person I'd fly three thousand miles to see.'

Oh my. I don't understand. He still wanted me as a sub then. My frown deepens.

'The feelings I have for you are very different from any I ever had for Elena,' he says by way of explanation.

'When did you know?'

He shrugs. 'Ironically, it was Elena who pointed it out to me. She encouraged me to go to Georgia.'

I knew it! I knew it in Savannah. I gaze at him, blankly.

What do I make of this? Maybe she is on my side and just worried that I'll hurt him. The thought is painful. I would never want to hurt him. She's right—he's been hurt enough.

Perhaps she's not so bad. I shake my head. I don't want to accept his relationship with her. I disapprove. Yes, that's what this is. She's an unsavory character who preyed on a vulnerable adolescent, robbing him of his teenage years, no matter what he says.

'So you desired her? When you were younger.'

'Yes.'

Oh.

'She taught me a great deal. She taught me to believe in myself.'

Oh. 'But she also beat the shit out of you.'

He smiles fondly. 'Yes, she did.'

'And you liked that?'

'At the time I did.'

'So much that you wanted to do it to others?'

His eyes grow wide and serious. 'Yes.'

'Did she help you with that?'

'Yes.'

'Did she sub for you?'

'Yes.'

Holy fuck. 'Do you expect me to like her?' My voice sounds brittle and bitter.

'No. Though it would make my life a hell of a lot easier,' he says wearily. 'I do understand your reticence.'

'Reticence! Jeez, Christian—if that were your son, how would you feel?'

He blinks at me as though he doesn't comprehend the question. He frowns. 'I didn't have to stay with her. It was my choice, too, Anastasia,' he murmurs.

This is getting me nowhere.

'Who's Linc?'

'Her ex-husband.'

'Lincoln Timber?'

'The very same,' he smirks.

'And Isaac?'

'Her current submissive.'

Oh no.

'He's in his mid-twenties, Anastasia. You

333

know—a consenting adult,' he adds quickly, correctly deciphering my look of disgust.

'Your age,' I mutter.

'Look, Anastasia, as I said to her, she's part of my past. You are my future. Don't let her come between us, please. And quite frankly, I'm really bored of this subject. I'm going to do some work.' He stands and gazes down at me. 'Let it go. Please.'

I stare mulishly up at him.

'Oh, I almost forgot,' he adds. 'Your car arrived a day early. It's in the garage. Taylor has the key.'

Whoa . . . the Saab? 'Can I drive it tomorrow?'

'No.'

'Why not?'

'You know why not. And that reminds me. If you are going to leave your office, let me know. Sawyer was there, watching you. It seems I can't trust you to look after yourself at all.' He scowls, making me feel like an errant child—again. And I would argue with him, but he's pretty worked up over Elena, and I don't want to push him any further, but I can't resist one comment.

'Seems I can't trust you either,' I mutter. 'You could have told me Sawyer was watching me.'

'Do you want to fight about that, too?' he snaps.

'I wasn't aware we were fighting. I thought we were communicating,' I mumble petulantly.

He closes his eyes briefly as he struggles to contain his temper. I swallow and watch anxiously. This could go either way.

'I have to work,' he says quietly, and with that, he leaves the room.

I exhale. I hadn't realized I'd been holding my breath. I flop back onto the bed, staring at the ceiling.

Can we ever have a normal conversation without it disintegrating into an argument? It's exhausting.

We just don't know each other that well. Do I really want to move in with him? I don't even know if I should make him a cup of tea or coffee while he's working. Should I disturb him at all? I have no idea of his likes and dislikes.

Evidently he's bored with the whole Elena thing—he's right, I need to move on. Let it go. Well, at least he's not expecting me to be friends with her, and I hope that she'll now stop hassling me for a meeting.

I get off the bed and wander to the window. Unlocking the balcony door, I open it and stroll over to the glass railing. Its transparency is unnerving. The air's chilly and fresh, as I'm up so high.

I gaze out over the twinkling lights of Seattle. He's so far removed from everything up here in his fortress. Answerable to no one. *He'd just told me he loves me, then all this crap comes up because of that dreadful woman.* I roll my eyes. His life is so complicated. He's so complicated.

With a heavy sigh and a last glance at Seattle spread like cloths of gold at my feet, I decide to call Ray. I haven't spoken to him for a while. It's a brief conversation as usual, but I ascertain he's fine and that I'm interrupting an important soccer match.

'Hope all is well with Christian,' he says casually, and I know he's fishing for information but doesn't really want to know.

'Yeah. We're cool.' Sort of, and I'm moving in with him. Though we haven't discussed a timetable.

'Love you, Dad.'

'Love you, too, Annie.'

I hang up and check my watch. It's only ten. Because of our discussion, I am feeling strangely innervated and restless.

I shower quickly, and back in the bedroom, decide to wear one of the nightdresses that Caroline Acton procured for me from Neiman Marcus. Christian's always moaning about my T-shirts. There are three. I choose the pale pink and put it on over my head. The fabric skims across my skin, caressing and clinging to me as it falls around my body. It feels luxurious—the finest, thinnest satin. *Whoa!* In the mirror, I look like a 1930s movie star. It's long, elegant—and very un-me.

I grab the matching robe and decide to hunt out a book in the library. I could read on my iPad—but right now, I want the comfort and reassurance of a physical book. I'll leave Christian alone. Perhaps he'll recover his good humor once he's finished working.

There are so many books in Christian's library. Scanning every title will take forever. I glance occasionally at the billiard table and flush as I recall our previous evening. I smile when I see that the ruler is still on the floor. Picking it up, I swat my palm. Ow! It stings.

Why can't I take a little more pain for my man? Disconsolately, I place it on the desk and continue my hunt for a good read.

Most of the books are first editions. How can he have amassed a collection like this in such a short time? Perhaps Taylor's job description includes book buying. I settle on *Rebecca* by Daphne du Maurier. I haven't read this for a long time. I smile as I curl up in one of the overstuffed armchairs and read the first line:

Last night I dreamt I went to Manderley again . . .

I am jostled awake as Christian lifts me in his arms.

'Hey,' he murmurs, 'you fell asleep. I couldn't find you.' He nuzzles my hair. Sleepily, I put my arms around his neck and breathe in his scent—oh, he smells so good—as he carries me back to the bedroom. He lays me down on the bed and covers me.

'Sleep, baby,' he whispers and he presses his lips against my forehead.

*   *   *

I wake suddenly from a disturbing dream and am momentarily disoriented. I find myself anxiously checking the end of the bed, but there's no one there. Drifting from the great room, I hear the faint strains of a complex melody from the piano.

What time is it? I check the alarm clock—two in the morning. Has Christian come to sleep at all? I disentangle my legs from my robe, which I'm still wearing, and clamber out of bed.

In the great room, I stand in the shadows, listening. Christian is lost to the music. He looks safe and secure in his bubble of light. And the tune he plays has a lilting melody, parts of which sound familiar, but so elaborate. *He's so good.* Why does this always take me by surprise?

The whole scene looks different somehow, and I realize that the piano lid is down, giving me an unhindered view. He glances up and our eyes lock,

337

his gray and softly luminous in the diffuse glow of the lamp. He continues to play, not faltering at all, as I make my way over to him. His eyes follow me, drinking me in, burning brighter. As I reach him, he stops.

'Why did you stop? That was lovely.'

'Do you have any idea how desirable you look at this moment?' he says, his voice soft.

Oh. 'Come to bed,' I whisper and his eyes heat as he holds out his hand. When I take it, he tugs unexpectedly so I fall into his lap. He wraps his arms around me and nuzzles my neck behind my ear, sending shivers down my spine.

'Why do we fight?' he whispers, as his teeth graze my earlobe.

My heart skips a beat, then starts pounding, coursing heat throughout my body.

'Because we're getting to know each other, and you're stubborn and cantankerous and moody and difficult,' I murmur breathlessly, shifting my head to give him better access to my throat. He runs his nose down my neck, and I feel his smile.

'I'm all those things, Miss Steele. It's a wonder you put up with me.' He nips my earlobe and I moan. 'Is it always like this?' he sighs.

'I have no idea.'

'Me neither.' He yanks the sash of my robe so it falls open, and his hand skims down my body, over my breast. My nipples harden beneath his gentle touch and strain against the satin. He continues down to my waist, down to my hip.

'You feel so fine under this material, and I can see everything—even this.' He tugs gently on my pubic hair through the fabric, making me gasp, while his other hand fists in my hair at my nape.

338

Pulling my head back, he kisses me, his tongue urgent, relentless, needy. I moan in response and caress his dear, dear face. His hand gently pulls my nightdress up, slowly, tantalizingly until he's fondling my naked behind and then running his thumbnail down the inside of my thigh.

Suddenly he rises, startling me, and he lifts me onto the piano. My feet rest on the keys, sounding discordant, disjointed notes, and his hands skim up my legs and part my knees. He grabs my hands.

'Lie back,' he orders, holding my hands while I sink back on top of the piano. The lid is hard and uncompromising against my back. He lets go and pushes my legs open wider, my feet dancing over the keys, over the lower and higher notes.

Oh, boy. I know what he's going to do, and the anticipation . . . I groan loudly as he kisses the inside of my knee, then kisses and sucks and nips his way higher up my leg to my thigh. The soft satin of my nightgown rises higher, skimming over my sensitized skin, as he pushes the fabric. I flex my feet and the chords sound again. Closing my eyes, I surrender myself to him as his mouth reaches the apex of my thighs.

He kisses me . . . *there* . . . *Oh, boy* . . . then gently blows before his tongue circles my clitoris. He pushes my legs wider. I feel so open—so exposed. He holds me in place, his hands just above my knees as his tongue tortures me, giving no quarter, no respite . . . no reprieve. Tilting my hips up, meeting and matching his rhythm, I am consumed.

'Oh, Christian, please.' I moan.

'Oh no, baby, not yet,' he teases, but I feel myself quicken as does he, and he stops.

'No,' I whimper.

'This is my revenge, Ana,' he growls softly. 'Argue with me, and I am going to take it out on your body somehow.' He trails kisses along my belly, his hands traveling up my thighs, stroking, kneading, tantalizing. His tongue circles my navel as his hands—*and his thumbs . . . oh his thumbs*—reach the summit of my thighs.

'Ah!' I cry out as he pushes one inside me. The other persecutes me, slowly, agonizingly, circling around and around. My back arches off the piano as I writhe beneath his touch. It's almost unbearable.

'Christian!' I cry, spiraling out of control with need.

He takes pity on me and stops. Lifting my feet off the keys, he pushes me; and suddenly, I'm sliding effortlessly up the piano, gliding on satin, and he's following me up there, briefly kneeling between my legs to roll on a condom. He hovers over me and I'm panting, gazing up at him with raging need, and I realize he's naked. When did he take off his clothes?

He stares down at me, and there's wonder in his eyes, wonder and love and passion, and it's breathtaking.

'I want you so badly,' he says and very slowly, exquisitely, he sinks into me.

*　　　*　　　*

I am sprawled on top of him, wrung out, my limbs heavy and languid, as we lie on top of his grand piano. *Oh my.* He's much more comfortable to lie on than the piano. Careful not to touch his chest, I rest my cheek against him and keep perfectly still.

340

He doesn't object, and I listen to his breathing as it slows like mine. Gently he strokes my hair.

'Do you drink tea or coffee in the evening?' I ask sleepily.

'What a strange question,' he says dreamily.

'I thought I could bring you tea in your study, and then I realized I didn't know what you would like.'

'Oh, I see. Water or wine in the evening, Ana. Though maybe I should try tea.'

His hand moves rhythmically down my back, stroking me tenderly.

'We really know very little about each other,' I murmur.

'I know,' he says, and his voice is mournful. I sit up to gaze at him.

'What is it?' I ask. He shakes his head as if to rid himself of some unpleasant thought, and raising his hand, he caresses my cheek, his eyes bright and earnest.

'I love you, Ana Steele,' he says.

~ § ~ ~ § ~ ~ § ~

The alarm goes off with the six a.m. traffic news, and I am rudely awakened from my disturbing dream of overly blonde and dark-haired women. I can't grasp what it's about, and I'm immediately distracted because Christian Grey is wrapped around me like silk, his unruly-haired head on my chest, his hand on my breast, his leg over me, holding me down. He's still asleep, and I am too warm. But I ignore my discomfort, tentatively reaching up to run my fingers gently through his hair, and he stirs. Raising bright gray eyes, he grins

341

sleepily. *Oh my . . . he's adorable.*

'Good morning, beautiful,' he says.

'Good morning, beautiful, yourself.' I smile back at him. He kisses me, disentangles himself, and leans up on his elbow, staring down at me.

'Sleep okay?' he asks.

'Yes, despite the interruption to my sleep last night.'

His grin broadens. 'Hmm. You can interrupt me like that anytime.' He kisses me again.

'How about you? Did you sleep well?'

'I always sleep well with you, Anastasia.'

'No more nightmares?'

'No.'

I frown and chance a question. 'What are your nightmares about?'

His brow creases and his grin fades. *Shit—my stupid curiosity.*

'They're flashbacks of my early childhood, or so Dr. Flynn says. Some vivid, some less so.' His voice drops and a distant, harrowed look crosses his face. Absentmindedly, he begins to trace my collarbone with his finger, distracting me.

'Do you wake up crying and screaming?' I try in vain to joke.

He looks at me, puzzled. 'No, Anastasia. I've never cried. As far as I can remember.' He frowns, as if reaching into the depths of his memories. Oh no—that's too dark a place to go at this hour, surely.

'Do you have any happy memories of your childhood?' I ask quickly, mainly to distract him. He looks pensive for a moment, still running his finger along my skin.

'I recall the crack whore baking. I remember the

smell. A birthday cake I think. For me. And then there's Mia's arrival with my mom and dad. My mom was worried about my reaction, but I adored baby Mia immediately. My first word was *Mia*. I remember my first piano lesson. Miss Kathie, my tutor, was awesome. She kept horses, too.' He smiles wistfully.

'You said your mom saved you. How?'

His reverie is broken, and he gazes at me as if I don't understand the elementary math of two plus two.

'She adopted me,' he says simply. 'I thought she was an angel when I first met her. She was dressed in white and so gentle and calm as she examined me. I'll never forget that. If she'd said no or if Carrick had said no . . .' He shrugs and glances over his shoulder at the alarm clock. 'This is all a little deep for so early in the morning,' he mutters.

'I have made a vow to get to know you better.'

'Did you, now, Miss Steele? I thought you wanted to know if I preferred coffee or tea.' He smirks. 'Anyway, I can think of one way you can get to know me.' He pushes his hips suggestively against me.

'I think I know you quite well enough that way.' My voice is haughty and scolding, and it makes him smile more broadly.

'I don't think I'll ever get to know you well enough that way,' he murmurs. 'There are definite advantages to waking up beside you.' His voice is soft and bone-meltingly seductive.

'Don't you have to get up?' My voice is low and husky. *Oh . . . what he does to me . . .*

'Not this morning. Only one place I want to be up right now, Miss Steele.' And his eyes sparkle salaciously.

'Christian!' I gasp, shocked. He shifts suddenly so that he's on top of me, pressing me into the bed. Grabbing my hands, he pulls them up above my head and begins to kiss my throat.

'Oh, Miss Steele.' He smiles against my skin, sending delicious tingles through me, as his hand travels down my body and starts to slowly hitch up my satin nightdress. 'Oh, what I'd like to do to you,' he murmurs.

And I am lost, interrogation over.

*   *   *

Mrs. Jones sets down my breakfast of pancakes and bacon, and for Christian an omelet and bacon. We sit side by side at the bar in a comfortable silence.

'When am I going to meet your trainer, Claude, and put him through his paces?' I ask. Christian glances down at me, grinning.

'Depends if you want to go to New York this weekend or not—unless you'd like to see him early one morning this week. I'll ask Andrea to check on his schedule and come back to you.'

'Andrea?'

'My PA.'

Oh yes. 'One of your many blondes,' I tease him.

'She's not mine. She works for me. You're mine.'

'I work for you,' I mutter sourly.

He grins as if he's forgotten. 'So you do.' His beaming smile is infectious.

'Maybe Claude can teach me to kickbox,' I warn.

'Oh yeah? To improve your odds against me?' Christian raises an eyebrow, amused. 'Bring it on, Miss Steele.' He is so damned happy compared to yesterday's foul mood after Elena left. It's totally disarming. Maybe it's all the sex . . . perhaps that's what's making him so buoyant.

I glance behind me at the piano, savoring the memory of last night. 'You put the lid of the piano back up.'

'I closed it last night so as not to disturb you. Guess it didn't work, but I'm glad it didn't.' Christian's lips twitch into a lascivious smile as he takes a bite of omelet. I go crimson and smirk back at him.

Oh yes . . . fun times on the piano.

Mrs. Jones leans over and places a paper bag containing my lunch in front of me, making me flush guiltily.

'For later, Ana. Tuna, okay?'

'Oh yes. Thank you, Mrs. Jones.' I give her a shy smile, which she reciprocates warmly before leaving the great room. I suspect it's to give us some privacy.

'Can I ask you something?' I turn back to Christian.

His amused expression slips. 'Of course.'

'And you won't be angry?'

'Is it about Elena?'

'No.'

'Then I won't be angry.'

'But I now have a supplementary question.'

'Oh?'

'Which is about her.'

He rolls his eyes. 'What?' he says, and now he's exasperated.

'Why do you get so mad when I ask you about her?'

'Honestly?'

I scowl at him. 'I thought you were always honest with me.'

'I endeavor to be.'

I narrow my eyes at him. 'That sounds like a very evasive answer.'

'I am always honest with you, Ana. I don't want to play games. Well, not those sorts of games,' he qualifies, as his eyes heat.

'What sort of games do you want to play?'

He inclines his head to one side and smirks at me. 'Miss Steele, you are so easily distracted.'

I giggle. He's right. 'Mr. Grey, you are distracting on so many levels.' I gaze at his dancing gray eyes alight with humor.

'My favorite sound in the whole world is your giggle, Anastasia. Now—what was your original question?' he asks smoothly, and I think he's laughing at me. I try to twist my mouth to show my displeasure, but I like playful Fifty—he's fun. I love some early morning banter. I frown, trying to recall my question.

'Oh yes. You only saw your subs on the weekends?'

'Yes, that's correct,' he says regarding me nervously.

I grin at him. 'So, no sex during the week.'

He laughs. 'Oh, that's where we're going with this.' He looks vaguely relieved. 'Why do you think I work out every weekday?' Now he really is laughing at me, but I don't care. I want to hug myself with glee. Another first—well, several firsts.

'You look very pleased with yourself, Miss Steele.'

'I am, Mr. Grey.'

'You should be.' He grins. 'Now eat your

breakfast.'

Oh, bossy Fifty . . . he's never far away.

*   *   *

We are in the back of the Audi. Taylor is driving
with the intention of dropping me off at work, then
Christian. Sawyer is riding shotgun.

'Didn't you say your roommate's brother was
arriving today?' Christian asks, almost casually, his
voice and expression giving nothing away.

'Oh, Ethan,' I gasp. 'I forgot. Oh Christian, thank
you for reminding me. I'll have to go back to the
apartment.'

His face falls. 'What time?'

'I'm not sure what time he's arriving.'

'I don't want you going anywhere on your own,'
he says sharply.

'I know,' I mutter and resist rolling my eyes at
Mr. Overreaction. 'Will Sawyer be spying—um
. . . patrolling today?' I glance slyly in Sawyer's
direction to see the backs of his ears turn red.

'Yes,' Christian snaps, his eyes glacial.

'If I were driving the Saab it would be easier,' I
mutter petulantly.

'Sawyer will have a car, and he can drive you to
your apartment, depending on what time.'

'Okay. I think Ethan will probably contact me
during the day. I'll let you know what the plans are
then.'

He gazes at me, saying nothing. Oh, what is he
thinking?

'Okay,' he acquiesces. 'Nowhere on your own.
Do you understand?' He waves a finger at me.

'Yes, dear,' I mutter.

347

There's a trace of a smile on his face. 'And maybe you should just use your BlackBerry—I'll e-mail you on it. That should prevent my IT guy having a thoroughly interesting morning, okay?' His voice is sardonic.

'Yes, Christian.' I can't resist. I roll my eyes at him, and he smirks at me.

'Why Miss Steele, I do believe you're making my palm twitch.'

'Ah, Mr. Grey, your perpetually twitching palm. What are we going to do with that?'

He laughs and then is distracted by his BlackBerry, which must be on vibrate because it doesn't ring. He frowns when he sees the caller ID.

'What is it?' he snaps into the phone, then listens intently. I use the opportunity to study his lovely features—his straight nose, his hair hanging scruffily over his forehead. I am distracted from my surreptitious ogling by his expression, which turns from incredulity to amusement. I pay attention.

'You're kidding . . . For a scene . . . When did he tell you this?' Christian chuckles, almost reluctantly. 'No, don't worry. You don't have to apologize. I'm glad there's a logical explanation. It did seem a ridiculously low amount of money . . . I have no doubt you've something evil and creative planned for your revenge. Poor Isaac.' He smiles. 'Good . . . Good-bye.' He snaps the phone shut and glances at me. His eyes are suddenly wary, but oddly, he looks relieved, too.

'Who was that?' I ask.

'You really want to know?' he asks quietly.

With that response, I know. I shake my head and stare out my window at the gray Seattle day, feeling forlorn. Why can't she leave him alone?

'Hey.' He reaches for my hand and kisses each of my knuckles in turn, and suddenly he's sucking my little finger, hard. Then biting it softly.

Whoa! He has a hotline to my groin, I gasp and glance nervously at Taylor and Sawyer, then at Christian, and his eyes are darker. He gives me a slow, carnal smile.

'Don't sweat it, Anastasia,' he murmurs. 'She's in the past.' And he plants a kiss in the center of my palm, sending tingles everywhere, and my momentary pique is forgotten.

*   *   *

'Morning, Ana,' Jack mutters as I make my way to my desk. 'Nice dress.'

I flush. The dress is part of my new wardrobe, courtesy of my incredibly rich boyfriend. It's a sleeveless shift dress of pale blue linen, quite fitted, and I'm wearing cream high-heeled sandals. Christian likes heels, I think. I smile secretly at the thought but quickly recover my bland professional smile for my boss.

'Good morning, Jack.'

I set about ordering a messenger to take his brochure to the printers. He pops his head around his office door.

'Could I have a coffee, please, Ana?'

'Sure.' I wander into the kitchen and bump into Claire from Reception, who is also fixing coffee.

'Hey, Ana,' she says cheerfully.

'Hi, Claire.'

We chat briefly about her extended-family gathering over the weekend, which she enjoyed immensely, and I tell her about sailing with

Christian.

'Your boyfriend is so dreamy, Ana,' she says, her eyes glazing over.

I am tempted to roll my eyes at her.

'He's not bad-looking.' I smile and we both start laughing.

*   *   *

'You took your time!' Jack snaps when I bring in his coffee.

Oh! 'I'm sorry.' I flush, then frown. I took the usual amount of time. What's his problem? Perhaps he's nervous about something.

He shakes his head. 'Sorry, Ana. I didn't mean to bark at you, honey.'

Honey?

'There's something going on at senior management level, and I don't know what it is. Keep your ear to the ground, okay? If you hear anything—I know how you girls talk.' He grins at me, and I feel slightly sick. He has no idea how we 'girls' talk. Besides, I know what's happening.

'You'll let me know, right?'

'Sure,' I mutter. 'I've sent the brochure to the printers. It will be back by two o'clock.'

'Great. Here.' He hands me a pile of manuscripts. 'All these need synopses of the first chapter, then filing.'

'I'll get on it.'

I am relieved to step out of his office and sit down at my desk. Oh, it's hard being in the know. What will he do when he finds out? My blood runs cold. Something tells me Jack will be annoyed. I glance at my BlackBerry and smile. There's an

350

e-mail from Christian.

From: Christian Grey
Subject: Sunrise
Date: June 14 2011 09:23
To: Anastasia Steele

I love waking up with you in the morning.

Christian Grey
Completely & Utterly Smitten CEO, Grey
Enterprises Holdings, Inc.

I think my face splits in two with my grin.

From: Anastasia Steele
Subject: Sundown
Date: June 14 2011 09:35
To: Christian Grey

Dear Completely & Utterly Smitten

I love waking up with you, too. But I love
being in bed with you and in elevators and
on pianos and billiard tables and boats
and desks and showers and bathtubs and
strange wooden crosses with shackles and
four-poster beds with red satin sheets and
boathouses and childhood bedrooms.

Yours

Sex Mad and Insatiable xx

From: Christian Grey
Subject: Wet Hardware
Date: June 14 2011 09:37
To: Anastasia Steele

Dear Sex Mad and Insatiable

I've just spat coffee all over my keyboard.

I don't think that's ever happened to me before.

I do admire a woman who concentrates on geography.

Am I to infer you just want me for my body?

Christian Grey
Completely & Utterly Shocked CEO, Grey Enterprises Holdings, Inc.

From: Anastasia Steele
Subject: Giggling—and wet too
Date: June 14 2011 09:42
To: Christian Grey

Dear Completely & Utterly Shocked

Always.

I have work to do.

Stop bothering me.

SM&I xx

From: Christian Grey
Subject: Do I have to?
Date: June 14 2011 09:50
To: Anastasia Steele

Dear SM&I

As ever, your wish is my command.

Love that you are giggling and wet.

Laters, baby.

x

Christian Grey,
Completely & Utterly Smitten, Shocked, and Spellbound CEO, Grey Enterprises Holdings, Inc.

I put the BlackBerry down and get on with my work.

*   *   *

At lunchtime Jack asks me to go down to the deli for him. I call Christian as soon as I leave Jack's office.

'Anastasia.' He answers immediately, his voice warm and caressing. How is it that this man can make me melt over the phone?

'Christian, Jack has asked me to get his lunch.'

'Lazy bastard,' Christian gripes.

I ignore him and continue. 'So, I'm going to get it. It might be handy if you gave me Sawyer's number, so I don't have to bother you.'

353

'It's no bother, baby.'

'Are you on your own?'

'No. There are six people staring at me right now wondering who the hell I'm talking to.'

Shit . . . 'Really?' I gasp, panicked.

'Yes. Really. My girlfriend,' he announces away from the phone.

Holy cow! 'They probably all thought you were gay, you know.'

He laughs. 'Yeah, probably.' I hear his grin.

'Er—I'd better go.' I am sure he can tell how embarrassed I am to be interrupting him.

'I'll let Sawyer know.' He laughs again. 'Have you heard from your friend?'

'Not yet. You'll be the first to know, Mr. Grey.'

'Good. Laters, baby.'

'Bye, Christian.' I grin. Every time he says that, it makes me smile . . . so un-Fifty, but somehow so him, too.

*   *   *

When I exit seconds later, Sawyer is waiting on the doorstep of the building.

'Miss Steele,' he greets me formally.

'Sawyer.' I nod in response and together we head down to the deli.

I don't feel as comfortable with Sawyer as I do with Taylor. He keeps scanning the street as we make our way along the block. It actually makes me more nervous, and I find myself mirroring his actions.

Is Leila out there? Or are we all infected by Christian's paranoia? Is this part of his fifty shades? What I'd give for half an hour of candid discussion with Dr. Flynn to find out.

There's nothing amiss, just lunchtime Seattle—people rushing for lunch, shopping, meeting friends. I watch two young women hug as they meet up.

I miss Kate. It's only been two weeks since she left for her vacation, but it feels like the longest two weeks of my life. So much has happened—she'll never believe me when I tell her. Well, tell her the edited, NDA-compliant version. I frown. I'll have to talk to Christian about that. What would Kate make of it? I blanch at the thought. Perhaps she'll be back with Ethan. I feel a rush of excitement at the thought, but I think it's unlikely. She'd probably stay on with Elliot.

'Where do you stand when you're waiting and watching outside?' I ask Sawyer as we get in line for lunch. Sawyer is in front of me, facing the door, continually monitoring the street and anyone who comes in. It's unnerving.

'I sit in the coffee shop directly across the street, Miss Steele.'

'Doesn't it get very boring?'

'Not to me, ma'am. It's what I do,' he says stiffly.

I flush. 'Sorry, I didn't mean to imply . . .' My voice trails off at his kind, understanding expression.

'Please, Miss Steele. My job is to protect you. And that's what I'll do.'

'So, no sign of Leila?'

'No, ma'am.'

I frown. 'How do you know what she looks like?'

'I've seen her photograph.'

'Oh, do you have it on you?'

'No, ma'am.' He taps his skull. 'Committed to

memory.'

Of course. I'd really like to examine a photograph of Leila to see what she looked like before she became Ghost Girl. I wonder if Christian would let me have a copy? Yes, he probably would—for my safety. I hatch a plan, and my subconscious gloats and nods approvingly.

*   *   *

The brochures arrive back at the office, and to my relief they look great. I take one into Jack's office. His eyes light up; I don't know if it's at me or the brochure. I choose to believe it's the latter.

'These look great, Ana.' Idly, he flicks through it. 'Yeah, good job. Are you seeing your boyfriend this evening?' His lip curls as he says 'boyfriend.'

'Yes. We live together.' It's sort of the truth. Well, we do at the moment. And I have officially agreed to move in, so it's not much of a white lie. I hope that it's enough to throw him off the scent.

'Would he object to you coming out for a quick drink tonight? To celebrate all your hard work?'

'I have a friend coming in from out of town tonight, and we're all going out for dinner.' And I'll be busy every night, Jack.

'I see.' He sighs, exasperated. 'Maybe when I'm back from New York, huh?' He raises his eyebrows in expectation, and his gaze darkens suggestively.

Oh no. I smile, noncommittal, stifling a shudder.

'Would you like some coffee or tea?' I ask.

'Coffee, please.' His voice is low and husky as if he's asking for something else. Fuck. He's not going to back off. I can see that now. *Oh . . . What to do?*

I breathe a long sigh of relief when I am out of

356

his office. He makes me tense. Christian is right about him, and part of me is pissed that Christian *is* right about him.

I sit down at my desk and my BlackBerry rings—a number I don't recognize.

'Ana Steele.'

'Hi, Steele!' Ethan's drawl catches me momentarily off guard.

'Ethan! How are you?' I almost squeal with delight.

'Glad to be back. I am seriously fed up with sunshine and rum punches, and my baby sister being hopelessly in love with the big guy. It's been hell, Ana.'

'Yeah! Sea, sand, sun, and rum punches sounds like *Dante's Inferno.*' I giggle. 'Where are you?'

'I'm at Sea-Tac, waiting for my bag. What are you doing?'

'I'm at work. Yes, I am gainfully employed,' I respond to his gasp. 'Do you want to come here and collect the keys? I can meet you later at the apartment.'

'Sounds great. I'll see you in about forty-five minutes, an hour maybe? What's the address?'

I give him SIP's address.

'See you soon, Ethan.'

'Laters,' he says and hangs up. What? Not Ethan, too? And it dawns on me that he's just spent a week with Elliot. I quickly type an e-mail to Christian.

From: Anastasia Steele
Subject: Visitors from Sunny Climes.
Date: June 14 2011 14:55

To: Christian Grey

Dearest Completely & Utterly SS&S

Ethan is back, and he's coming here to collect keys to the apartment.

I'd really like to make sure he's settled in okay.

Why don't you pick me up after work? We can go to the apartment, then we can ALL go out for a meal maybe?

My treat?

Your

Ana x

Still SM&I

Anastasia Steele
Assistant to Jack Hyde, Editor, SIP

From: Christian Grey
Subject: Dinner Out
Date: June 14 2011 15:05
To: Anastasia Steele

I approve of your plan. Except the part about you paying!

My treat.

I'll pick you up at 6:00.

x

PS: Why aren't you using your BlackBerry!!!

Christian Grey
Completely and Utterly Annoyed, CEO,
Grey Enterprises Holdings, Inc.

From: Anastasia Steele
Subject: Bossiness
Date: June 14 2011 15:11
To: Christian Grey

Oh, don't be so crusty and cross.

It's all in code.

I'll see you at 6:00.

Ana x

Anastasia Steele
Assistant to Jack Hyde, Editor, SIP

From: Christian Grey
Subject: Maddening Woman
Date: June 14 2011 15:18
To: Anastasia Steele

Crusty and cross!

I'll give you crusty and cross.

And look forward to it.

Christian Grey
Completely and Utterly More Annoyed, but
Smiling for Some Unknown Reason, CEO,
Grey Enterprises Holdings, Inc.

He doesn't reply, but then I don't expect him to. I imagine him moaning about mixed signals, and the thought makes me smile. I daydream briefly about what he might do to me but find myself shifting about in my chair. My subconscious gazes at me disapprovingly over her half-moon specs— get on with your work.

*   *   *

A little later, my phone buzzes. It's Claire at Reception.

'There's a real cute guy in Reception to see you. We must go out for drinks sometime, Ana. You sure know some hunky guys,' she hisses conspiratorially through the phone.

Ethan! Grabbing my keys from my purse, I hurry out to the foyer.

Holy shit—sun-bleached blond hair, a tan to die for, and glowing hazel eyes gaze up at me from the green leather couch. As soon as he sees me, his mouth drops open, and he's on his feet coming toward me.

'Wow, Ana.' He frowns at me as he bends to give me hug.

'You look well.' I grin up at him.

'You look . . . wow—different. Worldly, more sophisticated. What's happened? You changed your hair? Clothes? I don't know, Steele, but you look hot!'

I blush furiously. 'Oh, Ethan. I'm just in my work clothes,' I scold as Claire looks on with an arched eyebrow and a wry smile.

'How was Barbados?'

'Fun,' he says.

'When's Kate coming back?'

'She and Elliot are flying back Friday. They're pretty damn serious about each other.' Ethan rolls his eyes.

'I've missed her.'

'Yeah? How have you been doing with Mr. Mogul?'

'Mr. Mogul?' I snicker. 'Well, it's been interesting. He's taking us out for dinner this evening.'

'Cool.' Ethan seems genuinely pleased. Phew!

'Here.' I hand him the keys. 'You have the address?'

'Yeah. Laters.' He leans over and kisses my cheek.

'Elliot's expression?'

'Yeah, kind of grows on you.'

'It does. Laters.' I smile at him as he picks up his large over-the-shoulder bag from beside the green couch and exits the building.

When I turn, Jack is watching me from the far side of the foyer, his expression unreadable. I smile brightly at him and head back to my desk, feeling his eyes on me the whole time. This is beginning to get on my nerves. What to do? I have no idea. I'll have to wait until Kate is back. She's bound to come up with a plan. The thought dispels my bleak mood, and I pick up the next manuscript.

*   *   *

At five to six, my phone buzzes. It's Christian.

'Crusty and Cross here,' he says and I grin. He's still playful Fifty. My inner goddess is clapping her hands with glee like a small child.

'Well, this is Sex Mad and Insatiable. I take it you're outside?' I ask dryly.

'I am indeed, Miss Steele. Looking forward to seeing you.' His voice is warm and seductive, and my heart flutters wildly.

'Ditto, Mr. Grey. I'll be right out.' I hang up.

I switch off my computer and gather up my purse and cream cardigan.

'I'm off now, Jack,' I call through.

'Okay, Ana. Thanks for today! Have a great evening.'

'You, too.'

Why can't he be like that all the time? I don't understand him.

*   *   *

The Audi is parked at the curb, and Christian climbs out as I approach. He's taken off his jacket, and he's wearing his gray pants, my favorite ones

362

that hang from his hips—in that way. How can this Greek god be meant for me? I find myself grinning like a loon in answer to his own idiotic grin.

He's spent the whole day acting like a boyfriend in love—in love with me. This adorable, complex, flawed man is in love with me, and I with him. Joy bursts unexpectedly inside me, and I savor the moment as I feel briefly that I could conquer the world.

'Miss Steele, you look as captivating as you did this morning.' Christian pulls me into his arms and kisses me soundly.

'Mr. Grey, so do you.'

'Let's go get your friend.' He smiles down at me and opens the car door.

As Taylor heads to the apartment, Christian fills me in on his day—a much better one than yesterday, it seems. I gaze at him adoringly as he attempts to explain some breakthrough the environmental science department at WSU in Vancouver has made. His words mean very little to me, but I'm captivated by his passion and interest in this subject. Maybe this is what it will be like, good days and bad days, and if the good days are like this, I won't have much to complain about. He hands me a sheet of paper.

'These are the times that Claude is free this week,' he says.

Oh! The trainer.

As we pull up to my apartment building, he fishes his BlackBerry from his pocket.

'Grey,' he answers. 'Ros, what is it?' He listens intently, and I can tell it's an involved conversation.

'I'll go and get Ethan. I'll be two minutes,' I mouth at Christian and hold up two fingers.

He nods, obviously distracted by the call. Taylor opens my door, smiling at me warmly. I grin at him; even Taylor's feeling it. I press the entry phone and shout happily into it.

'Hi, Ethan, it's me. Let me in.'

The door buzzes, and I head upstairs to the apartment. It occurs to me that I have not been here since Saturday morning. That seems so long ago. Ethan has kindly left the front door open. I step into the apartment, and I don't know why, but I freeze instinctively as soon as I step inside. I take a moment to realize it's because the pale, wan figure standing by the kitchen island and holding a small revolver is Leila, and she's gazing impassively at me.

CHAPTER THIRTEEN

Holy fuck.

She's here, gazing at me with an unnerving blank expression, holding a gun. My subconscious swoons into a dead faint, and I don't think even smelling salts will bring her back.

I blink repeatedly at Leila as my mind goes into overdrive. How did she get in? Where's Ethan? Holy shit! Where is Ethan?

A creeping cold fear grips my heart, and my scalp prickles as each and every follicle on my head tightens with terror. What if she's harmed him? I start breathing rapidly as adrenaline and bone-numbing dread course through my body. *Keep calm, keep calm*—I repeat the mantra over and over in my head.

She tilts her head to one side, regarding me as if I'm an exhibit in a freak show. Jeez, I'm not the freak here.

It feels like an eon has passed while I process all this, though in reality it is only a split second. Leila's expression remains blank, and her appearance is as scruffy and ill-kempt as ever. She's still wearing that grubby trench coat, and she looks desperately in need of a shower. Her hair is greasy and lank, plastered against her head, and her eyes are a dull brown, cloudy, and vaguely confused.

Despite the fact that my mouth has no moisture in it whatsoever, I attempt to speak. 'Hi. Leila, isn't it?' I rasp. She smiles, but it's a disturbing curl of her lip rather than a true smile.

'She speaks,' she whispers, and her voice is soft and hoarse at the same time, an eerie sound.

'Yes, I speak,' I say gently as if to a child. 'Are you here alone?' Where is Ethan? My heart pounds at the thought that he might have come to some harm.

Her face falls, so much so that I think she's about to burst into tears—she looks so forlorn.

'Alone,' she whispers. 'Alone.' And the depth of sadness in that one word is heart wrenching. What does she mean? I am alone? She's alone? She's alone because she's harmed Ethan? Oh . . . no . . . I have to fight the choking fear clawing at my throat as tears threaten.

'What are you doing here? Can I help you?' My words are a calm, gentle interrogation despite the suffocating fear in my throat. Her brow furrows as if she's completely befuddled by my questions. But she makes no violent move against me. Her hand is still relaxed around her gun. I take a different tack, trying to ignore my tightening scalp.

'Would you like some tea?' Why am I asking her if she wants tea? It's Ray's answer to any emotional situation, resurfacing inappropriately. Jeez, he'd have a fit if he saw me right this minute. His army training would have kicked in, and he'd have disarmed her by now. She's not actually pointing that gun at me. Perhaps I can move. She shakes her head and tilts it from side to side as if stretching her neck.

I take a deep precious lungful of air, trying to calm my panicked breathing, and move toward the kitchen island. She frowns as if she can't quite understand what I am doing and shifts a little so she is still facing me. I reach the kettle and with a shaking hand fill it from the faucet. As I move, my breathing eases. Yes, if she wanted me dead, surely she would have shot me by now. She watches me with an absent, bemused curiosity. As I switch on the kettle, I'm plagued by the thought of Ethan. Is he hurt? Tied up?

'Is there anyone else in the apartment?' I ask tentatively.

She inclines her head the other way, and with her right hand—the hand not holding the revolver—she grabs a strand of her long greasy hair and starts twirling and fiddling with it, pulling and twisting. It's obviously a nervous habit, and while I am distracted by this, I am struck once again by how much she resembles me. I hold my breath, waiting for her answer, the anxiety building to an almost unbearable pitch.

'Alone. All alone,' she murmurs. I find this comforting. Maybe Ethan isn't here. The relief is empowering.

'Are you sure you don't want tea or coffee?'

'Not thirsty,' she answers softly, and she takes a cautious step toward me. My feeling of empowerment evaporates. Fuck! I start panting with fear again, feeling it surge thick and rough through my veins. In spite of this and feeling beyond brave, I turn and fetch a couple of cups from the cupboard.

'What do you have that I don't?' she asks, her voice assuming the singsong intonation of a child.

'What do you mean, Leila?' I ask as gently as I can.

'Master—Mr. Grey—he lets you call him by his given name.'

'I'm not his submissive, Leila. Er . . . Master understands that I am unable, inadequate to fulfill that role.'

She tilts her head to the other side. It's wholly unnerving and unnatural as a gesture.

'In-ad-e-quate.' She tests the word, sounding it out, seeing how it feels on her tongue. 'But Master is happy. I have seen him. He laughs and smiles. These reactions are rare . . . very rare for him.'

Oh.

'You look like me.' Leila changes tack, surprising me, her eyes seeming truly to focus on me for the first time. 'Master likes obedient ones who look like you and me. The others, all the same . . . all the same . . . and yet you sleep in his bed. I saw you.'

Shit! She was in the room. I didn't imagine it.

'You saw me in his bed?' I whisper.

'I never slept in Master's bed,' she murmurs. She's like a fallen ethereal wraith. Half a person. She looks so slight, and in spite of the fact that she's holding a gun, I suddenly feel overwhelmed

367

with sympathy for her. Her hands flex around the weapon, and my eyes widen, threatening to pop from my head.

'Why does Master like us like this? It makes me think something . . . something . . . Master is dark . . . Master is a dark man, but I love him.'

No, no, he's not. I bristle internally. He's not dark. He's a good man, and he's not in the dark. He's joined me in the light. And now she's here, trying to drag him back with some warped idea that she loves him.

'Leila, do you want to give me the gun?' I ask softly. Her hand grips it tightly, and she hugs it to her chest.

'This is mine. It's all I have left.' She gently caresses the gun. 'So she can join her love.'

Shit! Which love—Christian? It's like she's punched me in the stomach. I know he will be here momentarily to find out what's keeping me. Does she mean to shoot him? The thought is so horrific, I feel my throat swell and ache as a huge knot forms there, almost choking me, matching the fear that's balled tightly in my stomach.

Right on cue the door bursts open, and Christian is standing in the doorway, Taylor behind him.

Glancing at me briefly, Christian's eyes sweep over me from head to toe, and I notice the small spark of relief in his look. But his relief is fleeting as his gaze darts to Leila and stills, focusing on her, not wavering in the slightest. He glares at her with an intensity I have not seen before, his eyes wild, wide, angry, and scared.

Oh no . . . oh no.

Leila's eyes widen, and for a moment, it seems her reason returns. She blinks rapidly while her hand tightens once more around the gun.

My breath catches in my throat, and my heart starts thumping so loud that I hear the blood pounding in my ears. *No no no!*

My world teeters precariously in the hands of this poor, fucked-up woman. Will she shoot? Both of us? Just Christian? The thought is crippling.

But after an eternity, as time hangs suspended around us, her head dips slightly and she gazes up at him through her long lashes, her expression contrite.

Christian holds up his hand, signaling to Taylor to stay where he is. Taylor's blanched face betrays his fury. I have never seen him like this, but he stands stock-still as Christian and Leila stare at each other.

I realize I'm holding my breath. What will she do? What will he do? But they just continue to stare at each other. Christian's expression is raw, full of some unnamed emotion. It could be pity, fear, affection . . . or is it love? No, please, not love!

His eyes bore into her, and agonizingly slowly, the atmosphere in the apartment changes. The tension is building so that I can sense their connection, the charge between them.

No! Suddenly I feel *I'm* the interloper, intruding on them as they stand gazing at each other. I'm an outsider—a voyeur, spying on a forbidden, intimate scene behind closed curtains.

Christian's intense gaze burns brighter, and his bearing changes subtly. He looks taller, more angular somehow, colder, and more distant. I recognize this stance. I've seen him like this before—in his playroom.

My scalp prickles anew. This is Dominant

Christian, and how at ease he looks. Whether he was born to or made for this role, I just don't know, but with a sinking heart and sickened stomach, I watch as Leila responds, her lips parting, her breathing picking up as the first flush of color stains her cheeks. *No!* It's such an unwelcome glimpse into his past, agonizing to witness.

Finally he mouths a word at her. I can't make out what it is, but the effect on Leila is immediate. She drops to the floor on her knees, her head bowed, and the gun falls and skitters uselessly across the wooden floor. *Holy fuck.*

Christian walks calmly over to where the gun has fallen and bends gracefully to pick it up. He regards it with ill-disguised disgust, and then slips it into his jacket pocket. He gazes once more at Leila as she kneels compliantly beside the kitchen island.

'Anastasia, go with Taylor,' he commands. Taylor crosses the threshold and stares at me.

'Ethan,' I whisper.

'Downstairs.' He responds matter-of-factly, his eyes never leaving Leila.

Downstairs. Not here. Ethan's okay. Relief floods hard and fast through my blood, and for a moment I think I'm going to faint.

'Anastasia,' Christian's tone is clipped in warning.

I blink at him, and I'm suddenly unable to move. I don't want to leave him—leave him with her. He moves to stand beside Leila as she kneels at his feet. He's hovering over her, protectively. She's so still, it's unnatural. I can't take my eyes off the two of them—together . . .

'For the love of God, Anastasia, will you do as you're told for once in your life and go!' Christian's eyes lock with mine as he glowers at me, his voice a cold shard of ice. The anger beneath the quiet, deliberate delivery of his words is palpable.

Angry at me? No way. Please—no! I feel like he's slapped me hard. Why does he want to stay with her?

'Taylor. Take Miss Steele downstairs. Now.'

Taylor nods at him as I stare at Christian.

'Why?' I whisper.

'Go. Back to the apartment.' His eyes blaze frostily at me. 'I need to be alone with Leila.' He says it urgently.

I think he's trying to convey some kind of message, but I'm so thrown by all that's happened that I'm not sure. I glance down at Leila and notice a very small smile cross her lips, but otherwise she remains truly impassive. A complete submissive. *Fuck!* My heart chills.

This is what he needs. This is what he likes. *No!* I want to wail.

'Miss Steele. Ana.' Taylor holds his hand out to me, imploring me to come. I am immobilized by the horrific spectacle before me. It confirms my worst fears and plays on all my insecurities: Christian and Leila together—the Dom and his sub.

'Taylor,' Christian urges, and Taylor leans down and scoops me into his arms. The last thing I see as we leave is Christian gently stroking Leila's head as he murmurs something softly to her.

No!

As Taylor carries me down the stairs, I lie limply in his arms trying to grasp what's happened in the last ten minutes—or was it longer? Shorter? The concept of time has deserted me.

Christian and Leila, Leila and Christian . . .

371

together? What is he doing with her now?

'Jesus, Ana! What the fuck is going on?'

I am relieved to see Ethan as he paces the small lobby, still carrying his large bag. *Oh, thank heavens he's okay!* When Taylor sets me down, I practically throw myself at Ethan, wrapping my arms around his neck.

'Ethan. Oh, thank God!' I hug him, holding him close. I was so worried, and for a brief moment, I enjoy some respite from my rising panic at what is unfolding upstairs in my apartment.

'What the fuck is going on, Ana? Who's this guy?'

'Oh, sorry, Ethan, this is Taylor. He works with Christian. Taylor, this is Ethan, my roommate's brother.'

They nod at each other.

'Ana, upstairs, what's going on? I was fishing for the apartment keys when these guys jumped out of nowhere and grabbed them. One of them was Christian . . .' Ethan's voice trails off.

'You were late . . . Thank God.'

'Yeah. I met a friend from Pullman—we had a quick drink. What's going on up there?'

'There's a girl, an ex of Christian's. In our apartment. She's gone postal, and Christian is . . .' My voice cracks, and tears pool in my eyes.

'Hey,' Ethan whispers and pulls me close once more. 'Has anyone called the cops?'

'No, it's not like that.' I sob into his chest and now I've started, I can't stop crying, the tension of this latest episode releasing through my tears. Ethan tightens his arms around me, but I sense his bemusement.

'Hey, Ana, let's go get a drink.' He pats my back

awkwardly. Abruptly, I feel awkward, too, and embarrassed, and in all honesty, I want to be on my own. But I nod, accepting his offer. I want to be away from here, away from whatever's going on upstairs.

I turn to Taylor.

'Was the apartment checked?' I ask him tearfully, wiping my nose with the back of my hand.

'This afternoon.' Taylor shrugs apologetically as he hands me a handkerchief. He looks devastated. 'I'm sorry, Ana,' he murmurs.

I frown. Jeez, he looks so guilty. I don't want to make him feel worse.

'She does seem to have an uncanny ability to evade us,' he adds scowling again.

'Ethan and I will go for a quick drink and then head back to Escala.' I dry my eyes.

Taylor shuffles from foot to foot uncomfortably. 'Mr. Grey wanted you to go back to the apartment,' he says quietly.

'Well, we know where Leila is now.' I can't keep the bitterness out of my voice. 'So, no need for all the security. Tell Christian we'll see him later.'

Taylor opens his mouth to speak and then wisely closes it again.

'Do you want to leave your bag with Taylor?' I ask Ethan.

'No, I'll keep it with me, thanks.'

Ethan nods at Taylor, then ushers me out the front door. Too late, I remember that I've left my purse in the back of Audi. I have nothing.

'My purse—'

'Don't worry,' Ethan murmurs, his face full of concern. 'It's cool, it's on me.'

*   *   *

We choose a bar across the street, settling onto wooden barstools by the window. I want to see what's going on—who's coming, and more important, who's going. Ethan hands me a bottle of beer.

'Trouble with an ex?' he says gently.

'It's a bit more complicated than that,' I mutter, abruptly guarded. I can't talk about this—I have signed an NDA. And for the first time, I really resent that fact, plus that Christian's said nothing about rescinding it.

'I've got time,' Ethan says kindly and takes a long slug of his beer.

'She's an ex, from years back. She left her husband for some guy. Then a couple of weeks or so ago he was killed in a car crash, and now she's come after Christian.' I shrug. There, that didn't give too much away.

'Come after him?'

'She had a gun.'

'What the fuck!'

'She didn't actually threaten anyone with it. I think she meant to harm herself. But that's why I was so worried about you. I didn't know if you were in the apartment.'

'I see. She sounds unstable.'

'Yes, she is.'

'And what's Christian doing with her now?'

The blood drains from my face and bile rises in my throat. 'I don't know,' I whisper.

Ethan's eyes widen—at last he's got it.

This is the crux of my problem. What the fuck are they doing? Talking, I hope. Just talking. Yet

374

all I can see in my mind's eye is his hand, tenderly stroking her hair.

She's disturbed and Christian cares about her; that's all this is, I rationalize. But in the back of my mind, my subconscious is shaking her head sadly.

It's more than that. Leila was able to fulfill his needs in a way I cannot. The thought is depressing.

I try to focus on all we've done in the last few days—his declaration of love, his flirty humor, his playfulness. But Elena's words keep coming back to taunt me. It's true what they say about eavesdroppers.

Don't you miss it . . . your playroom?

I finish my beer in record time, and Ethan lines up another. I am not much of a companion, but to his credit he stays with me, chatting, trying to lift my spirits, talking about Barbados, about Kate and Elliot's antics, which is wonderfully distracting. But it's just that—a distraction.

My mind, my heart, my soul are all still in that apartment with my Fifty Shades and the woman who used to be his submissive. A woman who thinks she still loves him. A woman who looks like me.

During our third beer, a large cruiser with heavily-tinted windows pulls up next to the Audi in front of the apartment. I recognize Dr. Flynn as he climbs out, accompanied by a woman dressed in what look like pale blue scrubs. I glimpse Taylor as he lets them in through the front door.

'Who's that?' Ethan asks.

'His name's Dr. Flynn. Christian knows him.'

'What kind of doctor?'

'A shrink.'

'Oh.'

We both watch, and a few minutes later they are

back. Christian is carrying Leila, who is wrapped in a blanket. *What?* I watch horrified as they all climb into the cruiser, and it speeds away.

Ethan glances at me sympathetically, and I feel desolate, completely desolate.

'Can I have something a bit stronger?' I ask Ethan, my voice small.

'Sure. What would you like?'

'A brandy. Please.'

Ethan nods and retreats to the bar. I gaze through the window at the front door. Moments later Taylor emerges, climbs into the Audi, and heads off toward Escala . . . after Christian? I don't know.

Ethan places a large brandy in front of me.

'Come on, Steele. Let's get drunk.'

Sounds like the best offer I've had in a while. We clink glasses, and I take a gulp of the burning amber liquid, the fiery heat a welcome distraction from the hideous blossoming pain in my heart.

*   *   *

It's late and I feel fuzzy. Ethan and I are locked out of the apartment. He insists on walking me back to Escala, but he won't stay. He's called the friend he met earlier for a drink and arranged to crash with him.

'So, this is where the mogul lives.' Ethan whistles through his teeth, impressed.

I nod.

'Sure you don't want me to come in with you?' he asks.

'No, I need to face this—or just go to bed.'

'See you tomorrow?'

376

'Yes. Thanks, Ethan.' I hug him.

'You'll work it out, Steele,' he murmurs against my ear. He releases me and watches while I head into the building.

'Laters,' he calls. I offer him a weak smile and a wave, and then press the button to call the elevator.

I step out of the elevator and into Christian's apartment. Taylor is not waiting, which is unusual. Opening the double doors, I head toward the great room. Christian is on the phone, pacing the room near the piano.

'She's here,' he snaps. He turns to glare at me as he switches off his phone. 'Where the fuck have you been?' he growls but doesn't make a move toward me.

He's angry with me? He's the one that just spent God knows how long with his loony ex-girlfriend, and he's angry with me?

'Have you been drinking?' he asks, appalled.

'A bit.' I didn't think it was that obvious.

He gasps and runs his hand through his hair. 'I told you to come back here.' His voice is menacingly quiet. 'It's now fifteen after ten. I've been worried about you.'

'I went for a drink or three with Ethan while you attended to your ex,' I hiss at him. 'I didn't know how long you were going to be . . . with her.'

He narrows his eyes and takes a few paces toward me but stops.

'Why do you say it that like that?'

I shrug and stare down at my fingers.

'Ana, what's wrong?' And for the first time, I hear something other than anger in his voice. What? Fear?

I swallow, trying to work out what I want to say.

'Where's Leila?' I ask looking up at him.

'In a psychiatric hospital in Fremont,' he says, and his face is scrutinizing mine. 'Ana, what is it?' He moves toward me until he's standing right in front of me. 'What's wrong?' he breathes.

I shake my head. 'I'm no good for you.'

'What?' he breathes, his eyes widening in alarm. 'Why do you think that? How can you possibly think that?'

'I can't be everything you need.'

'You are everything I need.'

'Just seeing you with her . . .' My voice trails off.

'Why do you do this to me? This is not about you, Ana. It's about her.' He takes a sharp breath, running his hand through his hair again. 'Right now she's a very sick girl.'

'But I felt it . . . what you had together.'

'What? No.' He reaches for me, and I step back instinctively. He drops his hand, blinking at me. He looks as though he's seized with panic.

'You're running?' he whispers as his eyes widen with fear.

I say nothing as I try to collect my scattered thoughts.

'You can't,' he pleads.

'Christian . . . I . . .' I struggle to collect my thoughts. What am I trying to say? I need time, time to process this. Give me time.

'No. No!' he says.

'I . . .'

He looks wildly around the room. For inspiration? For divine intervention? I don't know.

'You can't go. Ana, I love you!'

'I love you, too, Christian, it's just—'

'No . . . no!' he says in desperation and puts both

378

hands on his head.

'Christian . . .'

'No,' he breathes, his eyes wide with panic, and suddenly he drops to his knees in front of me, head bowed, his hands spread out on his thighs. He takes a deep breath and doesn't move.

What? 'Christian, what are you doing?'

He continues to stare down, not looking at me.

'Christian! What are you doing?' I repeat in a high-pitched voice. He doesn't move. 'Christian, look at me!' I command in panic.

His head sweeps up without hesitation, and he regards me passively with his cool gray gaze—he's almost serene . . . expectant.

Holy Fuck . . . Christian. The submissive.

CHAPTER FOURTEEN

Christian on his knees at my feet, holding me with his steady gray gaze, is the most chilling and sobering sight I have ever seen—more so than Leila and her gun. The vague alcoholic fuzziness I'm suffering from evaporates in an instant, and is replaced by a prickling scalp and a creeping sense of doom as the blood drains from my face.

I inhale sharply with shock. *No. No, this is wrong, so wrong and so disturbing.*

'Christian, please, don't do this. I don't want this.'

He continues to regard me passively, not moving, saying nothing.

Oh, fuck. My poor Fifty. My heart squeezes and twists. What the hell have I done to him? Tears prick my eyes.

'Why are you doing this? Talk to me,' I whisper.

He blinks once.

'What would you like me to say?' he says softly, blandly, and for a moment I'm relieved that he's talking, but not like this—no. No.

Tears begin to ooze down my cheeks, and suddenly it is too much to see him in the same prostrate position as the pathetic creature that was Leila. The image of a powerful man who's really still a little boy, who was horrifically abused and neglected, who feels unworthy of love from his perfect family and his much-less-than-perfect girlfriend . . . my lost boy . . . it's heartbreaking.

Compassion, loss, and despair all swell in my heart, and I feel a choking sense of desperation. I am going to have to fight to bring him back, to bring back *my* Fifty.

The thought of me dominating anyone is appalling. The thought of dominating Christian is nauseating. It would make me like her—the woman who did this to him.

I shudder at that thought, fighting the bile in my throat. No way can I do that. No way do I want that.

As my thoughts clear, I can see only one way. Not taking my eyes off his, I sink to my knees in front of him.

The wooden floor is hard against my shins, and I dash my tears away roughly with the back of my hand.

Like this, we are equals. We're on a level. This is the only way I'm going to retrieve him.

His eyes widen fractionally as I stare up at him, but beyond that his expression and stance don't change.

'Christian, you don't have to do this,' I plead. 'I'm not going to run. I've told you and told you and told you, I won't run.' All that's happened . . . it's overwhelming. I just need some time to think . . . some time to myself. Why do you always assume the worst?' My heart clenches again because I know; it's because he's so doubting, so full of self-loathing.

Elena's words come back to haunt me. *'Does she know how negative you are about yourself? About all your issues?'*

Oh, Christian. Fear grips my heart once more and I start babbling, 'I was going to suggest going back to my apartment this evening. You never give me any time . . . time to just think things through,' I sob, and a ghost of a frown crosses his face. 'Just time to think. We barely know each other, and all this baggage that comes with you . . . I need . . . I need time to think it through. And now that Leila is . . . well, whatever she is . . . she's off the streets and not a threat . . . I thought . . . I thought . . .' My voice trails off and I stare at him. He regards me intently and I think he's listening

'Seeing you with Leila . . .' I close my eyes as the painful memory of his interaction with his ex-sub gnaws at me anew. 'It was such a shock. I had a glimpse into how your life has been . . . and . . .' I gaze down at my knotted fingers, tears still trickling down my cheeks. 'This is about me not being good enough for you. It was an insight into your life, and I am so scared you'll get bored with me, and then you'll go . . . and I'll end up like Leila . . . a shadow. Because I love you, Christian, and if you leave me, it will be like a world without light. I'll be in darkness. I don't want to run. I'm just so frightened you'll leave me . . .'

I realize as I say these words to him—in the hope that he's listening—what my real problem is. I just don't get why he likes me. I have *never* understood why he likes me.

'I don't understand why you find me attractive,' I murmur. 'You're, well, you're you . . . and I'm . . .' I shrug and gaze up at him. 'I just don't see it. You're beautiful and sexy and successful and good and kind and caring—all those things—and I'm not. And I can't do the things you like to do. I can't give you what you need. How could you be happy with me? How can I possibly hold you?' My voice is a whisper as I express my darkest fears. 'I have never understood what you see in me. And seeing you with her, it brought all that home.' I sniff and wipe my nose with the back of my hand, gazing at his impassive expression.

Oh, he's so exasperating. *Talk to me, damn it!*

'Are you going to kneel here all night? Because I'll do it, too,' I snap at him.

I think his expression softens—maybe he looks vaguely amused. But it's so hard to tell.

I could reach across and touch him, but this would be a gross abuse of the position he's put me in. I don't want that, but I don't know what he wants, or what he's trying to say to me. I just don't understand.

'Christian, please, please . . . talk to me,' I beseech him, wringing my hands in my lap. I am uncomfortable on my knees, but I continue to kneel, staring into his serious, beautiful, gray eyes, and I wait.

And wait.

And wait.

'Please,' I beg once more.

His intense gaze darkens suddenly and he blinks.

'I was so scared,' he whispers.

Oh, thank the Lord! My subconscious staggers back into her armchair, sagging with relief, and takes a large swig of gin.

He's talking! Gratitude overwhelms me, and I swallow, trying to contain my emotion and the fresh bout of tears that threatens.

His voice is soft and low. 'When I saw Ethan arrive outside, I knew someone had let you into your apartment. Both Taylor and I leapt out of the car. We knew, and to see her there like that with you—and armed. I think I died a thousand deaths, Ana. Someone threatening you . . . all my worst fears realized. I was so angry, with her, with you, with Taylor, with myself.'

He shakes his head revealing his agony. 'I didn't know how volatile she would be. I didn't know what to do. I didn't know how she'd react.' He stops and frowns. 'And then she gave me a clue; she looked so contrite. And I just knew what I had to do.' He pauses, gazing at me, trying to gauge my reaction.

'Go on,' I whisper.

He swallows. 'Seeing her in that state, knowing that I might have something to do with her mental breakdown . . .' He closes his eyes once more. 'She was always so mischievous and lively.' He shudders and takes a rasping breath, almost like a sob. This is torture to listen to, but I kneel, attentive, lapping up this insight.

'She might have harmed you. And it would have been my fault.' His eyes drift off, filled with uncomprehending horror, and he's silent once more.

383

'But she didn't,' I whisper. 'And you weren't responsible for her being in that state, Christian.' I blink up at him, encouraging him to continue.

Then it dawns on me that everything he did was to keep me safe, and perhaps Leila, too, because he also cares for her. But how much does he care for her? The question lingers in my head, unwelcome. He says he loves me, but then he was so harsh, throwing me out of my own apartment.

'I just wanted you gone,' he murmurs, with his uncanny ability to read my thoughts. 'I wanted you away from the danger, and . . . You. Just. Wouldn't. Go,' he hisses through clenched teeth and shakes his head. His exasperation is palpable.

He gazes at me intently. 'Anastasia Steele, you are the most stubborn woman I know.' He closes his eyes and shakes his head once more in disbelief.

Oh, he's back. I breathe a long, cleansing sigh of relief.

He opens his eyes again, and his expression is forlorn—sincere. 'You weren't going to run?' he asks.

'No!'

He closes his eyes again and his whole body relaxes. When he opens his eyes, I can see his pain and anguish.

'I thought—' He stops. 'This is me, Ana. All of me . . . and I'm all yours. What do I have to do to make you realize that? To make you see that I want you any way I can get you. That I love you.'

'I love you, too, Christian, and to see you like this is . . .' I choke and my tears start anew. 'I thought I'd broken you.'

'Broken? Me? Oh no, Ana. Just the opposite.' He reaches out and takes my hand. 'You're my lifeline,' he whispers, and he kisses my knuckles before pressing my palm against his.

With his eyes wide and full of fear, he gently tugs my hand and places it on his chest over his heart—in the forbidden zone. His breathing quickens. His heart is beating a frantic, pounding tattoo beneath my fingers. He doesn't take his eyes off mine; his jaw is tense, his teeth clenched.

I gasp. *Oh, my Fifty!* He's letting me touch him. And it's like all the air in my lungs has vaporized—gone. The blood is pounding in my ears as the rhythm of my heart rises to match his.

He releases my hand, leaving it in place over his heart. I flex my fingers slightly, feeling the warmth of his skin beneath the thin fabric of his shirt. He's holding his breath. I can't bear it. I make to move my hand.

'No,' he says quickly and places his hand once more over mine, pressing my fingers against him. 'Don't.'

Emboldened by these two words, I shuffle closer so our knees are touching and tentatively raise my other hand so that he knows exactly what I intend to do. His eyes grow wider but he doesn't stop me.

Gently I start to undo the buttons on his shirt. It's tricky with one hand. I flex my fingers beneath his hand and he lets go, allowing me to use both hands to undo his shirt. My eyes don't leave his as I pull his shirt wide open, revealing his chest.

He swallows, and his lips part as his breathing increases, and I sense his rising panic, but he doesn't pull away. Is he still in sub mode? I have no idea.

Should I do this? I don't want to hurt him, physically or mentally. The sight of him like this, offering himself to me, has been a wake-up call.

I reach up, and my hand hovers over his chest, and I stare at him . . . asking his permission. Very subtly he tilts his head to one side, steeling himself in anticipation of my touch, and the tension radiates from him, but this time it's not in anger—it's in fear.

I hesitate. Can I really do this to him?

'Yes,' he breathes—again with the weird ability to answer my unspoken questions.

I extend my fingertips into his chest hair and lightly brush them down his sternum. He closes his eyes, and his face creases as if he's experiencing intolerable pain. It's unbearable to witness, so I lift my fingers immediately, but he quickly grabs my hand and replaces it firmly, flat on his bare chest so that the hair tickles my palm.

'No,' he says, his voice strained. 'I need to.'

His eyes are screwed up so tightly. This must be agony. It's truly tormenting to watch. Carefully I let my fingers stroke across his chest to his heart, marveling at the feel of him, terrified that this is a step too far.

He opens his eyes, and they are gray fire, blazing at me.

Holy cow. His look is blistering, feral, beyond intense, and his breathing is rapid. It stirs my blood. I squirm under his gaze.

He hasn't stopped me, so I run my fingertips across his chest again, and his mouth goes slack. He's panting, and I don't know if it's from fear, or something else.

I've wanted to kiss him there for so long that I lean up on my knees and hold his gaze for a moment, making my intention perfectly clear. Then

I bend and gently plant a soft kiss above his heart, feeling his warm, sweet-smelling skin beneath my lips.

His strangled groan moves me so much that I sit back on my heels, fearful of what I'll see on his face. His eyes are screwed tightly shut, but he hasn't moved.

'Again,' he whispers, and I lean into his chest once more, this time to kiss one of his scars. He gasps, and I kiss another and another. He groans loudly, and suddenly his arms are around me, and his hand is in my hair, pulling my head up painfully so that my lips meet his insistent mouth. And we're kissing, my fingers knotting into his hair.

'Oh, Ana,' he breathes, and he twists and pulls me down on to the floor so that I am underneath him. I bring my hands up to cup his beautiful face, and in that moment, I feel his tears.

He's crying . . . no. No!

'Christian, please don't cry. I meant it when I said I'd never leave you. I did. If I gave you any other impression, I'm so sorry . . . please, please forgive me. I love you. I will always love you.'

He looms over me, gazing down into my face, and his expression is so pained.

'What is it?'

His eyes grow larger.

'What is this secret that makes you think I'll run for the hills? That makes you so determined to believe I'll go?' I plead, my voice tremulous. 'Tell me, Christian, *please* . . . '

He sits up, though this time he crosses his legs and I follow suit, my legs outstretched. Vaguely I wonder if we can get off the floor. But I don't want to interrupt his train of thought. He's finally going to confide in me.

He gazes down at me, and he looks utterly desolate. *Oh, shit—it's bad.*

'Ana . . .' He pauses, searching for the words, his expression pained . . . Where the hell is this going?

He takes a deep breath and swallows. 'I'm a sadist, Ana. I like to whip little brown-haired girls like you because you all look like the crack whore—my birth mother. I'm sure you can guess why.' He says it in a rush as if he's had the sentence in his head for days and days and is desperate to be rid of it.

My world stops. *Oh no.*

This is not what I expected. This is bad. Really bad. I gaze at him, trying to understand the implication of what he's just said. It does explain why we all look the same.

My immediate thought is that Leila was right— *'Master is dark.'*

I recall the first conversation I had with him about his tendencies when we were in the Red Room of Pain.

'You said you weren't a sadist,' I whisper, desperately trying to understand . . . make some excuse for him.

'No, I said I was a Dominant. If I lied to you, it was a lie of omission. I'm sorry.' He looks briefly down at his manicured fingernails.

I think he's mortified. Mortified about lying to me? Or about what he is?

'When you asked me that question, I had envisioned a very different relationship between us,' he murmurs. I can tell by his gaze that he's terrified.

Then it hits me like a wrecking ball. If he's a

388

sadist, he really needs all that whipping and caning shit. Oh, fuck. I put my head in my hands.

'So it's true,' I whisper, glancing up at him. 'I can't give you what you need.' This is it—this really does mean we are incompatible.

The world starts falling away at my feet, collapsing around me as panic grips my throat. This is it. We can't do this.

He frowns. 'No no no. Ana. No. You can. You *do* give me what I need.' He clenches his fists. 'Please believe me,' he murmurs, his words an impassioned plea.

'I don't know what to believe, Christian. This is so fucked-up,' I whisper, my throat hoarse and aching as it closes in, choking me with unshed tears.

His eyes are wide and luminous when he looks at me again.

'Ana, believe me. After I punished you and you left me, my worldview changed. I wasn't joking when I said I would avoid ever feeling like that again.' He gazes at me with pained entreaty. 'When you said you loved me, it was a revelation. No one's ever said it to me before, and it was as if I'd laid something to rest—or maybe you'd laid it to rest, I don't know. Dr. Flynn and I are still in deep discussion about it.'

Oh. Hope flares briefly in my heart. Perhaps we'll be okay. I want us to be okay. *Don't I?* 'What does that all mean?' I whisper.

'It means I don't need it. Not now.'

What? 'How do you know? How can you be so sure?'

'I just know. The thought of hurting you . . . in any real way . . . it's abhorrent to me.'

'I don't understand. What about rulers and

389

spanking and all that kinky fuckery?'

He runs a hand through his hair and almost smiles but instead sighs ruefully. 'I'm talking about the heavy shit, Anastasia. You should see what I can do with a cane or a cat.'

My mouth drops open, stunned. 'I'd rather not.'

'I know. If you wanted to do that, then fine . . . but you don't and I get it. I can't do all that shit with you if you don't want to. I told you once before, you have all the power. And now, since you came back, I don't feel that compulsion at all.'

I gape at him for a moment trying to take this all in. 'When we met, that's what you wanted, though?'

'Yes, undoubtedly.'

'How can your compulsion just go, Christian? Like I'm some kind of panacea, and you're—for want of a better word—cured? I don't get it.'

He sighs once more. 'I wouldn't say "cured" . . . You don't believe me?'

'I just find it—unbelievable. Which is different.'

'If you'd never left me, then I probably wouldn't feel this way. Your walking out on me was the best thing you ever did . . . for us. It made me realize how much I want you, just you, and I mean it when I say I'll take you any way I can have you.'

I gaze at him. Can I believe this? My head hurts just trying to think this all through, and deep down I feel . . . numb.

'You're still here. I thought you would be out of the door by now,' he whispers.

'Why? Because I might think you're a sicko for whipping and fucking women who look like your mother? Whatever would give you that impression?' I hiss, lashing out.

He blanches at my harsh words.

390

'Well, I wouldn't have put it quite like that, but yes,' he says, his eyes wide and hurt.

His expression is sobering and I regret my outburst. I frown, feeling a pang of guilt.

Oh, what am I going to do? I gaze at him and he looks contrite, sincere . . . he looks like my Fifty.

And unbidden, I recall the photograph in his childhood bedroom, and in that moment realize why the woman in it looked so familiar. She looked like him. She must have been his biological mother.

His easy dismissal of her comes to mind: *No one of consequence* . . . She's responsible for all this . . . and I look like her . . . *Fuck!*

He stares at me, eyes raw, and I know he's waiting for my next move. He seems genuine. He's said he loves me, but I'm really confused.

This is all so fucked-up. He's reassured me about Leila, but now I know with more certainty than ever how she was able to give him his kicks. The thought is wearying and unpalatable.

'Christian, I'm exhausted. Can we discuss this tomorrow? I want to go to bed.'

He blinks at me in surprise. 'You're not going?'

'Do you want me to go?'

'No! I thought you would leave once you knew.'

All the times he's alluded to my leaving once I knew his darkest secrets flash through my mind . . . and now I know. Shit. Master *is* dark.

Should I leave? I gaze at him, this crazy man that I love—yes, love.

Can I leave him? I left him once before, and it nearly broke me . . . and him. I love him. I know that in spite of this revelation.

'Don't leave me,' he whispers.

'Oh, for crying out loud—*no*! I am not going to

go!' I shout, and it's cathartic. There, I've said it. I am not leaving.

'Really?' His eyes widen.

'What can I do to make you understand I will not run? What can I say?'

He gazes at me, revealing his fear and anguish again. He swallows. 'There is one thing you can do.'

'What?' I snap.

'Marry me,' he whispers.

What? Did he really just—

For the second time in less than half an hour my world stops.

Holy fuck. I stare at the deeply damaged man I love. I can't believe what he's just said.

Marriage? He's proposing marriage? Is he kidding? I can't help it—a small, nervous, disbelieving giggle erupts from deep inside. I bite my lip to stop it from turning into full-scale hysterical laughter and fail miserably. I lie back flat on the floor and surrender myself to the laughter, laughing as I've never laughed before, huge healing cathartic howls of laughter.

And for a moment I am on my own, looking down at this absurd situation, a giggling, overwhelmed girl beside a beautiful, disturbed boy. I drape my arm across my eyes, as my laughter turns to scalding tears. *No, no . . . this is too much.*

As the hysteria subsides, Christian gently lifts my arm off my face. I turn and gaze up at him.

He's leaning over me. His mouth is twisted with wry amusement, but his eyes are a burning gray, maybe wounded. *Oh no.*

He gently wipes away a stray tear with the back of his knuckles. 'You find my proposal amusing, Miss Steele?'

Oh, Fifty! Reaching up, I caress his cheek tenderly, enjoying the feel of the stubble beneath my fingers. Lord, I love this man.

'Mr. Grey . . . Christian. Your sense of timing is without doubt . . .' I gaze up at him as words fail me.

He smirks at me, but the crinkling around his eyes shows me that he's hurt. It's sobering.

'You're cutting me to the quick here, Ana. Will you marry me?'

I sit up and lean over him, placing my hands on his knees. I stare into his lovely face. 'Christian, I've met your psycho ex with a gun, been thrown out of my apartment, had you go thermonuclear Fifty on me—'

He opens his mouth to speak, but I hold up my hand. He obediently shuts his mouth.

'You've just revealed some quite frankly shocking information about yourself, and now you've asked me to marry you.'

He moves his head from side to side as if considering the facts. He's amused. Thank heavens.

'Yes, I think that's a fair and accurate summary of the situation,' he says dryly.

I shake my head at him. 'Whatever happened to delayed gratification?'

'I got over it, and I'm now a firm advocate of instant gratification. Carpe diem, Ana,' he whispers.

'Look, Christian, I've known you for about three minutes, and there's so much more I need to know. I've had too much to drink, I'm hungry, I'm tired, and I want to go to bed. I need to consider your proposal just as I considered that contract you gave me. And'—I press my lips together to show my displeasure but also to lighten the mood between us—'that wasn't the most romantic proposal.'

He tilts his head to one side and his lips quirk up in a smile. 'Fair point well made, as ever, Miss Steele,' he breathes, his voice laced with relief. 'So, that's not a no?'

I sigh. 'No, Mr. Grey, it's not a no, but it's not a yes, either. You're only doing this because you're scared, and you don't trust me.'

'No, I'm doing this because I've finally met someone I want to spend the rest of my life with.'

Oh. My heart skips a beat and inside, I melt. How is it that in the middle of the most bizarre situations he can say the most romantic things? My mouth pops open in shock.

'I never thought that would happen to me,' he continues, his expression radiating pure undiluted sincerity.

I gape at him, searching for the right words.

'Can I think about it . . . please? And think about everything else that's happened today? What you've just told me? You asked for patience and faith. Well, back at you, Grey. I need those now.'

His eyes search mine and after a beat, he leans forward and tucks my hair behind my ear.

'I can live with that.' He kisses me quickly on the lips. 'Not very romantic, eh?' He raises his eyebrows, and I give him an admonishing shake of my head. 'Hearts and flowers?' he asks softly.

I nod and he gives me a slight smile.

'You're hungry?'

'Yes.'

'You didn't eat.' His eyes frost and his jaw hardens.

'No, I didn't eat.' I sit back on my heels and

regard him passively. 'Being thrown out of my apartment after witnessing my boyfriend interacting intimately with his ex-submissive considerably suppressed my appetite.' I glare at him and fist my hands on my hips.

Christian shakes his head and rises gracefully to his feet. *Oh, finally we can get off the floor.* He holds his hand out to me.

'Let me fix you something to eat,' he says.

'Can't I just go to bed?' I mutter wearily as I place my hand in his.

He pulls me up. I am stiff. He gazes down at me, his expression soft.

'No, you need to eat. Come.' Bossy Christian is back, and it's a relief.

He leads me to the kitchen area and ushers me toward a barstool as he heads to the fridge. I glance at my watch and it's nearly eleven thirty and I have to get up for work in the morning.

'Christian, I'm really not hungry.'

He studiously ignores me as he ferrets through the enormous fridge. 'Cheese?' he asks.

'Not at this hour.'

'Pretzels?'

'In the fridge? No,' I snap.

He turns and grins at me. 'You don't like pretzels?'

'Not at eleven thirty. Christian, I'm going to bed. You can rummage around in your refrigerator for the rest of the night if you want. I'm tired, and I've had far too interesting a day. A day I'd like to forget.' I slide off the stool and he scowls at me, but right now I don't care. I want to go to bed—I'm exhausted.

'Macaroni and cheese?' He holds up a white

bowl lidded with foil. He looks so hopeful and endearing.

'You like macaroni and cheese?' I ask.

He nods enthusiastically, and my heart melts. He looks so young all of a sudden. Who would have thought? Christian Grey likes nursery food.

'You want some?' he asks, sounding hopeful. I can't resist him, and I'm hungry.

I nod and give him a weak smile. His answering grin is breathtaking. He takes the foil off the bowl and pops it into the microwave. I perch back on the stool and watch the beauty that is Mr. Christian Grey—the man who wants to marry me—move gracefully and with ease around his kitchen.

'So you know how to use the microwave, then?' I tease softly.

'If it's in a packet, I can usually do something with it. It's real food I have a problem with.'

I cannot believe this is the same man who was on his knees in front of me not half an hour before. He's his usual mercurial self. He sets out plates, cutlery, and place mats on the breakfast bar.

'It's very late,' I mutter.

'Don't go to work tomorrow.'

'I have to go to work tomorrow. My boss is leaving for New York.'

Christian frowns. 'Do you want to go there this weekend?'

'I checked the weather forecast, and it looks like rain,' I say, shaking my head.

'Oh, so what do you want to do?'

The microwave's *ping* announces that our supper is warmed through.

'I just want to get through one day at a time right now. All this excitement is . . . tiring.' I raise an eyebrow at him, which he judiciously ignores.

Christian places the white bowl in between our place settings and takes his seat beside me. He looks deep in thought, distracted. I dish the macaroni onto our plates. It smells divine, and my mouth waters in anticipation. I am famished.

'Sorry about Leila,' he murmurs.

'Why are you sorry?' Mmm, the macaroni tastes as good as it smells. My stomach grumbles gratefully.

'It must have been a terrible shock for you, finding her in your apartment. Taylor swept through it earlier himself. He's very upset.'

'I don't blame Taylor.'

'Neither do I. He's been out looking for you.'

'Really? Why?'

'I didn't know where you were. You left your purse, your phone. I couldn't even track you. Where did you go?' he asks. His voice is soft, but there's an ominous undercurrent to his words.

'Ethan and I just went to a bar across the street. So I could watch what was happening.'

'I see.' The atmosphere between us has changed subtly. It's no longer light.

Okay, well . . . two can play that game. Let's just bring this back to you, Fifty. Trying to sound nonchalant, wanting to assuage my burning curiosity but dreading the answer, I ask, 'So, what did you do with Leila in the apartment?'

I glance up at him, and he freezes with his forkful of macaroni suspended in midair. *Oh no, that's not good.*

'You really want to know?'

A knot tightens in my gut and my appetite vanishes. 'Yes,' I whisper. *Do you? Do you really?*

My subconscious has thrown her empty bottle of gin on the floor and is sitting up in her armchair, glaring at me in horror.

Christian's mouth flattens into a line, and he hesitates. 'We talked, and I gave her a bath.' His voice is hoarse, and he continues quickly when I make no response. 'And I dressed her in some of your clothes. I hope you don't mind. But she was filthy.'

Holy fuck. He bathed her?

What an inappropriate thing to do. I'm reeling, staring down at my uneaten macaroni. The sight of it now makes me nauseous.

Try to rationalize this, my subconscious coaches. That cool, intellectual part of my brain knows that he just did that because she was dirty, but it's too hard. My fragile, jealous self can't bear it.

Suddenly I want to cry—not succumb to ladylike tears that trickle decorously down my cheeks, but howling-at-the-moon crying. I take a deep breath to suppress the urge, but my throat is arid and uncomfortable from my unshed tears and sobs.

'It was all I could do, Ana,' he says softly.

'You still have feelings for her?'

'No!' he says, appalled, and closes his eyes, his expression one of anguish. I turn away, staring once more at my sickening food. I can't bear to look at him.

'To see her like that—so different, so broken. I care about her, one human being to another.' He shrugs as if to shake off an unpleasant memory. Jeez, is he expecting my sympathy?

'Ana, look at me.'

I can't. I know that if I do, I will burst into tears. This is just too much to absorb. I'm like an overflowing tank of gasoline—full, beyond capacity. There is no room for any more. I simply cannot cope with any more crap. I will combust and explode, and it will be ugly if I try. Jeez!

Christian caring for his ex-sub in such an intimate fashion—the image flashes through my brain. Bathing her, for fuck's sake—naked. A harsh, painful shudder wracks my body.

'Ana.'

'What?'

'Don't. It doesn't mean anything. It was like caring for a child, a broken, shattered child,' he mutters.

What the hell would he know about caring for a child? This was a woman he had a very full-on, deviant sexual relationship with.

Oh, this hurts. I take a deep, steadying breath. Or perhaps he's referring to himself. He's the broken child. That makes more sense . . . or maybe it makes no sense at all. Oh, this is so fucked-up, and suddenly I'm bone-crushingly tired. I need sleep.

'Ana?'

I stand, take my plate to the sink, and scrape the contents into the trash.

'Ana, please.'

I whirl around and face him. 'Just stop, Christian! Just stop with the "Ana, please"!' I shout at him, and my tears start to trickle down my face. 'I've had enough of all this shit today. I am going to bed. I am tired and emotional. Now let me be.'

I turn on my heel and practically run to the bedroom, taking with me the memory of his wide-eyed, shocked stare. Nice to know I can shock him, too. I strip out of my clothes in double-quick time, and after rifling through his chest of drawers, drag on one of his T-shirts and head for the bathroom.

I gaze at myself in the mirror, hardly recognizing the gaunt, pink-eyed, blotchy-cheeked harridan staring back at me, and it's too much. I sink to the floor and surrender to the overwhelming emotion I can no longer contain, sobbing huge chest-wrenching sobs, finally letting my tears flow unrestrained.

CHAPTER FIFTEEN

'Hey,' Christian's says gently as he pulls me into his arms, 'please don't cry, Ana, please,' he begs. He's on the bathroom floor, and I am in his lap. I put my arms around him and weep into his neck. Cooing softly into my hair, he gently strokes my back, my head.

'I'm sorry, baby,' he whispers, and that makes me cry harder and hug him tighter.

We sit like this forever. Eventually, when I'm all cried out, Christian staggers to his feet, holding me, and carries me into his room where he lays me down in the bed. In a few seconds he's beside me and the lights are off. He pulls me into his arms, hugging me tightly, and I finally drift off into a dark and troubled sleep.

*   *   *

I awake with a jolt. My head is fuzzy and I'm too warm. Christian is wrapped around me like a vine. He grumbles in his sleep as I slip out of his arms, but he doesn't wake. Sitting up, I glance at the alarm clock. It's three in the morning. I need an Advil and a drink. I swing my legs out of bed and make my way to the kitchen in the great room.

In the fridge I find a carton of orange juice and pour myself a glass. Mmm . . . it's delicious, and my fuzzy head eases immediately. I hunt through the cupboards looking for some painkillers and eventually come across a plastic box full of meds. I sink two Advil and pour myself another orange juice.

Wandering to the great wall of glass, I look out on a sleeping Seattle. The lights twinkle and wink beneath Christian's castle in the sky, or should I say fortress? I press my forehead against the cool window—it's a relief. I have so much to think about after all the revelations of yesterday. I place my back against the glass and slide down onto the floor. The great room is cavernous in the dark, the only light coming from the three lamps above the kitchen island.

Could I live here, married to Christian? After all that he's done here? All the history this place holds for him?

Marriage. It's almost unbelievable and completely unexpected. But then, everything about Christian is unexpected. My lips smirk with irony of this reality. Christian Grey, expect the unexpected—fifty shades of fucked-up.

My smile fades. I look like his mother. This wounds me deeply, and the air leaves my lungs in a rush. We all look like his mom.

How the hell do I move on from the disclosure of that little secret? No wonder he didn't want to tell me. But certainly he can't remember much of his mother. I wonder once more if I should talk to

401

Dr. Flynn. Would Christian let me? Perhaps he could fill in the gaps.

I shake my head. I feel world-weary, but I'm enjoying the calm serenity of the great room and its beautiful works of art—cold and austere, but in their own way, still beautiful in the shadows and surely worth a fortune. Could I live here? For better, for worse? In sickness and in health? I close my eyes, lean my head back against the glass, and take a deep, cleansing breath.

The peaceful tranquility is shattered by a visceral, primeval cry that makes every single hair on my body stand to attention. *Christian! Holy fuck—what's happened?* I am on my feet, running back to the bedroom before the echoes of that horrible sound have died away, my heart thumping with fear.

I flip one of the light switches, and Christian's bedside light comes to life. He's tossing and turning, writhing in agony. *No!* He cries out again, and the eerie, devastating sound lances through me anew.

Shit—a nightmare!

'Christian!' I lean over him, grab his shoulders, and shake him awake. He opens his eyes, and they are wild and vacant, scanning quickly around the empty room before coming back to rest on me.

'You left, you left, you must have left,' he mumbles—his wide-eyed stare becoming accusatory—and he looks so lost, it wrenches at my heart. Poor Fifty.

'I'm here.' I sit down on the bed beside him. 'I'm here,' I murmur softly in an effort to reassure him. I reach out to place my palm on the side of his face, trying to soothe him.

'You were gone,' he whispers rapidly. His eyes are still wild and frightened, but he seems to be calming.

'I went to get a drink. I was thirsty.'

He closes his eyes and rubs his face. When he opens them again, he looks so desolate.

'You're here. Oh, thank God.' He reaches for me, and grabbing me tightly, he pulls me down on the bed beside him.

'I just went for a drink,' I murmur.

Oh, the intensity of his fear . . . I can feel it. His T-shirt is drenched in sweat, and his heart is pounding as he hugs me close. He's gazing at me as if reassuring himself that I am really here. I gently stroke his hair and then his cheek.

'Christian, please. I'm here. I'm not going anywhere,' I say soothingly.

'Oh, Ana,' he breathes. He grasps my chin to hold me in place, and then his mouth is on mine. Desire sweeps through him, and unbidden my body responds—it's so tied and attuned to him. His lips are at my ear, my throat, then back at my mouth, his teeth gently pulling at my lower lip, his hand traveling up my body from my hip to my breast, dragging my T-shirt up. Caressing me, feeling his way through the dips and shallows of my skin, he elicits the same familiar reaction, his touch sending shivers through me. I moan as his hand cups my breast and his fingers tighten over my nipple.

'I want you,' he murmurs.

'I'm here for you. Only you, Christian.'

He groans and kisses me once more, passionately, with a fervor and desperation I've not felt from him before. Grabbing the hem of his T-shirt, I tug and he helps me pull it off over his

403

head. Kneeling between my legs, he hastily pulls me upright and drags my T-shirt off.

His eyes are serious, wanting, full of dark secrets—exposed. He cups his hands around my face and kisses me, and we sink down into the bed once more, his thigh between both of mine so that he's half lying on top of me. His erection is rigid against my hip through his boxer briefs. He wants me, but his words from earlier choose this moment to come back and haunt me, what he said about his mother. And it's like a bucket of cold water on my libido. Fuck. I can't do this. Not now.

'Christian . . . Stop. I can't do this,' I whisper urgently against his mouth, my hands pushing on his upper arms.

'What? What's wrong?' he murmurs and starts kissing my neck, running the tip of his tongue lightly down my throat. *Oh . . .*

'No, please. I can't do this, not now. I need some time, please.'

'Oh, Ana, don't overthink this,' he whispers as he nips my earlobe.

'Ah!' I gasp, feeling it in my groin, and my body bows, betraying me. This is so confusing.

'I am just the same, Ana. I love you and I need you. Touch me. Please.' He rubs his nose against mine, and his quiet heartfelt plea moves me and I melt.

Touch him. Touch him while we make love. Oh my.

He rears up over me, gazing down, and in the half-light from the dimmed bedside light, I can tell that he's waiting for my decision, and he's caught in my spell.

I reach up and tentatively place my hand on the

soft patch of hair over his sternum. He gasps and scrunches his eyes closed as if in pain, but I don't take my hand away this time. I move it up to his shoulders, feeling the tremor run through him. He groans, and I pull him down to me and place both my hands on his back, where I've never touched him before, on his shoulder blades, holding him to me. His strangled moan arouses me like nothing else.

He buries his head in my neck, kissing and sucking and biting me, before trailing his nose up my chin and kissing me, his tongue possessing my mouth, his hands moving over my body once more. His lips move down . . . down . . . down to my breasts, worshipping as they go, and my hands stay on his shoulders and his back, enjoying the flex and ripple of his finely honed muscles, his skin still damp from his nightmare. His lips close over my nipple, pulling and tugging, so that it rises to greet his glorious skilled mouth.

I groan and run my fingernails across his back. And he gasps, a strangled moan.

'Oh, fuck, Ana,' he chokes, and it's a half cry, half groan. It tears at my heart, but also deep inside me, tightening all the muscles below my waist. Oh, what I can do to him! I'm panting now, matching his tortured breaths with my own.

His hand travels south, over my belly, down to my sex—and his fingers are on me, then in me. I groan as he moves his fingers around inside me, in that way, and I push my pelvis up to welcome his touch.

'Ana,' he breathes. He suddenly releases me and sits up; he removes his boxer briefs and leans over to the bedside table to grab a foil packet. His eyes are a blazing gray as he passes me the condom. 'You want to do this? You can still say no. You can always say no,' he murmurs.

'Don't give me a chance to think, Christian. I want you, too.' I rip the packet open with my teeth as he kneels between my legs, and with trembling fingers I slide it onto him.

'Steady,' he says. 'You are going to unman me, Ana.'

I marvel at what I can do to this man with my touch. He stretches out over me, and for now my doubts are pushed down and locked away in the dark, scary depths at the back of my mind. I'm intoxicated with this man, my man, my Fifty Shades. He shifts suddenly, completely taking me by surprise, so I am on top. *Whoa.*

'You—take me,' he murmurs, his eyes glowing with a feral intensity.

Oh my. Slowly, oh so slowly, I sink down onto him. He tilts his head back and closes his eyes as he groans. I grab his hands and start to move, reveling in the fullness of my possession, reveling in his reaction, watching him unravel beneath me. I feel like a goddess. I lean down and kiss his chin, running my teeth along his stubbled jaw. He tastes delicious. He clasps my hips and steadies my rhythm, slow and easy.

'Ana, touch me . . . please.'

Oh. I lean forward and steady myself with my hands on his chest. And he calls out, his cry almost a sob, and he thrusts deep inside me.

'Ahh,' I whimper and run my fingernails gently over his chest, through the hair there, and he groans loudly and twists abruptly so I am once more beneath him.

'Enough.' He moans. 'No more, please.' And it's a heartfelt plea.

Reaching up, I clasp his face in my hands, feeling the dampness on his cheeks, and pull him down to my lips so that I can kiss him. I curl my hands around his back.

He groans deep and low in his throat as he moves inside me, pushing me onward and upward, but I can't find my release. My head is too cloudy with issues. I am too wrapped up in him.

'Let go, Ana,' he urges me.

'No.'

'Yes,' he snarls. He shifts slightly and gyrates his hips, again and again.

Jeez . . . argh!

'Come on baby, I need this. Give it to me.'

And I explode, my body a slave to his, and wrap myself around him, clinging to him like a vine as he cries out my name, and climaxes with me, then collapses, his full weight pressing me into the mattress.

*   *   *

I cradle Christian in my arms, his head on my chest, as we lie in the afterglow of our lovemaking. I run my fingers through his hair as I listen to his breathing return to normal.

'Don't ever leave me,' he whispers, and I roll my eyes in the full knowledge that he can't see me.

'I know you're rolling your eyes at me,' he murmurs, and I hear the trace of humor in his voice.

'You know me well,' I murmur.

'I'd like to know you better.'

'Back at you, Grey. What was your nightmare about?'

'The usual.'

'Tell me.'

He swallows and tenses before he issues a drawn-out sigh. 'I must be about three, and the crack whore's pimp is mad as hell again. He smokes and smokes, one cigarette after another, and he can't find an ashtray.' He stops, and I freeze as a creeping chill grips my heart.

'It hurt,' he says, 'It's the pain I remember. That's what gives me nightmares. That, and the fact that she did nothing to stop him.'

Oh no. This is unbearable. I tighten my grip around him, my legs and arms holding him to me, and I try not to let my despair choke me. How could anyone treat a child like that? He raises his head and pins me with his intense gray gaze.

'You're not like her. Don't ever think that. Please.'

I blink back at him. It's very reassuring to hear. He puts his head on my chest again, and I think he's finished, but he surprises me by continuing.

'Sometimes in the dreams she's just lying on the floor. And I think she's asleep. But she doesn't move. She never moves. And I'm hungry. Really hungry.'

Oh, fuck.

'There's a loud noise and he's back, and he hits me so hard, cursing the crack whore. His first reaction was always to use his fists or his belt.'

'Is that why you don't like to be touched?'

He closes his eyes and hugs me tighter. 'That's complicated,' he murmurs. He nuzzles me between my breasts, inhaling deeply, trying to distract me.

408

'Tell me,' I prompt.

He sighs. 'She didn't love me. I didn't love me. The only touch I knew was . . . harsh. It stemmed from there. Flynn explains it better than I can.'

'Can I see Flynn?'

He raises his head to look at me. 'Fifty Shades rubbing off on you?'

'And then some. I like how it's rubbing off right now.' I wriggle provocatively underneath him and he smiles.

'Yes, Miss Steele, I like that, too.' He leans up and kisses me. He gazes at me for a moment.

'You are so precious to me, Ana. I was serious about marrying you. We can get to know each other then. I can look after you. You can look after me. We can have kids if you want. I will lay my world at your feet, Anastasia. I want you, body and soul, forever. Please think about it.'

'I will think about it, Christian. I will,' I reassure him, reeling once more. *Kids? Jeez.* 'I'd really like to talk to Dr. Flynn, though, if you don't mind.'

'Anything for you, baby. Anything. When would you like to see him?'

'Sooner rather than later.'

'Okay. I'll make the arrangements in the morning.' He glances at the clock. 'It's late. We should sleep.' He shifts to switch off his bedside light and pulls me against him.

I glance at the alarm clock. Crap, it's three forty-five.

He curls his arms around me, his front to my back, and nuzzles my neck. 'I love you, Ana Steele, and I want you by my side, always,' he murmurs as he kisses my neck. 'Now go to sleep.'

I close my eyes.

Reluctantly, I open my heavy eyelids and bright light fills the room. I groan. I feel cloudy, disconnected from my leaden limbs, and Christian is wrapped around me like ivy. As usual, I'm too warm. It can't be later than five in the morning; the alarm has not gone off yet. I stretch out to free myself from his heat, turning in his arms, and he mumbles something unintelligible in his sleep. I glance at the clock. Eight forty-five.

Shit, I'm going to be late. *Fuck.* I scramble out of bed and dash to the bathroom. I am showered and out within four minutes.

Christian sits up in bed watching me with ill-concealed amusement coupled with wariness as I continue to dry myself while gathering my clothes. Perhaps he's waiting for me to react to yesterday's revelations. Right now, I just don't have time.

I check my clothes—black slacks, black shirt—all a bit Mrs. R, but I don't have a second to change my mind. I hastily don black bra and panties, conscious that he's watching my every move. It's . . . unnerving. The panties and bra will do.

'You look good,' Christian purrs from the bed. 'You can call in sick, you know.' He gives me his devastating, lopsided, 150 percent panty-busting smile. Oh, he's so tempting. My inner goddess pouts provocatively at me.

'No, Christian, I can't. I am not a megalomaniac CEO with a beautiful smile who can come and go as he pleases.'

'I like to come as I please.' He smirks and cranks his glorious smile up another notch so it's in full

410

HD IMAX.

'Christian!' I scold. I throw my towel at him and he laughs.

'Beautiful smile, huh?'

'Yes. You know the effect you have on me.' I put on my watch.

'Do I?' he blinks innocently.

'Yes, you do. The same effect you have on all women. Gets really tiresome, watching them all swoon.'

'Does it?' He cocks his eyebrow at me, more amused.

'Don't play the innocent, Mr. Grey, it really doesn't suit you,' I mutter distractedly as I scoop my hair into a ponytail and pull on my black high-heeled shoes. There, that will do.

When I bend to kiss him good-bye, he grabs me and pulls me down onto the bed, leaning over me and smiling from ear to ear. *Oh my.* He's so beautiful—eyes bright with mischief, floppy just-fucked-again hair, that dazzling smile. Now he's playful.

I'm tired, still reeling from all the disclosures of yesterday, while he's bright as a button and sexy as fuck. Oh, exasperating Fifty.

'What can I do to tempt you to stay?' he says softly, and my heart skips a beat and begins to pound. He is temptation personified.

'You can't,' I grumble, struggling to sit back up. 'Let me go.'

He pouts and I give up. Grinning, I trace my fingers over his sculptured lips—my Fifty Shades. I love him so in all his monumental, fuckedupness. I haven't even begun to process yesterday's events and how I feel about them.

411

I lean up to kiss him, thankful that I have brushed my teeth. He kisses me long and hard and then swiftly sets me on my feet, leaving me dazed, breathless, and slightly wobbly.

'Taylor will take you. Quicker than finding somewhere to park. He's waiting outside the building,' Christian says kindly, and he seems relieved. Is he worried about my reaction this morning? Surely last night—er, this morning—proved that I am not going to run.

'Okay. Thank you,' I mutter, disappointed that I am upright on my feet, confused by his hesitancy, and vaguely irritated that once again I won't be driving my Saab. But he's right, of course—it will be quicker with Taylor.

'Enjoy your lazy morning, Mr. Grey. I wish I could stay, but the man who owns the company I work for would not approve of his staff ditching just for hot sex.' I grab my purse.

'Personally, Miss Steele, I have no doubt that he would approve. In fact he might insist on it.'

'Why are you staying in bed? It's not like you.'

He crosses his hands behind his head and grins at me.

'Because I can, Miss Steele.'

I shake my head at him. 'Laters, baby.' I blow him a kiss, and I am out the door.

*   *   *

Taylor is waiting for me, and he seems to understand that I am late because he drives like a bat out of hell to get me to work by nine fifteen. I am grateful when he pulls up at the curb—grateful to be alive–his driving was scary. And grateful that I

412

am not hideously late—only fifteen minutes.

'Thank you, Taylor,' I mutter, ashen-faced. I remember Christian telling me he drove tanks; maybe he drives for NASCAR, too.

'Ana.' He nods a farewell, and I dash into my office, realizing as I open the door to Reception that Taylor seems to have overcome the Miss Steele formality. It makes me smile.

Claire grins at me as I rush through Reception and make my way to my desk.

'Ana!' Jack calls me. 'Get in here.'

Oh, shit.

'What time do you call this?' he snaps.

'I'm sorry. I overslept.' I flush crimson.

'Don't let it happen again. Fix me some coffee, and then I need you to do some letters. Jump to it,' he shouts, making me flinch.

Why is he so mad? What's his problem? What have I done? I hurry to the kitchen to fix his coffee. Maybe I should have ditched. I could be . . . well, doing something hot with Christian, or having breakfast with him, or just talking—that would be novel.

Jack barely acknowledges my presence when I venture back into his office to deliver his coffee. He thrusts a sheet of paper at me—it's handwritten in a barely legible scrawl.

'Type this up, have me sign, then copy and mail it to all our authors.'

'Yes, Jack.'

He doesn't look up as I leave. Boy, is he mad.

It is with some relief that I finally sit down at my desk. I take a sip of tea as I wait for my computer to boot up. I check my e-mails.

From: Christian Grey
Subject: Missing you
Date: June 15 2011 09:05
To: Anastasia Steele

Please use your BlackBerry.

x

Christian Grey
CEO, Grey Enterprises Holdings, Inc.

From: Anastasia Steele
Subject: All Right for Some
Date: June 15 2011 09:27
To: Christian Grey

My boss is mad.

I blame you for keeping me up late with your . . . shenanigans.

You should be ashamed of yourself.

Anastasia Steele
Assistant to Jack Hyde, Editor, SIP

From: Christian Grey
Subject: Shenaniwhatagans?
Date: June 15 2011 09:32
To: Anastasia Steele

You don't have to work, Anastasia.

You have no idea how appalled I am at my shenanigans.

But I like keeping you up late ;)

Please use your BlackBerry.

Oh, and marry me, please.

Christian Grey
CEO, Grey Enterprises Holdings, Inc.

From: Anastasia Steele
Subject: Living to make
Date: June 15 2011 09:35
To: Christian Grey

I know your natural inclination is toward nagging, but just stop.

I need to talk to your shrink.

Only then will I give you my answer.

I am not opposed to living in sin.

Anastasia Steele
Assistant to Jack Hyde, Editor, SIP

From: Christian Grey
Subject: BLACKBERRY
Date: June 15 2011 09:40
To: Anastasia Steele

Anastasia, if you are going to start discussing Dr. Flynn, then USE YOUR BLACKBERRY.

This is not a request.

Christian Grey,
Now Pissed CEO, Grey Enterprises
Holdings, Inc.

Oh shit. Now he's mad at me, too. Well, he can stew for all I care. I take my BlackBerry out of my purse and eye it with skepticism. As I do, it starts ringing. Can't he leave me alone?

'Yes,' I snap.

'Ana, hi—'

'José! How are you?' Oh, it's good to hear his voice.

'I'm fine, Ana. Look, are you still seeing that Grey guy?'

'Er—yes . . . Why?' Where is he going with this?

'Well, he's bought all your photos, and I thought I could deliver them up to Seattle. The exhibition closes Thursday, so I could bring them up Friday evening and drop them off, you know. And maybe we could catch a drink or something. Actually, I was hoping for a place to crash, too.'

'José, that's cool. Yeah, I'm sure we could work something out. Let me talk to Christian and call you back, okay?'

'Cool, I'll wait to hear from you. Bye, Ana.'

'Bye.' And he's gone.

Holy cow. I haven't seen or heard from José since his show. I didn't even ask him how it went or if he sold any more pictures. Some friend I am.

416

So, I could spend the evening with José on Friday. How will Christian like that? I become aware that I am biting my lip till it hurts. Oh, that man has double standards. He can—I shudder at the thought—bathe his batshit ex-lover, but I will probably get a truckload of grief for wanting to have a drink with José. How am I going to handle this?

'Ana!' Jack pulls me abruptly out of my reverie. Is he still mad? 'Where's that letter?'

'Er—coming.' Shit. What is eating him?

I type up his letter in double-quick time, print it out, and nervously make my way into his office.

'Here you go.' I place it on his desk and turn to leave. Jack quickly casts his critical, piercing eyes over it.

'I don't know what you're doing out there, but I pay you to work,' he barks.

'I'm aware of that, Jack,' I mutter apologetically. I feel a slow flush creep up my skin.

'This is full of mistakes,' he snaps. 'Do it again.'

Fuck. He's beginning to sound like someone I know, but rudeness from Christian I can tolerate. Jack is beginning to piss me off.

'And get me another coffee while you're at it.'

'Sorry,' I whisper and scurry out of his office as quickly as I can.

Holy fuck. He's being unbearable. I sit back down at my desk, hastily redo his letter, which had two mistakes in it, and check it thoroughly before printing. Now it's perfect. I fetch him another coffee, letting Claire know with a roll of my eyes that I am in deep doo-doo. Taking a deep breath, I approach his office again.

'Better,' he mumbles reluctantly as he signs the

letter. 'Photocopy it, file the original, and mail out to all authors. Understand?'

'Yes.' I am not an idiot. 'Jack, is there something wrong?'

He glances up, his blue eyes darkening as his gaze runs up and down my body. My blood chills.

'No.' His answer is concise, rude, and dismissive. I stand there like the idiot I professed not to be and then shuffle back out of his office. Perhaps he, too, suffers from a personality disorder. Sheesh, I'm surrounded by them. I make my way to the copy machine—which, of course, is suffering from a paper jam—and when I've fixed it, I find it's out of paper. This is not my day.

When I am finally back at my desk, stuffing envelopes, my BlackBerry buzzes. I can see through the glass wall that Jack is on the phone. I answer—it's Ethan.

'Hi, Ana. How'd it go last night?'

Last night. A quick montage of images flashes through my mind—Christian kneeling, his revelation, his proposal, macaroni and cheese, my weeping, his nightmare, *the sex,* touching him . . .

'Eh . . . fine,' I mutter unconvincingly.

Ethan pauses and decides to collude in my denial. 'Cool. Can I pick up the keys?'

'Sure.'

'I'll be over in about half an hour. Will you have time to grab a coffee?'

'Not today. I was late getting in, and my boss is like an angry bear with a sore head and poison ivy up his ass.'

'Sounds nasty.'

'Nasty and ugly.' I giggle.

Ethan laughs and my mood lifts a little. 'Okay.

See you in thirty.' He hangs up.

I glance up at Jack and he's staring at me. Oh, shit. I studiously ignore him and continue to stuff envelopes.

Half an hour later my phone buzzes. It's Claire. 'He's here again, in Reception. The blond god.'

Ethan is a joy to see after all the angst of yesterday and the bad temper my boss is inflicting on me today, but all too soon, he's saying good-bye.

'Will I see you this evening?'

'I'll probably stay with Christian.' I flush.

'You have got it bad,' Ethan observes good-naturedly.

I shrug. That's not the half of it, and in that moment I realize, I have it more than bad. I have it for life. And amazingly, Christian seems to feel the same. Ethan gives me a swift hug.

'Laters, Ana.'

I return to my desk, wrestling with my realization. Oh, what I would do for a day on my own, to just think all this through.

'Where have you been?' Jack is suddenly looming over me.

'I had some business to attend to in Reception.' He is really getting on my nerves.

'I want my lunch. The usual,' he says abruptly and stomps back into his office.

Why didn't I stay home with Christian? My inner goddess crosses her arms and purses her lips; she wants to know the answer to that one, too. Picking up my purse and my BlackBerry, I head for the door. I check my messages.

From: Christian Grey
Subject: Missing you
Date: June 15 2011 09:06
To: Anastasia Steele

My bed is too big without you.

Looks like I'll have to go to work after all.

Even megalomaniac CEOs need something to do.

x

Christian Grey
Twiddling His Thumbs CEO, Grey Enterprises Holdings, Inc.

And there's another from him, from later this morning.

From: Christian Grey
Subject: Discretion
Date: June 15 2011 09:50
To: Anastasia Steele

Is the better part of valor.

Please use discretion . . . your work e-mails are monitored.

HOW MANY TIMES DO I HAVE TO TELL YOU THIS?

Yes. Shouty capitals as you say. USE YOUR BLACKBERRY.

Dr. Flynn can see us tomorrow evening.

x

Christian Grey,
Still Pissed CEO, Grey Enterprises Holdings,
Inc.

And an even later one . . . Oh no.

From: Christian Grey
Subject: Crickets
Date: June 15 2011 12:15
To: Anastasia Steele

I haven't heard from you.

Please tell me you are okay.

You know how I worry.

I will send Taylor to check!

x

Christian Grey,
Overanxious CEO, Grey Enterprises
Holdings, Inc.

I roll my eyes, and call him. I don't want him to worry.

'Christian Grey's phone, Andrea Parker speaking.'

Oh. I am so disconcerted that it's not Christian who answers that it halts me in the street, and the

421

young man behind me mutters angrily as he swerves to avoid bumping into me. I stand under the green awning of the deli.

'Hello? Can I help you?' Andrea fills the void of awkward silence.

'Sorry . . . Er . . . I was hoping to speak to Christian—'

'Mr. Grey is in a meeting at this time.' She bristles with efficiency. 'Can I take a message?'

'Can you tell him Ana called?'

'Ana? As in Anastasia Steele?'

'Er . . . Yes.' Her question confuses me.

'Hold one second please, Miss Steele.'

I listen attentively as she puts the phone down, but I can't tell what's going on. A few seconds later Christian is on the line. 'Are you okay?'

'Yes, I'm fine.'

He releases his held breath, relieved.

'Christian, why wouldn't I be okay?' I whisper reassuringly.

'You're normally so quick at responding to my e-mails. After what I told you yesterday, I was worried,' he says quietly, and then he's talking to someone in his office.

'No, Andrea. Tell them to wait,' he says sternly. Oh, I know that tone of voice.

I can't hear Andrea's response.

'No. I said wait,' he snaps.

'Christian, you're obviously busy. I only called to let you know that I'm okay, and I mean that—just very busy today. Jack has been cracking the whip. Er . . . I mean . . .' I flush and fall silent.

Christian says nothing for a minute.

'Cracking the whip, eh? Well, there was a time when I would have called him a lucky man.' His voice is full of dry humor. 'Don't let him get on top of you, baby.'

'Christian!' I scold him and I know he's grinning.

'Just watch him, that's all. Look, I'm glad you're okay. What time should I pick you up?'

'I'll e-mail you.'

'From your BlackBerry,' he says sternly.

'Yes, Sir,' I snap back.

'Laters, baby.'

'Bye . . .'

He's still hanging on.

'Hang up,' I scold, smiling.

He sighs heavily down the phone. 'I wish you'd never gone to work this morning.'

'Me, too. But I am busy. Hang up.'

'You hang up.' I hear his smile. Oh, playful Christian. I love playful Christian. Hmm . . . I love Christian, period.

'We've been here before.'

'You're biting your lip.'

Shit, he's right. How does he know?

'You see, you think I don't know you, Anastasia. But I know you better than you think,' he murmurs seductively in that way that makes me weak, and wet.

'Christian, I'll talk to you later. Right now, I really wish I hadn't left this morning, too.'

'I'll wait for your e-mail, Miss Steele.'

'Good day, Mr. Grey.'

Hanging up, I lean against the cold, hard glass of the deli store window. Oh my, even on the phone he owns me. Shaking my head to clear it of all thoughts Grey, I head into the deli, depressed by all thoughts Jack.

He is scowling when I get back.

'Is it okay if I go to lunch now?' I ask tentatively. He gazes up at me and his scowl deepens.

'If you must,' he snaps. 'Forty-five minutes. Make up the time you lost this morning.'

'Jack, can I ask you something?'

'What?'

'You seem kind of out of sorts today. Have I done something to offend you?'

He blinks at me momentarily. 'I don't think I'm in the mood to list your misdemeanors right now. I'm busy.' He continues to stare at his computer screen, effectively dismissing me.

Whoa . . . What have I done?

I turn and leave his office, and for a minute I think I'm going to cry. Why has he taken such a sudden and intense dislike to me? A very unwelcome idea pops into my head, but I ignore it. I don't need his shit right now—I have enough of my own.

I head out of the building to the nearby Starbucks, order a latte, and sit down in the window. Taking my iPod from my purse, I plug my headphones in. I choose a song haphazardly and press 'repeat' so it will play over and over again. I need music to think by.

My mind drifts. Christian the sadist. Christian the submissive. Christian the untouchable. Christian's Oedipal impulses. Christian bathing Leila. I groan and close my eyes while that last image haunts me.

Can I really marry this man? He's so much to take in. He's complex and difficult, but deep down

I know I don't want to leave him despite all his issues. I could never leave him. I love him. It would be like cutting off my right arm.

Right now, I have never felt so alive, so vital. I've encountered all manner of perplexing, profound feelings and new experiences since I met him. It's never a dull moment with Fifty.

Looking back on my life before Christian, it's as if everything was in black and white, like José's pictures. Now my whole world is in rich, bright, saturated color. I am soaring in a beam of dazzling light, Christian's dazzling light. I am still Icarus, flying too close to his sun. I snort to myself. Flying with Christian—who can resist a man who can fly?

Can I give him up? Do I want to give him up? It's as if he's flipped a switch and lit me up from within. It's been an education knowing him. I have discovered more about myself in the last few weeks than ever before. I've learned about my body, my hard limits, my soft limits, my tolerance, my patience, my compassion, and my capacity for love.

And it strikes me like a thunderbolt—that's what he needs from me, what he's entitled to— unconditional love. He never received it from the crack whore—it's what he needs. Can I love him unconditionally? Can I accept him for who he is regardless of his revelations last night?

I know he's damaged, but I don't think he's irredeemable. I sigh, recalling Taylor's words. *'He's a good man, Miss Steele.'*

I've seen the weighty evidence of his goodness— his charity work, his business ethics, his generosity—and yet he doesn't see it in himself. He doesn't feel deserving of any love. Given his history and his predilections, I have an inkling of his self-loathing—that's why he's never let anyone in. *Can I get past this?*

He said once that I couldn't begin to understand the depths of his depravity. Well, he's told me now, and given the first few years of his life, it doesn't surprise me . . . though it was still a shock to hear it out loud. At least he's told me—and he seems happier now that he has. I know everything.

Does it devalue his love for me? No, I don't think so. He's never felt this way before and neither have I. We've both come so far.

Tears prick and pool in my eyes as I recall his final barriers crumbling last night when he let me touch him. And it took Leila and all her craziness to get us to there.

Perhaps I should be grateful. The fact that he bathed her is not quite such a bitter taste on my tongue now. I wonder which clothes he gave her. I hope it wasn't the plum dress. I liked that.

So can I love this man with all his issues unconditionally? Because he deserves nothing less. He still needs to learn boundaries and little things like empathy, and to be less controlling. He says he no longer feels the compulsion to hurt me; perhaps Dr. Flynn will be able to cast some light on that.

Fundamentally, that's what concerns me most— that he needs that and has always found like-minded women who need it, too. I frown. Yes, this is the reassurance I need. I want to be all things to this man, his Alpha and his Omega and everything in between, because he is all things to me.

I hope Flynn will have the answers, and maybe then I can say yes. Christian and I can find our own slice of heaven close to the sun.

I gaze out at bustling, lunchtime Seattle. Mrs.

426

Christian Grey—who would have thought? I glance at my watch. *Shit!* I leap up from my seat and dash to the door—a whole hour of just sitting—where did the time go? Jack is going to go ballistic!

*   *   *

I slink back to my desk. Fortunately he's not in his office. It looks like I've gotten away with it. I gaze intently at my computer screen, unseeing, trying to reassemble my thoughts into work mode.

'Where were you?'

I jump. Jack is standing, arms crossed, behind me.

'I was in the basement, photocopying,' I lie. Jack's lips press into a thin, uncompromising line.

'I'm leaving for my plane at six thirty. I need you to stay until then.'

'Okay.' I smile as sweetly as I can manage.

'I'd like my itinerary for New York printed out and photocopied ten times. And get the brochures packaged up. And get me some coffee!' he snarls and stalks into his office.

I breathe a sigh of relief and stick my tongue out at him as he closes the door. Bastard.

*   *   *

At four o'clock, Claire rings from Reception.

'I have Mia Grey on the line for you.'

Mia? I hope she doesn't want to hang at the mall.

'Hi, Mia!'

'Ana, hi. How are you?' Her excitement is stifling.

'Good. Busy today. You?'

427

'I am so bored! I need to find something to do, so I'm arranging a birthday party for Christian.'

Christian's birthday? Jeez, I had no idea. 'When is it?'

'I knew it. I knew he wouldn't tell you. It's on Saturday. Mom and Dad want everyone over for a meal to celebrate. I'm officially inviting you.'

'Oh, that's lovely. Thank you, Mia.'

'I've already called Christian and told him, and he gave me your number here.'

'Cool.' My mind is in a flat spin—what the hell am I going to get Christian for his birthday? What do you buy the man who has everything?

'And maybe sometime next week we can go out for lunch?'

'Sure. How about tomorrow? My boss is away in New York.'

'Oh, that would be cool, Ana. What time?'

'Twelve forty-five?'

'I'll be there. Bye, Ana.'

'Bye.' I hang up.

Christian. Birthday. What on earth should I get him?

From: Anastasia Steele
Subject: Antediluvian
Date: June 15 2011 16:11
To: Christian Grey

Dear Mr. Grey

When, exactly, were you going to tell me?

What shall I get my old man for his birthday?

428

Perhaps some new batteries for his hearing aid?

A x

Anastasia Steele
Assistant to Jack Hyde, Editor, SIP

From: Christian Grey
Subject: Prehistoric
Date: June 15 2011 16:20
To: Anastasia Steele

Don't mock the elderly.

Glad you are alive and kicking.

And that Mia has been in touch.

Batteries are always useful.

I don't like celebrating my birthday.

x

Christian Grey,
Deaf as a Post CEO, Grey Enterprises
Holdings, Inc.

From: Anastasia Steele
Subject: Hmmm.
Date: June 15 2011 16:24
To: Christian Grey

Dear Mr. Grey

I can imagine you pouting as you wrote that last sentence.

That does things to me.

A xox

Anastasia Steele
Assistant to Jack Hyde, Editor, SIP

From: Christian Grey
Subject: Rolling Eyes
Date: June 15 2011 16:29
To: Anastasia Steele

Miss Steele

WILL YOU USE YOUR BLACKBERRY!!!

x

Christian Grey,
Twitchy Palmed, CEO, Grey Enterprises
Holdings, Inc.

I roll my eyes. Why is he so touchy about e-mails?

From: Anastasia Steele
Subject: Inspiration
Date: June 15 2011 16:33
To: Christian Grey

Dear Mr. Grey

Ah . . . your twitchy palms can't stay still for long, can they?

I wonder what Dr. Flynn would say about that?

But now I know what to give you for your birthday—and I hope it makes me sore . . .

;)

A x

From: Christian Grey
Subject: Angina
Date: June 15 2011 16:38
To: Anastasia Steele

Miss Steele

I don't think my heart could stand the strain of another e-mail like that, or my pants for that matter.

Behave.

x

Christian Grey
CEO, Grey Enterprises Holdings, Inc.

From: Anastasia Steele
Subject: Trying
Date: June 15 2011 16:42
To: Christian Grey

Christian

I am trying to work for my very trying boss.

Please stop bothering me and being trying yourself.

Your last e-mail nearly made me combust.

x

PS: Can you pick me up at 6:30?

From: Christian Grey
Subject: I'll Be There
Date: June 15 2011 16:47
To: Anastasia Steele

Nothing would give me greater pleasure.

Actually, I can think of any of number of things that would give me greater pleasure, and they all involve you.

x

Christian Grey
CEO, Grey Enterprises Holdings, Inc.

I flush reading his response and shake my head. E-mail banter is all well and good, but we really need to talk. Perhaps once we've seen Flynn. I put my BlackBerry down and finish my petty cash reconciliation.

*   *   *

By six fifteen, the office is deserted. I have everything ready for Jack. His cab to the airport is booked, and I just have to hand him his documents. I glance anxiously through the glass, but he's still deep in his telephone call, and I don't want to interrupt him—not in the mood he's in today.

As I wait for him to finish, it occurs to me that I have not eaten today. Oh shit, that's not going to go down well with Fifty. I quickly skip down to the kitchen to see if there are any cookies left.

As I'm opening the communal cookie jar, Jack appears unexpectedly in the kitchen doorway, startling me.

Oh. What's he doing here?

He stares at me. 'Well, Ana, I think this might be a good time to discuss your misdemeanors.' He steps in, closing the door behind him, and my mouth instantly dries as alarm bells ring loud and piercing in my head.

Oh, fuck.

His lips twitch into a grotesque smile, and his eyes gleam deep, dark cobalt. 'At last, I have you on your own,' he says, and he slowly licks his lower lip.

What?

'Now . . . are you going to be a good girl and listen very carefully to what I say?'

CHAPTER SIXTEEN

Jack's eyes flash the darkest blue, and he sneers as he casts a leering look down my body.

Fear chokes me. What is this? What does he want? From somewhere deep inside and despite my dry mouth, I find the resolve and courage to squeeze out some words, my self-defense class 'Keep them talking' mantra circling my brain like an ethereal sentinel.

'Jack, now might not be a good time for this. Your cab is due in ten minutes, and I need to give you all your documents.' My voice is quiet but hoarse, betraying me.

He smiles, and it's a despotic fuck-you smile that finally touches his eyes. They glint in the harsh fluorescent glow of the strip light above us in the drab windowless room. He takes a step toward me, glaring, his eyes never leaving mine. His pupils are dilating as I watch—the black eclipsing the blue. Oh no. My fear escalates.

'You know I had to fight with Elizabeth to give you this job . . .' His voice trails off as he takes another step toward me, and I step back against the dingy wall cupboards. *Keep him talking, keep him talking, keep him talking.*

'Jack, what exactly is your problem? If you want to air your grievances, then perhaps we should ask HR to get involved. We could do this with Elizabeth in a more formal setting.'

Where is Security? Are they in the building yet?

'We don't need HR to overmanage this situation, Ana.' He sneers. 'When I hired you, I thought you would be a hard worker. I thought you had potential. But now, I don't know. You've become distracted and sloppy. And I wondered . . . is it your *boyfriend* who's leading you astray?' He says 'boyfriend' with chilling contempt.

'I decided to check through your e-mail account to see if I could find any clues. And you know what I found, Ana? What was out of place? The only personal e-mails in your account were to your hotshot boyfriend.' He pauses, assessing my reaction. 'And I got to thinking . . . where are the e-mails from him? There are none. Nada. Nothing. So what's going on, Ana? How come his e-mails to you aren't on our system? Are you some company spy, planted in here by Grey's organization? Is that what this is?'

Holy shit, the e-mails. *Oh no.* What have I said?

'Jack, what are you talking about?' I try for bewildered, and I'm pretty convincing. This conversation is not going as I expected, and I don't trust him in the slightest. Some subliminal pheromone that Jack is exuding has me on high alert. This man is angry, volatile, and totally unpredictable. I try to reason with him.

'You just said that you had to persuade Elizabeth to hire me. So how could I be planted as a spy? Make up your mind, Jack.'

'But Grey fucked the New York trip, didn't he?' *Oh, shit.*

'How did he manage that, Ana? What did your rich, Ivy League boyfriend do?'

What little blood remains in my face drains away, and I think I'm going to faint. 'I don't know what you're talking about, Jack,' I whisper. 'Your cab will be here shortly. Shall I fetch your things?' Oh,

435

please, let me go. Stop this.

Jack continues, enjoying my discomfort. 'And he thinks I'd make a pass at you?' He smirks and his eyes heat. 'Well, I want you to think about something while I'm in New York. I gave you this job, and I expect you to show me some gratitude. In fact, I'm entitled to it. I had to fight to get you. Elizabeth wanted someone better qualified, but I—I saw something in you. So, we need to work out a deal. A deal where you keep me happy. D'you understand what I'm saying, Ana?'

Fuck!

'Look at it as refining your job description if you like. And if you keep me happy, I won't dig any further into how your boyfriend is pulling strings, milking his contacts, or cashing in some favor from one of his Ivy League frat-boy sycophants.'

My mouth drops open. *He's blackmailing me. For sex!* And what can I say? News of Christian's takeover is embargoed for another three weeks. I can barely believe this. Sex—with me!

Jack moves closer until he's standing right in front of me, staring down into my eyes. His cloying sweet cologne invades my nostrils—it's nauseating—and if I'm not mistaken, the bitter stench of alcohol is on his breath. *Fuck, he's been drinking . . . when?*

'You are such a tight-assed, cock-blocking, prick tease, you know, Ana,' he whispers through clenched teeth.

What? Prick tease . . . Me?

'Jack, I have no idea what you're talking about,' I whisper, as I feel the adrenaline surge through my body. He's closer now. I am waiting to make my move. Ray will be proud. Ray taught me what to do.

436

Ray knows his self-defense. If Jack touches me—if he even breathes too close to me—I will take him down. My breath is shallow. *I must not faint, I must not faint.*

'Look at you.' He gives me a leering look. 'You're so turned on, I can tell. You've really led me on. Deep down you want it. I know.'

Holy fuck. The man is completely delusional. My fear rises to DEFCON 1, threatening to overwhelm me. 'No, Jack. I have never led you on.'

'You have, you prick-teasing bitch. I can read the signs.' Reaching up, he gently strokes my face with the back of his knuckles, down to my chin. His index finger strokes my throat, and my heart leaps into my mouth as I fight my gag reflex. He reaches the dip at the base of my neck, where the top button of my black shirt is open, and presses his hand against my chest.

'You want me. Admit it, Ana.'

Keeping my eyes firmly fixed on his and concentrating on what I have to do—rather than my mushrooming revulsion and dread—I place my hand gently over his in a caress. He smiles in triumph. I grab his little finger and twist it back, pulling it sharply down backward to his hip.

'Arrgh!' he cries out in pain and surprise, and as he leans off balance, I bring my knee, swift and hard, up into his groin, and make perfect contact with my goal. I dodge deftly to my left as his knees buckle, and he collapses with a groan onto the kitchen floor, grasping himself between his legs.

'Don't you ever touch me again,' I snarl at him. 'Your itinerary and the brochures are packaged on my desk. I am going home now. Have a nice trip. And in the future, get your own damn coffee.'

'You fucking bitch!' he half screams, half groans at me, but I am already out the door.

I run full tilt to my desk, grab my jacket and my purse, and dash to Reception, ignoring the moans and curses emanating from the bastard still prostrate on the kitchen floor. I burst out of the building and stop for a minute as the cool air hits my face. I take a deep breath and compose myself. But I haven't eaten all day, and as the very unwelcome surge of adrenaline recedes, my legs give out beneath me and I sink to the ground.

I watch with mild detachment the slow motion movie that plays out in front of me: Christian and Taylor in dark suits and white shirts, leaping out of the waiting car and running toward me. Christian sinks to his knees at my side, and on some unconscious level, all I can think is: *He's here. My love is here.*

'Ana, Ana! What's wrong?' He scoops me into his lap, running his hands up and down my arms, checking for any signs of injury. Grabbing my head between his hands, he stares with wide, terrified, gray eyes into mine. I sag against him, suddenly overwhelmed with relief and fatigue. Oh, Christian's arms. There is no place I'd rather be.

'Ana.' He shakes me gently. 'What's wrong? Are you sick?'

I shake my head as I realize I need to start communicating.

'Jack,' I whisper, and I sense rather than see Christian's swift glance at Taylor, who abruptly disappears into the building.

'Fuck!' Christian enfolds me in his arms. 'What did that sleazeball do to you?'

And from somewhere just the right side of crazy,

438

a giggle bubbles in my throat. I recall Jack's utter shock as I grabbed his finger.

'It's what I did to him.' I start giggling and I can't stop.

'Ana!' Christian shakes me again, and my giggling fit ceases. 'Did he touch you?'

'Only once.'

Christian's muscles bunch and tense as rage sweeps through him, and he stands up swiftly, powerfully—rock steady—with me in his arms. He's furious. *No!*

'Where is that fucker?'

From inside the building we hear muffled shouting. Christian sets me on my feet.

'Can you stand?'

I nod.

'Don't go in. Don't, Christian.' Suddenly my fear is back, fear of what Christian will do to Jack.

'Get in the car,' he barks at me.

'Christian, no.' I grab his arm.

'Get in the goddamned car, Ana.' He shakes me off.

'No! Please!' I plead with him. 'Stay. Don't leave me on my own.' I deploy my ultimate weapon.

Seething, Christian runs his hand through his hair and glares down at me, clearly wracked with indecision. The shouting inside the building escalates, and then stops suddenly.

Oh no. What has Taylor done?

Christian fishes out his BlackBerry.

'Christian, he has my e-mails.'

'What?'

'My e-mails to you. He wanted to know where your e-mails to me were. He was trying to blackmail me.'

Christian's look is murderous.

Oh, shit.

'Fuck!' he splutters and narrows his eyes at me. He punches a number into his BlackBerry.

Oh no. I'm in trouble. Who's he calling?

'Barney. Grey. I need you to access the SIP main server and wipe all Anastasia Steele's e-mails to me. Then access the personal data files of Jack Hyde and check they aren't stored there. If they are, wipe them . . . Yes, all of them. Now. Let me know when it's done.'

He stabs the 'off' button then dials another number.

'Roach. Grey. Hyde—I want him out. Now. This minute. Call Security. Get him to clear his desk immediately, or I will liquidate this company first thing in the morning. You already have all the justification you need to give him his pink slip. Do you understand?' He listens briefly and hangs up, seemingly satisfied.

'BlackBerry,' he hisses at me through clenched teeth.

'Please don't be mad at me.' I blink up at him.

'I am so mad at you right now,' he snarls and once more sweeps his hand through his hair. 'Get in the car.'

'Christian, please—'

'Get in the fucking car, Anastasia, or so help me I'll put you in there myself,' he threatens, his eyes blazing with fury.

Oh, shit. 'Don't do anything stupid, please,' I beg.

'*STUPID!*' he explodes. 'I told you to use your fucking BlackBerry. Don't talk to me about stupid. Get in the motherfucking car, Anastasia—*NOW!*' he snarls, and a frisson of fear runs through me.

This is Very Angry Christian. I've not seen him this mad before. He's barely holding on to his self-control.

'Okay,' I mutter, placating him. 'But please, be careful.'

Pressing his lips together in a hard line, he points angrily to the car, glaring at me.

Jeez, okay, I get the message.

'Please be careful. I don't want anything to happen to you. It would kill me,' I murmur. He blinks rapidly and stills, lowering his arm while he takes a deep breath.

'I'll be careful,' he says, his eyes softening. Oh, thank the Lord. His eyes burn into me as I head to the car, open the front passenger door, and climb in. Once I'm safely in the comfort of the Audi, he disappears into the building, and my heart leaps again into my throat. What's he planning to do?

I sit and wait. And wait. And wait. Five eternal minutes. Jack's cab pulls up in front of the Audi. Ten minutes. Fifteen. Jeez, what are they doing in there, and how is Taylor? The wait is agonizing.

Twenty-five minutes later, Jack emerges from the building, clutching a cardboard storage box. Behind him is the security guard. Where was he earlier? And after them come Christian and Taylor. Jack looks sick. He heads straight for the cab, and I'm grateful for the Audi's heavily tinted windows so he cannot see me. The cab drives off—presumably not to Sea-Tac—as Christian and Taylor reach the car.

Opening the driver's door, Christian slides smoothly into the seat, presumably because I am in the front, and Taylor gets in behind me. Neither of them says a word as Christian starts the car and pulls out into the traffic. I risk a quick glance at

Fifty. His mouth is set in a firm line, but he seems distracted. The car phone rings.

'Grey,' Christian snaps.

'Mr. Grey, Barney here.'

'Barney, I'm on speakerphone, and there are others in the car,' Christian warns.

'Sir, it's all done. But I need to talk to you about what else I found on Mr. Hyde's computer.'

'I'll call you when I reach my destination. And thanks, Barney.'

'No problem, Mr. Grey.'

Barney hangs up. He sounds much younger than I expected.

What else is on Jack's computer?

'Are you talking to me?' I ask quietly.

Christian glances at me, before fixing his eyes back on the road ahead, and I can tell he's still mad.

'No,' he mutters sullenly.

Oh, there we go . . . how childish. I wrap my arms around myself and stare unseeing out the window. Perhaps I should just ask him to drop me off at my apartment; then he can 'not talk' to me from the safety of Escala and save us both the inevitable quarrel. But even as I think it, I know I don't want to leave him to brood, not after yesterday.

Eventually we pull up in front of his apartment building, and Christian climbs out of the car. Moving with easy grace around to my side, he opens my door.

'Come,' he orders as Taylor clambers into the driver's seat. I take his proffered hand and follow him through the grand foyer to the elevator. He doesn't let go of me.

'Christian, why are you so mad at me?' I whisper as we wait.

442

'You know why,' he mutters as we step into the elevator, and he punches in the code to his floor. 'God, if something had happened to you, he'd be dead by now.' Christian's tone chills me to the bone. The doors close.

'As it is, I'm going to ruin his career so he can't take advantage of young women anymore, miserable excuse for a man that he is.' He shakes his head. 'Jesus, Ana!' He grabs me suddenly, imprisoning me in the corner of the elevator.

His hands fist in my hair as he pulls my face up to his, and his mouth is on mine, a passionate desperation in his kiss. I don't know why this takes me by surprise, but it does. I taste his relief, his longing, and his residual anger while his tongue possesses my mouth. He stops, gazing down at me, resting his weight against me so I can't move. He leaves me breathless, clinging to him for support, staring up into that beautiful face etched with determination and without any trace of humor.

'If anything had happened to you . . . If he'd harmed you . . .' I feel the shudder that runs through him. 'BlackBerry,' he commands quietly. 'From now on. Understand?'

I nod, swallowing, unable to break eye contact from his grim, mesmerizing look.

He straightens, releasing me as the elevator comes to a stop. 'He said you kicked him in the balls.' Christian's tone is lighter with a trace of admiration, and I think I'm forgiven.

'Yes,' I whisper, still reeling from the intensity of his kiss and his impassioned command.

'Good.'

'Ray is ex-army. He taught me well.'

'I'm very glad he did,' he breathes and adds,

443

arching a brow, 'I'll need to remember that.' Taking my hand, he leads me out of the elevator and I follow, relieved. I think that's as bad as his mood is going to get.

'I need to call Barney. I won't be long.' He disappears into his study, leaving me stranded in the vast living room. Mrs. Jones is adding the finishing touches to our meal. I realize I am famished, but I need something to do.

'Can I help?' I ask.

She laughs. 'No, Ana. Can I fix you a drink or something? You look beat.'

'I'd love a glass of wine.'

'White?'

'Yes, please.'

I perch on one of the barstools, and she hands me a glass of chilled wine. I don't know what it is, but it's delicious and slides down easily, soothing my shattered nerves. What was I thinking about earlier today? How alive I have felt since I met Christian. How exciting my life has become. Jeez, could I just have a few boring days?

What if I'd never met Christian? I'd be holed up in my apartment, talking it through with Ethan, completely freaked by my encounter with Jack, knowing I would have to face the sleazeball again on Friday. As it is, there's every chance I'll never set eyes on him again. But who will I work for now? I frown. I hadn't thought of that. Shit, do I even have a job?

'Evening, Gail,' Christian says as he comes back into the great room, dragging me from my thoughts. Heading straight to the fridge, he pours himself a glass of wine.

'Good evening, Mr. Grey. Dinner in ten, sir?'

'Sounds good.'

Christian raises his glass.

'To ex-military men who train their daughters well,' he says and his eyes soften.

'Cheers,' I mutter, raising my glass.

'What's wrong?' Christian asks.

'I don't know if I still have a job.'

He cocks his head to the side. 'Do you still want one?'

'Of course.'

'Then you still have one.'

Simple. See? He is master of my universe. I roll my eyes at him and he smiles.

*   *   *

Mrs. Jones makes a mean chicken potpie. She has left us to enjoy the fruits of her labors, and I feel much better now I've had something to eat. We are sitting at the breakfast bar, and despite my best cajoling, Christian won't tell me what Barney has found on Jack's computer. I drop the subject, and decide to tackle instead the thorny issue of José's impending visit.

'José called,' I say nonchalantly.

'Oh?' Christian turns to face me.

'He wants to deliver your photos on Friday.'

'A personal delivery. How accommodating of him,' Christian mutters.

'He wants to go out. For a drink. With me.'

'I see.'

'And Kate and Elliot should be back,' I add quickly.

Christian puts his fork down, frowning at me.

'What exactly are you asking?'

445

I bristle. 'I'm not asking anything. I'm informing you of my plans for Friday. Look, I want to see José, and he wants to stay over. Either he stays here or he can stay at my place, but if he does, I should be there, too.'

Christian's eyes widen. He looks dumbfounded.

'He made a pass at you.'

'Christian, that was weeks ago. He was drunk, I was drunk, you saved the day—it won't happen again. He's no Jack, for heaven's sake.'

'Ethan's there. He can keep him company.'

'He wants to see me, not Ethan.'

Christian scowls at me.

'He's just a friend.' My voice is emphatic.

'I don't like it.'

So what? Jeez, he's irritating sometimes. I take a deep breath. 'He's my friend, Christian. I haven't seen him since his show. And that was too brief. I know you don't have any friends, apart from that god-awful woman, but I don't moan about you seeing her,' I snap. Christian blinks, shocked. 'I want to see him. I've been a poor friend to him.' My subconscious is alarmed. *Are you stamping your little foot? Steady now!*

Gray eyes blaze at me. 'Is that what you think?' he breathes.

'Think about what?'

'Elena. You'd rather I didn't see her?'

'Exactly. I'd rather you didn't see her.'

'Why didn't you say?'

'Because it's not my place to say. You think she's your only friend.' I shrug in exasperation. He really doesn't get it. How did this turn into a conversation about her? I don't even want to think about her. I try to steer us back to José. 'Just as it's not your place to say if I can or can't see José. Don't you see that?'

Christian gazes at me, perplexed, I think. *Oh, what is he thinking?*

'He can stay here, I suppose,' he mutters. 'I can keep an eye on him.' He sounds petulant.

Hallelujah!

'Thank you! You know, if I am going to live here, too . . .' I trail off. Christian nods. He knows what I'm trying to say. 'It's not like you haven't got the space.' I smirk.

His lips turn up slowly. 'Are you smirking at me, Miss Steele?'

'Most definitely, Mr. Grey.' I get up just in case his palms start twitching, clear our plates, and then load them into the dishwasher.

'Gail will do that.'

'I've done it now.' I stand up and gaze at him. He's watching me intently.

'I have to work for a while,' he says apologetically.

'Cool. I'll find something to do.'

'Come here,' he orders, but his voice is soft and seductive, his eyes heated. I don't hesitate to walk into his arms, clasping him around his neck as he perches on his barstool. He wraps his arms around me, crushes me to him, and just holds me.

'Are you okay?' he whispers into my hair.

'Okay?'

'After what happened with that fucker? After what happened yesterday?' he adds, his voice quiet and earnest.

I gaze into dark, serious, eyes. *Am I okay?* 'Yes,' I whisper.

His arms tighten around me, and I feel safe,

cherished, and loved all at once. It's blissful. Closing my eyes, I enjoy the feel of being in his arms. I love this man. I love his intoxicating scent, his strength, his mercurial ways—my Fifty.

'Let's not fight,' he murmurs. He kisses my hair and inhales deeply. 'You smell heavenly as usual, Ana.'

'So do you,' I whisper and kiss his neck.

All too soon he releases me. 'I should only be a couple of hours.'

*   *   *

I wander listlessly through the apartment. Christian is still working. I have showered and dressed in some sweats and a T-shirt of my own, and I'm bored. I don't want to read. If I sit still, I'll recall Jack and his fingers on me.

I check out my old bedroom, the subs' room. José can sleep here—he'll like the view. It's about eight fifteen, and the sun is beginning to sink into the west. The lights of the city twinkle below me. It's glorious. Yes, José will like it here. I wonder idly where Christian will hang José's pictures of me. I'd rather he didn't. I am not keen on looking at myself.

Back down the hallway I find myself outside the playroom, and without thinking, I try the door handle. Christian normally keeps it locked, but to my surprise, the door opens. How strange. Feeling like a child playing hooky and straying into the forbidden forest, I walk in. It's dark. I flick the switch and the lights under the cornice light up with a soft glow. It's as I remember it. A womblike room.

Memories of the last time I was in here flash

through my mind. The belt . . . I wince at the recollection. Now it hangs innocently, lined up with others, on the rack beside the door. Tentatively I run my fingers over the belts, the floggers, the paddles, and the whips. Sheesh. This is what I need to square with Dr. Flynn. Can someone in this lifestyle just stop? It seems so improbable. Wandering over to the bed, I sit on soft red satin sheets, gazing around at all the apparatuses.

Beside me is the bench, above that the assortment of canes. *So many! Surely one is enough?* Well, the less said about that, the better. And the large table. We never tried that, whatever he does on it. My eyes fall on the chesterfield, and I move over to sit on it. It's just a couch, nothing extraordinary about it—nothing to fasten anything to, not that I can see. Glancing behind me, I spy the museum chest. My curiosity is piqued. What does he keep in there?

As I pull open the top drawer I realize my blood is pounding through my veins. Why am I so nervous? This feels so illicit, as if I'm trespassing, which of course I am. But if he wants to marry me, well . . .

Holy fuck, what's all this? An array of instruments and bizarre implements—I don't have a clue what they are, or what they're for—are carefully laid out in the display drawer. I pick one up. It's bullet-shaped with a sort of handle. *Hmm . . . what the hell do you do with that?* My mind boggles, though I think I have an idea. There are four different sizes! My scalp prickles and I glance up.

Christian is standing in the doorway, staring at me, his face unreadable. How long has he been

449

there? I feel like I've been caught with my hand in the cookie jar.

'Hi.' I smile nervously, and I know my eyes are wide and that I'm deathly pale.

'What are you doing?' he says softly, but there's an undercurrent in his tone.

Oh shit. Is he mad? I flush. 'Er . . . I was bored and curious,' I mutter, embarrassed to be found out. He said he'd be two hours.

'That's a very dangerous combination.' He runs his index finger across his lower lip in quiet contemplation, not taking his eyes off me. I swallow and my mouth is dry.

Slowly he enters the room and closes the door quietly behind him, his eyes liquid gray fire. *Oh my.* He leans casually over the chest of drawers, but I think his stance is deceptive. My inner goddess doesn't know whether it's fight-or-flight time.

'So, what exactly are you curious about, Miss Steele? Perhaps I could enlighten you.'

'The door was open . . . I—' I gaze at Christian as I hold my breath and blink, uncertain as ever of his reaction or what I should say. His eyes are dark. I think he's amused, but it's difficult to tell. He places his elbows on the museum chest and rests his chin on his clasped hands.

'I was in here earlier today wondering what to do with it all. I must have forgotten to lock it.' He scowls momentarily, as if leaving the door unlocked is a terrible lapse in judgment. I frown—it's not like him to be forgetful.

'Oh?'

'But now here you are, curious as ever.' His voice is soft, puzzled.

'You're not mad?' I whisper, using my remaining

breath.

He cocks his head to one side, and his lips twitch in amusement.

'Why would I be mad?'

'I feel like I'm trespassing . . . and you're always mad at me.' My voice is quiet, though I'm relieved. Christian's brow creases once more.

'Yes, you're trespassing, but I'm not mad. I hope that one day you'll live with me here, and all this'—he gestures vaguely around the room with one hand—'will be yours, too.'

My playroom . . .? I gape at him—that's a lot to take in.

'That's why I was in here today. Trying to decide what to do.' He taps his lips with his index finger. 'Am I angry with you all the time? I wasn't this morning.'

Oh, that's true. I smile at the memory of Christian when we woke, and it distracts me from the thought of what will become of the playroom. He was such fun Fifty this morning.

'You were playful. I like playful Christian.'

'Do you, now?' He arches an eyebrow, and his lovely mouth curves up in a smile, a shy smile. Wow!

'What's this?' I hold up the silver bullet thing.

'Always hungry for information, Miss Steele. That's a butt plug,' he says gently.

'Oh . . .'

'Bought for you.'

What? 'For me?'

He nods slowly, his face now serious and wary.

I frown. 'You buy new, er . . . toys . . . for each submissive?'

'Some things. Yes.'

'Butt plugs?'

'Yes.'

Okay . . . I swallow. Butt plug. It's solid metal— surely that's uncomfortable? I remember our discussion about sex toys and hard limits after I graduated. I think at the time I said I would try. Now, actually seeing one, I don't know if it's something I want to do. I examine it once more and place it back in the drawer.

'And this?' I take out a long, black, rubbery object made of gradually diminishing spherical bubbles joined together, the first one large and the last much smaller. Eight bubbles in total.

'Anal beads,' says Christian, watching me carefully.

Oh! I examine them with fascinated horror. All of these, inside me . . . *there!* I had no idea.

'They have quite an effect if you pull them out mid-orgasm,' he adds matter-of-factly.

'This is for me?' I whisper.

'For you.' He nods slowly.

'This is the butt drawer?'

He smirks. 'If you like.'

I close it quickly, feeling myself turning red as a stoplight.

'Don't you like the butt drawer?' he asks innocently, amused. I gaze at him and shrug, trying to brazen out my shock.

'It's not top of my Christmas card list,' I mutter nonchalantly. Tentatively, I open the second drawer. He grins.

'Next drawer down holds a selection of vibrators.'

I shut the drawer quickly.

'And the next?' I whisper, ashen once more, but this time with embarrassment.

'That's more interesting.'

Oh! Hesitantly I pull the drawer open, not taking my eyes off his beautiful but rather smug face. Inside there are an assortment of metal items and some clothespins. Clothespins! I pick up a large metal cliplike device.

'Genital clamp,' Christian says. He stands up and moves casually around so that he's beside me. I put it back immediately and choose something more delicate—two small clips on a chain.

'Some of these are for pain, but most are for pleasure,' he murmurs.

'What's this?'

'Nipple clamps—that's for both.'

'Both? Nipples?'

Christian smirks at me. 'Well, there are two clamps, baby. Yes, both nipples, but that's not what I meant. These are for both pleasure and pain.'

Oh. He takes it from me.

'Hold out your little finger.'

I do as he asks, and he clamps one clip to the tip of my finger. It's not too harsh.

'The sensation is very intense, but it's when taking them off that they are at their most painful and pleasurable.' I remove the clip. Hmm, that might be nice. I squirm at the thought.

'I like the look of these,' I murmur and Christian smiles.

'Do you now, Miss Steele? I think I can tell.'

I nod shyly and put the clips back in the drawer. Christian leans forward to pull out two more.

'These are adjustable.' He holds them up for me to inspect.

'Adjustable?'

'You can wear them very tight . . . or not.

Depending on your mood.'

How does he make that sound so erotic? I swallow, and to divert his attention, pull out a device that looks like a spiky pastry cutter.

'This?' I frown. No baking in the playroom, surely.

'That's a Wartenberg pinwheel.'

'For?'

He reaches over and takes it from me. 'Give me your hand. Palm up.'

I offer him my left hand and he takes it gently, skating his thumb over my knuckles. A shiver runs through me. His skin against mine, it never fails to thrill me. He runs the wheel over my palm.

'Ah!' The prongs bite into my skin—there's more than just pain. In fact, it tickles.

'Imagine that over your breasts,' Christian murmurs lasciviously.

Oh! I flush and snatch my hand back. My breathing and heart rate increase.

'There's a fine line between pleasure and pain, Anastasia,' he says softly as he leans down and puts the device back in the drawer.

'Clothespins?' I whisper.

'You can do a great deal with a clothespin.' His eyes burn.

I lean against the drawer so it closes.

'Is that all?' Christian looks amused.

'No . . .' I pull open the fourth drawer to be confounded by a mass of leather and straps. I tug at one of the straps . . . it appears to be attached to a ball.

'Ball gag. To keep you quiet,' says Christian, amused once more.

'Soft limit,' I mutter.

454

'I remember,' he says. 'But you can still breathe. Your teeth clamp over the ball.' Taking it from me, he replicates a mouth clamping down on the ball with his fingers.

'Have you worn one of these?' I ask.

He stills and gazes down at me. 'Yes.'

'To mask your screams?'

He closes his eyes, and I think it's in exasperation. 'No, that's not what they're about.'

Oh?

'It's about control, Anastasia. How helpless would you be if you were tied up and couldn't speak? How trusting would you have to be, knowing I had that much power over you? That I had to read your body and your reaction, rather than hear your words? It makes you more dependent, puts me in ultimate control.'

I swallow.

'You sound like you miss it.'

'It's what I know,' he murmurs. His eyes are wide and serious, and the atmosphere between us has changed, as if he's at confessional.

'You have power over me. You know you do,' I whisper.

'Do I? You make me feel . . . helpless.'

'No!' *Oh, Fifty* . . . 'Why?'

'Because you're the only person I know who could really hurt me.' He reaches up and tucks my hair behind my ear.

'Oh, Christian . . . that works both ways. If you didn't want me—' I shudder, glancing down at my twisting fingers. Therein lies my other dark reservation about us. If he wasn't so . . . broken, would he want me? I shake my head. I must try not to think like that.

'The last thing I want to do is hurt you. I love you,' I murmur, reaching up with both hands to run my fingers through his sideburns and gently stroke his cheeks. He leans his face into my touch, drops the gag back in the drawer, and reaches for me, his hands around my waist. He pulls me against him.

'Have we finished show-and-tell?' he asks, his voice soft and seductive. His hand moves up my back to the nape of my neck.

'Why? What did you want to do?'

He bends and kisses me gently, and I melt against him, grasping his arms.

'Ana, you were nearly attacked today.' His voice is soft but wary.

'So?' I ask, enjoying the feel of his hand at my back and his proximity. He pulls his head back and scowls down at me.

'What do you mean, "so?"' he rebukes.

I gaze up into his lovely, grumpy face, and I'm dazzled.

'Christian, I'm fine.'

He wraps me in his arms, holding me close. 'When I think what might have happened,' he breathes, burying his face in my hair.

'When will you learn that I'm stronger than I look?' I whisper reassuringly into his neck, inhaling his delicious scent. There is nothing better on the planet than being in Christian's arms.

'I know you're strong,' Christian muses quietly. He kisses my hair, but then to my great disappointment, releases me. *Oh?*

Bending down I fish another item out of the open drawer. Several cuffs attached to a bar. I hold it up.

'That,' says Christian, his eyes darkening, 'is a

456

spreader bar with ankle and wrist restraints.'

'How does it work?' I ask, genuinely intrigued.

'You want me to show you?' he breathes in surprise, closing his eyes briefly.

I blink at him. When he opens his eyes, they are blazing.

'Yes, I want a demonstration. I like being tied up,' I whisper as my inner goddess pole vaults from the bunker onto her chaise longue.

'Oh, Ana,' he murmurs. He looks pained all of a sudden.

'What?'

'Not here.'

'What do you mean?'

'I want you in my bed, not in here. Come.' He grabs the bar and my hand, then leads me promptly out of the room.

Why are we leaving? I glance behind me as we exit. 'Why not in there?'

Christian stops on the stairs and gazes up at me, his expression grave.

'Ana, you may be ready to go back in there, but I'm not. Last time we were in there, you left me. I keep telling you—when will you understand?' He frowns, releasing me so that he can gesticulate with his free hand.

'My whole attitude has changed as a result. My whole outlook on life has radically shifted. I've told you this. What I haven't told you is—' He stops and runs his hand through his hair, searching for the correct words. 'I'm like a recovering alcoholic, okay? That's the only comparison I can draw. The compulsion has gone, but I don't want to put temptation in my way. I don't want to hurt you.'

He looks so remorseful, and in that moment, a

sharp nagging pain lances through me. What have I done to this man? Have I improved his life? He was happy before he met me, wasn't he?

'I can't bear to hurt you because I love you,' he adds, gazing up at me, his expression one of absolute sincerity like a small boy telling a very simple truth.

He's completely guileless, and he takes my breath away. I adore him more than anything or anyone. I *do* love this man unconditionally.

I launch myself at him so hard that he has to drop what he's carrying to catch me as I push him up against the wall. Grabbing his face between my hands, I pull his lips to mine tasting his surprise as I push my tongue into his mouth. I am standing on the step above him—we're at the same level, and I feel euphorically empowered. Kissing him passionately, my fingers twisting into his hair, I want to touch him, everywhere, but restrain myself, knowing his fear. Regardless, my desire unfurls, hot and heavy, blossoming deep inside me. He groans and grabs my shoulders, pushing me away.

'Do you want me to fuck you on the stairs?' he mutters, his breathing ragged. 'Because right now, I will.'

'Yes,' I murmur and I'm sure my dark gaze matches his.

He glares at me, his eyes hooded and heavy. 'No. I want you in my bed.' He scoops me up suddenly over his shoulder, making me squeal loudly, and smacks me hard on my behind, so that I squeal again. As he heads down the stairs, he stoops to pick up the fallen spreader bar.

Mrs. Jones is coming out of the utility room when we pass through the hall. She smiles at us,

458

and I give her an apologetic upside-down wave. I don't think Christian notices her.

In the bedroom he sets me down on my feet and drops the spreader onto the bed.

'I don't think you'll hurt me,' I breathe.

'I don't think I'll hurt you, either,' he says. He takes my head in his hands and kisses me, long and hard, igniting my already heated blood.

'I want you so much,' he whispers against my mouth, panting. 'Are you sure about this—after today?'

'Yes. I want you, too. I want to undress you.' I can't wait to get my hands on him—my fingers are itching to touch him.

His eyes widen and for a second he hesitates, perhaps to consider my request.

'Okay,' he says cautiously.

I reach for the second button on his shirt and hear him catch his breath.

'I won't touch you if you don't want me to,' I whisper.

'No,' he responds quickly. 'Do. It's fine. I'm good,' he mutters.

I gently undo the button and my fingers glide down his shirt to the next. His eyes are large and luminous, his lips parted as his breathing shallows. He is so beautiful, even in his fear . . . because of his fear. I undo the third button and notice his soft hair poking through the large V of the shirt.

'I want to kiss you there,' I murmur.

He inhales sharply. 'Kiss me?'

'Yes,' I murmur.

He gasps as I undo the next button and very slowly lean forward, making my intention clear. He's holding his breath, but stands stock-still as I plant a gentle kiss among the soft, exposed curls. I undo the final button and lift my face to him. He's gazing at me, and there's a look of satisfaction, calm, and . . . wonder on his face.

'It's getting easier, isn't it?' I whisper.

He nods as I slowly push his shirt off his shoulders and let it fall to the floor.

'What have you done to me, Ana?' he murmurs. 'Whatever it is, don't stop.' And he gathers me in his arms, thrusting both his hands into my hair and pulling my head right back so that he can have easy access to my throat.

He runs his lips up to my jaw, nipping softly. I groan. Oh, I want this man. My fingers fumble at his waistband, undoing the button and pulling down the zipper.

'Oh, baby,' he breathes as he kisses me behind my ear. I feel his erection, firm and hard, straining against me. I want him—in my mouth. I step back abruptly and drop to my knees.

'Whoa!' he gasps.

I tug his pants and boxers sharply, and he springs free. Before he can stop me, I take him into my mouth, sucking hard, enjoying his shocked astonishment as his mouth drops open. He gazes down at me, watching my every move, eyes so dark and filled with carnal bliss. Oh my. I sheath my teeth and suck harder. He closes his eyes and surrenders to this blissful carnal pleasure. I know what I do to him, and it's hedonistic, liberating, and sexy as hell. The feeling is heady; I'm not just powerful—I'm omniscient.

'Fuck,' he hisses and gently cradles my head, flexing his hips so he moves deeper inside my mouth. Oh yes, I want this and I swirl my tongue around him, pulling hard . . . over and over.

'Ana.' He tries to step back.

Oh no you don't, Grey. I want you. I grab his hips firmly, doubling my efforts, and I can tell he's close.

'Please,' he pants. 'I'm gonna come, Ana,' he groans.

Good. My inner goddess's head is thrown back in ecstasy, and he comes, loudly and wetly, into my mouth.

He opens his bright gray eyes, gazing down at me, and I smile up at him, licking my lips. He grins back at me, a wicked, salacious grin.

'Oh, so this is the game we're playing, Miss Steele?' He bends, hooks his hands under my arms, and pulls me to my feet. Suddenly his mouth is on mine. He groans.

'I can taste myself. You taste better,' he murmurs against my lips. He tugs my T-shirt off and throws it carelessly onto the floor, then picks me up and tosses me onto the bed. Grabbing the end of my sweats, he tugs abruptly so that they come off in one swift move. I'm naked underneath, sprawled across his bed. Waiting. Wanting. His eyes drink me in, and slowly he removes his remaining clothes, not taking his eyes off me.

'You are one beautiful woman, Anastasia,' he murmurs appreciatively.

Hmm . . . I tilt my head coquettishly to one side and beam at him.

'You are one beautiful man, Christian, and you taste mighty fine.'

He gives me a wicked grin and reaches for the spreader bar. Grabbing my left ankle, he quickly cuffs it, strapping the buckle tightly, but not too tight. He tests how much room I have by sliding

461

his little finger between the cuff and my ankle. He doesn't take his eyes off mine; he doesn't need to see what he's doing. Hmm . . . he's done this before.

'We'll have to see how you taste. If I recall, you're a rare, exquisite delicacy, Miss Steele.'

Oh.

Grasping my other ankle, he quickly and efficiently cuffs that one as well, so that my feet are about two feet apart.

'The good thing about this spreader is, it expands,' he murmurs. He clicks something on the bar, then pushes, so my legs spread further. Whoa, three feet apart. My mouth drops open, and I take a deep breath. Fuck, this is hot. I'm on fire, restless and needy.

Christian licks his lower lip.

'Oh, we're going to have some fun with this, Ana.' Reaching down he grasps the bar and twists it so I flip onto my front. It takes me by surprise.

'See what I can do to you?' he says darkly and twists it again abruptly, so I am once more on my back, gaping up at him, breathless.

'These other cuffs are for your wrists. I'll think about that. Depends if you behave or not.'

'When do I not behave?'

'I can think of a few infractions,' he says softly, running his fingers up the soles of my feet. It tickles, but the bar holds me in place, though I try to writhe away from his fingers.

'Your BlackBerry, for one.'

I gasp. 'What are you going to do?'

'Oh, I never disclose my plans.' He smirks, his eyes alight with pure mischief.

Wow. He's so mind-bogglingly sexy, it takes my breath away. He crawls up the bed so that he's

462

kneeling between my legs, gloriously naked, and I'm helpless.

'Hmm. You are so exposed, Miss Steele.' He runs the fingers of both his hands up the inside of each of my legs, slowly, surely, making small circular patterns. Never breaking eye contact with me.

'It's all about anticipation, Ana. What will I do to you?' His softly spoken words penetrate right to the deepest, darkest, part of me. I wriggle on the bed and moan. His fingers continue their slow assault up my legs, past the backs of my knees. Instinctively, I want to close my legs but I can't.

'Remember, if you don't like something, just tell me to stop,' he murmurs. Bending over, he kisses my belly, soft, sucking kisses, while his hands continue their slow tortuous journey north up my inner thighs, touching and teasing.

'Oh, please, Christian,' I plead.

'Oh, Miss Steele. I've discovered you can be merciless in your amorous assaults upon me. I think I should return the favor.'

My fingers clutch the comforter as I surrender myself to him, his mouth gently heading south, his fingers north, to the vulnerable and exposed apex of my thighs. I groan as he eases his fingers inside me, and buck my pelvis up to meet them. Christian moans in response.

'You never cease to amaze me, Ana. You're so wet,' he murmurs against the line where my pubic hair joins my belly. My body bows as his mouth finds me.

Oh my.

He begins a slow and sensual assault, his tongue swirling around and around while his fingers move

463

inside me. Because I can't close my legs, or move, it's intense, really intense. My back arches as I try to absorb the sensations.

'Oh, Christian,' I cry.

'I know, baby,' he whispers, and to ease up on me, he blows softly on the most sensitive part of my body.

'Arrgh! Please!' I beg.

'Say my name,' he commands.

'Christian,' I call, hardly recognizing my own voice—it's so high-pitched and needy.

'Again,' he breathes.

'Christian, Christian, Christian Grey,' I call out loudly.

'You are mine.' His voice is soft and deadly and with one last flick of his tongue, I fall—spectacularly—embracing my orgasm, and because my legs are so far apart, it goes on and on and I am lost.

Vaguely, I'm aware that Christian has flipped me onto my stomach.

'We're going to try this, baby. If you don't like it, or it's too uncomfortable, tell me and we'll stop.'

What? I am too lost in the afterglow to form any sentient or coherent thoughts. I am sitting on Christian's lap. How did that happen?

'Lean down, baby,' he murmurs at my ear. 'Head and chest on the bed.'

In a daze I do as I'm told. He pulls both my hands backward and cuffs them to the bar, next to my ankles. *Oh* . . . My knees are drawn up, my ass in the air, utterly vulnerable, completely his.

'Ana, you look so beautiful.' His voice is full of wonder, and I hear the rip of foil. He runs his fingers from the base of my spine down toward my

464

sex and pauses a beat over my ass.

'When you're ready, I want this, too.' His finger is hovering over me. I gasp loudly as I feel myself tense under his gentle probing. 'Not today, sweet Ana, but one day . . . I want you every way. I want to possess every inch of you. You're mine.'

I think about the butt plug, and everything tightens deep inside me. His words make me groan, and his fingers move down and around to more familiar territory.

Moments later, he's slamming into me. 'Aagh! Gently,' I cry, and he stills.

'You okay?'

'Gently . . . let me get used to this.'

He eases slowly out of me then eases gently back, filling me, stretching me, twice, thrice, and I am helpless.

'Yes, good, I've got it now,' I murmur, relishing the feeling.

He groans, and picks up his rhythm. Moving, moving . . . relentless . . . onward, inward, filling me . . . and it's exquisite. There's joy in my helplessness, joy in my surrender to him, and to know that he can lose himself in me the way he wants to. I can do this. He takes me to these dark places, places I didn't know existed, and together we fill them with blinding light. Oh yes . . . blazing, blinding light.

And I let go, glorying in what he does to me, finding my sweet, sweet release, as I come again, loudly, screaming his name. And he stills, pouring his heart and soul into me.

'Ana, baby,' he cries and collapses beside me.

*   *   *

His fingers deftly undo the straps, and he rubs my ankles then my wrists. When he's finished and I'm finally free, he pulls me into his arms and I drift, exhausted.

When I surface again, I am curled beside him and he's gazing at me. I have no idea what the time is.

'I could watch you sleep forever, Ana,' he murmurs and he kisses my forehead.

I smile and shift languorously beside him.

'I never want to let you go,' he says softly and wraps his arms around me.

Hmm. 'I never want to go. Never let me go,' I mutter sleepily, my eyelids refusing to open.

'I need you,' he whispers, but his voice is a distant, ethereal part of my dreams. He needs me . . . needs me . . . and as I finally slip into the darkness, my last thoughts are of a small boy with gray eyes and dirty, messy, copper-colored hair smiling shyly at me.

CHAPTER SEVENTEEN

Hmm.

Christian is nuzzling my neck as I slowly wake.

'Morning, baby,' he whispers and nips at my earlobe. My eyes flutter open and close again quickly. Bright early morning light floods the room, and his hand is softly caressing my breast, gently teasing me. Moving down he grasps my hip as he lies behind me, holding me close.

I stretch out beside him, relishing his touch, and feel his erection against my behind. *Oh my.* A

Christian Grey wake-up call.

'You're pleased to see me,' I mumble sleepily, squirming suggestively against him. I feel his grin against my jaw.

'I'm very pleased to see you,' he says as he skates his hand over my stomach and down to cup my sex and explore with his fingers. 'There are definite advantages to waking up beside you, Miss Steele,' he teases and gently pulls me around so that I'm lying on my back.

'Sleep well?' he asks as his fingers continue their sensual torture. He's smiling down at me—his dazzling, all-American-drop-dead-male-model-perfect-teeth smile. He takes my breath away.

My hips begin to sway to the rhythm of the dance his fingers have begun. He kisses me chastely on the lips and then moves down my neck, nipping slowly, kissing, and sucking as he goes. I moan. He's gentle and his touch is light and heavenly. His intrepid fingers move down, and slowly he eases one inside me, hissing quietly in awe.

'Oh, Ana,' he murmurs reverentially against my throat. 'You're always ready.' He moves his finger in time with his kisses as his lips journey leisurely across my clavicle and then down to my breast. He torments first one, then the other nipple with teeth and lips, but oh so gently, and they tighten and lengthen in sweet response.

I groan.

'Hmm,' he growls softly and raises his head to give me a blazing gray-eyed look. 'I want you now.' He reaches over to the bedside table. He shifts on top of me, taking his weight on his elbows, and rubs his nose along mine while easing my legs apart with his. He kneels up and rips open the foil packet.

467

'I can't wait until Saturday,' he says, his eyes glowing with salacious delight.

'Your party?' I pant.

'No. I can stop using these fuckers.'

'Aptly named.' I giggle.

He smirks at me as he rolls on the condom. 'Are you giggling, Miss Steele?'

'No.' I try and fail to straighten my face.

'Now is not the time for giggling.' He shakes his head in admonishment and his voice is low, stern, but his expression—*holy cow*—is glacial and volcanic at once.

My breath catches in my throat. 'I thought you liked it when I giggle,' I whisper hoarsely, gazing into the dark depths of his stormy eyes.

'Not now. There's a time and a place for giggling. This is neither. I need to stop you, and I think I know how,' he says ominously, and his body covers mine.

*   *   *

'What would you like for breakfast, Ana?'

'I'll just have some granola. Thank you, Mrs. Jones.'

I flush as I take my place at the breakfast bar beside Christian. The last time I set eyes on the very prim and proper Mrs. Jones, I was being unceremoniously dragged into the bedroom over Christian's shoulder.

'You look lovely,' Christian says softly. I'm wearing my gray pencil skirt and gray silk blouse again.

'So do you.' I smile shyly at him. He's wearing a pale blue shirt and jeans, and he looks cool and

468

fresh and perfect, as always.

'We should buy you some more skirts,' he says matter-of-factly. 'In fact—I'd love to take you shopping.'

Hmm—shopping. I hate shopping. But with Christian, maybe it won't be so bad. I decide on distraction as the best form of defense.

'I wonder what will happen at work today?'

'They'll have to replace the sleazeball.' Christian frowns, scowling as if he's just stepped in something extraordinarily unpleasant.

'I hope they take on a woman as my new boss.'

'Why?'

'Well, you're less likely to object to me going away with her,' I tease him.

His lips twitch and he starts on his omelet.

'What's so funny?' I ask.

'You are. Eat your granola, all of it, if that's all you're having.'

Bossy as ever. I purse my lips at him but dig in.

*   *   *

'So, the key goes here.' Christian points out the ignition beneath the gearshift.

'Strange place,' I mutter. But I'm delighted with every little detail, practically bouncing like a small child in the comfortable leather seat. Christian is finally letting me drive my car.

He regards me coolly, though his eyes are alight with humor. 'You're quite excited about this, aren't you?' he murmurs, amused.

I nod, grinning like a fool. 'Just smell that new car smell. This is even better than the Submissive Special . . . um, the A3,' I add quickly, blushing.

Christian's mouth twists. 'Submissive Special, eh? You have such a way with words, Miss Steele.' He leans back with a faux look of disapproval, but he can't fool me. I know he's enjoying himself.

'Well, let's go.' He waves his hand toward the entrance of the garage.

I clap my hands, start the car, and the engine purrs to life. Putting the gearshift into drive, I ease my foot off the brake and the Saab moves smoothly forward. Taylor starts up the Audi behind us and once the garage barrier lifts, follows us out of Escala onto the street.

'Can we have the radio on?' I ask as we wait at the first stop sign.

'I want you to concentrate,' he says sharply.

'Christian, please, I can drive with music on.' I roll my eyes. He scowls for a minute and then reaches for the radio.

'You can play your iPod and MP3 discs as well as CDs on this,' he murmurs.

The too-loud dulcet tones of the Police suddenly fill the car. Christian turns the music down. *Hmm* . . . 'King of Pain.'

'Your anthem,' I tease him, then instantly regret it when his mouth tightens in a thin line. *Oh no*. 'I have this album, somewhere.' I continue hastily to distract him. Hmm . . . somewhere in the apartment I have spent very little time in.

I wonder how Ethan is. I should try to call him today. I won't have much to do at work.

Anxiety blooms in my stomach. What will happen when I get to the office? Will everyone know about Jack? Will everyone know of Christian's involvement? Will I still have a job? Sheesh, if I have no job, what will I do?

470

Marry the gazillionaire, Ana! My subconscious has her snarky face on. I ignore her—rapacious bitch.

'Hey, Miss Smart-mouth. Come back.' Christian drags me into the here and now as I pull up at the next traffic light.

'You're very distracted. Concentrate, Ana,' he scolds. 'Accidents happen when you don't concentrate.'

Oh, for heaven's sake—and suddenly I'm catapulted back in time to when Ray was teaching me to drive. I don't need another father. A husband maybe, a kinky husband. *Hmm.*

'I'm just thinking about work.'

'Baby, you'll be fine. Trust me.' Christian smiles.

'Please don't interfere—I want to do this on my own. Christian, please. It's important to me,' I say as gently as I can. I don't want to argue. His mouth sets once more into a hard stubborn line, and I think he's going to berate me again.

Oh no.

'Let's not argue, Christian. We've had such a wonderful morning. And last night was'—words fail me, last night was—'heaven.'

He says nothing. I glance over at him and his eyes are closed.

'Yes. Heaven,' he says softly. 'I meant what I said.'

'What?'

'I don't want to let you go.'

'I don't want to go.'

He smiles and it's this new, shy smile that dissolves everything in its path. Boy, it's powerful.

'Good,' he says simply, and he visibly relaxes.

I drive into the parking lot half a block from SIP.

'I'll walk you to work. Taylor will take me

471

from there,' Christian offers. I climb awkwardly out of the car, restricted by my pencil skirt, while Christian climbs out gracefully, at ease with his body or at least giving the impression of someone at ease with his body. Hmm . . . someone who can't bear to be touched can't be that at ease. I frown at my errant thought.

'Don't forget we're seeing Flynn at seven this evening,' he says as he holds his hand out to me. I press the remote door lock and take his hand.

'I won't forget. I'll compile a list of questions for him.'

'Questions? About me?'

I nod.

'I can answer any questions you have about me.' Christian looks affronted.

I smile at him. 'Yes, but I want the unbiased, expensive charlatan's opinion.'

He frowns and suddenly pulls me into his embrace, holding both my hands tightly behind my back.

'Is this a good idea?' he says, his voice low and husky. I lean back to see the anxiety looming large and wide in his eyes. It tears at my soul.

'If you don't want me to, I won't.' I stare at him, blinking, wanting to caress the concern out of his face. I tug on one of my hands and he frees it. I touch his cheek tenderly—it's smooth from shaving this morning.

'What are you worried about?' I ask, my voice soft and soothing.

'That you'll go.'

'Christian, how many times do I have to tell you—I'm not going anywhere. You've already told me the worst. I'm not leaving you.'

'Then why haven't you answered me?'

'Answered you?' I murmur disingenuously.

'You know what I'm talking about, Ana.'

I sigh. 'I want to know that I'm enough for you, Christian. That's all.'

'And you won't take my word for it?' he says, exasperated, releasing me.

'Christian, this has all been so quick. And by your own admission, you're fifty shades of fucked-up. I can't give you what you need,' I mutter. 'It's just not for me. But that makes me feel inadequate, especially seeing you with Leila. Who's to say that one day you won't meet someone who likes doing what you do? And who's to say you won't, you know . . . fall for her? Someone much better suited to your needs.' The thought of Christian with anyone else sickens me. I stare down at my knotted fingers.

'I knew several women who like doing what I like to do. None of them appealed to me the way you do. I've never had an emotional connection with any of them. It's only ever been you, Ana.'

'Because you never gave them a chance. You've spent too long locked up in your fortress, Christian. Look, let's discuss this later. I have to go to work. Maybe Dr. Flynn can offer us his insight.' This is all far too heavy a discussion for a parking lot at eight fifty in the morning, and Christian, for once, seems to agree. He nods but his eyes are wary.

'Come,' he orders, holding out his hand.

*   *   *

When I reach my desk, I find a note asking me to go straight to Elizabeth's office. My heart leaps into my mouth. Oh, this is it. I'm going to get fired.

473

'Anastasia.' Elizabeth smiles kindly, waving me into a chair before her desk. I sit and gaze at her expectantly, hoping that she can't hear my thumping heart. She smoothes her thick black hair and regards me with somber, clear blue eyes.

'I have some rather sad news.'

Sad! Oh no.

'I've called you in to inform you that Jack has left the company rather suddenly.'

I flush. This isn't sad for me. Should I tell her that I know?

'His rather hasty departure has left a vacancy, and we'd like you to fill it for now, until we find a replacement.'

What? I feel the blood rush from my head. *Me?*

'But I've only been here for a week or so.'

'Yes, Anastasia, I understand, but Jack was always a champion of your abilities. He had high hopes for you.'

I stop breathing. He had high hopes of getting me on my back, sure.

'Here's a detailed job description. Have a good look through it, and we can discuss it later today.'

'But—'

'Please, I know this is sudden, but you've already made contact with Jack's key authors. Your chapter notes haven't gone unnoticed by the other editors. You have a shrewd mind, Anastasia. We all think you can do it.'

'Okay.' *This is unreal.*

'Look, think about it. In the meantime you can take Jack's office.'

She stands, effectively dismissing me, and holds out her hand. I shake it in a complete daze.

'I'm glad he's gone,' she whispers and a haunted

look crosses her face. *Holy shit.* What did he do to her?

Back at my desk, I grab my BlackBerry and call Christian.

He answers on the second ring. 'Anastasia. You okay?' he asks, concerned.

'They've just given me Jack's job—well, temporarily,' I blurt out.

'You're kidding,' he whispers, shocked.

'Did you have anything to do with this?' My voice is sharper than I mean it to be.

'No—no, not at all. I mean, with all due respect, Anastasia, you've only been there for a week or so—and I don't mean that unkindly.'

'I know.' I frown. 'Apparently Jack really rated me.'

'Did he, now?' Christian's tone is frosty and then he sighs.

'Well, baby, if they think you can do it, I'm sure you can. Congratulations. Perhaps we should celebrate after we've seen Flynn.'

'Hmm. Are you sure you had nothing to do with this?'

He is silent for a minute, and then he says in a low menacing voice, 'Do you doubt me? It angers me that you do.'

I swallow. Boy, he gets mad so easily. 'I'm sorry,' I breathe, chastened.

'If you need anything, let me know. I'll be here. And Anastasia?'

'What?'

'Use your BlackBerry,' he adds tersely.

'Yes, Christian.'

He doesn't hang up as I expect him to but takes a deep breath.

'I mean it. If you need me, I'm here.' His words are much softer, conciliatory. Oh, he's so mercurial . . . his mood swings are like a metronome set at presto.

'Okay,' I murmur. 'I'd better go. I have to move offices.'

'If you need me. I mean it,' he murmurs.

'I know. Thank you, Christian. I love you.'

I sense his grin at the other end of the phone. I've won him back.

'I love you, too, baby.' Oh, will I ever tire of him saying those words to me?

'I'll talk to you later.'

'Laters, baby.'

I hang up and glance at Jack's office. My office. Holy cow—Anastasia Steele, Acting Editor. Who would have thought? I should ask for more money.

What would Jack think if he knew? I shudder at the thought and wonder idly how he's spending his morning, obviously not in New York as he expected. I stroll into my new office, sit down at the desk, and start reading the job description.

At twelve thirty, Elizabeth buzzes me.

'Ana, we need you in a meeting at one o'clock in the boardroom. Jerry Roach and Kay Bestie will be there—you know, the company president and vice president? All the editors will be attending.'

Shit!

'Do I need to prepare anything?'

'No, this is just an informal gathering we do once a month. Lunch will be provided.'

'I'll be there.' I hang up.

Holy shit! I check through the current roster of Jack's authors. Yes, I've pretty much got those nailed. I have the five manuscripts he was

476

championing, plus two more, which should really be considered for publication. I take a deep breath—I cannot believe it's lunchtime already. The day has flown by, and I'm loving it. There has been so much to absorb this morning. A *ping* from my calendar announces an appointment.

Oh no—Mia! In all the excitement I have forgotten about our lunch. I fish out my BlackBerry and try frantically to find her phone number.

My phone buzzes.

'It's him, in Reception.' Claire's voice is hushed.

'Who?' For a second, I think it might be Christian.

'The blond god.'

'Ethan?'

Oh, what does he want? I immediately feel guilty for not having called him.

Ethan, dressed in a checked blue shirt, white T-shirt, and jeans, beams at me when I appear.

'Wow! You look hot, Steele,' he says, nodding appreciatively. He gives me a quick hug.

'Is everything okay?' I ask.

He frowns. 'Everything's fine, Ana. I just wanted to see you. I haven't heard from you in a while, and I wanted to check how Mr. Mogul was treating you.'

I flush and can't help my smile.

'Okay!' Ethan exclaims, holding up his hands. 'I can tell by the secret smile. I don't want to know any more. I came by on the off chance you could do lunch. I'm enrolling at Seattle for psych courses in September. For my master's.'

'Oh, Ethan. So much has happened. I have a ton to tell you, but right now I can't. I have a meeting.' An idea hits me hard. 'And I wonder if you can do me a really, really, really big favor?' I clasp my

477

hands together in supplication.

'Sure,' he says, bemused by my pleading.

'I'm supposed to be having lunch with Christian and Elliot's sister—but I can't get hold of her, and this meeting's just been sprung on me. Please will you take her for lunch? Please?'

'Aw, Ana! I don't want to babysit some brat.'

'Please, Ethan.' I give him the biggest-bluest-longest-eyelashed look that I can manage. He rolls his eyes and I know I've got him.

'You'll cook me something?' he mutters.

'Sure, whatever, whenever.'

'So where is she?'

'She's due here now.' And as if on cue, I hear her voice.

'Ana!' she calls from the front door.

We both turn, and there she is—all curvaceous and tall with her sleek black bob—wearing a mint green minidress and matching high-heeled pumps with straps around her slim ankles. She looks stunning.

'The brat?' he whispers, gaping at her.

'Yes. The brat that needs babysitting,' I whisper back. 'Hi, Mia.' I give her a quick hug as she stares rather blatantly at Ethan.

'Mia—this is Ethan, Kate's brother.'

He nods, his eyebrows raised in surprise. Mia blinks several times as she gives him her hand.

'Delighted to meet you,' Ethan murmurs smoothly and Mia blinks again—silent for once. She blushes.

Oh my. I don't think I've ever seen her blush.

'I can't make lunch,' I say lamely. 'Ethan has agreed to take you, if that's okay? Can we have a rain check?'

'Sure,' she says quietly. Mia quiet, this is novel.

'Yeah, I'll take it from here. Laters, Ana,' Ethan says, offering Mia his arm. She accepts it with a shy smile.

'Bye, Ana.' Mia turns to me and mouths, 'Oh. My. God!' giving me an exaggerated wink.

She likes him! I wave at them as they leave the building. I wonder what Christian's attitude is about his sister dating. The thought makes me uneasy. She's my age, so he can't object, can he?

This is Christian we're dealing with. My snarky subconscious is back, hatchet-mouthed, cardigan on, and purse in the crook of her arm. I shake off the image. Mia is a grown woman and Christian can be reasonable, can't he? I dismiss the thought and head back to Jack's . . . er . . . my office to prep for the meeting.

It's three thirty when I return. The meeting went well. I have even secured approval to accept the two manuscripts I was championing. It's a heady feeling.

On my desk is an enormous wicker basket crammed with stunning white and pale pink roses. Wow—the fragrance alone is heavenly. I smile as I pick up the card. I know who sent them.

Congratulations, Miss Steele
And all on your own!
No help from your overfriendly, neighborhood,
megalomaniac CEO
Love
Christian

I pick up my BlackBerry to e-mail him.

From: Anastasia Steele
Subject: Megalomaniac . . .
Date: June 16 2011 15:43
To: Christian Grey

. . . is my favorite type of maniac. Thank you for the beautiful flowers. They've arrived in a huge wicker basket that makes me think of picnics and blankets.

x

From: Christian Grey
Subject: Fresh Air
Date: June 16 2011 15:55
To: Anastasia Steele

Maniac, eh? Dr. Flynn may have something to say about that.

You want to go on a picnic?

We could have fun in the great outdoors, Anastasia . . .

How is your day going, baby?

Christian Grey
CEO, Grey Enterprises Holdings, Inc.

Oh my. I flush reading his response.

From: Anastasia Steele
Subject: Hectic
Date: June 16 2011 16:00
To: Christian Grey

The day has flown by. I have hardly had a moment to myself to think about anything other than work. I think I can do this! I'll tell you more when I'm home. Outdoors sounds . . . interesting.
Love you.

A x

PS: Don't worry about Dr. Flynn.

My phone buzzes. It's Claire from Reception, desperate to know who sent the flowers and what happened to Jack. Holed up in the office all day, I have missed the gossip. I tell her quickly that the flowers are from my boyfriend and that I know very little about Jack's departure. My BlackBerry buzzes and I have another e-mail from Christian.

From: Christian Grey
Subject: I'll try . . .
Date: June 16 2011 16:09
To: Anastasia Steele

. . . not to worry.
Laters, baby. x

Christian Grey
CEO, Grey Enterprises Holdings, Inc.

At five thirty, I clean up my desk. I can't believe how quickly the day has gone. I have to get back to Escala and prepare to meet Dr. Flynn. I haven't even had time to think of questions. Perhaps today we can have an initial meeting, and maybe Christian will let me see him again. I shrug off the thought as I dash out of the office, waving a quick good-bye to Claire.

I've also got Christian's birthday to think about. I know what I'm going to give him. I'd like him to have it tonight before we meet Flynn, but how? Beside the parking lot is a small store selling touristy trinkets. Inspiration hits me and I duck inside.

*   *   *

Christian is on his BlackBerry, standing and staring out the glass wall as I enter the great room half an hour later. Turning, he beams at me and wraps up his call.

'Ros, that's great. Tell Barney and we'll go from there . . . Good-bye.'

He strides over to me as I stand shyly in the entryway. He's changed now into a white T-shirt and jeans, all bad boy and smoldering. *Whoa.*

'Good evening, Miss Steele,' he murmurs and he bends to kiss me. 'Congratulations on your promotion.' He wraps his arms around me. He smells delicious.

'You've showered.'

'I've just had a workout with Claude.'

482

'Oh.'

'Managed to knock him on his ass twice.' Christian beams, boyish and pleased with himself. His grin is infectious.

'That doesn't happen often?'

'No. Very satisfying when it does. Hungry?'

I shake my head.

'What?' He frowns at me.

'I'm nervous. About Dr. Flynn.'

'Me, too. How was your day?' He releases me, and I give him a brief summary. He listens attentively.

'Oh—there's one more thing I should tell you,' I add. 'I was supposed to have lunch with Mia.'

He raises his eyebrows, surprised. 'You never mentioned that.'

'I know, I forgot. I couldn't make it because of the meeting, and Ethan took her out to lunch instead.'

His face darkens. 'I see. Stop biting your lip.'

'I'm going to freshen up,' I say, changing the subject and turning to leave before he can react any further.

* * *

Dr. Flynn's office is a short drive from Christian's apartment. *Very handy*, I muse, *for emergency sessions.*

'I usually run here from home,' Christian says as he parks my Saab. 'This is a great car.' He smiles at me.

'I think so, too.' I smile back at him. 'Christian . . . I—' I gaze anxiously at him.

'What is it, Ana?'

'Here.' I pull the small black gift box from my purse. 'This is for you for your birthday. I wanted to give it to you now—but only if you promise not to open it until Saturday, okay?'

He blinks at me in surprise and swallows. 'Okay,' he murmurs cautiously.

Taking a deep breath, I hand it to him, ignoring his bemused expression. He shakes the box, and it produces a very satisfactory rattle. He frowns. I know he's desperate to see what it contains. Then he grins, his eyes alight with youthful, carefree excitement. *Oh boy* . . . he looks his age—and so beautiful.

'You can't open it until Saturday,' I warn him.

'I get it,' he says. 'Why are you giving this to me now?' He pops the box into the inside pocket of his blue pinstriped jacket, close to his heart.

How apt, I muse. I smirk at him.

'Because I can, Mr. Grey.'

His mouth twists with wry amusement.

'Why, Miss Steele, you stole my line.'

We are ushered into Dr. Flynn's palatial office by a brisk and friendly receptionist. She greets Christian warmly, a little too warmly for my taste—she's old enough to be his mother—and he knows her name.

The room is understated: pale green with two dark green couches facing two leather winged chairs, and it has the atmosphere of a gentlemen's club. Dr. Flynn is seated at a desk at the far end of the room.

As we enter, he stands and walks over to join us in the seating area. He wears black pants and a pale blue open-necked shirt—no tie. His bright blue eyes seem to miss nothing.

'Christian.' He smiles amicably.

'John.' Christian shakes his hand. 'You remember Anastasia?'

'How could I forget? Anastasia, welcome.'

'Ana, please,' I mumble as he shakes my hand firmly. I do love his English accent.

'Ana,' he says kindly, ushering us toward the couches.

Christian gestures to one of them for me. I sit, trying to look relaxed, resting my hand on the armrest, and he sprawls on the other couch beside me so that we're at right angles to each other. A small table with a simple lamp is between us. I note with interest a box of tissues beside the lamp.

This isn't what I expected. I had in my mind's eye a stark white room with a black leather chaise longue.

Looking relaxed and in control, Dr. Flynn takes a seat in one of the winged chairs and picks up a leather notepad. Christian crosses his legs, his ankle resting on his knee, and stretches one arm along the back of the couch. Reaching across with his other hand, he finds my hand on the armrest and gives it a reassuring squeeze.

'Christian has requested that you accompany him to one of our sessions,' Dr. Flynn begins gently. 'Just so you know, we treat these sessions with absolute confidentiality—'

I raise my eyebrow at Flynn, halting him mid-speech.

'Oh—um . . . I've signed an NDA,' I murmur, embarrassed that he's stopped. Both Flynn and Christian stare at me, and Christian releases my hand.

'A nondisclosure agreement?' Dr. Flynn's brow

furrows, and he glances quizzically at Christian.

Christian shrugs.

'You start all your relationships with women with an NDA?' Dr. Flynn asks him.

'The contractual ones, I do.'

Dr. Flynn's lip twitches. 'You've had other types of relationships with women?' he asks, and he looks amused.

'No,' Christian answers after a beat, and he looks amused, too.

'As I thought.' Dr. Flynn turns his attention back to me. 'Well, I guess we don't have to worry about confidentiality, but may I suggest that the two of you discuss this at some point? As I understand, you're no longer entering into that kind of contractual relationship.'

'Different kind of contract, hopefully,' says Christian softly, glancing at me. I flush and Dr. Flynn narrows his eyes.

'Ana. You'll have to forgive me, but I probably know a lot more about you than you think. Christian has been very forthcoming.'

I glance nervously at Christian. What has he said?

'An NDA?' he continues. 'That must have shocked you.'

I blink at him. 'Oh, I think the shock of that has paled into insignificance, given Christian's most recent revelations,' I answer, my voice soft and hesitant. I sound so nervous.

'I'm sure.' Dr. Flynn smiles kindly at me. 'So, Christian, what would you like to discuss?'

Christian shrugs like a surly teen. 'Anastasia wanted to see you. Perhaps you should ask her.'

Dr. Flynn's face registers his surprise once more,

and he gazes shrewdly at me.

Holy shit. This is mortifying. I gaze down at my fingers.

'Would you be more comfortable if Christian left us for a while?'

My eyes dart to Christian and he's gazing at me expectantly.

'Yes,' I whisper.

Christian frowns and opens his mouth but closes it again quickly and stands in one swift graceful movement.

'I'll be in the waiting room,' he says, his mouth a flat, grumpy line.

Oh no.

'Thank you, Christian,' Dr. Flynn says impassively.

Christian gives me one long, searching look, then stalks out of the room—but he doesn't slam the door. Phew. I immediately relax.

'He intimidates you?'

'Yes. But not as much as he used to.' I feel disloyal, but it's the truth.

'That doesn't surprise me, Ana. What can I help you with?'

I stare down at my knotted fingers. What can I ask?

'Dr. Flynn, I've never been in a relationship before, and Christian is . . . well, he's Christian. And over the last week or so, a great deal has happened. I haven't had a chance to think things through.'

'What do you need to think through?'

I glance up at him, and his head is cocked to one side as he gazes at me with compassion, I think.

'Well . . . Christian tells me that he's happy to give up . . . er—' I stumble and pause. This is so much more difficult to discuss than I'd imagined.

Dr. Flynn sighs. 'Ana, in the very limited time that you've known him, you've made more progress with my patient than I have in the last two years. You have had a profound effect on him. You must see that.'

'He's had a profound effect on me, too. I just don't know if I'm enough. To fulfill his needs,' I whisper.

'Is that what you need from me? Reassurance?'

I nod.

'Needs change,' he says simply. 'Christian has found himself in a situation where his methods of coping are no longer effective. Very simply, you've forced him to confront some of his demons and rethink.'

I blink at him. This echoes what Christian has told me.

'Yes, his demons,' I murmur.

'We don't dwell on them—they're in the past. Christian knows what his demons are, as do I—and now I'm sure you do, too. I'm much more concerned with the future and getting Christian to a place where he wants to be.'

I frown and he raises an eyebrow.

'The technical term is SFBT—sorry.' He smiles. 'That stands for Solution-Focused Brief Therapy. Essentially, it's goal oriented. We concentrate on where Christian wants to be and how to get him there. It's a dialectical approach. There's no point in breast-beating about the past—all that's been picked over by every physician, psychologist, and psychiatrist Christian's ever seen. We know why he's the way he is, but it's the future that's important. Where Christian envisages himself, where he wants to be. It took you walking out on him to make him take this form of therapy seriously. He realizes that his goal is a loving relationship with you. It's that simple, and that's what we're working on now. Of course there are obstacles—his haphephobia, for one.'

His what? I gasp.

'I'm sorry. I mean his fear of being touched,' Dr. Flynn says, shaking his head as if scolding himself. 'Which I'm sure you're aware of.'

I flush and nod. *Oh, that!*

'He has a morbid self-abhorrence. I'm sure that comes as no surprise to you. And of course there's the parasomnia . . . um—night terrors, sorry, to the layperson.'

I blink at him, trying to absorb all these long words. I know about all of this. But Flynn hasn't mentioned my central concern.

'But he's a sadist. Surely, as such, he has needs that I can't fulfill.'

Dr. Flynn actually rolls his eyes, and his mouth presses into a hard line. 'That's no longer recognized as a psychiatric term. I don't know how many times I have told him that. It's not even classified as a paraphilia anymore, not since the nineties.'

Dr. Flynn has lost me again. I blink at him. He smiles kindly at me.

'This is a pet peeve of mine.' He shakes his head. 'Christian just thinks the worst of any given situation. It's part of his self-abhorrence. Of course, there's such a thing as sexual sadism, but it's not a disease; it's a lifestyle choice. And if it's practiced in a safe, sane relationship between consenting adults, then it's a nonissue. My understanding

489

is that Christian has conducted all of his BDSM relationships in this manner. You're the first lover who hasn't consented, so he's not willing to do it.'

Lover!

'But surely it's not that simple.'

'Why not?' Dr. Flynn shrugs good-naturedly.

'Well . . . the reasons he does it.'

'Ana, that's the point. In terms of solution-focused therapy, it is that simple. Christian wants to be with you. In order to do that, he needs to forgo the more extreme aspects of that kind of relationship. After all, what you're asking for is not unreasonable . . . is it?'

I flush. No, it's not unreasonable, is it?

'I don't think so. But I worry that he does.'

'Christian recognizes that and has acted accordingly. He's not insane.' Dr. Flynn sighs. 'In a nutshell, he's not a sadist, Ana. He's an angry, frightened, brilliant young man, who was dealt a shit hand of cards when he was born. We can all beat our breasts about it, and analyze the who, the how, and the why to death—or Christian can move on and decide how he wants to live. He'd found something that worked for him for a few years, more or less, but since he met you, it no longer works. And as a consequence, he's changing his modus operandi. You and I have to respect his choice and support him in it.'

I gape at him. 'That's my reassurance?'

'As good as it gets, Ana. There are no guarantees in this life.' He smiles. 'And that is my professional opinion.'

I smile, too, weakly. Doctor jokes . . . jeez.

'But he thinks of himself as a recovering alcoholic.'

'Christian will always think the worst of himself. As I said, it's part of his self-abhorrence. It's in his makeup, no matter what. Naturally he's anxious about making this change in his life. He's potentially exposing himself to a whole world of emotional pain, which, incidentally, he had a taste of when you left him. Naturally he's apprehensive.' Dr. Flynn pauses. 'I don't mean to stress how important a role you have in his Damascene conversion—his road to Damascus. But you have. Christian would not be in this place if he had not met you. Personally I don't think that an alcoholic is a very good analogy, but if it works for him for now, then I think we should give him the benefit of the doubt.'

Give Christian the benefit of the doubt. I frown at the thought.

'Emotionally, Christian is an adolescent, Ana. He bypassed that phase in his life totally. He's channeled all his energies into succeeding in the business world, and he has beyond all expectations. His emotional world has to play catch-up.'

'So how do I help?'

Dr. Flynn laughs. 'Just keep doing what you're doing.' He grins at me. 'Christian is head over heels. It's a delight to see.'

I flush, and my inner goddess is hugging herself with glee, but something bothers me.

'Can I ask you one more thing?'

'Of course.'

I take a deep breath. 'Part of me thinks that if he wasn't this broken he wouldn't . . . want me.'

Dr. Flynn's eyebrows shoot up in surprise. 'That's a very negative thing to say about yourself, Ana. And frankly it says more about you than it

491

does about Christian. It's not quite up there with his self-loathing, but I'm surprised by it.'

'Well, look at him . . . and then look at me.'

Dr. Flynn frowns. 'I have. I see an attractive young man, and I see an attractive young woman. Ana, why don't you think of yourself as attractive?'

Oh no . . . I don't want this to be about me. I stare down at my fingers. There's a sharp knock on the door that makes me jump. Christian comes back into the room, glaring at both of us. I flush and glance quickly at Flynn, who is smiling benignly at Christian.

'Welcome back, Christian,' he says.

'I think time is up, John.'

'Nearly, Christian. Join us.'

Christian sits down, beside me this time, and places his hand possessively on my knee. His action does not go unnoticed by Dr. Flynn.

'Did you have any other questions, Ana?' Dr. Flynn asks and his concern is obvious. Shit . . . I should not have asked that question. I shake my head.

'Christian?'

'Not today, John.'

Flynn nods.

'It may be beneficial if you both come again. I'm sure Ana will have more questions.'

Christian nods reluctantly.

I flush. Shit . . . he wants to delve. Christian clasps my hand and regards me intently.

'Okay?' he asks softly.

I smile at him, nodding. Yes, we're going for the benefit of the doubt, courtesy of the good doctor from England.

Christian squeezes my hand and turns to Flynn.

'How is she?' he asks softly.

Me?

'She'll get there,' he says reassuringly.

'Good. Keep me updated of her progress.'

'I will.'

Holy fuck. They're talking about Leila.

'Should we go and celebrate your promotion?' Christian asks me pointedly.

I nod shyly as Christian stands.

We say our quick good-byes to Dr. Flynn, and Christian ushers me out with unseemly haste.

*   *   *

In the street, he turns to me. 'How was that?' His voice is anxious.

'It was good.'

He regards me suspiciously. I cock my head to one side.

'Mr. Grey, please don't look at me that way. Under doctor's orders I am going to give you the benefit of the doubt.'

'What does that mean?'

'You'll see.'

His mouth twists and his eyes narrow. 'Get in the car,' he orders while opening the passenger door of the Saab.

Oh, change of direction. My BlackBerry buzzes. I haul it out of my purse.

Shit, José!

'Hi!'

'Ana, hi . . .'

I stare at Fifty, who is eyeing me suspiciously. 'José,' I mouth at him. He stares impassively at me, but his eyes harden. Does he think I don't notice? I

493

turn my attention back to José.

'Sorry I haven't called you. Is it about tomorrow?' I ask José, but stare up at Christian.

'Yeah, listen—I spoke with some guy at Grey's place, so I know where I'm delivering the photos, and I should get there between five and six . . . after that, I'm free.'

Oh.

'Well, I'm actually staying with Christian right now, and if you want to, he says you can stay at his place.'

Christian presses his mouth in a hard line. Hmm—some host he is.

José is silent for a minute, absorbing this news. I cringe. I haven't had a chance to talk to him about Christian.

'Okay,' he says eventually. 'This thing with Grey, it's serious?'

I turn away from the car and pace to the other side of the sidewalk.

'Yes.'

'How serious?'

I roll my eyes and pause. Why does Christian have to be listening?

'Serious.'

'Is he with you now? That why you're speaking in monosyllables?'

'Yes.'

'Okay. So are you allowed out tomorrow?'

'Of course I am.' I hope. I automatically cross my fingers.

'So where should I meet you?'

'You could pick me up from work,' I offer.

'Okay.'

'I'll text you the address.'

'What time?'

'Six?'

'Sure. I'll see you then, Ana. Looking forward to it. I miss you.'

I grin. 'Cool. I'll see you then.' I switch the phone off and turn.

Christian is leaning against the car watching me carefully, his expression impossible to read.

'How's your friend?' he asks coolly.

'He's well. He'll pick me up from work, and I think we'll go for a drink. Would you like to join us?'

Christian hesitates, his gray eyes cool. 'You don't think he'll try anything?'

'No!' My tone is exasperated—but I refrain from rolling my eyes.

'Okay.' Christian holds his hands up in defeat. 'You hang out with your friend, and I'll see you later in the evening.'

I was expecting a fight, and his easy acquiescence throws me off balance.

'See? I can be reasonable.' He smirks.

My mouth twists. We'll see about that.

'Can I drive?'

Christian blinks at me, surprised by my request.

'I'd rather you didn't.'

'Why, exactly?'

'Because I don't like to be driven.'

'You managed this morning, and you seem to tolerate Taylor driving you.'

'I trust Taylor's driving implicitly.'

'And not mine?' I put my hands on my hips. 'Honestly—your control-freakishness knows no bounds. I've been driving since I was fifteen.'

He shrugs in response, as if this is of

no consequence whatsoever. Oh—he's so exasperating! Benefit of the doubt? Well, screw that.

'Is this my car?' I demand.

He frowns at me. 'Of course it's your car.'

'Then give me the keys, please. I've driven it twice, and only to and from work. Now you're having all the fun.' I am in full-on pout mode. Christian's lips twitch with a repressed smile.

'But you don't know where we're going.'

'I'm sure you can enlighten me, Mr. Grey. You've done a great job of it so far.'

He gazes at me, stunned, and then smiles, his new shy smile that totally disarms me and takes my breath away.

'Great job, eh?' he murmurs.

I blush. 'Mostly yes.'

'Well, in that case.' He hands me the keys, walks around to the driver's door, and opens it for me.

*   *   *

'Left here,' Christian orders, and we head north toward I-5. 'Hell—gently, Ana.' He grabs hold of the dashboard.

Oh, for heaven's sake. I roll my eyes but don't turn to look at him. Van Morrison croons in the background over the car sound system.

'Slow down!'

'I am slowing down!'

Christian sighs. 'What did Flynn say?' I hear his anxiety leaching into his voice.

'I told you. He says I should give you the benefit of the doubt.' Damn—maybe I should have let Christian drive. Then I could watch him. In fact . . .

496

I signal to pull over.

'What are you doing?' he snaps, alarmed.

'Letting you drive.'

'Why?'

'So I can look at you.'

He laughs. 'No, no—you wanted to drive. So, you drive, and I'll look at you.'

I scowl at him. 'Keep your eyes on the road!' he shouts.

My blood boils. Right! I pull over to the curb just before a traffic light and storm out of the car, slamming the door, and stand on the sidewalk, arms crossed. I glare at him. He climbs out of the car.

'What are you doing?' he asks angrily, staring down at me.

'No. What are you doing?'

'You can't park here.'

'I know that.'

'So why have you?'

'Because I've had it with you barking orders. Either you drive or you shut up about my driving!'

'Anastasia, get back in the car before we get a ticket.'

'No.'

He blinks at me, at a total loss, then runs his hands through his hair, and his anger becomes bewilderment. He looks so comical all of a sudden, and I can't help but smile at him. He frowns.

'What?' he snaps once more.

'You.'

'Oh, Anastasia! You are the most frustrating female on the planet.' He throws his hands in the air. 'Fine—I'll drive.' I grab the edges of his jacket and pull him to me.

'No—you are the most frustrating man on the

497

planet, Mr. Grey.'

He gazes down at me, his eyes dark and intense, then he snakes his arms around my waist and embraces me, holding me close.

'Maybe we're meant for each other, then,' he says softly and inhales deeply, his nose in my hair. I wrap my arms around him and close my eyes. For the first time since this morning, I feel myself relax.

'Oh . . . Ana, Ana, Ana,' he breathes, his lips pressed against my hair. I tighten my arms around him, and we stand, immobile, enjoying a moment of unexpected tranquility, on the street. Releasing me, he opens the passenger door. I climb in and sit quietly, watching him walk around the car.

Restarting the car, Christian pulls out into the traffic, absentmindedly humming along to Van Morrison.

Whoa. I've never heard him sing, not even in the shower, ever. I frown. He has a lovely voice—of course. Hmm . . . has he heard me sing?

He wouldn't be asking you to marry him if he had! My subconscious has her arms crossed and is wearing Burberry check. The song finishes and Christian grins.

'You know, if we had gotten a ticket, the title of this car is in your name.'

'Well, good thing I've been promoted—I can afford the fine,' I say smugly, staring at his lovely profile. His lips twitch. Another Van Morrison song starts playing as he takes the on-ramp to I-5, heading north.

'Where are we going?'

'It's a surprise. What else did Flynn say?'

I sigh. 'He talked about FFFSTB or something.'

'SFBT. The latest therapy option,' he mutters.

498

'You've tried others?'

Christian snorts. 'Baby, I've been subjected to them all. Cognitivism, Freud, functionalism, Gestalt, behaviorism . . . You name it, over the years I've done it,' he says and his tone betrays his bitterness. The rancor in his voice is distressing.

'Do you think this latest approach will help?'

'What did Flynn say?'

'He said not to dwell on your past. Focus on the future—on where you want to be.'

Christian nods but shrugs at the same time, his expression cautious.

'What else?' he persists.

'He talked about your fear of being touched, although he called it something else. And about your nightmares and your self-abhorrence.' I glance at him, and in the evening light, he's pensive, chewing on his thumbnail as he drives. He glances quickly at me.

'Eyes on the road, Mr. Grey,' I admonish, my eyebrow cocked at him.

He looks amused and slightly exasperated. 'You were talking forever, Anastasia. What else did he say?'

I swallow. 'He doesn't think you're a sadist,' I whisper.

'Really?' Christian says quietly and frowns. The atmosphere in the car takes a nosedive.

'He says that term's not recognized in psychiatry. Not since the nineties,' I mutter, quickly trying to rescue the mood between us.

Christian's face darkens, and he exhales slowly.

'Flynn and I have differing opinions on this,' he says quietly.

'He said you always think the worst of yourself.

499

I know that's true,' I murmur. 'He also mentioned sexual sadism—but he said that was a lifestyle choice, not a psychiatric condition. Maybe that's what you're thinking about.'

His eyes flash toward me again, and his mouth sets in a grim line.

'So—one talk with the good doctor and you're an expert,' he says acidly and turns his eyes forward.

Oh dear . . . I sigh.

'Look—if you don't want to hear what he said, don't ask me,' I mutter softly.

I don't want to argue. Anyway he's right—what the hell do I know about all his shit? Do I even want to know? I can list the salient points—his control-freakishness, his possessiveness, his jealousy, his overprotectiveness—and I completely understand where he's coming from. I can even understand why he doesn't like to be touched—I've seen the physical scars. I can only imagine the mental ones, and I've only glimpsed his nightmares once. And Dr. Flynn said—

'I want to know what you discussed.' Christian interrupts my thoughts as he heads off I-5 on exit 172, heading west toward the slowly sinking sun.

'He called me your lover.'

'Did he, now?' His tone is conciliatory. 'Well, he's nothing if not fastidious about his terms. I think that's an accurate description. Don't you?'

'Did you think of your subs as lovers?'

Christian's brow creases once more, but this time he's thinking. He turns the Saab smoothly north once again. *Where are we going?*

'No. They were sexual partners,' he murmurs, his voice cautious again. 'You're my only lover. And I want you to be more.'

Oh ... there's that magical word again, brimming with possibility. It makes me smile, and inside I hug myself, trying to contain my joy.

'I know,' I whisper, trying hard to hide my excitement. 'I just need some time, Christian. To get my head around these last few days.' He glances at me oddly, perplexed, his head inclined to one side.

After a beat, the traffic light we're stopped at turns green. He nods and turns the music up, and our discussion is over.

Van Morrison is still singing—more optimistically now—about it being a marvelous night for moondancing. I gaze out the windows at the pines and spruce dusted gold by the fading light of the sun, their long shadows stretching across the road. Christian has turned onto a more residential street, and we're heading west toward the Sound.

'Where are we going?' I ask again as we turn onto a road. I catch a road sign—9TH AVE NW. I am baffled.

'Surprise,' he says and smiles mysteriously.

CHAPTER EIGHTEEN

Christian continues to drive past single-story, well-kept clapboard houses where kids play basketball in their yards or cycle and run around in the street. It all looks affluent and wholesome with the houses nestling among the trees. Perhaps we're going to visit someone? Who?

A few minutes later, Christian turns sharply left, and we're confronted by two ornate white metal gates set in a six-foot-high sandstone wall. Christian presses a button on his door handle and the electric window hums quietly down into the doorframe. He punches a number into the keypad and the gates swing open in welcome.

He glances at me, and his expression has changed. He looks uncertain, even nervous.

'What is it?' I ask, and I can't mask the concern in my voice.

'An idea,' he says quietly and eases the Saab through the gates.

We head up a tree-lined lane just wide enough for two cars. On one side the trees ring a densely wooded area, and on the other there's a vast area of grassland where a once-cultivated field has been left fallow. Grass and wildflowers have reclaimed it, creating a rural idyll—a meadow, where the late evening breeze softly ripples through the grass and the evening sun gilds the wildflowers. It's lovely, utterly tranquil, and suddenly I imagine myself lying in the grass and gazing up at a clear blue summer sky. The thought is tantalizing, yet makes me feel homesick for some strange reason. How odd.

The lane curves around and opens into a sweeping driveway in front of an impressive Mediterranean-style house of soft pink sandstone. It's palatial. All the lights are on, each window brightly illuminated in the dusk. There's a smart black BMW parked in front of the four-car garage, but Christian pulls up outside the grand portico.

Hmm . . . I wonder who lives here. Why are we visiting?

Christian glances anxiously at me as he switches off the car engine.

'Will you keep an open mind?' he asks.

I frown.

'Christian, I've needed an open mind since the day I met you.'

He smiles ironically and nods. 'Fair point well made, Miss Steele. Let's go.'

The dark wood doors open, and a woman with dark brown hair, a sincere smile, and a sharp lilac suit stands waiting. I'm grateful I changed into my new navy shift dress to impress Dr. Flynn. Okay, I'm not wearing killer heels like her—but still, I'm not in jeans.

'Mr. Grey.' She smiles warmly and they shake hands.

'Miss Kelly,' he says politely.

She smiles at me and holds out her hand, which I shake. Her isn't-he-dreamily-gorgeous-wish-he-were-mine flush does not go unnoticed.

'Olga Kelly,' she announces breezily.

'Ana Steele,' I mutter back at her. Who is this woman? She stands aside, welcoming us into the house. It's a shock when I step in. The place is empty—completely empty. We find ourselves in a large entrance hall. The walls are a faded primrose yellow with scuff marks where pictures must once have hung. All that remains are the old-fashioned crystal light fixtures. The floors are dull hardwood. There are closed doors to either side of us, but Christian gives me no time to assimilate what's happening.

'Come,' he says, and taking my hand, he leads me through the archway in front of us into a larger inner vestibule. It's dominated by a curved, sweeping staircase with an intricate iron balustrade, but still he doesn't stop. He takes me through to the main living area, which is empty save for a large

503

faded gold rug—the biggest rug I have ever seen. Oh—and there are four crystal chandeliers.

But Christian's intention is now clear as we head across the room and outside through open French doors to a large stone terrace. Below us there's half a football field of manicured lawn, but beyond that is the view. *Wow.*

The panoramic, uninterrupted vista is breath-taking—staggering even: twilight over the Sound. In the distance lies Bainbridge Island, and farther still on this crystal-clear evening, the setting sun sinks slowly, glowing blood and flame orange, beyond Olympic National Park. Vermilion hues bleed into the cerulean sky, with opals and aquamarines, and meld with the darker purples of the scant wispy clouds and the land beyond the Sound. It is nature's best, a visual symphony orchestrated in the sky and reflected in the deep, still waters of the Sound. I am lost to the view—staring, trying to absorb such beauty.

I realize I'm holding my breath in awe, and Christian is still holding my hand. As I reluctantly turn my eyes away from the view, he's gazing anxiously at me.

'You brought me here to admire the view?' I whisper.

He nods, his expression serious.

'It's staggering, Christian. Thank you,' I murmur, letting my eyes feast on it once more. He releases my hand.

'How would you like to look at it for the rest of your life?' he breathes.

What? I whip my face back to his, startled blue eyes to pensive gray. I think my mouth drops open, and I gape at him blankly.

504

'I've always wanted to live on the coast. I sail up and down the Sound coveting these houses. This place hasn't been on the market long. I want to buy it, demolish it, and build a new house—for us,' he whispers, and his eyes glow, translucent with his hopes and dreams.

Holy cow. Somehow I remain upright. I'm reeling. *Live here! In this beautiful haven! For the rest of my life . . .*

'It's just an idea,' he adds cautiously.

I glance back to assess the interior of the house. How much is it worth? It must be what—five, ten million dollars? I have no idea. Holy shit.

'Why do you want to demolish it?' I ask, looking back at him. His face falls. *Oh no.*

'I'd like to make a more sustainable home, using the latest ecological techniques. Elliot could build it.'

I gaze back at the room again. Miss Olga Kelly is on the far side, hovering by the entrance. She's the Realtor, of course. I notice the room is huge and double height, a little like the great room at Escala. There's a balcony above—that must be the landing on the second floor. There's a huge fireplace and a whole line of French doors opening onto the terrace. It has an old-world charm.

'Can we look around the house?'

He blinks at me. 'Sure.' He shrugs, puzzled.

Miss Kelly's face lights up like Christmas when we head back in. She's delighted to take us on a tour and gives us the spiel.

The house is enormous: twelve thousand square feet on six acres of land. As well as the main living room, there's the eat-in—no, banquet-in—kitchen with family room attached—*family!*—a music room,

505

a library, a study and, much to my amazement, an indoor pool and exercise suite with sauna and steam room attached. Downstairs in the basement there's a cinema—*jeez*—and game room. Hmm . . . what sort of games could we play in here?

Miss Kelly points out all sorts of features, but basically the house is beautiful and was obviously at one time a happy family home. It's a little shabby now, but nothing that some TLC couldn't cure.

As we follow Miss Kelly up the magnificent main stairs to the second floor, I can hardly contain my excitement . . . this house has everything I could ever wish for in a home.

'Couldn't you make the existing house more ecological and self-sustaining?'

Christian blinks at me, nonplussed. 'I'd have to ask Elliot. He's the expert in all this.'

Miss Kelly leads us into the master suite, where full-height windows open onto a balcony, and the view is still spectacular. I could sit in bed and gaze out all day, watching the sailing boats and the changing weather.

There are five additional bedrooms on this floor. *Kids!* I push the thought hastily to one side. I have too much to process already. Miss Kelly is busily suggesting to Christian how the grounds could accommodate riding stables and a paddock. *Horses!* Terrifying images of my few riding lessons flash through my mind, but Christian doesn't appear to be listening.

'The paddock would be where the meadow is now?' I ask.

'Yes,' Miss Kelly says brightly.

To me the meadow looks like somewhere to lie in the long grass and have picnics, not for some four-legged fiend of Satan to roam.

Back in the main room, Miss Kelly discreetly disappears, and Christian leads me out once more onto the terrace. The sun has set and lights from the towns on the Olympic peninsula are twinkling on the far side of the Sound.

Christian pulls me into his arms and tips my chin up with his index finger, staring intently down at me.

'Lot to take in?' he asks, his expression unreadable.

I nod.

'I wanted to check that you liked it before I bought it.'

'The view?'

He nods.

'I love the view, and I like the house that's here.'

'You do?'

I smile shyly. 'Christian, you had me at the meadow.'

His lips part as he inhales sharply, then his face transforms with a grin, and his hands are suddenly thrusting into my hair and his mouth is on mine.

*   *   *

Back in the car as we head for Seattle, Christian's mood has lifted considerably.

'So, you're going to buy it?' I ask.

'Yes.'

'You'll put Escala on the market?'

He frowns. 'Why would I do that?'

'To pay for . . .' My voice trails off—of course. I flush.

He smirks at me. 'Trust me, I can afford it.'

507

'Do you like being rich?'

'Yes. Show me someone who doesn't,' he says darkly.

Okay, get off that subject quickly.

'Anastasia, you're going to have to learn to be rich, too, if you say yes,' he says softly.

'Wealth isn't something I've ever aspired to, Christian.' I frown.

'I know. I love that about you. But then again, you've never been hungry,' he says simply. His words are sobering.

'Where are we going?' I ask brightly, changing the subject.

'To celebrate.' Christian relaxes.

Oh! 'Celebrate what, the house?'

'Have you forgotten already? Your acting editor role.'

'Oh yes.' I grin. Unbelievably, I had forgotten.

'Where?'

'Up high at my club.'

'Your club?'

'Yes. One of them.'

*   *   *

The Mile High Club is on the seventy-sixth floor of Columbia Tower, higher even than Christian's apartment. It's very trendy and has the most head-spinning views over Seattle.

'Cristal, ma'am?' Christian hands me a glass of chilled champagne as I sit perched on a barstool.

'Why, thank you, *Sir.*' I stress the last word flirtatiously, batting my eyelashes at him deliberately.

He gazes at me and his face darkens. 'Are you

flirting with me, Miss Steele?'

'Yes, Mr. Grey, I am. What are you going to do about it?'

'I'm sure I can think of something,' he says, his voice low. 'Come—our table's ready.'

As we approach the table, Christian stops me, his hand on my elbow.

'Go and take your panties off,' he whispers.

Oh? A delicious tingle runs down my spine.

'Go,' he commands quietly.

Whoa, what? He's not smiling—he's dead serious. Every muscle below my waistline tightens. I hand him my glass of champagne, turn sharply on my heel, and head for the restroom.

Shit. What's he going to do? Perhaps this club is aptly named.

The restrooms are the height of modern design—all dark wood, black granite, and pools of light from strategically placed halogens. In the privacy of the stall, I smirk as I divest myself of my underwear. Again I'm grateful I changed into the navy blue shift dress. I thought it appropriate attire to meet the good Dr. Flynn—I hadn't expected the evening to take this unexpected course.

I am excited already. Why does he affect me so? I slightly resent how easily I fall under his spell. I know now that we won't be spending the evening talking through all our issues and recent events . . . but how can I resist him?

Checking my appearance in the mirror, I am bright-eyed and flushed with excitement. *Issues, schmissues.*

I take a deep breath and head back out into the club. I mean, it's not as if I haven't gone pantyless before. My inner goddess is draped in a pink feather boa and diamonds, strutting her stuff in fuck-me shoes.

Christian stands politely when I return to the table, his expression unreadable. He looks his usual perfect, cool, calm, and collected self. Of course, I now know differently.

'Sit beside me,' he says. I slide into the seat and he sits. 'I've ordered for you. I hope you don't mind.' He hands me my half-finished glass of champagne, regarding me intently, and under his scrutiny, my blood heats anew. He rests his hands on his thighs. I tense and part my legs slightly.

The waiter arrives with a dish of oysters on crushed ice. *Oysters.* The memory of the two of us in the private dining room at the Heathman fills my mind. We were discussing his contract. Oh, boy. We've come a long way since then.

'I think you liked oysters last time you tried them.' His voice is low, seductive.

'Only time I've tried them.' I'm all breathy, my voice exposing me. His lips twitch with a smile.

'Oh, Miss Steele—when will you learn?' he muses.

He takes an oyster from the dish and lifts his other hand from his thigh. I flinch in anticipation, but he reaches for a slice of lemon.

'Learn what?' I ask. Jeez, my pulse is racing. His long, skilled fingers gently squeeze the lemon over the shellfish.

'Eat,' he says, holding the shell close to my mouth. I part my lips, and he gently places the shell on my bottom lip. 'Tip your head back slowly,' he murmurs. I do as he asks and the oyster slips down my throat. He doesn't touch me, only the shell does.

Christian helps himself to one, then feeds me another. We continue this torturous routine until all twelve are gone. His skin never connects with mine. It's driving me crazy.

'Still like oysters?' he asks as I swallow the final one.

I nod, flushed, craving his touch.

'Good.'

I squirm in my seat. Why is this so hot?

He puts his hand casually on his own thigh again, and I melt. Now. Please. Touch me. My inner goddess is on her knees, naked except for her panties—begging. He runs his hand up and down his thigh, lifts it, then places it back where it was.

The waiter tops up our champagne glasses and whisks away our plates. Moments later he's back with our entrées, sea bass—*I don't believe it*—served with asparagus, sautéed potatoes, and a hollandaise sauce.

'A favorite of yours, Mr. Grey?'

'Most definitely, Miss Steele. Though I believe it was cod at the Heathman.' His hand moves up and down his thigh. My breathing spikes, but still he doesn't touch me. It's so frustrating. I try to concentrate on our conversation.

'I seem to remember we were in a private dining room then, discussing contracts.'

'Happy days,' he says, smirking. 'This time I hope to get to fuck you.' He moves his hand to pick up his knife.

Gah!

He takes a bite out of his sea bass. He's doing this on purpose.

'Don't count on it,' I mutter with a pout and he glances at me, amused. 'Speaking of contracts,' I add. 'The NDA.'

'Tear it up,' he says simply.

Whoa.

'What? Really?'

'Yes.'

'You're sure I'm not going to run to the *Seattle Times* with an exposé?' I tease.

He laughs and it's a wonderful sound. He looks so young.

'No. I trust you. I'm going to give you the benefit of the doubt.'

Oh. I grin shyly at him. 'Ditto,' I breathe.

His eyes light up. 'I'm very glad you're wearing a dress,' he murmurs. And bam—desire courses through my already overheated blood.

'Why haven't you touched me, then?' I hiss.

'Missing my touch?' he asks, grinning. He's amused . . . the bastard.

'Yes,' I seethe.

'Eat,' he orders.

'You're not going to touch me, are you?'

'No.' He shakes his head.

What? I gasp out loud.

'Just imagine how you'll feel when we're home,' he whispers. 'I can't wait to get you home.'

'It will be your fault if I combust here on the seventy-sixth floor,' I mutter through gritted teeth.

'Oh, Anastasia. We'd find a way to put the fire out,' he says, grinning salaciously at me.

Fuming, I dig into my sea bass, and my inner goddess narrows her eyes in quiet, devious contemplation. We can play this game, too. I learned the basics during our meal at the Heathman. I take a bite out of my sea bass. It is melt-in-the-mouth delicious. I close my eyes,

512

savoring the taste. When I open them, I begin my seduction of Christian Grey, very slowly hitching my skirt up, exposing more of my thighs.

Christian pauses momentarily, a forkful of fish suspended midair.

Touch me.

After a beat, he resumes eating. I take another bite of sea bass, ignoring him. Then, putting down my knife, I run my fingers up the inside of my lower thigh, lightly tapping my skin with my fingertips. It's distracting even to me, especially as I am craving his touch. Christian pauses once more.

'I know what you're doing.' His voice is low and husky.

'I know that you know, Mr. Grey,' I reply softly. 'That's the point.' I pick up an asparagus stalk, gaze sideways at him from beneath my lashes, then dip the asparagus into the hollandaise sauce, swirling the tip around and around.

'You're not turning the tables on me, Miss Steele.' Smirking he reaches over and takes the spear from me—amazingly and annoyingly managing not to touch me again. No, this isn't right—this is not going according to plan. *Gah!*

'Open your mouth,' he commands.

I am losing this battle of wills. I glance up at him again, and his eyes blaze bright gray. Parting my lips a fraction, I run my tongue across my lower lip. Christian smiles and his eyes darken further.

'Wider,' he breathes, his lips parting so that I can see his tongue. I groan inwardly and bite my bottom lip, then do as he asks.

I hear his sharp intake of breath—he's not so immune. Good, I am finally getting to him.

Keeping my eyes locked on his, I take the spear

513

in my mouth, and suck gently . . . delicately . . . on the end. The hollandaise sauce is mouthwatering. I bite down, moaning quietly in appreciation.

Christian closes his eyes. *Yes!* When he opens them again, his pupils have dilated. The effect on me is immediate. I groan and reach out to touch his thigh. To my surprise, he uses his other hand to grab my wrist.

'Oh no you don't, Miss Steele,' he murmurs softly. Raising my hand to his mouth, he gently brushes my knuckles with his lips, and I squirm. Finally! More, please.

'Don't touch,' he scolds me quietly, and places my hand back on my knee. It's so frustrating—this brief unsatisfactory contact.

'You don't play fair.' I pout.

'I know.' He picks up his champagne glass to propose a toast, and I mirror his actions.

'Congratulations on your promotion, Miss Steele.' We clink glasses and I blush.

'Yes, kind of unexpected,' I mutter. He frowns as if some unpleasant thought has crossed his mind.

'Eat,' he orders. 'I am not taking you home until you've finished your meal, and then we can really celebrate.' His expression is so heated, so raw, so commanding. I am melting.

'I'm not hungry. Not for food.'

He shakes his head, thoroughly enjoying himself, but narrows his eyes at me just the same.

'Eat, or I'll put you across my knee, right here, and we'll entertain the other diners.'

His words make me squirm. He wouldn't dare! Him and his twitchy palm. I press my mouth into a hard line and stare at him. Picking up an asparagus stalk, he dips the head into the hollandaise.

'Eat this,' he murmurs, his voice low and seductive.

I willingly comply.

'You really don't eat enough. You've lost weight since I've known you.' His tone is gentle.

I don't want to think about my weight; truth is, I like being this slim. I swallow the asparagus.

'I just want to go home and make love,' I mutter disconsolately. Christian grins.

'So do I, and we will. Eat up.'

Reluctantly, I turn back to my food and start to eat. Honestly, I've taken my panties off and everything. I feel like a child who has been denied candy. He is such a tease, a delicious, hot, naughty tease, and all mine.

He quizzes me about Ethan. As it turns out, Christian does business with Kate and Ethan's father. Hmm . . . it's a small world. I'm relieved he doesn't mention Dr. Flynn or the house, as I'm finding it difficult to concentrate on our conversation. I want to go home.

The carnal anticipation is unfurling between us. He's so good at this. Making me wait. Setting the scene. Between bites, he places his hand on his thigh, so close to mine, but still doesn't touch me just to tease me further.

Bastard! Finally I finish my food and place my knife and fork on the plate.

'Good girl,' he murmurs, and those two words hold so much promise.

I frown at him. 'What now?' I ask, desire clawing at my belly. Oh, I want this man.

'Now? We leave. I believe you have certain expectations, Miss Steele. Which I intend to fulfill to the best of my ability.'

Whoa!

'The best . . . of your a . . . bil . . . ity?' I stutter. *Holy shit.*

He grins and stands.

'Don't we have to pay?' I ask, breathless.

He cocks his head to one side. 'I am a member here. They'll bill me. Come, Anastasia, after you.' He steps aside, and I stand to leave, conscious that I am not wearing my panties.

He gazes at me darkly, like he's undressing me, and I glory in his carnal appraisal. It just makes me feel so sexy—this beautiful man desires me. Will I always get a kick out of this? Deliberately stopping in front of him, I smooth my dress over my hips.

Christian whispers in my ear, 'I can't wait to get you home.' But he still doesn't touch me.

On the way out he murmurs something about the car to the maître d', but I'm not listening; my inner goddess is incandescent with anticipation. Jeez, she could light up Seattle.

Waiting by the elevators, we are joined by two middle-aged couples. When the doors open, Christian takes my elbow and steers me to the back. I glance around, and we're surrounded by dark smoked-glass mirrors. As the other couples enter, one man in a rather unflattering brown suit greets Christian.

'Grey.' He nods politely. Christian nods in return but is silent.

The couples stand in front of us, facing the elevator doors. They are obviously friends—the women chat loudly, excited and animated after their meal. I think they're all a little tipsy.

As the doors close, Christian briefly stoops down beside me to tie his shoelace. Odd, his shoelaces aren't undone. Discreetly he places his hand on my ankle, startling me, and as he stands his hand travels swiftly up my leg, skating deliciously over my skin—whoa—right up. I have to stifle my gasp of surprise as his hand reaches my backside. Christian moves behind me.

Oh my. I gape at the people in front of us, staring at the backs of their heads. They have no idea what we're up to. Wrapping his free arm around my waist, Christian pulls me to him, holding me in place as his fingers explore. *Holy fucking shit . . . in here?* The elevator travels smoothly down, stopping at the fifty-third floor to let some more people on, but I am not paying attention. I am focused on every little move his fingers make. Circling around . . . now moving forward, questing, as we shuffle back.

Again I stifle a groan when his fingers find their goal.

'Always so ready, Miss Steele,' he whispers as he slips a finger inside me. I squirm and gasp. How can he do this with all these people here?

'Keep still and quiet,' he warns, murmuring in my ear.

I'm flushed, warm, wanting, trapped in an elevator with seven people, six of them oblivious to what's occurring in the corner. His finger slides in and out of me, again and again. My breathing . . . Jeez, it's embarrassing. I want to tell him to stop . . . and continue . . . and stop. I sag against him, and he tightens his arm around me, his erection against my hip.

We halt again at the forty-fourth floor. *Oh . . . how long is this torture going to continue? In . . . out . . . in . . . out . . .* Subtly I grind myself against his

517

persistent finger. After all this time of not touching me, he chooses now! Here! And it makes me feel so—wanton.

'Hush,' he breathes, seemingly unaffected as yet two more people come aboard. The elevator is getting crowded. Christian moves us both farther back so that we're now pressed into the corner, holding me in place and torturing me further. He nuzzles my hair. I'm sure we look like a young couple in love, canoodling in the corner, if anyone could be bothered to turn around and see what we're doing . . . And he eases a second finger inside me.

Fuck! I groan, and I'm thankful that the gaggle of people in front of us are still chatting away, totally oblivious.

Oh, Christian, what you do to me. I lean my head against his chest, closing my eyes and surrendering to his unrelenting fingers.

'Don't come,' he whispers. 'I want that later.' He splays his hand out on my belly, pressing down slightly, as he continues his sweet persecution. The feeling is exquisite.

Finally the elevator reaches the first floor. With a loud *ping* the doors open, and almost instantly the passengers start exiting. Christian slowly slips his fingers out of me and kisses the back of my head. I glance around at him, and he smiles, then nods again at Mr. Badly Fitted Brown Suit, who returns his nod of acknowledgment as he shuffles out of the elevator with his wife. I barely notice, concentrating instead on staying upright and trying to manage my panting. Jeez, I feel aching and bereft. Christian releases me, leaving me to stand on my own two feet without leaning on him.

518

Turning, I gaze up at him. He looks cool and unruffled, his usual composed self. Hmm . . . This is so not fair.

'Ready?' he asks. His eyes gleam wickedly as he slips first his index, then his middle finger into his mouth and sucks on them. 'Mighty fine, Miss Steele,' he whispers. I nearly convulse on the spot.

'I can't believe you just did that,' I murmur, and I'm practically coming apart at the seams.

'You'd be surprised what I can do, Miss Steele,' he says. Reaching out, he tucks a lock of hair behind my ear, a slight smile betraying his amusement.

'I want to get you home, but maybe we'll only make it as far as the car.' He grins down at me as he takes my hand and leads me out of the elevator.

What! Sex in the car? Can't we just do it here on the cool marble of the lobby floor . . . please?

'Come.'

'Yes, I want to.'

'Miss Steele!' he admonishes me with mock-amused horror.

'I've never had sex in a car,' I mumble. Christian halts and places those same fingers under my chin, tipping my head back and glaring down at me.

'I'm very pleased to hear that. I have to say I'd be very surprised, not to say mad, if you had.'

I flush, blinking up at him. Of course; I've only had sex with him. I frown.

'That's not what I meant.'

'What did you mean?' His tone is unexpectedly harsh.

'Christian, it was just an expression.'

'The famous expression, "I've never had sex in a car." Yes, it just trips off the tongue.'

What's his problem?

'Christian, I wasn't thinking. For heaven's sake, you've just . . . um, done that to me in an elevator full of people. My wits are scattered.'

He raises his eyebrows. 'What did I do to you?' he challenges.

I scowl at him. He wants me to say it.

'You turned me on, big time. Now take me home and fuck me.'

His mouth drops open then he laughs, surprised. Now he looks young and carefree. Oh, to hear him laugh. I love it because it's so rare.

'You're a born romantic, Miss Steele.' He takes my hand, and we head out of the building to where the valet stands by my Saab.

*   *   *

'So you want sex in a car,' Christian murmurs as he switches on the ignition.

'Quite frankly, I would have been happy with the lobby floor.'

'Trust me, Ana, so would I. But I don't enjoy being arrested at this time of night, and I didn't want to fuck you in a restroom. Well, not today.'

What! 'You mean there was a possibility?'

'Oh yes.'

'Let's go back.'

He turns to gaze at me and laughs. His laughter is infectious; soon we're both laughing—wonderful, cathartic, head-held-back laughter. Reaching over, he places his hand on my knee, caressing it gently with skilled fingers. I stop laughing.

'Patience, Anastasia,' he murmurs and pulls into the Seattle traffic.

He parks the Saab in the Escala garage and turns off the engine. Suddenly, in the confines of the car, the atmosphere between us changes. With wanton anticipation, I glance at him, trying to contain my palpitating heart. He's turned toward me, leaning against the door, his elbow propped on the steering wheel.

He pulls his lower lip with his thumb and index finger. His mouth is so distracting. I want it on me. He's watching me intently, his eyes dark gray. My mouth goes dry. He smiles a slow sexy smile.

'We will fuck in the car at a time and place of my choosing. Right now, I want to take you on every available surface of my apartment.'

It's like he's addressing me below the waist . . . my inner goddess performs four *arabesques* and a *pas de basque*.

'Yes.' Jeez, I sound so breathy, desperate.

He leans forward a fraction. I close my eyes, waiting for his kiss, thinking—finally. But nothing happens. After an interminable few seconds, I open my eyes to find him gazing at me. I can't figure out what he's thinking, but before I can say anything, he distracts me once more.

'If I kiss you now, we won't make it into the apartment. Come.'

Gah! Could this man be any more frustrating? He climbs out of the car.

*   *   *

Once again, we wait for the elevator, my body

thrumming with anticipation. Christian holds my hand, running his thumb rhythmically across my knuckles, each stroke echoing through me. Oh, I want his hands on all of me. He's tortured me long enough.

'So, what happened to instant gratification?' I murmur while we wait.

'It's not appropriate in every situation, Anastasia.'

'Since when?'

'Since this evening.'

'Why are you torturing me so?'

'Tit for tat, Miss Steele.'

'How am I torturing you?'

'I think you know.'

I gaze up at him and his expression is difficult to read. *He wants my answer . . . that's it.*

'I'm into delayed gratification, too,' I whisper, smiling shyly.

He tugs my hand unexpectedly, and suddenly I am in his arms. He grabs the hair at the nape of my neck, pulling gently so my head tips back.

'What can I do to make you say yes?' he asks fervently, throwing me off balance once more. I blink at him—at his lovely, serious, desperate expression.

'Give me some time . . . please,' I murmur. He groans and finally kisses me, long and hard. Then we're in the elevator, and we're all hands and mouths and tongues and lips and fingers and hair. Desire, thick and strong, lances through my blood, clouding all my reason. He pushes me against the wall, pinning me with his hips, one hand in my hair, the other at my chin, holding me in place.

'You own me,' he whispers. 'My fate is in your

hands, Ana.'

His words are intoxicating, and in my overheated state, I want to rip off his clothes. I push off his jacket, and as the elevator arrives at the apartment, we tumble out into the foyer.

Christian pins me to the wall by the elevator, his jacket falling to the floor, and his hand travels up my leg, his lips never leaving mine. He hoists up my dress.

'First surface here,' he breathes and abruptly he lifts me. 'Wrap your legs around me.'

I do as I'm told, and he turns and lays me down on the foyer table, so he's standing between my legs. I'm aware that the usual vase of flowers is missing. *Huh?* Reaching into his jeans pocket, he fishes out a foil packet and hands it to me, undoing his fly.

'Do you know how much you turn me on?'

'What?' I pant. 'No . . . I . . .'

'Well, you do,' he mutters, 'all the time.' He grabs the foil packet from my hands. Oh, this is so quick, but after all his tantalizing teasing, I want him badly—right now. He gazes down at me as he rolls on the condom, then puts his hands under my thighs, spreading my legs wider.

Positioning himself, he pauses. 'Keep your eyes open. I want to see you,' he whispers, and clasping both my hands with his, he sinks slowly into me.

I try, I really do, but the feeling is so exquisite. What I've been waiting for after all his teasing. *Oh, the fullness, this feeling . . .* I groan and arch my back off the table.

'Open!' he growls, tightening his hands on mine and thrusting sharply into me so that I cry out.

I blink my eyes open, and he stares down at me

wide-eyed. Slowly he withdraws, then sinks into me once more, his mouth slackening and then forming an *Ah . . .* , but he says nothing. Seeing his arousal, his reaction to me—I light up inside, my blood scorching through my veins. His gray eyes burn into mine. He picks up the rhythm, and I revel in it, glory in it, watching him, watching me—his passion, his love—as we come apart, together.

I call out as I explode around him, and Christian follows.

'Yes, Ana!' he cries. He collapses on me, releasing my hands and resting his head on my chest. My legs are still wrapped around him, and under the patient, maternal eyes of the Madonna paintings, I cradle his head against me and struggle to catch my breath.

He raises his head to look at me. 'I'm not finished with you yet,' he murmurs and leaning up, he kisses me.

*   *   *

I lie naked in Christian's bed, sprawled over his chest, panting. Holy cow—does his energy ever wane? Christian trails his fingers up and down my back.

'Satisfied, Miss Steele?'

I murmur my assent. I have no energy left for talking. Raising my head, I turn unfocused eyes to him and bask in his warm, fond gaze. Very deliberately, I angle my head down so he knows I am going to kiss his chest.

He tenses momentarily, and I plant a soft kiss in his chest hair, breathing in his unique Christian smell, mixed with sweat and sex. It's heady. He

524

rolls onto his side so I'm lying beside him and gazes down at me.

'Is sex like this for everyone? I'm surprised anyone ever goes out,' I murmur, feeling suddenly shy.

He grins. 'I can't speak for everyone, but it's pretty damned special with you, Anastasia.' He bends and kisses me.

'That's because you're pretty damned special, Mr. Grey,' I agree, smiling and caressing his face. He blinks down at me, at a loss.

'It's late. Go to sleep,' he says. He kisses me, then lies down and pulls me to him so we're spooning in bed.

'You don't like compliments.'

'Go to sleep, Anastasia.'

Hmm . . . But he is pretty damned special. Jeez . . . why doesn't he realize this?

'I loved the house,' I murmur.

He says nothing for a minute, but I sense his grin.

'I love you. Go to sleep.' He nuzzles my hair, and I drift into sleep, safe in his arms, dreaming of sunsets and French doors and wide staircases . . . and a small copper-haired boy running through a meadow, laughing and giggling as I chase him.

~ § ~   ~ § ~   ~ § ~

'Gotta go, baby.' Christian kisses me just below my ear.

I open my eyes; it's morning. I turn to face him, but he's up and dressed and fresh and delicious, leaning over me.

'What time is it?' *Oh no . . . I don't want to be*

late.

'Don't panic. I have a breakfast meeting.' He rubs his nose against mine.

'You smell good,' I murmur, stretching out beneath him, my limbs pleasurably tight and creaky from all our exploits yesterday. I wrap my arms around his neck.

'Don't go.'

He cocks his head to one side and raises his eyebrow. 'Miss Steele—are you trying to keep a man from an honest day's work?'

I nod sleepily at him, and he smiles his new shy smile.

'As tempting as you are, I have to go.' He kisses me and stands. He's wearing a really sharp dark navy suit, white shirt, and navy tie, and he looks every inch the CEO . . . the hot CEO.

'Laters, baby,' he murmurs and he's off.

Glancing at the clock, I note it's already seven—I must have slept through the alarm. Well, time to get up.

*   *   *

In the shower, inspiration hits me. I've thought of another birthday present for Christian. It's so difficult to buy something for the man who has everything. I've already given him my main present, and I still have the other item I bought at the tourist shop, but this is one present that will really be for me. I hug myself in anticipation as I switch off the shower. I just have to prepare it.

In the walk-in closet, I put on a dark red fitted dress with a square neckline, cut quite low. Yes, this will do for work.

Now for Christian's present. I start rummaging through his drawers, looking for his ties. In the bottom drawer I find those faded, ripped jeans, the ones he wears in the playroom—the ones he looks so hot in. I stroke them gently, using my whole hand. Oh my, the material is so soft.

Beneath them, I find a large, black, flat cardboard box. It piques my interest immediately. What's in here? I stare at it, feeling like I'm trespassing again. Taking it out, I shake it. It's heavy as if it holds papers or manuscripts. I cannot resist, I open the lid—and quickly shut it again. Holy fuck—photographs from the Red Room. The shock makes me sit back on my heels as I try to wipe the image from my brain. *Why did I open the box? Why has he kept them?*

I shudder. My subconscious scowls at me—*this is before you. Forget them.*

She's right. When I stand up I notice his ties are hanging at the end of his clothes rail. I find my favorite and exit quickly.

Those photos are BA—Before Ana. My subconscious nods with approval, but it's with a heavier heart that I head into the main room for breakfast. Mrs. Jones smiles at me warmly and then frowns.

'Everything all right, Ana?' she asks kindly.

'Yes,' I murmur, distracted. 'Do you have a key to the . . . um, playroom?'

She pauses momentarily, surprised.

'Yes, of course.' She unclips a small bunch of keys from her belt. 'What would you like for breakfast, dear?' she asks as she hands me the keys.

'Just granola. I won't be long.'

I feel more ambivalent about this gift now, but

527

only since the discovery of those photographs. *Nothing's changed!* my subconscious barks at me again, glaring at me over her half-moon winged glasses. That one picture you saw was hot, my inner goddess chips in, and mentally I scowl at her. Yes it was—too hot for me.

What else does he have hidden away? Quickly I ferret through the museum chest, take what I need, and lock the playroom door behind me. Wouldn't do for José to discover this!

I hand the keys back to Mrs. Jones and sit down to devour my breakfast, feeling odd that Christian is absent. The photographic image dances, unwelcome, around my mind. I wonder who it was. Leila, perhaps?

* * *

On my drive in to work, I debate whether or not to tell Christian I found his photographs. *No,* screams my subconscious, her Edvard Munch face on. I decide she's probably right.

* * *

As I sit down at my desk, my BlackBerry buzzes.

From: Christian Grey
Subject: Surfaces
Date: June 17 2011 08:59
To: Anastasia Steele

I calculate that there are at least 30 surfaces

to go. I am looking forward to each and every one of them. Then there's the floors, the walls—and let's not forget the balcony.

After that there's my office . . .

Miss you. x

Christian Grey
Priapic CEO, Grey Enterprises Holdings, Inc.

His e-mail makes me smile, and all my earlier reservations evaporate. It's me he wants now, and memories of last night's sexcapades flood my mind *. . . the elevator, the foyer, the bed.* Priapic is right. I wonder idly what the female equivalent might be?

From: Anastasia Steele
Subject: Romance?
Date: June 17 2011 09:03
To: Christian Grey

Mr. Grey

You have a one-track mind.

I missed you at breakfast.

But Mrs. Jones was very accommodating.

A x

From: Christian Grey
Subject: Intrigued

Date: June 17 2011 09:07
To: Anastasia Steele

What was Mrs. Jones accommodating about?

What are you up to, Miss Steele?

Christian Grey
Curious CEO, Grey Enterprises Holdings, Inc.

How does he know?

From: Anastasia Steele
Subject: Tapping Nose
Date: June 17 2011 09:10
To: Christian Grey

Wait and see—it's a surprise.

I need to work . . . let me be.

Love you.

A x

From: Christian Grey
Subject: Frustrated
Date: June 17 2011 09:12
To: Anastasia Steele

I hate it when you keep things from me.

Christian Grey
CEO, Grey Enterprises Holdings, Inc.

I stare at the small screen of my BlackBerry. The vehemence implicit in his e-mail takes me by surprise. Why does he feel like this? It's not like I'm hiding erotic photographs of my exes.

From: Anastasia Steele
Subject: Indulging you
Date: June 17 2011 09:14
To: Christian Grey

It's for your birthday.

Another surprise.

Don't be so petulant.

A x

He doesn't reply immediately, and I'm called into a meeting so I can't dwell on it for too long.

*   *   *

When I next glance at my BlackBerry, to my horror I realize it's four in the afternoon. Where has the day gone? Still no message from Christian. I decide to e-mail him again.

From: Anastasia Steele
Subject: Hello
Date: June 17 2011 16:03
To: Christian Grey

Are you not talking to me?

Don't forget I am going for a drink with José, and that he's staying with us tonight.

Please rethink about joining us.

A x

He doesn't reply, and I feel a frisson of unease. I hope he's okay. Calling his cell phone, I get his voice mail. The announcement simply says 'Grey, leave a message' in his most clipped tone.

'Hi . . . um . . . it's me. Ana. Are you okay? Call me,' I stutter through my message. I've never had to leave one for him before. I flush as I hang up. *Of course he'll know it's you, idiot!* My subconscious rolls her eyes at me. I am tempted to ring his PA, Andrea, but decide that's a step too far. Reluctantly I continue my work.

*　　　*　　　*

My phone rings unexpectedly and my heart jumps. *Christian!* But no—it's Kate, my best friend, finally!

'Ana!' she shouts from wherever she is.

'Kate! Are you back? I've missed you.'

'Me, too. I have so much to tell you. We're at Sea-Tac—me and my man.' She giggles in a most un-Kate-like way.

'Cool. I have so much to tell you, too.'

'See you back at the apartment?'

'I'm having drinks with José. Join us.'

'José's in town? Sure! Text me where.'

'Okay.' I beam.

'You good, Ana?'

'Yeah, I'm fine.'

'Still with Christian?'

'Yes.'

'Good. Laters!'

Oh, not her, too. Elliot's influence knows no bounds.

'Yeah—laters, baby.' I grin and she hangs up.

Wow. Kate is home. How am I going to tell her all that has happened? I should write it down so I don't forget anything.

*   *   *

An hour later my office phone rings—*Christian*? No, it's Claire.

'You should see the guy asking for you in Reception. How come you know all these hot guys, Ana?'

José must be here. I glance at the clock—it's five fifty-five, and a small thrill of excitement pulses through me. I haven't seen him in ages.

'Ana, wow! You look great. So grown-up.' He grins at me.

Just because I'm wearing a smart dress . . . jeez!

He hugs me hard. 'And tall,' he mutters in amazement.

'It's just the shoes, José. You don't look so bad yourself.'

He's wearing jeans, a black T-shirt, and a black-

and-white- checked flannel shirt.

'I'll grab my things and we can go.'

'Cool. I'll wait here.'

*   *   *

I pick up two Rolling Rocks from the crowded bar and head over to the table where José is seated.

'You found Christian's place okay?'

'Yeah. I haven't been inside. I just delivered the photos to the service elevator. Some guy named Taylor took them up. Looks like quite a place.'

'It is. You should see inside.'

'Can't wait. *Salud,* Ana. Seattle agrees with you.'

I flush as we clink bottles. It's Christian that agrees with me. '*Salud.* Tell me about your show and how it went.'

He beams and launches into the story. He sold all but three of his photos, which has taken care of his student loans and left him with some money to spare.

'And I've been commissioned to do some landscapes for the Portland Tourist Board. Pretty cool, huh?' he finishes proudly.

'Oh, José—that's wonderful. Not interfering with your studies though?' I frown at him.

'Nah. Now that you guys have gone, plus three of the guys I used to hang out with, I have more time.'

'No hot babe to keep you busy? Last time I saw you, you had half a dozen women hanging on your every word.' I arch an eyebrow at him.

'Nah, Ana. None of them are woman enough for me.' He's all bravado.

'Oh sure. José Rodriguez, lady-killer.' I giggle.

'Hey—I have my moments, Steele.' He looks

534

vaguely hurt, and I am chastened.

'Sure you do.' I mollify him.

'So, how's Grey?' he asks, his tone changing, becoming cooler.

'He's good. We're good,' I murmur.

'Serious, you say?'

'Yes. Serious.'

'He's not too old for you?'

'Oh, José. You know what my mom says—I was born old.'

José's mouth twists wryly.

'How is your mom?' And like that, we are out of the danger zone.

'Ana!'

I turn and there's Kate with Ethan. She looks gorgeous: bleached strawberry-blonde hair, golden tan, and beaming white smile, and so shapely in her white camisole and tight white jeans. All eyes are on Kate. I leap up from my seat to give her a hug. Oh, how I've missed this woman!

She pushes me away from her and holds me at arm's length, examining me closely. I flush under her intense gaze.

'You've lost weight. A lot of weight. And you look different. Grown-up. What's been going on?' she says, all mother hen. 'I like your dress. Suits you.'

'A lot's happened since you went away. I'll tell you later, when we're on our own.' I am not ready for the Katherine Kavanagh Inquisition just yet. She regards me suspiciously.

'You're okay?' she asks gently.

'Yes.' I smile, though I'd be happier knowing where Christian is.

'Cool.'

'Hi, Ethan.' I grin at him, and he gives me a quick hug.

'Hi, Ana,' he whispers in my ear.

José frowns at him.

'How was lunch with Mia?' I ask Ethan.

'Interesting,' he says cryptically.

Oh?

'Ethan—you know José?'

'We've met once,' José mutters, assessing Ethan as they shake hands.

'Yeah, at Kate's place in Vancouver,' Ethan says, smiling pleasantly at José. 'Right—who's for a drink?'

*   *   *

I make my way to the restrooms. While there I text Christian our location; perhaps he'll join us. There are no missed calls from him and no e-mails. This is not like him.

'Whassup, Ana?' José asks as I come back to the table.

'I can't reach Christian. I hope he's okay.'

'He'll be fine. Like another beer?'

'Sure.'

Kate leans across. 'Ethan says some mad stalker ex-girlfriend was in the apartment with a gun?'

'Well . . . yeah.' I shrug apologetically. Oh jeez—do we have to do this now?

'Ana—what the hell's been going on?' Kate stops abruptly and checks her phone.

'Hi, baby,' she says when she answers it. *Baby!* She frowns and looks at me. 'Sure,' she says and turns to me. 'It's Elliot . . . he wants to talk to you.'

'Ana.' Elliot's voice is clipped and quiet, and my

536

scalp prickles ominously.

'What's wrong?'

'It's Christian. He's not back from Portland.'

'What? What do you mean?'

'His helicopter has gone missing.'

'*Charlie Tango*?' I whisper as all the breath leaves my body. 'No!'

CHAPTER NINETEEN

I stare at the flames, mesmerized. They dance and weave bright blazing orange with tips of cobalt blue in the fireplace in Christian's apartment. And despite the heat pumping out of the fire and the blanket draped around my shoulders, I'm cold. Bone-chillingly cold.

I'm aware of hushed voices, many hushed voices. But they're in the background, a distant buzz. I don't hear the words. All I can hear, all I can focus on, is the soft hiss of the gas from the fire.

My thoughts turn to the house we saw yesterday and the huge fireplaces—real fireplaces for burning wood. I'd like to make love with Christian in front of a real fire. I'd like to make love with Christian in front of this fire. Yes, that would be fun. No doubt, he'd think of some way to make it memorable, like all the times we've made love. I snort wryly to myself, even the times when we were just fucking. Yes, those were pretty memorable, too. *Where is he?*

The flames shimmy and flicker, holding me captive, keeping me numb. I focus solely on their flaring, scorching beauty. They are bewitching.

Anastasia, you've bewitched me.

He said that the first time he slept with me in my bed. *Oh no . . .*

I wrap my arms around myself, and the world falls away from me and reality bleeds into my consciousness. The creeping emptiness inside expands some more. *Charlie Tango* is missing.

'Ana. Here,' Mrs. Jones gently coaxes me, her voice bringing me back into the room, into the now, into the anguish. She gives me a cup of tea. I take the cup and saucer gratefully, the rattle betraying my shaking hands.

'Thank you,' I whisper, my voice hoarse from unshed tears and the large lump in my throat.

Mia sits across from me on the larger-than-large U-shaped couch, holding hands with Grace. They gaze at me, pain and anxiety etched on their lovely faces. Grace looks older—a mother worried for her son. I blink dispassionately at them. I can't offer a reassuring smile, a tear even—there's nothing, just blankness and the growing emptiness. I gaze at Elliot, José, and Ethan, who stand around the breakfast bar, all serious faces, talking quietly. Discussing something in soft subdued voices. Behind them Mrs. Jones busies herself in the kitchen.

Kate is in the TV room, monitoring the local news. I hear the faint squawk from the big plasma TV. I can't bear to see the news item again—CHRISTIAN GREY MISSING—his beautiful face on TV.

Idly it occurs to me that I've never seen so many people in this room, yet they are still dwarfed by its sheer size. Little islands of lost, anxious people in my Fifty's home. What would he think about their being here?

Somewhere, Taylor and Carrick are talking to the authorities who are drip-feeding us information, but it's all meaningless. The fact is, he's missing. He's been missing for eight hours. No sign, no word from him. The search has been called off—this much I do know. It's just too dark. And we don't know where he is. He could be hurt, hungry, or worse. *No!*

I offer another silent prayer to God. *Please let Christian be okay. Please let Christian be okay.* I repeat it over and over in my head—my mantra, my lifeline, something concrete to cling to in my desperation. I refuse to think the worst. No, don't go there. There is hope.

'You're my lifeline.'

Christian's words come back to haunt me. Yes, there is always hope. I must not despair. His words echo through my mind.

'I'm now a firm advocate of instant gratification. Carpe diem, Ana.'

Why didn't I seize the day?

'I'm doing this because I've finally met someone I want to spend the rest of my life with.'

I close my eyes in silent prayer, rocking gently. *Please let the rest of his life not be this short. Please, please.* We haven't had enough time . . . we need more time. We've done so much in the last few weeks, come so far. It can't end. All our tender moments: the lipstick, when he made love to me for the first time at the Olympic hotel, on his knees in front of me offering himself to me, finally touching him.

'I am just the same, Ana. I love you and I need you. Touch me. Please.'

Oh, I love him so. I will be nothing without him,

nothing but a shadow—all the light eclipsed. *No no no . . . my poor Christian.*

'This is me, Ana. All of me . . . and I'm all yours. What do I have to do to make you realize that? To make you see that I want you any way I can get you. That I love you.'

And I you, my Fifty Shades.

I open my eyes and gaze unseeing into the fire once more, memories of our time together flitting through my mind: his boyish joy when we were sailing and gliding; his suave, sophisticated, hot-as-hell look at the masked ball; dancing, oh yes, dancing here in the apartment to Sinatra, whirling around the room; his quiet, anxious hope yesterday at the house—that stunning view.

'I will lay my world at your feet, Anastasia. I want you, body and soul, forever.'

Oh, please, let him be okay. He cannot be gone. He is the center of my universe.

An involuntary sob escapes my throat, and I clutch my hand to my mouth. No. I must be strong.

José is suddenly at my side, or has he been there a while? I have no idea.

'Do you want to call your mom or dad?' he asks gently.

No! I shake my head and clutch José's hand. I cannot speak, I know I will dissolve if I do, but the warmth and gentle squeeze of his hand offers me no solace.

Oh, Mom. My lip trembles at the thought of my mother. Should I call her? No. I couldn't deal with her reaction. Maybe Ray; he wouldn't get emotional—he never gets emotional, not even when the Mariners lose.

Grace rises to join the boys, distracting me. That

must be the longest she's sat still. Mia comes to sit beside me, too, and grabs my other hand.

'He will come back,' she says, her voice initially determined but cracking on the last word. Her eyes are wide and red-rimmed, her face pale and pinched from lack of sleep.

I gaze up at Ethan, who is watching Mia and Elliot, who has his arms around Grace. I glance at the clock. It's after eleven, heading toward midnight. *Damn time!* With each passing hour, the clawing emptiness expands, consuming me, choking me. I know deep down inside I am preparing myself for the worst. I close my eyes and offer up another silent prayer, clasping both Mia's and José's hands.

Opening my eyes again, I stare into the flames once more. I can see his shy smile—my favorite of all his expressions, a glimpse of the real Christian, my real Christian. He is so many people: control freak, CEO, stalker, sex god, Dom—and at the same time—such a boy with his toys. I smile. His car, his boat, his plane, his *Charlie Tango* helicopter . . . my lost boy, truly lost right now. My smile fades and pain lances through me. I remember him in the shower, wiping away the lipstick marks.

'I'm nothing, Anastasia. I'm a husk of a man. I don't have a heart.'

The lump in my throat expands. Oh, Christian, you do, you do have a heart, and it's mine. I want to cherish it forever. Even though he's so complex and difficult, I love him. I will always love him. There will never be anyone else. Ever.

I remember sitting in Starbucks weighing up my Christian pros and cons. All those cons, even those photographs I found this morning, melt into insignificance now. There's just him and whether he'll come back. *Oh please, Lord, bring him back, please let him be okay. I'll go to church . . . I'll do anything.* Oh, if I get him back, I shall seize the day. His voice echoes around in my head once more: '*Carpe diem, Ana.*'

I gaze deeper into the fire, the flames still licking and curling around each other, blazing brightly. Then Grace shrieks, and everything goes into slow motion.

'Christian!'

I turn my head in time to see Grace barreling across the great room from where she had been pacing somewhere behind me, and there in the entrance stands a dismayed Christian. He's dressed in just his shirtsleeves and suit pants, and he's holding his navy jacket, shoes, and socks. He looks tired, dirty, and utterly beautiful.

Holy fuck . . . Christian. He's alive. I gaze numbly at him, trying to work out if I'm hallucinating or if he's really here.

His expression is one of utter bewilderment. He deposits his jacket and shoes on the floor in time to catch Grace, who throws her arms around his neck and kisses him hard on the cheek.

'Mom?'

Christian gazes down at her, completely at a loss.

'I thought I'd never see you again,' Grace whispers, voicing our collective fear.

'Mom, I'm here.' I hear the consternation in his voice.

'I died a thousand deaths today,' she whispers, her voice barely audible, echoing my thoughts. She gasps and sobs, no longer able to hold back her tears. Christian frowns, horrified or mortified—I don't know which—then after a beat, envelops her

542

in a huge hug, holding her close.

'Oh, Christian,' she chokes, wrapping her arms around him, weeping into his neck—all self-restraint forgotten—and Christian doesn't balk. He just holds her, rocking to and fro, comforting her. Scalding tears pool in my eyes. Carrick hollers from the hallway.

'He's alive! Shit—you're here!' He appears from Taylor's office, clutching his cell phone, and embraces both of them, his eyes closed in sweet relief.

'Dad?'

Mia squeals something unintelligible from beside me, then she's up and runs to join her parents, hugging all of them, too.

Finally the tears start to cascade down my cheeks. He's here, he's fine. But I cannot move.

Carrick is the first to pull away, wiping his eyes and clapping Christian on the shoulder. Mia releases them then, and Grace steps back.

'Sorry,' she mumbles.

'Hey, Mom—it's okay,' Christian says, consternation still evident on his face.

'Where were you? What happened?' Grace cries and puts her head in her hands.

'Mom,' Christian mutters. He draws her into his arms again and kisses the top of her head. 'I'm here. I'm good. It's just taken me a hell of a long time to get back from Portland. What's with the welcoming committee?' He looks up and scans the room until his eyes lock with mine.

He blinks and glances briefly at José, who lets go of my hand. Christian's mouth tightens. I drink in the sight of him and relief courses through me, leaving me spent, exhausted, and completely

543

elated. Yet my tears don't stop. Christian turns his attention back to his mother.

'Mom, I'm good. What's wrong?' Christian says reassuringly. She places her hands on either side of his face.

'Christian, you've been missing. Your flight plan—you never made it to Seattle. Why didn't you contact us?'

Christian's eyebrows shoot up in surprise. 'I didn't think it would take this long.'

'Why didn't you call?'

'No power in my cell.'

'You didn't stop . . . call collect?'

'Mom—it's a long story.'

'Oh, Christian! Don't you ever do that to me again! Do you understand?' she half shouts at him.

'Yes, Mom.' He wipes her tears away with his thumbs and hugs her once more. When she composes herself, he releases her to hug Mia, who slaps him hard on the chest.

'You had us so worried!' she blurts out, and she, too, is in tears.

'I'm here now, for heaven's sake,' Christian mutters.

As Elliot comes forward, Christian relinquishes Mia to Carrick, who already has one arm around his wife. He curls the other around his daughter. Elliot hugs Christian briefly, much to Christian's surprise, and slaps him hard on the back.

'Great to see you,' Elliot says loudly, if a little gruffly, trying to hide his emotion.

As the tears stream down my face, I can see it all. The great room is bathed in it—unconditional love. He has it in spades; he's just never accepted it before, and even now he's at a total loss.

Look, Christian, all these people love you! Perhaps now you'll start believing it.

Kate is standing behind me—she must have left the TV room—and she gently strokes my hair.

'He's really here, Ana,' she murmurs comfortingly.

'I'm going to say hi to my girl now,' Christian tells his parents. Both of them nod, smile, and step aside.

He moves toward me, gray eyes bright though weary and still bemused. From somewhere deep inside, I find the strength to stagger to my feet and bolt into his open arms.

'Christian!' I sob.

'Hush,' he says and holds me, burying his face in my hair and inhaling deeply. I raise my tearstained face to his, and he kisses me far too briefly.

'Hi,' he murmurs.

'Hi,' I whisper back, the lump in the back of my throat burning.

'Miss me?'

'A bit.'

He grins. 'I can tell.' And with a gentle touch of his hand, he wipes away the tears that refuse to stop running down my cheeks.

'I thought . . . I thought—' I choke.

'I can see. Hush . . . I'm here. I'm here . . .' he murmurs and kisses me chastely again.

'Are you okay?' I ask, releasing him and touching his chest, his arms, his waist—oh, the feel of this warm, vital, sensual man beneath my fingers— reassures me that he's here, standing in front of me. He's back. He doesn't so much as flinch. He just regards me intently.

'I'm okay. I'm not going anywhere.'

545

'Oh, thank God.' I clasp him around his waist again, and he hugs me once more. 'Are you hungry? Do you need something to drink?'

'Yes.'

I step back to get him something, but he doesn't let me go. He tucks me under his arm and extends a hand to José.

'Mr. Grey,' says José evenly.

Christian snorts. 'Christian, please,' he says.

'Christian, welcome back. Glad you're okay . . . and, um—thanks for letting me stay.'

'No problem.' Christian narrows his eyes, but he's distracted by Mrs. Jones, who is suddenly at his side. It only occurs to me now that she's not her usual smart self. I hadn't noticed it before. Her hair is loose, and she's in soft gray leggings and a large gray sweatshirt with WSU COUGARS emblazoned on the front that dwarfs her. She looks years younger.

'Can I get you something, Mr. Grey?' She wipes her eyes with a tissue.

Christian smiles fondly at her. 'A beer, please, Gail—Budvar—and a bite to eat.'

'I'll get it,' I murmur, wanting to do something for my man.

'No. Don't go,' he says softly, tightening his arm around me.

The rest of his family closes in, and Ethan and Kate join us. He shakes Ethan's hand and gives Kate a quick peck on the cheek. Mrs. Jones returns with a bottle of beer and a glass. He takes the bottle but shakes his head at the glass. She smiles and returns to the kitchen.

'Surprised you don't want something stronger,' mutters Elliot. 'So what the fuck happened to you? First I knew was when Dad called me to say the chopper was missing.'

'Elliot!' Grace scolds.

'Helicopter,' Christian growls, correcting Elliot, who grins, and I suspect this is a family joke.

'Let's sit and I'll tell you.' Christian pulls me over to the couch, and everyone sits down, all eyes on Christian. He takes a long drink of his beer. He spies Taylor hovering at the entrance and nods. Taylor nods back.

'Your daughter?'

'She's fine now. False alarm, sir.'

'Good.' Christian smiles.

Daughter? What happened to Taylor's daughter?

'Glad you're back, sir. Will that be all?'

'We have a helicopter to pick up.'

Taylor nods. 'Now? Or will the morning do?'

'Morning, I think, Taylor.'

'Very good, Mr. Grey. Anything else, sir?'

Christian shakes his head and raises his bottle to him. Taylor gives him a rare smile—rarer than Christian's, I think—and heads out, presumably to his office or up to his room.

'Christian, what happened?' Carrick demands.

Christian launches into his story. He was flying in *Charlie Tango* with Ros, his number two, to deal with a funding issue at WSU in Vancouver. I can barely keep up, I'm so dazed. I just hold Christian's hand and stare at his manicured fingernails, his long fingers, the creases on his knuckles, his wristwatch—an Omega with three small dials. I gaze up at his beautiful profile as he continues his tale.

'Ros had never seen Mount Saint Helens, so on the way back as a celebration, we took a quick detour. I heard the temporary flight restriction was lifted a while back, and I wanted to take a look. Well, it's fortunate that we did. We were flying low, about two hundred feet above ground level, when the instrument panel lit up. We had a fire in the tail—I had no choice but to cut all the electronics and land.' He shakes his head. 'I set her down by Silver Lake, got Ros out, and managed to put the fire out.'

'A fire? Both engines?' Carrick is horrified.

'Yep.'

'Shit! But I thought—'

'I know,' Christian interrupts him. 'It was sheer luck I was flying so low,' he murmurs. I shudder. He releases my hand and puts his arm around me.

'Cold?' he asks me. I shake my head.

'How did you put out the fire?' asks Kate, her Carla Bernstein instincts kicking in. Jeez, she sounds terse sometimes.

'Extinguisher. We have to carry them—by law,' Christian answers levelly.

His words from long ago circle my mind. *I thank Divine Providence every day that it was you who came to interview me and not Katherine Kavanagh.*

'Why didn't you call or use the radio?' Grace asks.

Christian shakes his head. 'With the electronics out, we had no radio. And I wasn't going to risk turning them on because of the fire. GPS was still working on the BlackBerry, so I was able to navigate to the nearest road. Took us four hours to walk there. Ros was in heels.' Christian's mouth presses into a disapproving flat line.

'We had no cell reception. There's no coverage at Gifford. Ros's battery died first. Mine dried up on the way.'

548

Holy hell. I tense and Christian pulls me into his lap.

'So how did you get back to Seattle?' Grace asks, blinking slightly at the sight of the two of us, no doubt. I flush.

'We hitched and pooled our resources. Between us, Ros and I had six hundred dollars, and we thought we'd have to bribe someone to drive us back, but a truck driver stopped and agreed to bring us home. He refused the money and shared his lunch with us.' Christian shakes his head in dismay at the memory. 'Took forever. He didn't have a cell—weird but true. I didn't realize.' He stops, gazing at his family.

'That we'd worry?' Grace scoffs. 'Oh, Christian!' she scolds him. 'We've been going out of our minds!'

'You've made the news, bro.'

Christian rolls his eyes. 'Yeah. I figured that much when I arrived to this reception and the handful of photographers outside. I'm sorry, Mom—I should have asked the driver to stop so I could phone. But I was anxious to be back.' He glances at José.

Oh, that's why, because José is staying here. I frown at the thought. Jeez—all that worry.

Grace shakes her head. 'I'm just glad you're back in one piece, darling.'

I start to relax, resting my head against his chest. He smells outdoorsy, slightly sweaty, of body wash—of Christian, the most welcome scent in the world. Tears start to trickle down my face again, tears of gratitude.

'Both engines?' Carrick says again, frowning in disbelief.

'Go figure.' Christian shrugs and runs his hand down my back.

'Hey,' he whispers. He puts his fingers under my chin and tilts my head back. 'Stop with the crying.'

I wipe my nose with the back of my hand in a most unladylike way. 'Stop with the disappearing.' I sniff and his lips quirk up.

'Electrical failure . . . that's odd, isn't it?' Carrick says again.

'Yes, crossed my mind, too, Dad. But right now, I'd just like to go to bed and think about all that shit tomorrow.'

'So the media know that *the* Christian Grey has been found safe and well?' Kate says.

'Yes. Andrea and my PR people will deal with the media. Ros called her after we dropped her home.'

'Yes, Andrea called me to let me know you were still alive.' Carrick grins.

'I must give that woman a raise. Sure is late,' says Christian.

'I think that's a hint, ladies and gentlemen, that my dear bro needs his beauty sleep,' Elliot scoffs suggestively. Christian grimaces at him.

'Cary, my son is safe. You can take me home now.'

Cary? Grace looks adoringly at her husband.

'Yes. I think we could use the sleep,' Carrick replies, smiling down at her.

'Stay,' Christian offers.

'No, sweetheart, I want to get home. Now that I know you're safe.'

Christian reluctantly eases me onto the couch and stands. Grace hugs him once more, presses her head against his chest, and closes her eyes, content.

550

He wraps his arms around her.

'I was so worried, darling,' she whispers.

'I'm okay, Mom.'

She leans back and studies him intently while he holds her. 'Yes. I think you are,' she says slowly, glances at me, and smiles. I flush.

We follow Carrick and Grace as they make their way to the foyer. Behind me, I'm aware that Mia and Ethan are having a heated whispered conversation, but I can't hear it.

Mia is smiling shyly at Ethan, and he's gaping at her and shaking his head. Suddenly she crosses her arms and turns on her heel. He rubs his forehead with one hand, obviously frustrated.

'Mom, Dad—wait for me,' Mia calls sullenly. Perhaps she's as mercurial as her brother.

Kate hugs me hard. 'I can tell some serious shit's been going down while I've been blissfully ignorant in Barbados. It's kind of obvious you two are nuts about each other. I'm glad he's safe. Not just for him, Ana—for you, too.'

'Thank you, Kate,' I whisper.

'Yeah. Who knew we'd find love at the same time?' She grins. Wow. She's admitted it.

'With brothers!' I giggle.

'We could end up sisters-in-law,' she quips.

I tense, then mentally kick myself as Kate stands back to gaze at me with her what-aren't-you-telling-me look. I flush. Damn, should I tell her he's asked me?

'Come on, baby,' Elliot summons her from the elevator.

'Let's talk tomorrow, Ana. You must be exhausted.'

I am reprieved. 'Sure. You, too, Kate—you've

traveled such a long distance today.'

We hug once more, then she and Elliot follow the Greys into the elevator. Ethan shakes Christian's hand and gives me a quick hug. He looks distracted, but he follows them into the elevator and the doors close.

José is hovering in the hallway as we come out of the foyer.

'Look. I'll turn in . . . leave you guys,' he says.

I blush. Why is this awkward?

'Do you know where to go?' Christian asks.

José nods.

'Yeah, the housekeeper—'

'Mrs. Jones,' I prompt.

'Yeah, Mrs. Jones, she showed me earlier. Quite a place you have here, Christian.'

'Thank you,' Christian says politely as he comes to stand beside me, placing his arm around my shoulders. Leaning over, he kisses my hair.

'I'm going to eat whatever Mrs. Jones has put out for me. Good night, José.' Christian wanders back into the great room, leaving José and me at the entrance.

Wow! Left alone with José.

'Well, good night.' José looks uncomfortable all of a sudden.

'Good night, José, and thank you for staying.'

'Sure, Ana. Any time your rich, hotshot boyfriend goes missing—I'll be there.'

'José!' I admonish him.

'Only kidding. Don't get mad. I'll be leaving early in the morning. I'll see you sometime, yeah? I've missed you.'

'Sure, José. Soon, I hope. Sorry tonight was so . . . shitty.' I smirk apologetically.

'Yeah.' He grins. 'Shitty.' He hugs me. 'Seriously, Ana, I'm glad you're happy, but I'm here if you need me.'

I gaze up at him. 'Thank you.'

He flashes me a sad, bittersweet smile, and then he goes upstairs.

I turn back to the great room. Christian stands beside the couch, watching me with an unreadable expression on his face. We're finally alone and we gaze at each other.

'He's still got it bad, you know,' he murmurs.

'And how would you know that, Mr. Grey?'

'I recognize the symptoms, Miss Steele. I believe I have the same affliction.'

'I thought I'd never see you again,' I whisper. There—the words are out. All my worst fears packaged neatly in one short sentence now exorcised.

'It wasn't as bad as it sounds.'

I pick up his suit jacket and shoes from where they lie on the floor and move toward him.

'I'll take that,' he whispers, reaching for his jacket.

Christian gazes down at me as if I'm his reason for living and mirrors my look, I'm sure. He is here, really here. He pulls me into his arms and wraps himself around me.

'Christian,' I gasp, and my tears start anew.

'Hush,' he soothes, kissing my hair. 'You know . . . in the few seconds of sheer terror before I landed, all my thoughts were of you. You're my talisman, Ana.'

'I thought I'd lost you,' I breathe. We stand, holding each other, reconnecting and reassuring each other. As I tighten my arms around him, I

553

realize I'm still holding his shoes. I drop them noisily to the floor.

'Come and shower with me,' he murmurs.

'Okay.' I glance up at him. I don't want to let go. Reaching down, he tilts my chin up with his fingers.

'You know, even tearstained, you are beautiful, Ana Steele.' He leans down and kisses me gently. 'And your lips are so soft.' He kisses me again, deepening it.

Oh my . . . and to think I could have lost . . . no . . . I stop thinking and surrender myself.

'I need to put my jacket down,' he murmurs.

'Drop it,' I murmur against his lips.

'I can't.'

I lean back to gaze up at him, puzzled.

He smirks at me. 'This is why.' From the inside breast pocket he pulls out the small box I gave him that contains my present. He slings the jacket over the back of the couch and places the box on top.

Seize the day, Ana, my subconscious prods me. Well, it's after midnight, so technically it's his birthday.

'Open it,' I whisper, and my heart starts pounding.

'I was hoping you'd say that,' he murmurs. 'This has been driving me crazy.'

I grin impishly at him. I feel giddy. He gives me his shy smile, and I melt despite my thumping heart, delighting in his amused yet intrigued expression. With deft fingers, he unwraps and opens the box. His brow creases as he fishes out a small, rectangular, plastic key chain featuring a picture made up of tiny pixels that flash on and off like an LED screen. It depicts the Seattle skyline with the word SEATTLE written boldly across the landscape.

He stares at it for a minute and then gazes at me, bemused, a frown marring his lovely brow.

'Turn it over,' I whisper, holding my breath.

He does, and his eyes shoot to mine, wide and gray, alive with wonder and joy. His lips part in disbelief.

The word YES flashes on and off on the key ring.

'Happy birthday,' I whisper.

CHAPTER TWENTY

'You'll marry me?' he whispers, incredulous.

I nod nervously, flushing and anxious and not quite believing his reaction—this man whom I thought I'd lost. How could he not understand how much I love him?

'Say it,' he orders softly, his gaze intense and hot.

'Yes, I'll marry you.'

He inhales sharply and moves suddenly, grabbing me and swinging me around in a most un-Fifty-like manner. He's laughing, young and carefree, radiating joyful elation. I grab his arms to hold on, feeling his muscles ripple beneath my fingers, and his infectious laughter sweeps me up—dizzy, addled, a girl totally and utterly smitten with her man. He puts me down and kisses me. Hard. His hands are on either side of my face, his tongue insistent, persuasive . . . arousing.

'Oh, Ana,' he breathes against my lips, and it's an exultation that leaves me reeling. He loves me, of that I have no doubt, and I savor the taste of this delicious man, this man I thought I might never see again. His joy is evident—his eyes shining, his youthful smile—and his relief almost palpable.

'I thought I'd lost you,' I murmur, still dazzled and breathless from his kiss.

'Baby, it will take more than a malfunctioning 135 to keep me away from you.'

'135?'

'*Charlie Tango*. She's a Eurocopter EC135, the safest in its class.' Some unnamed but dark emotion crosses his face briefly, distracting me. What isn't he saying? Before I can ask him, he stills and looks down at me, frowning, and for a second I think he's going to tell me. I blink up into his speculative gray eyes.

'Wait a minute. You gave this to me before we saw Flynn,' he says, holding up the key chain. He looks almost horrified.

Oh dear, where's he going with this? I nod, keeping a straight face.

His mouth drops open.

I shrug apologetically. 'I wanted you to know that whatever Flynn said, it wouldn't make a difference to me.'

Christian blinks at me in disbelief. 'So all yesterday evening, when I was begging you for an answer, I had it already?' He's dismayed. I nod again, trying desperately to gauge his reaction. He gazes at me in stupefied wonder, but then narrows his eyes and his mouth twists with amused irony.

'All that worry,' he whispers ominously. I grin at him and shrug once more. 'Oh, don't try and get cute with me, Miss Steele. Right now, I want . . .' He runs his hand through his hair, then shakes his head and changes tack.

'I can't believe you left me hanging.' His whisper is laced with disbelief. His expression alters subtly, his eyes gleaming wickedly, his mouth twitching into a carnal smile.

Holy hell. A thrill runs through me. What's he thinking?

'I believe some retribution is in order, Miss Steele,' he says softly.

Retribution? Oh shit! I know he's playing—but I take a cautious step back from him anyway.

He grins. 'Is that the game?' he whispers. 'Because I will catch you.' And his eyes burn with a bright playful intensity. 'And you're biting your lip,' he adds threateningly.

All of my insides tighten at once. *Oh my.* My future husband wants to play. I take another step back, then turn to run—but in vain. Christian grabs me in one easy swoop while I squeal with delight, surprise, and shock. He hoists me over his shoulder and heads down the hall.

'Christian!' I hiss, mindful that José is upstairs, though whether he can hear us is doubtful. I steady myself by clasping his lower back, then on a brave impulse, I swat his behind. He swats me right back.

'Ow!' I yelp.

'Shower time,' he declares triumphantly.

'Put me down!' I try and fail to sound disapproving. My struggle is futile—his arm is firmly clamped over my thighs—and for some reason I cannot stop giggling.

'Fond of these shoes?' he asks, amused, as he opens the door to his bathroom.

'I prefer them to be touching the floor.' I attempt to snarl at him, but it's not very effective as I can't keep the laughter out of my voice.

'Your wish is my command, Miss Steele.' Without putting me down, he slips off both of my shoes and lets them clatter to the tile floor. Pausing by the vanity, he empties his pockets—dead BlackBerry, keys, wallet, the key chain. I can only imagine what I look like in the mirror from this angle. When he's finished, he marches directly into his oversized shower.

'Christian!' I scold loudly—his intent is now clear.

He switches the water on to max. *Jeez!* Arctic water spurts over my backside, and I squeal—then stop, mindful once more that José is above us. It's cold and I'm fully clothed. The chilling water soaks into my dress, my panties, and my bra. I'm drenched and once more I cannot stop giggling.

'No!' I squeal. 'Put me down!' I swat him again, harder this time, and Christian releases me, letting me slide down his now soaked body. His white shirt is stuck to his chest and his suit pants are sodden. I am soaked, too, flushed, giddy, and breathless, and he's grinning down at me, looking so . . . so unbelievably hot.

He sobers, his eyes shining, and cups my face again, drawing my lips to his. His kiss is gentle, cherishing, and totally distracting. I no longer care that I am fully clothed and soaking wet in Christian's shower. It's just the two of us beneath the cascading water. He's back, he's safe, he's mine.

My hands move involuntarily to his shirt as it clings to every line and sinew of his chest, revealing the hair scrunched beneath the white wetness. I yank the shirt hem out of his pants, and he groans against my mouth, but his lips do not leave mine. As I start to unbutton his shirt, he reaches for my zipper, slowly sliding the clasp down my dress. His lips become more insistent, more provocative, his tongue invading my mouth—and my body explodes with desire. I tug his shirt hard, ripping it open. The buttons fly everywhere, ricocheting off the tiles and disappearing onto the shower floor. As I strip the wet fabric off his shoulders and down his arms, I press him into the wall, hampering his attempts to undress me. 'Cufflinks,' he murmurs, holding up his wrists where his shirt hangs sodden and limp.

With scrambling fingers I release first one and then the other gold cufflink, letting them fall carelessly to the tiled floor, and his shirt follows. His eyes search mine through the cascading water, his gaze burning, carnal, heated like the water. I reach for the waistband of his pants, but he shakes his head and grabs my shoulders, spinning me around so I am facing away from him. He finishes the long journey south with my zipper, smoothes my wet hair away from my neck, and runs his tongue up my neck to my hairline and back again, kissing and sucking as he goes.

I moan and slowly he peels my dress off my shoulders and down past my breasts, kissing my neck beneath my ear. He unclasps my bra and pushes it off, freeing my breasts. His hands reach around and cup each one as he murmurs his appreciation in my ear.

'So beautiful,' he whispers.

My arms are trapped by my bra and dress, which hang unfastened below my breasts; my arms are still in the sleeves, but my hands are free. I roll my head, giving Christian better access to my neck and push my breasts into his magical hands. I reach around behind me and welcome his sharp intake of breath as my inquisitive fingers make contact with his erection. He pushes his groin into my welcoming hands. Dammit, why didn't he let me take his pants off?

He tugs on my nipples, and as they harden and stretch under his expert touch, all thoughts of his pants disappear and pleasure spikes sharp and libidinous in my belly. I lean my head back against him and groan.

'Yes,' he breathes and turns me once more, capturing my mouth with his. He peels my bra, dress, and panties down so they join his shirt in a soggy heap on the shower floor.

I grab the body wash beside us. Christian stills as he realizes what I am about to do. Staring him straight in the eye, I squirt some of the sweet-smelling gel into my palm and hold my hand up in front of his chest, waiting for an answer to my unspoken question. His eyes widen, then he gives me an almost imperceptible nod.

Gently I place my hand on his sternum and start to rub the soap into his skin. His chest rises as he inhales sharply, but he stands stock-still. After a beat, his hands clasp my hips, but he doesn't push me away. He watches me warily, his look intense more than scared, but his lips are parted as his breathing increases.

'Is this okay?' I whisper.

'Yes.' His short, breathy reply is almost a gasp. I am reminded of the many showers we've had together, but the one at the Olympic is a bittersweet memory. Well, now I can touch him. I wash him using gentle circles, cleaning my man, moving to his underarms, over his ribs, down his flat firm belly, toward his happy trail and the waistband of his pants.

'My turn,' he whispers and reaches for the

shampoo, shifting us out of range of the stream of water and squirting some onto the top of my head.

I think this is my cue to stop washing him, so I hook my fingers into his waistband. He works the shampoo into my hair, his firm, long fingers massaging my scalp. Groaning in appreciation, I close my eyes and give myself over to the heavenly sensation. After all the stress of the evening, this is just what I need.

He chuckles and I open one eye to find him smiling down at me. 'You like?'

'Hmm . . .'

He grins. 'Me, too,' he says and leans over to kiss my forehead, his fingers continuing their sweet, firm kneading of my scalp.

'Turn around,' he says authoritatively. I do as I'm told, and his fingers slowly work over my head, cleansing, relaxing, loving me as they go. Oh, this is bliss. He reaches for more shampoo and gently washes the long tresses down my back. When he's finished, he pulls me back under the shower.

'Lean your head back,' he orders quietly.

I willingly comply, and he carefully rinses out the suds. When he's done, I face him once more and make a beeline for his pants.

'I want to wash all of you,' I whisper. He smiles that lopsided smile and lifts his hands in a gesture that says 'I'm all yours, baby.' I grin; it feels like Christmas. I make short work of his zipper, and soon his pants and boxers join the rest of our clothing. I stand and reach for the body wash and the freshwater sponge.

'Looks like you're pleased to see me,' I murmur dryly.

'I'm always pleased to see you, Miss Steele.' He

smirks at me.

I soap the sponge, then retrace my journey over his chest. He's more relaxed—maybe because I'm not actually touching him. I head south with the sponge, across his belly, along the happy trail, through his pubic hair, and over and up his erection.

I peek up at him, and he regards me with hooded eyes and sensual longing. *Hmm . . . I like this look.* I drop the sponge and use my hands, grasping him firmly. He closes his eyes, tips his head back, and groans, thrusting his hips into my hands.

Oh yes! It's so arousing. My inner goddess has resurfaced after her evening of rocking and weeping in the corner, and she's wearing harlot-red lipstick.

His burning eyes suddenly lock with mine. He's remembered something.

'It's Saturday,' he exclaims, eyes alight with salacious wonder, and he grasps my waist, pulling me to him and kissing me savagely.

Whoa—change of pace!

His hands sweep down my slick, wet body, around to my sex, his fingers exploring, teasing, and his mouth is relentless, leaving me breathless. His other hand is in my wet hair, holding me in place while I bear the full force of his passion unleashed. His fingers move inside me.

'Ahh,' I moan into his mouth.

'Yes,' he hisses, and lifts me, his hands beneath my backside. 'Wrap your legs around me, baby.' My legs obey, and I cling like a limpet to his neck. He braces me against the wall of the shower and pauses, gazing down at me.

'Eyes open,' he murmurs. 'I want to see you.'

I blink up at him, my heart hammering, my blood pulsing hot and heavy through my body, desire, real and rampant, surging through me. Then he eases into me oh so slowly, filling me, claiming me, skin against skin. I push down against him and groan loudly. Once fully inside me, he pauses once more, his face strained, intense.

'You are mine, Anastasia,' he whispers.

'Always.'

He smiles victoriously and shifts, making me gasp.

'And now we can let everyone know, because you said yes.' His voice is reverential, and he leans down, capturing my mouth with his, and starts to move . . . slow and sweet. I close my eyes and tilt my head back as my body bows, my will submitting to his, slave to his intoxicating slow rhythm.

His teeth graze my jaw, my chin, and down my neck as he picks up the pace, pushing me onward, upward—away from this earthly plane, the teeming shower, the evening's chilling fright. It's just me and my man moving in unison, moving as one— each completely absorbed in the other—our gasps and grunts mingling. I revel in the exquisite feeling of his possession as my body blooms and flowers around him.

I could have lost him . . . and I love him . . . I love him so much, and I'm suddenly overcome by the enormity of my love and the depth of my commitment to him. I will spend the rest of my life loving this man, and with that awe-inspiring thought, I detonate around him—a healing, cathartic orgasm, crying out his name as tears flow down my cheeks.

He reaches his climax and pours himself into

me. With his face buried in my neck, he sinks to the floor, holding me tightly, kissing my face, and kissing away my tears as the warm water spills down around us, washing us clean.

* * *

'My fingers are pruny,' I murmur, postcoital and sated as I lean against his chest. He raises my fingers to his lips and kisses each in turn.

'We should really get out of this shower.'

'I'm comfortable here.' I'm sitting between his legs and he's holding me close. I don't want to move.

Christian murmurs his assent. But suddenly I'm bone tired, world-weary. So much has happened this last week—enough for a lifetime of drama—and now I'm getting married. A disbelieving giggle escapes my lips.

'Something amusing you, Miss Steele?' he asks fondly.

'It's been a busy week.'

He grins. 'That it has.'

'I thank God you're back in one piece, Mr. Grey,' I whisper, sobering at the thought of what might have been. He tenses and I immediately regret reminding him.

'I was scared,' he confesses much to my surprise.

'Earlier?'

He nods, his expression serious.

Holy shit. 'So you made light of it to reassure your family?'

'Yes. I was too low to land well. But somehow I did.'

Crap. My eyes sweep up to his, and he looks

564

grave as the water cascades over us. 'How close a call was it?' He gazes down at me.

'Close.' He pauses. 'For a few awful seconds, I thought I'd never see you again.'

I hug him tightly. 'I can't imagine my life without you, Christian. I love you so much it frightens me.'

'Me, too,' he breathes. 'My life would be empty without you. I love you so much.' His arms tighten around me and he nuzzles my hair. 'I won't ever let you go.'

'I don't want to go, ever.' I kiss his neck, and he leans down and kisses me gently.

After a moment, he shifts. 'Come—let's get you dry and into bed. I'm exhausted and you look beat.'

I lean back and arch an eyebrow at his choice of words. He cocks his head to one side and smirks at me.

'You have something to say, Miss Steele?'

I shake my head and rise unsteadily to my feet.

*   *   *

I am sitting up in bed. Christian insisted on drying my hair—he's quite skilled at it. How that happened is an unpleasant thought, so I dismiss it immediately. It's after two in the morning, and I am ready to sleep. Christian gazes down at me and reexamines the key chain before climbing into bed. He shakes his head, incredulous once more.

'This is so neat. The best birthday present I've ever had.' He glances at me, his eyes soft and warm. 'Better than my signed Guiseppe DeNatale poster.'

'I would have told you earlier, but since it was going to be your birthday . . . What do you give the man who has everything? I thought I'd give you . . .

565

me.'

He puts the key chain down on the bedside table and snuggles in beside me, pulling me into his arms against his chest so that we're spooning.

'It's perfect. Like you.'

I smirk, though he can't see my expression. 'I am far from perfect, Christian.'

'Are you smirking at me, Miss Steele?'

How does he know? 'Maybe.' I giggle. 'Can I ask you something?'

'Of course.' He nuzzles my neck.

'You didn't call on your trip back from Portland. Was that really because of José? You were worried about me being here alone with him?'

Christian says nothing. I turn to face him, and his eyes are wide as I reproach him.

'Do you know how ridiculous that is? How much stress you put your family and me through? We all love you very much.'

He blinks a couple of times and then gives me his shy smile. 'I had no idea you'd all be so worried.'

I purse my lips. 'When are you going to get it through your thick skull that you are loved?'

'Thick skull?' His eyebrows widen in surprise.

I nod. 'Yes. Thick skull.'

'I don't think the bone density of my head is significantly higher than anywhere else in my body.'

'I'm serious! Stop trying to make me laugh. I am still a little mad at you, though that's partially eclipsed by the fact that you're home safe and sound when I thought . . .' My voice fades as I recall those anxious few hours. 'Well, you know what I thought.'

His eyes soften and he reaches up to caress my face. 'I'm sorry. Okay.'

'Your poor mom, too. It was very moving, seeing you with her,' I whisper.

He smiles shyly. 'I've never seen her that way.' He blinks at the memory. 'Yes, that was really something. She's normally so self-possessed. It was quite a shock.'

'See? Everyone loves you.' I smile. 'Perhaps now you'll start believing it.' I lean down and kiss him gently. 'Happy birthday, Christian. I'm glad you're here to share your day with me. And you haven't seen what I've got for you tomorrow . . . um . . . today.' I smirk.

'There's more?' he says, astounded, and his face erupts into a breathtaking grin.

'Oh yes, Mr. Grey, but you'll have to wait until then.'

*   *   *

I wake suddenly from a dream or nightmare, and my pulse is thumping. I turn, panicked, and to my relief, Christian is fast asleep beside me. Because I've shifted, he stirs and reaches out in his sleep, draping his arm over me, and rests his head on my shoulder, sighing softly.

The room is flooded with light. It's eight o'clock. Christian never sleeps this late. I lie back and let my racing heart calm. Why the anxiety? Is it the aftermath of last night?

I turn and stare at him. He's here. He's safe. I take a deep steadying breath and gaze at his lovely face. A face that is now so familiar, all its dips and shadows eternally etched on my mind.

He looks much younger when he's asleep, and I grin because today he's a whole year older. I hug myself, thinking about my present. Oooh . . . what will he do? Perhaps I should start by bringing him breakfast in bed. Besides, José may still be here.

I find José at the counter, eating a bowl of cereal. I can't help but flush when I see him. He knows I've spent the night with Christian. Why do I suddenly feel so shy? It's not as if I'm naked or anything. I'm wearing my floor-length silk wrap.

'Morning, José.' I smile, brazening it out.

'Hey, Ana!' His face lights up, genuinely pleased to see me. There's no hint of teasing or salacious contempt in his expression.

'Sleep well?' I ask.

'Sure. Some view from up here.'

'Yeah. It's pretty special.' Like the owner of this apartment. 'Want a real man's breakfast?' I tease.

'Love some.'

'It's Christian's birthday today—I'm making him breakfast in bed.'

'He awake?'

'No, I think he's fried from yesterday.' I quickly glance away from him and head to the fridge so he can't see my blush. *Jeez, it's only José.* When I take the eggs and bacon out of the fridge, José is grinning at me.

'You really like him, don't you?'

I purse my lips. 'I love him, José.'

His eyes widen momentarily then he grins. 'What's not to love?' he asks, gesturing around the great room.

I scowl at him. 'Gee, thanks!'

'Hey, Ana, just kidding.'

Hmm . . . will I always have this leveled at me? That I'm marrying Christian for his money?

'Seriously, I'm kidding. You've never been that

kind of girl.'

'Omelet good for you?' I ask, changing the subject. I don't want to argue.

'Sure.'

'And me,' Christian says as he saunters into the great room. Holy fuck, he's wearing only pajama bottoms that hang in that totally hot way off his hips.

'José.' He nods.

'Christian.' José returns his nod solemnly.

Christian turns to me and smirks as I stare. He's done this on purpose. I narrow my eyes, desperately trying to recover my equilibrium, and Christian's expression alters subtly. He knows that I know what he's up to, and he doesn't care.

'I was going to bring you breakfast in bed.'

Swaggering over, he wraps his arm around me, tilts my chin up, and plants a loud wet kiss on my lips. Very un-Fifty!

'Good morning, Anastasia,' he says. I want to scowl at him and tell him to behave—but it's his birthday. I flush. Why is he so territorial?

'Good morning, Christian. Happy birthday.' I give him a smile, and he smirks at me.

'I'm looking forward to my other present,' he says and that's it. I flush the color of the Red Room of Pain and glance nervously at José, who looks like he's swallowed something unpleasant. I turn away and start preparing the food.

'So what are your plans today, José?' Christian asks, seemingly casual as he sits down on a barstool.

'I'm heading up to see my dad and Ray, Ana's dad.'

Christian frowns.

'They know each other?'

569

'Yeah, they were in the army together. They lost contact until Ana and I were in college together. It's kinda cute. They're best buds now. We're going on a fishing trip.'

'Fishing?' Christian is genuinely interested.

'Yeah—some great catches in these coastal waters. The steelheads can grow way big.'

'True. My brother, Elliot, and I landed a thirty-four-pound steelhead once.'

They're talking fishing? What is it about fishing? I have never understood it.

'Thirty-four pounds? Not bad. Ana's father though, he holds the record. A forty-three-pounder.'

'You're kidding! He never said.'

'Happy birthday, by the way.'

'Thanks. So, where do you like to fish?'

I zone out. This I do not need to know. But at the same time I'm relieved. See, Christian? José's not so bad.

*   *   *

By the time José makes to leave, both of them are much more relaxed with each other. Christian quickly changes into T-shirt and jeans, and barefoot, he accompanies José and me to the foyer.

'Thanks for letting me crash here,' José says to Christian as they shake hands.

'Anytime.' Christian smiles.

José hugs me quickly. 'Stay safe, Ana.'

'Sure. Great to see you. Next time we'll have a real evening out.'

'I'll hold you to that.' He waves at us from inside the elevator and then he's gone.

'See, he's not so bad.'

'He still wants into your panties, Ana. But can't say I blame him.'

'Christian, that's not true!'

'You have no idea, do you?' He smirks down at me. 'He wants you. Big-time.'

I frown. 'Christian, he's just a friend, a good friend.' And I'm suddenly aware that I sound like Christian when he's talking about Mrs. Robinson. The thought is unsettling.

Christian holds up his hands in a placating gesture.

'I don't want to fight,' he says softly.

Oh! We're not fighting . . . are we? 'Me neither.'

'You didn't tell him we were getting married.'

'No. I figured I ought to tell Mom and Ray first.' *Shit.* It's the first time I've thought about this since I said yes. Jeez—what are my parents going to say?

Christian nods. 'Yes, you're right. And I . . . um, I should ask your father.'

I laugh. 'Oh, Christian—this isn't the eighteenth century.'

Holy shit. What will Ray say? The thought of that conversation fills me with horror.

'It's traditional.' Christian shrugs.

'Let's talk about that later. I want to give you your other present.' My aim is to distract him. The thought of my present is burning a hole in my consciousness. I need to give it to him and see how he reacts.

He gives me his shy smile, and my heart skips a beat. For as long as I live, I'll never tire of looking at that smile.

'You're biting your lip again,' he says and pulls on my chin.

A thrill runs through my body as his fingers touch me. Without a word, and while I still have a modicum of courage, I take his hand and lead him back to the bedroom. I drop his hand, leaving him standing by the bed, and from under my side of the bed, I take out the two remaining gift boxes.

'Two?' he says, surprised.

I take a deep breath. 'I bought this before the, um . . . incident yesterday. I'm not sure about it now.' I quickly hand him one of the parcels before I can change my mind. He gazes at me, puzzled, sensing my uncertainty.

'Sure you want me to open it?'

I nod, anxious.

Christian tears off the packaging and gazes in surprise at the box.

'*Charlie Tango*,' I whisper.

He grins. The box contains a small wooden helicopter with a large, solar-powered rotor blade. He opens it up.

'Solar powered,' he murmurs. 'Wow.' And before I know it he's sitting on the bed assembling it. It snaps together quickly, and Christian holds it up in the palm of his hand. A blue wooden helicopter. He looks up at me and gives me his glorious, all-American-boy smile, then heads to the window so that the little helicopter is bathed in sunlight and the rotor starts to spin.

'Look at that,' he breathes, examining it closely. 'What we can already do with this technology.' He holds it at eye level, watching the blades spin. He's fascinated and fascinating to watch as he loses himself in thought, staring at the little helicopter. What is he thinking?

'You like it?'

'Ana, I love it. Thank you.' He grabs me and kisses me swiftly, then turns back to watch the rotor spin. 'I'll add it to the glider in my office,' he says distractedly, watching the blades spin. He moves his hand out of the sunlight, and the blades slows down and comes to a stop.

I can't help my face-splitting grin, and I want to hug myself. He loves it. Of course, he's all about alternative technologies. I'd forgotten that in my haste to buy it. Placing it on the chest of drawers, he turns to face me.

'It'll keep me company while we salvage *Charlie Tango*.'

'Is it salvageable?'

'I don't know. I hope so. I'll miss her, otherwise.'

Her? I am shocked at myself for the small pang of jealousy I feel for an inanimate object. My subconscious snorts with derisive laughter. I ignore her.

'What's in the other box?' he asks, his eyes wide with almost childish excitement.

Holy fuck. 'I'm not sure if this present is for you or me.'

'Really?' he asks, and I know I have piqued his interest. Nervously I hand him the second box. He shakes it gently and we both hear a heavy rattle. He glances up at me.

'Why are you so nervous?' he asks, bemused. I shrug, embarrassed and excited as I flush. He raises an eyebrow.

'You have me intrigued, Miss Steele,' he whispers, and his voice runs right through me, desire and anticipation spawning in my belly. 'I have to say I'm enjoying your reaction. What have you been up to?' He narrows his eyes speculatively.

573

I remain tight-lipped as I hold my breath.

He removes the lid of the box and takes out a small card. The rest of the contents are wrapped in tissue. He opens the card, and his eyes dart quickly to mine—widening with shock or surprise, I just don't know.

'Do rude things to you?' he murmurs. I nod and swallow. He cocks his head to one side warily, assessing my reaction, and frowns. Then he turns his attention back to the box. He tears through the pale blue tissue paper and fishes out an eye mask, some nipple clamps, a butt plug, his iPod, his silver gray tie—and last but by no means least—the key to his playroom.

He gazes at me, his expression dark, unreadable. *Oh shit*. Is this a bad move?

'You want to play?' he asks softly.

'Yes,' I breathe.

'For my birthday?'

'Yes.' Could my voice sound any smaller?

Myriad emotions cross his face, none of which I can place, but he settles for anxious. *Hmm* . . . Not quite the reaction I was expecting.

'You're sure?' he asks.

'Not the whips and stuff.'

'I understand that.'

'Yes, then. I'm sure.'

He shakes his head and gazes down at the contents of the box. 'Sex mad and insatiable. Well, I think we can do something with this lot,' he murmurs almost to himself, then puts the contents back in the box. When he glances at me again, his expression has completely changed. Holy cow, his eyes burn, and his mouth lifts in a slow erotic smile. He holds out his hand.

574

'Now,' he says, and it's not a request. My belly clenches, tight and hard, deep, deep down.

I put my hand in his.

'Come,' he orders, and I follow him out of the bedroom, my heart in my mouth. Desire races slick and hot through my blood as my insides tighten with hungry anticipation. Finally!

CHAPTER TWENTY-ONE

Christian pauses outside the playroom.

'You're sure about this?' he asks, his gaze heated yet anxious.

'Yes,' I murmur, smiling shyly at him.

His eyes soften. 'Anything you don't want to do?'

I'm derailed by his unexpected question, and my mind goes into overdrive. One thought occurs. 'I don't want you to take photos of me.'

He stills, and his expression hardens as he cocks his head to one side and eyes me speculatively.

Oh, shit. I think he's going to ask me why, but fortunately he doesn't.

'Okay,' he murmurs. His brow furrows as he unlocks the door, then stands aside to usher me into the room. I feel his eyes on me as he follows me inside and closes the door.

Placing the gift box on the chest of drawers, he takes out the iPod, switches it on, then waves at the music center on the wall so that the smoked glass doors glide silently open. He presses some buttons, and the sound of a subway train echoes around the room. He turns it down so that the slow, hypnotic electronic beat that follows becomes ambient.

A woman starts to sing, I don't know who she is but her voice is soft yet rasping and the beat is measured, deliberate . . . erotic. *Oh my.* It's music to make love to.

Christian turns to face me as I stand in the middle of the room, my heart pounding, my blood singing in my veins, pulsing—or so it feels—in time to the music's seductive beat. He saunters casually over to me and tugs on my chin so I'm no longer biting my lip.

'What do you want to do, Anastasia?' he murmurs, planting a soft chaste kiss at the corner of my mouth, his fingers still grasping my chin.

'It's your birthday. Whatever you want,' I whisper. He traces his thumb along my lower lip, his brow creased once more.

'Are we in here because you think I want to be in here?' His words are softly spoken, but he regards me intently.

'No,' I whisper. 'I want to be in here, too.'

His gaze darkens, growing bolder as he assesses my response. After what seems an eternity, he speaks.

'Oh, there are so many possibilities, Miss Steele.' His voice is low, excited. 'But let's start with getting you naked.' He pulls the sash of my robe so that it falls open, revealing my silk nightdress, then steps back and sits down nonchalantly on the arm of the chesterfield couch.

'Take your clothes off. Slowly.' He gives me a sensual, challenging look.

I swallow compulsively, pressing my thighs together. I'm already damp between my legs. My inner goddess is stripped naked and standing in line, ready and waiting and begging me to play catch-up. I pull the robe away from my shoulders, my eyes never leaving his, and shrug, letting it fall billowing to the floor. His mesmerizing gray eyes heat, and he runs his index finger over his lips as he gazes at me.

Slipping the spaghetti straps of my gown off my shoulders, I gaze at him for a beat, then release them. My nightdress skims and ripples softly down my body, pooling at my feet. I am naked and practically panting and oh-so-ready.

Christian pauses for a moment, and I marvel at the frankly carnal appreciation in his expression. Standing up, he makes his way over to the chest and picks up his silver gray tie—my favorite tie. He pulls it through his fingers as he turns and strolls casually toward me, a smile playing on his lips. When he stands in front of me, I expect him to ask for my hands, but he doesn't.

'I think you're underdressed, Miss Steele,' he murmurs. He places the tie around my neck, and slowly but dexterously ties it in what I assume is a fine Windsor knot. As he tightens the knot, his fingers brush the base of my throat and electricity shoots through me, making me gasp. He leaves the wide end of the tie long, long enough so the tip skims my pubic hair.

'You look mighty fine now, Miss Steele,' he says and bends to kiss me gently on my lips. It's a swift kiss, and I want more, desire spiraling wantonly through my body.

'What shall we do with you now?' he says, and then picking up the tie, he yanks sharply so that I'm forced forward into his arms. His hands dive into my hair and pull my head back, and he really kisses me, hard, his tongue unforgiving and merciless.

577

One of his hands roams freely down my back to cup my behind. When he pulls away, he's panting too and gazing down at me, his eyes molten gray; I'm left wanting, gasping for breath, my wits thoroughly scattered. I'm sure my lips will be swollen after his sensual assault.

'Turn around,' he orders gently and I obey. Pulling my hair free of the tie, he quickly braids and secures it. He tugs the braid so my head tilts up.

'You have beautiful hair, Anastasia,' he murmurs and kisses my throat, sending shivers running up and down my spine. 'You just have to say stop. You know that, don't you?' he whispers against my throat.

I nod, my eyes closed, and relish his lips on me. He turns me around once more and picks up the end of the tie.

'Come,' he says, tugging gently, leading me over to the chest where the rest of the box's contents are on display.

'Anastasia, these objects.' He holds up the butt plug. 'This is a size too big. As an anal virgin, you don't want to start with this. We want to start with this.' He holds up his pinkie finger, and I gasp, shocked. Fingers . . . *there?* He smirks at me, and the unpleasant thought of the anal fisting mentioned in the contract comes to mind.

'Just finger—singular,' he says softly with that uncanny ability he has to read my mind. My eyes dart to his. How does he do that?

'These clamps are vicious.' He prods the nipple clamps. 'We'll use these.' He places a different pair of clamps on the chest. They look like giant black hairpins but with little jet jewels hanging down. 'They're adjustable,' Christian murmurs, his voice laced with gentle concern.

I blink up at him, wide-eyed. Christian, my sexual mentor. He knows so much more about all of this than I do. I'll never catch up. I frown. He knows more than me about most things . . . except cooking.

'Clear?' he asks.

'Yes,' I whisper, my mouth dry. 'Are you going to tell me what you intend to do?'

'No. I'm making this up as I go along. This isn't a scene, Ana.'

'How should I behave?'

His brow creases. 'However you want to.'

Oh!

'Were you expecting my alter ego, Anastasia?' he asks, his tone vaguely mocking and bemused at once. I blink at him.

'Well, yes. I like him,' I murmur. He smiles his private smile and reaches up to run his thumb down my cheek.

'Do you now,' he breathes and runs his thumb across my lower lip. 'I'm your lover, Anastasia, not your Dom. I love to hear your laugh and your girlish giggle. I like you relaxed and happy, like you are in José's photos. That's the girl that fell into my office. That's the girl I fell in love with.'

My mouth drops open, and a welcome warmth blooms in my heart. It's joy—pure joy.

'But having said all that, I also like to do rude things to you, Miss Steele, and my alter ego knows a trick or two. So, do as you're told and turn around.' His eyes glint wickedly, and the joy moves sharply south, seizing me tightly and gripping every sinew below my waist. I do as I'm told. Behind me, he opens one of the drawers and a moment later he's in front of me again.

'Come,' he orders and tugs on the tie, leading me to the table. As we walk past the couch, I notice for the first time that all the canes have vanished. It distracts me. Were they there yesterday when I came in? I don't remember. Did Christian move them? Mrs. Jones? Christian interrupts my train of thought.

'I want you to kneel up on this,' he says when we're at the table.

Oh, okay. What does he have in mind? My inner goddess can't wait to find out—she's already scissor-kicked onto the table and is watching him with adoration.

He gently lifts me onto the table, and I fold my legs beneath me and kneel in front of him, surprised by my own grace. Now we are eye to eye. He runs his hands down my thighs, grasps my knees, and pulls my legs apart and stands directly in front of me. He looks very serious, his eyes darker, hooded . . . lustful.

'Arms behind your back. I'm going to cuff you.'

He produces some leather cuffs from his back pocket and reaches around me. This is it. Where's he going to take me this time?

His proximity is intoxicating. This man is going to be my husband. Can one lust after one's husband like this? I don't remember reading about that anywhere. I can't resist him, and I run my parted lips along his jaw, feeling the stubble, a heady combination of prickly and soft, under my tongue. He stills and closes his eyes. His breathing falters and he pulls back.

'Stop. Or this will be over far quicker than either of us wants,' he warns. For a moment, I think he might be angry but then he smiles, and his heated eyes are alight with amusement.

'You're irresistible.' I pout.

'Am I now?' he says dryly.

I nod.

'Well—don't distract me, or I'll gag you.'

'I like distracting you,' I whisper, looking mulishly at him, and he cocks his eyebrow at me.

'Or spank you.'

Oh! I try to hide my smile. There was a time, not very long ago, when I would have been subdued by this threat. I would never have had the nerve to kiss him, unbidden, while he was in this room. I realize now, I'm no longer intimidated by him. It's a revelation. I grin mischievously, and he smirks at me.

'Behave,' he growls and stands back, gazing at me and slaps the leather cuffs across his palm. And the warning is there, implicit in his actions. I try for contrite, and I think I succeed. He approaches me again.

'That's better,' he breathes and leans behind me once more with the cuffs. I resist touching him but inhale his glorious Christian scent, still fresh from last night's shower. *Hmm* . . . I should bottle this.

I expect him to cuff my wrists, but he attaches each cuff above my elbows. It makes me arch my back, pushing my breasts forward, though my elbows are by no means together. When he's finished, he stands back to admire me.

'Feel okay?' he asks. It's not the most comfortable of positions, but I'm so wired with anticipation to see where he's going with this that I nod, weak with wanting.

'Good.' He pulls the mask from his back pocket.

'I think you've seen enough now,' he murmurs. He slides the mask over my head, covering my eyes. My breathing spikes. *Wow.* Why is not being able to see so erotic? I am here, trussed up and kneeling on a table, waiting—sweet anticipation hot and heavy deep in my belly. I can still hear, though, and the melodic steady beat of the track continues. It resonates through my body. I hadn't noticed before. He must have it on repeat.

Christian steps away. What is he doing? He moves back to the chest and opens a drawer, then closes it again. A moment later he's back, and I sense him in front of me. There's a pungent, rich, musky scent in the air. It's delicious, almost mouthwatering.

'I don't want to ruin my favorite tie,' he murmurs. It slowly unravels as he undoes it.

I inhale sharply as the tail of the tie travels up my body, tickling me in its wake. Ruin his tie? I listen acutely to determine what he's going to do. He's rubbing his hands together. His knuckles suddenly brush over my cheek, down to my jaw following my jawline.

My body leaps to attention as his touch sends a delicious shiver through me. His hand flexes over my neck, and it's slick with sweet-smelling oil so his hand glides smoothly down my throat, across my clavicle, and up to my shoulder, his fingers kneading gently as they go. Oh, I'm getting a massage. Not what I expected.

He places his other hand on my other shoulder and begins another slow teasing journey across my clavicle. I groan softly as he works his way down toward my increasingly aching breasts, aching for his touch. It's tantalizing. I arch my body farther into his deft touch, but his hands glide to my sides, slow, measured, in time to the beat of the music, and studiously avoid my breasts. I groan, but I don't know if it's from pleasure or frustration.

'You are so beautiful, Ana,' he murmurs, his voice low and husky, his mouth next to my ear. His nose follows along my jaw as he continues to massage me—beneath my breasts, across my belly, down . . . He kisses me fleetingly on my lips, then he runs his nose down my neck, my throat. *Holy cow, I'm on fire . . .* his nearness, his hands, his words.

'And soon you'll be my wife to have and to hold,' he whispers.

Oh my.

'To love and to cherish.'

Jeez.

'With my body, I will worship you.'

I tip my head back and moan. His fingers run through my pubic hair, over my sex, and he rubs the palm of his hand against my clitoris.

'Mrs. Grey,' he whispers as his palm works against me.

I groan.

'Yes,' he breathes as his palm continues to tease me. 'Open your mouth.'

My mouth is already open from panting. I open wider, and he slips a large cool metal object between my lips. Shaped like an oversized baby's pacifier, it has small grooves or carvings, and what feels like a chain at the end. It's big.

'Suck,' he commands softly. 'I'm going to put this inside you.'

Inside me? Inside me where? My heart lurches into my mouth.

'Suck,' he repeats and he stops palming me.

No, don't stop! I want to shout, but my mouth is full. His oiled hands glide back up my body and finally cup my neglected breasts.

'Don't stop sucking.'

Gently he rolls my nipples between his thumbs and forefingers, and they harden and lengthen under his expert touch, sending synaptic waves of pleasure all the way to my groin.

'You have such beautiful breasts, Ana,' he murmurs, and my nipples harden further in response. He murmurs his approval and I moan. His lips move down from my neck toward one breast, trailing soft bites and sucks over and over, down toward my nipple, and suddenly I feel the pinch of the clamp.

'Ah!' I garble my groan through the device in my mouth. Holy cow, the feeling is exquisite, raw, painful, pleasurable . . . oh—the pinch. Gently, he laves the restrained nipple with his tongue, and as he does so, he applies the other. The bite of the second clamp is equally harsh . . . but just as good. I groan loudly.

'Feel it,' he whispers.

Oh, I do. I do. I do.

'Give me this.' He tugs gently on the ornate metal pacifier in my mouth, and I release it. His hands once more trail down my body toward my sex. He's reoiled his hands. They glide around to my backside.

I gasp. What's he going to do? I tense up on my knees as he runs his fingers between my buttocks.

'Hush, easy,' he breathes close to my ear and kisses my neck as his fingers stroke and tease me.

What's he going to do? His other hand glides down my belly to my sex, palming me once more.

He eases his fingers inside me, and I moan loudly, appreciatively.

'I'm going to put this inside you,' he murmurs. 'Not here.' His fingers trail between my buttocks, spreading oil. 'But here.' He moves his fingers around and around, in and out, hitting the front wall of my vagina. I moan and my restrained nipples swell.

'Ah.'

'Hush now.' Christian removes his fingers and slides the object into me. He cups my face and kisses me, his mouth invading mine, and I hear a very faint click. Instantly the plug inside me starts to vibrate—*down there*! I gasp. The feeling is extraordinary—beyond anything I've felt before.

'Ah!'

'Easy,' Christian calms me, stifling my gasps with his mouth. His hands move down and tug very gently on the clamps. I cry out loudly.

'Christian, please!'

'Hush, baby. Hang in there.'

This is too much—all this overstimulation, everywhere. My body starts to climb, and on my knees, I'm unable to control the buildup. *Oh my . . .* Will I be able to handle this?

'Good girl,' he soothes.

'Christian,' I pant, sounding desperate even to my own ears.

'Hush, feel it, Ana. Don't be afraid.' His hands are now on my waist, holding me, but I can't concentrate on his hands, what's inside me, and the clamps, too. My body is building, building to an explosion—with the relentless vibrations and the sweet, sweet torture of my nipples. *Holy hell.* It will be too intense. His hands move from my hips, down and around, slick and oiled, touching, feeling, kneading my skin—kneading my behind.

'So beautiful,' he murmurs and suddenly he gently pushes an anointed finger inside me . . . *there*! Into my backside. *Fuck*. It feels alien, full, forbidden . . . but oh . . . so . . . good. And he moves slowly, easing in and out, while his teeth graze my upturned chin.

'So beautiful, Ana.'

I'm suspended high—high above a wide, wide ravine, and I'm soaring then falling giddily at the same time, plunging to the Earth. I can hold on no more, and I scream as my body convulses and climaxes at the overwhelming fullness. As my body explodes, I'm nothing but sensation—everywhere. Christian releases first one and then the other clamp, causing my nipples to sing with a surge of sweet, sweet painful feeling, but it's oh-so-good and causing my orgasm, this orgasm, to go on and on. His finger stays where it is, gently easing in and out.

'Argh!' I cry out, and Christian wraps himself around me, holding me, as my body continues to pulse mercilessly inside.

'*No!*' I shout again, pleading, and this time he tugs the vibrator out of me, and his finger, too, as my body continues to convulse.

He unstraps one of the cuffs so that my arms fall forward. My head lolls on his shoulder, and I am lost, lost to all this overwhelming sensation. I'm all shattered breath, exhausted desire, and sweet, welcome oblivion.

Vaguely, I'm aware that Christian lifts me, carries me over to the bed, and lays me down on the cool satin sheets. After a moment, his hands, still oiled, gently rub the backs of my thighs, my knees, my calves, and my shoulders. I feel the bed dip as he stretches out beside me.

He pulls the mask off, but I don't have the energy to open my eyes. Finding my braid, he undoes the hair tie and leans forward, kissing me softly on my lips. Only my erratic breathing disturbs the silence in the room and steadies as I float gently back to Earth. The music has stopped.

'So beautiful,' he murmurs.

When I persuade one eye to open, he's gazing down at me, smiling softly.

'Hi,' he says. I manage a grunt in response, and his smile broadens. 'Rude enough for you?'

I nod and give him a reluctant grin. Jeez, any ruder and I'd have to spank the pair of us.

'I think you're trying to kill me,' I mutter.

'Death by orgasm.' He smirks. 'There are worse ways to go,' he says but then frowns ever so slightly as an unpleasant thought crosses his mind. It distresses me. I reach up and caress his face.

'You can kill me like this anytime,' I whisper. I notice that he's gloriously naked and ready for action. When he takes my hand and kisses my knuckles, I lean up and capture his face between my hands and pull his mouth to mine. He kisses me briefly, then stops.

'This is what I want to do,' he murmurs and reaches beneath his pillow for the music center remote. He presses a button and the soft strains of a guitar echo around the walls.

'I want to make love to you,' he says, gazing down at me, his gray eyes burning with bright, loving sincerity. Softly in the background, a familiar voice starts to sing 'The First Time Ever I Saw Your Face.' And his lips find mine.

As I tighten around him, finding my release once more, Christian unravels in my arms, his head thrown back as he calls out my name. He clasps me tightly to his chest as we sit nose to nose in the middle of his vast bed, me astride him. And in this moment—this moment of joy with this man to this music—the intensity of my experience this morning in here with him and all that has occurred during the past week overwhelms me anew, not just physically but emotionally. I am completely overcome with all these feelings. I am so deeply in love with him. For the first time I'm offered a glimmer of understanding as to how he feels about my safety.

Recalling his close call with *Charlie Tango* yesterday, I shudder at the thought and tears pool in my eyes. If anything ever happened to him—I love him so. My tears run unchecked down my cheeks. So many sides of Christian—his sweet, gentle persona and his rugged, I-can-do-what-I-fucking-well-like-to-you-and-you'll-come-like-a-train Dominant side—his fifty shades—all of him. All spectacular. All mine. And I'm aware we don't know each other well, and we have a mountain of issues to overcome, but I know for each other, we will—and we'll have a lifetime to do it.

'Hey,' he breathes, clasping my head in his hands, gazing down at me. He's still inside me. 'Why are you crying?' His voice is filled with concern.

'Because I love you so much,' I whisper. He half closes his eyes as if drugged, absorbing my words. When he opens them again, they blaze with his love.

'And I you, Ana. You make me . . . whole.' He kisses me gently as Roberta Flack finishes her song.

*   *   *

We have talked and talked and talked, sitting upright together on the bed in the playroom, me in his lap, our legs curled around each other. The red satin sheet is draped around us like a royal cocoon, and I have no idea how much time has passed. Christian is laughing at my impersonation of Kate during the photo shoot at the Heathman.

'To think it could have been her who came to interview me. Thank the Lord for the common cold,' he murmurs and kisses my nose.

'I believe she had the flu, Christian,' I scold him, trailing my fingers idly through his chest hair and marveling that he's tolerating it so well. 'All the canes have gone,' I murmur, recalling my distraction from earlier. He tucks my hair behind my ear for the umpteenth time.

'I didn't think you'd ever get past that hard limit.'

'No, I don't think I will,' I whisper wide-eyed, then find myself glancing over at the whips, paddles, and floggers lining the opposite wall. He follows my gaze.

'You want me to get rid of them, too?' He's amused but sincere.

'Not the crop . . . the brown one. Or that suede flogger.' I flush.

He smiles down at me.

'Okay, the crop and the flogger. Why, Miss Steele, you're full of surprises.'

'As are you, Mr. Grey. It's one of the things I

love about you.' I kiss him gently at the corner of his mouth.

'What else do you love about me?' he asks and his eyes widen.

I know it's a huge deal for him to ask this question. It humbles me and I blink at him. I love everything about him—even his fifty shades. I know that life with Christian will never be boring.

'This.' I stroke my index finger across his lips. 'I love this, and what comes out of it, and what you do to me with it. And what's in here.' I caress his temple. 'You're so smart and witty and knowledgeable, competent in so many things. But most of all, I love what's in here.' I press my palm gently against his chest, feeling his steady beating heart. 'You are the most compassionate man I've met. What you do. How you work. It's awe-inspiring,' I whisper.

'Awe-inspiring?' He's puzzled, but there's a trace of humor on his face. Then his face transforms, and his shy smile appears as if he's embarrassed, and I want to launch myself at him. So I do.

*   *   *

I am dozing, wrapped in satin and Grey. Christian nuzzles me awake.

'Hungry?' he whispers.

'Hmm, famished.'

'Me, too.'

I lean up to gaze down at him sprawled on the bed.

'It's your birthday, Mr. Grey. I'll cook you something. What would you like?'

'Surprise me.' He runs his hand down my back,

stroking me gently. 'I should check my BlackBerry for all the messages I missed yesterday.' He sighs and starts to sit up, and I know this special time is over . . . for now.

'Let's shower,' he says.

Who am I to turn down the birthday boy?

*   *   *

Christian is in his study on the phone. Taylor is with him, looking serious but casual in jeans and a tight black T-shirt. I busy myself in the kitchen fixing lunch. I have found salmon steaks in the fridge, and I'm poaching them in lemon, making a salad, and boiling some baby potatoes. I feel extraordinarily relaxed and happy, on top of the world—literally. Turning toward the large window, I stare out at the glorious blue sky. *All that talking . . . all that sexing . . . hmm.* A girl could get used to that.

Taylor emerges from the study, interrupting my reverie. I turn down my iPod and take out an earbud.

'Hi, Taylor.'

'Ana.' He nods.

'Your daughter okay?'

'Yes, thanks. My ex-wife thought she had appendicitis, but she was overreacting as usual.' Taylor rolls his eyes, surprising me. 'Sophie's fine, though she has a nasty stomach bug.'

'I'm sorry.'

He smiles.

'Has *Charlie Tango* been located?'

'Yes. The recovery team is on its way. She should be back at Boeing Field late tonight.'

'Oh, good.'

591

He gives me a tight smile. 'Will that be all, ma'am?'

'Yes, yes, of course.' I flush . . . will I ever get used to Taylor calling me ma'am? It makes me feel so old, at least thirty.

He nods and heads out of the great room. Christian is still on the phone. I am waiting for the potatoes to boil. It gives me an idea. Fetching my purse, I fish out my BlackBerry. There's a text from Kate.

> *C U this evening. Looking forward to a looooong chat*

I text back.

> *Same here*

It will be good to talk to Kate.

Calling up the e-mail program, I type a quick message to Christian.

From: Anastasia Steele
Subject: Lunch
Date: June 18 2011 13:12
To: Christian Grey

Dear Mr. Grey

I am e-mailing to inform you that your lunch is nearly ready.

And that I had some mind-blowing, kinky fuckery earlier today.

Birthday kinky fuckery is to be recommended.

And another thing—I love you.

A x

(Your fiancée)

I listen carefully for a reaction, but he's still on the phone. I shrug. Perhaps he's just too busy. My BlackBerry vibrates.

From: Christian Grey
Subject: Kinky Fuckery
Date: June 18 2011 13:15
To: Anastasia Steele

What aspect was most mind-blowing?

I'm taking notes.

Christian Grey
Famished and Wasting Away After the Morning's Exertions CEO, Grey Enterprises Holdings, Inc.

PS: I love your signature

PPS: What happened to the art of conversation?

Dear Mr. Grey

May I draw your attention to the first line of my previous e-mail informing you that your lunch is indeed almost ready . . . so none of this famished and wasting away nonsense. With regard to the mind-blowing aspects of the kinky fuckery . . . frankly—all of it. I'd be interested in reading your notes. And I like my bracketed signature, too.

A x

(Your fiancée)

PS: Since when have you been so loquacious? And you're on the phone!

I press send and look up, and he's standing in front of me, smirking. Before I can say anything, he bounds around the kitchen island, sweeps me up in his arms, and kisses me soundly.

'That is all, Miss Steele,' he says, releasing me, and he saunters—in his jeans, bare feet, and untucked white shirt—back to his office, leaving me breathless.

*   *   *

I've made a watercress, cilantro, and sour cream dip

to accompany the salmon, and I've set the breakfast bar. I hate interrupting him while he's working, but now I stand in the doorway of his office. He's still on the phone, all thoroughly fucked hair and bright gray eyes—a visually nourishing feast. He looks up when he sees me and doesn't take his eyes off me. He frowns slightly, and I don't know if it's at me or because of his conversation.

'Just let them in and leave them alone. Do you understand, Mia?' he hisses and rolls his eyes. 'Good.'

I mime eating, and he grins at me and nods.

'I'll see you later.' He hangs up. 'One more call?' he asks.

'Sure.'

'That dress is very short,' he adds.

'You like it?' I give him a quick twirl. It's one of Caroline Acton's purchases. A soft turquoise sundress, probably more suitable for the beach, but it's such a lovely day on so many levels. He frowns and my face falls.

'You look fantastic in it, Ana. I just don't want anyone else to see you like that.'

'Oh!' I scowl at him. 'We're at home, Christian. No one but the staff.'

His mouth twists, and either he's trying to hide his amusement or he really doesn't think that's funny. But eventually he nods, reassured. I shake my head at him—he's actually being serious? I head back to the kitchen.

Five minutes later, he's back in front of me, holding the phone.

'I have Ray for you,' he murmurs, his eyes wary.

All the air leaves my body at once. I take the phone and cover the mouthpiece.

'You told him!' I hiss. Christian nods, and his eyes widen at my obvious look of distress.

Shit! I take a deep breath. 'Hi, Dad.'

'Christian has just asked me if he can marry you,' Ray says.

The silence stretches between us as I desperately think of what to say. Ray as usual stays silent, giving me no clue as to his reaction to this news.

'What did you say?' I crack first.

'I said I wanted to talk to you. It's kind of sudden, don't you think, Annie? You've not known him long. I mean, he's a nice guy, knows his fishing . . . but so soon?' His voice is calm and measured.

'Yes. It is sudden . . . hang on.' Hastily, I leave the kitchen area, away from Christian's anxious gaze, and head toward the great window. The doors to the balcony are open, and I step out into the sunshine. I can't quite walk to the edge. It's just too far up.

'I know it's sudden and all—but . . . well, I love him. He loves me. He wants to marry me, and there'll never be anyone else for me.' I flush thinking this is probably the most intimate conversation I have ever had with my stepfather.

Ray is silent on the other end of the phone.

'Have you told your mother?'

'No.'

'Annie . . . I know he's all kinds of rich and eligible, but marriage? It's such a big step. You're sure?'

'He's my happily ever after,' I whisper.

'Whoa,' Ray says after a moment, his tone softer.

'He's everything.'

'Annie, Annie, Annie. You're such a headstrong young woman. I hope to God you know what you're

596

doing. Hand me back to him, will you?'

'Sure, Dad, and will you give me away at the wedding?' I ask quietly.

'Oh, honey.' His voice cracks, and he's quiet for a few moments, the emotion in his voice bringing tears to my eyes. 'Nothing would give me greater pleasure,' he says eventually.

Oh, Ray. I love you so much . . . I swallow to keep from crying. 'Thank you, Dad. I'll hand you back to Christian. Be gentle with him. I love him,' I whisper.

I think Ray is smiling on the other end of the line, but it's hard to tell. It's always hard to tell with Ray.

'Sure thing, Annie. And come and visit this old man and bring that Christian with you.'

I march back into the room—pissed at Christian for not warning me—and hand him the phone, my expression letting him know just how annoyed I am. He's amused as he takes the phone and heads back into his study.

Two minutes later, he reappears.

'I have your stepfather's rather begrudging blessing,' he says proudly, so proudly, in fact, that it makes me giggle, and he grins at me. He's acting like he's just negotiated a major new merger or acquisition, which I suppose on one level, he has.

*   *   *

'Damn, you're a good cook, woman.' Christian swallows his last mouthful and raises his glass of white wine to me. I blossom under his praise, and it occurs to me I'll only get to cook for him on weekends. I frown. I enjoy cooking. Perhaps

597

I should have made him a cake for his birthday. I check my watch. I still have time.

'Ana?' He interrupts my thoughts. 'Why did you ask me not to take your photo?' His question startles me all the more because his voice is deceptively soft.

Oh . . . shit. The photos. I stare down at my empty plate, twisting my fingers in my lap. What can I say? I'd promised myself not to mention that I'd found his version of *Penthouse Pets*.

'Ana,' he snaps. 'What is it?' He makes me jump, and his voice commands me to look at him. When did I think he didn't intimidate me?

'I found your photos,' I whisper.

His eyes widen in shock. 'You've been in the safe?' he asks, incredulous.

'Safe? No. I didn't know you had a safe.'

He frowns. 'I don't understand.'

'In your closet. The box. I was looking for your tie, and the box was under your jeans . . . the ones you normally wear in the playroom. Except today.' I flush.

He gapes at me, appalled, and nervously runs his hand through his hair as he processes this information. He rubs his chin, lost in thought, but he can't mask the perplexed annoyance etched on his face. Abruptly he shakes his head, exasperated—but amused, too—and a faint smile of admiration kisses the corner of his mouth. He steeples his hands in front of him and focuses on me once more.

'It's not what you think. I'd forgotten all about them. That box had been moved. Those photographs belong in my safe.'

'Who moved them?' I whisper.

He swallows. 'There's only one person who could have done that.'

'Oh. Who? And what do you mean, 'It's not what I think'?'

He sighs and tilts his head to one side, and I think he's embarrassed. *So he should be!* my subconscious snarls.

'This is going to sound cold, but—they're an insurance policy,' he whispers, steeling himself for my response.

'Insurance policy?'

'Against exposure.'

The penny drops and rattles uncomfortably around and around in my empty head.

'Oh,' I murmur, because I can't think of what else to say. I close my eyes. This is it. This is fifty shades of fucked-up, right here, right now. 'Yes. You're right,' I mutter. 'That does sound cold.' I stand to clear our dishes. I don't want to know any more.

'Ana.'

'Do they know? The girls . . . the subs?'

He frowns. 'Of course they know.'

Oh, well, that's something. He reaches out, grabbing me and pulling me to him.

'Those photos are supposed to be in the safe. They're not for recreational use.' He stops. 'Maybe they were when they were taken originally. But—' He stops, imploring me. 'They don't mean anything.'

'Who put them in your closet?'

'It could only have been Leila.'

'She knows your safe combination?'

He shrugs. 'It wouldn't surprise me. It's a very long combination, and I use it so rarely. It's the one number I have written down and haven't changed.' He shakes his head. 'I wonder what else she knows and if she's taken anything else out of there.' He frowns, then turns his attention back to me. 'Look, I'll destroy the photos. Now if you like.'

'They're your photos, Christian. Do with them as you wish,' I mutter.

'Don't be like that,' he says, taking my head in his hands and holding my gaze to his. 'I don't want that life. I want our life, together.'

Holy cow. How does he know that beneath my horror about these photos is my paranoia?

'Ana, I thought we exorcised all those ghosts this morning. I feel that way. Don't you?'

I blink at him, recalling our very, very pleasurable and romantic and downright dirty morning in his playroom.

'Yes.' I smile. 'Yes, I feel like that, too.'

'Good.' He leans forward and kisses me, folding me in his arms. 'I'll shred them,' he murmurs. 'And then I have to go to work. I'm sorry, baby, but I have a mountain of business to get through this afternoon.'

'It's cool. I have to call my mother.' I grimace. 'Then I want to do some shopping and bake you a cake.'

He grins and his eyes light up like a small boy's.

'A cake?'

I nod.

'A chocolate cake?'

'You want a chocolate cake?' His grin is infectious.

He nods.

'I'll see what I can do, Mr. Grey.'

He kisses me once more.

Carla is stunned into silence.

'Mom, say something.'

'You're not pregnant, are you, Ana?' she whispers in horror.

'No no no, nothing like that.' Disappointment slices through my heart, and I'm saddened that she would think that of me. But then I remember with an ever-sinking feeling that she was pregnant with me when she married my father.

'I'm sorry, darling. This is just so sudden. I mean, Christian is quite a catch, but you're so young, and you should see a little of the world.'

'Mom, can't you just be happy for me? I love him.'

'Darling, I just need to get used to the idea. It's a shock. I could tell in Georgia that there was something very special between you two, but marriage . . .?'

In Georgia he wanted me to be his submissive, but I won't tell her that.

'Have you set a date?'

'No.'

'I wish your father was alive,' she whispers. Oh no . . . not this. Not this, now.

'I know, Mom. I would have liked to know him, too.'

'He only held you once, and he was so proud. He thought you were the most beautiful girl in the world.' Her voice is a deathly hush as the familiar tale is retold . . . again. She will be in tears next.

'I know, Mom.'

'And then he died.' She sniffs, and I know this

601

has set her off as it does every time.

'Mom,' I whisper, wanting to reach down the phone and hold her.

'I'm a silly old woman,' she murmurs and she sniffs again. 'Of course I am happy for you, darling. Does Ray know?' she adds, and she seems to have recovered her equilibrium.

'Christian's just asked him.'

'Oh, that's sweet. Good.' She sounds melancholic, but she's making an effort.

'Yes, it was,' I murmur.

'Ana, darling, I love you so much. I *am* happy for you. And you must both visit.'

'Yes, Mom. I love you, too.'

'Bob is calling me, I have to go. Let me have a date. We need to plan . . . are you having a big wedding?'

Big wedding, crap. I haven't even thought about that. Big wedding? No. I don't want a big wedding.

'I don't know yet. As soon as I do, I'll call.'

'Good. You take care now and be safe. You two need to have some fun . . . plenty of time for kids later.'

Kids! *Hmm* . . . and there it is again—a not-so-veiled reference to the fact that she had me so early.

'Mom, I didn't really ruin your life, did I?'

She gasps. 'Oh no, Ana, never think that. You were the best thing that ever happened to your father and me. I just wish he was here to see you so grown-up and getting married.' She's wistful and maudlin again.

'I wish that, too.' I shake my head, thinking about my mythical father. 'Mom, I'll let you go. I'll call soon.'

'Love you, darling.'
'Me, too, Mom. Good-bye.'

*   *   *

Christian's kitchen is a dream to work in. For a man who knows nothing about cooking, he seems to have everything. I suspect Mrs. Jones loves to cook, too. The only thing I need is some high-quality chocolate for the frosting. I leave the two halves of the cake on a cooling rack, grab my purse, and pop my head around Christian's study door. He's concentrating on his computer screen. He looks up and smiles at me.

'I'm just heading to the store to pick up some ingredients.'

'Okay.' He frowns at me.

'What?'

'You going to put some jeans on or something?'

Oh, come on. 'Christian, they're just legs.'

He gazes at me, not amused. This is going to be a fight. And it's his birthday. I roll my eyes at him, feeling like an errant teenager.

'What if we were at the beach?' I take a different tack.

'We're not at the beach.'

'Would you object if we were at the beach?'

He considers this for a moment. 'No,' he says simply.

I roll my eyes again and smirk at him. 'Well, just imagine we are. Laters.' I turn and bolt for the foyer. I make it to the elevator before he catches up with me. As the doors close, I wave at him, grinning sweetly as he watches, helpless—but fortunately amused—with narrowed eyes. He shakes his head

603

in exasperation, then I can see him no more.

Oh, that was exciting. Adrenaline is pounding through my veins, and my heart feels like it wants to exit my chest. But as the elevator descends, so do my spirits. Shit, what have I done?

I have a tiger by the tail. He's going to be mad when I get back. My subconscious is glaring at me over her half-moon glasses, a willow switch in her hand. Shit. I think about what little experience I have with men. I've never lived with a man before—well, except Ray—and for some reason he doesn't count. He's my dad . . . well, the man I consider my dad.

And now I have Christian. He's never really lived with anyone, I think. I'll have to ask him—if he's still talking to me.

But I feel strongly that I should wear what I like. I remember his rules. Yes, this must be hard for him, but he sure as hell paid for this dress. He should have given Neimans better instructions: nothing too short!

This skirt isn't that short, is it? I check in the large mirror in the lobby. Damn. Yes, it is quite short, but I've made a stand now. And no doubt I'll have to face the consequences. I wonder idly what he'll do, but first I need cash.

*   *   *

I stare at my receipt from the ATM: $51,689.16. That's $50,000 too much! *Anastasia, you're going to have to learn to be rich, too, if you say yes.* And so it begins. I take my paltry fifty dollars and make my way to the store

* * *

I head straight to the kitchen when I arrive back, and I can't help feeling a frisson of alarm. Christian is still in his study. Jeez, that's most of the afternoon. I decide my best option is to face him and see how much damage I've done. I peek cautiously around his study door. He's on the phone, staring out the window.

'And the Eurocopter specialist is due Monday afternoon? . . . Good. Just keep me informed. Tell them that I'll need their initial findings either Monday evening or Tuesday morning.' He hangs up and swivels his chair around, but stills when he sees me, his expression impassive.

'Hi,' I whisper. He says nothing, and my heart free-falls into my stomach. Gingerly I walk into his study and around his desk to where he's sitting. He still says nothing, his eyes never leaving mine. I stand in front of him, feeling fifty shades of foolish.

'I'm back. Are you mad at me?'

He sighs, reaches out for my hand, and pulls me into his lap, wrapping his arms around me. He buries his nose in my hair.

'Yes,' he says.

'I'm sorry. I don't know what came over me.' I curl up in his lap, inhaling his heavenly Christian smell, feeling safe regardless of the fact that he's mad.

'Me, neither. Wear what you like,' he murmurs. He runs his hand up my bare leg to my thigh. 'Besides, this dress has its advantages.' He bends to kiss me, and as our lips touch, passion or lust or a deep-seated need to make amends lances through me and desire flares in my blood. I seize his head

605

in my hands, thrusting my fingers in his hair. He groans as his body responds, and he hungrily nips at my lower lip—my throat, my ear, his tongue invading my mouth, and before I'm even aware of it he's unzipping his pants, pulling me astride his lap, and sinking into me. I grasp the back of the chair, my feet just touching the ground . . . and we start to move.

*   *   *

'I like your version of sorry,' he breathes into my hair.

'And I like yours.' I giggle, snuggling against his chest. 'Have you finished?'

'Christ, Ana, you want more?'

'No! Your work.'

'I'll be done in about half an hour. I heard your message on my voice mail.'

'From yesterday.'

'You sounded worried.'

I hug him tightly.

'I was. It's not like you not to respond.'

He kisses my hair.

'Your cake should be ready in half an hour.' I smile at him and climb off his lap.

'Looking forward to it. It smelled delicious, evocative even, while it was baking.'

I smile shyly down at him, feeling a little self-conscious, and he mirrors my expression. Jeez, are we really so different? Perhaps it's his early memories of baking. Leaning down, I plant a swift kiss on the corner of his mouth and make my way back to the kitchen.

I am all prepared when I hear him come out of his study, and I light the solitary gold candle on his cake. He gives me an ear-splitting grin as he saunters toward me, and I softly sing 'Happy Birthday' to him. Then he leans over and blows it out, closing his eyes.

'I've made my wish,' he says as he opens them again, and for some reason his look makes me flush.

'The frosting is still soft. I hope you like it.'

'I can't wait to taste it, Anastasia,' he murmurs, and he makes that sound so sexy. I cut us each a slice, and we dig in with small pastry forks.

'Mmm,' he groans in appreciation. 'This is why I want to marry you.'

And I laugh with relief . . . he likes it.

*　　　*　　　*

'Ready to face my family?' Christian switches the R8 ignition off. We're parked in his parents' driveway.

'Yes. Are you going to tell them?'

'Of course. I'm looking forward to seeing their reactions.' He smiles wickedly at me and climbs out of the car.

It is seven thirty, and though it's been a warm day, there's a cool evening breeze blowing off the bay. I pull my wrap around me as I step out of the car. I'm wearing an emerald green cocktail dress I found this morning while I was rummaging through the closet. It has a wide matching belt. Christian takes my hand, and we head to the front door.

607

Carrick opens it wide before he can knock.

'Christian, hello. Happy birthday, son.' He takes Christian's proffered hand but pulls him into a brief hug, surprising him.

'Er . . . thanks, Dad.'

'Ana, how lovely to see you again.' He hugs me, too, and we follow him into the house.

Before we can set foot in the living room, Kate comes barreling down the hallway toward the two of us. She looks furious.

Oh no!

'You two! I want to talk to you,' she snarls in her you-better-not-fucking-mess-with-me voice. I glance nervously at Christian, who shrugs and decides to humor her as we follow her into the dining room, leaving Carrick bemused on the threshold of the living room. She shuts the door and turns on me.

'What the fuck is this?' she hisses and waves a piece of paper at me. Completely at a loss, I take it from her and scan it quickly. My mouth dries. *Holy shit*. It's my e-mail response to Christian, discussing the contract.

CHAPTER TWENTY-TWO

All the color drains from my face as my blood turns to ice and fear lances through my body. Instinctively I step between her and Christian.

'What is it?' Christian murmurs, his tone wary.

I ignore him. I cannot believe Kate is doing this.

'Kate! This has nothing to do with you.' I glare venomously at her, anger replacing my fear. How dare she do this? Not now, not today. Not on Christian's birthday. Surprised by my response, she blinks at me, green eyes wide.

'Ana, what is it?' Christian says again, his tone more menacing.

'Christian, would you just go, please?' I ask him.

'No. Show me.' He holds out his hand, and I know he's not to be argued with—his voice is cold and hard. Reluctantly I give him the e-mail.

'What's he done to you?' Kate asks, ignoring Christian. She looks so apprehensive. I flush as myriad erotic images flit quickly across my mind.

'That's none of your business, Kate.' I can't keep the exasperation out of my voice.

'Where did you get this?' Christian asks, his head cocked to one side, his face expressionless, but his voice . . . so menacingly soft. Kate flushes.

'That's irrelevant.' At his stony glare, she hastily continues. 'It was in the pocket of a jacket—which I assume is yours—that I found on the back of Ana's bedroom door.' Faced with Christian's burning gray gaze, Kate's steeliness slips a little, but she seems to recover and scowls at him.

She's a beacon of hostility in a slinky, bright red dress. She looks magnificent. But why the hell is she going through my clothes? It's usually the other way around.

'Have you told anyone?' Christian's voice is like a silk glove.

'No! Of course not,' Kate snaps, affronted. Christian nods and appears to relax. He turns and heads toward the fireplace. Wordlessly Kate and I watch as he picks up a lighter from the mantelpiece, sets fire to the e-mail, and releases it, letting it float afire slowly into the grate until it is no more. The silence in the room is oppressive.

'Not even Elliot?' I ask, turning my attention back to Kate.

'No one,' Kate says emphatically, and for the first time she looks puzzled and hurt. 'I just want to know you're okay, Ana,' she whispers.

'I'm fine, Kate. More than fine. Please, Christian and I are good, really good—this is old news. Please ignore it.'

'Ignore it?' she says. 'How can I ignore that? What's he done to you?' And her green eyes are so full of heartfelt concern.

'He hasn't done anything to me, Kate. Honestly—I'm good.'

She blinks at me.

'Really?' she asks.

Christian wraps an arm around me and draws me close, not taking his eyes off Kate.

'Ana has consented to be my wife, Katherine,' he says quietly.

'Wife!' Kate squeaks, her eyes widening in disbelief.

'We're getting married. We're going to announce our engagement this evening,' he says.

'Oh!' Kate gapes at me. She's stunned. 'I leave you alone for sixteen days, and this happens? It's very sudden. So yesterday, when I said—' She gazes at me, lost. 'Where does that e-mail fit into all this?'

'It doesn't, Kate. Forget it—please. I love him and he loves me. Don't do this. Don't ruin his party and our night,' I whisper. She blinks and unexpectedly her eyes are shining with tears.

'No. Of course I won't. You're okay?' She wants reassurance.

'I've never been happier,' I whisper. She reaches

610

forward and grabs my hand regardless of Christian's arm wrapped around me.

'You really are okay?' she asks hopefully.

'Yes.' I grin at her, my joy returning. She's back onside. She smiles at me, my happiness reflecting back on her. I step out of Christian's hold, and she hugs me suddenly.

'Oh, Ana—I was so worried when I read this. I didn't know what to think. Will you explain it to me?' she whispers.

'One day, not now.'

'Good. I won't tell anyone. I love you so much, Ana, like my own sister. I just thought . . . I didn't know what to think. I'm sorry. If you're happy, then I'm happy.' She looks directly at Christian and repeats her apology. He nods at her, his eyes glacial, and his expression does not change. Oh, shit, he's still mad.

'I really am sorry. You're right, it's none of my business,' she whispers to me.

There's a knock on the door that startles Kate and I apart. Grace pokes her head around.

'Everything okay, darling?' she asks Christian.

'Everything's fine, Mrs. Grey,' Kate says immediately.

'Fine, Mom,' Christian says.

'Good.' Grace enters. 'Then you won't mind if I give my son a birthday hug.' She beams at both of us. He hugs her tightly and thaws immediately.

'Happy birthday, darling,' she says softly, closing her eyes in his embrace. 'I'm so glad you're still with us.'

'Mom, I'm fine.' Christian smiles down at her. She pulls back, looks at him closely, and grins.

'I'm so happy for you,' she says and caresses his

611

face.

He grins at her—his thousand-megawatt smile.

She knows! When did he tell her?

'Well, kids, if you've all finished your tête-à-tête, there's a throng of people here to check that you really are in one piece, Christian, and to wish you a happy birthday.'

'I'll be right there.'

Grace glances anxiously at Kate and me and seems reassured by our smiles. She winks at me as she holds the door open for us. Christian holds out his hand to me and I take it.

'Christian, I really do apologize,' Kate says humbly. Humble Kate is something to behold. Christian nods at her, and we follow her out.

In the hallway, I gaze anxiously up at Christian. 'Does your mother know about us?'

'Yes.'

'Oh.' And to think our evening could have been derailed by the tenacious Miss Kavanagh. I shudder at the thought—the ramifications of Christian's lifestyle revealed to all.

'Well, that was an interesting start to the evening.' I smile sweetly at him. He glances down at me—and it's back, his amused look. Thank heavens.

'As ever, Miss Steele, you have a gift for understatement.' He raises my hand to his lips and kisses my knuckles as we walk into the living room to a sudden, spontaneous, and deafening round of applause.

Crap. How many people are here?

I scan the room quickly: all the Greys, Ethan with Mia, Dr. Flynn and his wife, I assume. There's Mac from the boat, a tall, handsome African

American—I remember seeing him in Christian's office the first time I met Christian—Mia's bitchy friend Lily, two women I don't recognize at all, and . . . *oh no*. My heart sinks. *That* woman . . . Mrs. Robinson.

Gretchen materializes with a tray of champagne. She's wearing a low-cut black dress, hair in an updo instead of pigtails, flushing and fluttering her eyelashes at Christian. The applause dies down, and Christian squeezes my hand as all eyes turn to him expectantly.

'Thank you, everyone. Looks like I'll need one of these.' He grabs two drinks off Gretchen's tray and gives her a brief smile. I think Gretchen's going to expire or swoon. He hands a glass to me.

Christian raises his glass to the rest of the room, and immediately everyone surges forward. Leading the charge is the evil woman in black. Does she ever wear any other color?

'Christian, I was so worried.' Elena gives him a brief hug and kisses both his cheeks. He doesn't let me go despite the fact I try to free my hand.

'I'm good, Elena,' Christian mutters coolly.

'Why didn't you call me?' Her plea is desperate, her eyes searching his.

'I've been busy.'

'Didn't you get my messages?'

Christian shifts uncomfortably and pulls me closer, putting his arm around me. His face remains impassive as he regards Elena. She can no longer ignore me, so she nods politely in my direction.

'Ana,' she purrs. 'You look lovely, dear.'

'Elena,' I purr back. 'Thank you.'

I catch Grace's eye. She frowns, watching the three of us.

'Elena, I need to make an announcement,' Christian says, eyeing her dispassionately.

Her clear blue eyes cloud. 'Of course.' She fakes a smile and steps back.

'Everyone,' Christian calls. He waits for a moment until the buzz in the room dies down and all eyes are once more on him.

'Thank you for coming today. I have to say I was expecting a quiet family dinner, so this is a pleasant surprise.' He stares pointedly at Mia, who grins and gives him a little wave. Christian shakes his head in exasperation and continues.

'Ros and I'—he acknowledges the red-haired woman standing nearby with a small bubbly blonde—'we had a close call yesterday.'

Oh, that's the Ros that works with him. She grins and raises her glass to him. He nods back at her.

'So I'm especially glad to be here today to share with all of you my very good news. This beautiful woman'—he glances down at me—'Miss Anastasia Rose Steele, has consented to be my wife, and I'd like you all to be the first to know.'

There are general gasps of astonishment, the odd cheer, and then a round of applause! Jeez—this is really happening. I think I am the color of Kate's dress. Christian grasps my chin, lifts my lips to his, and kisses me quickly.

'You'll soon be mine.'

'I am already,' I whisper.

'Legally,' he mouths at me and gives me a wicked grin.

Lily, who is standing beside Mia, looks crestfallen; Gretchen looks like she's eaten something nasty and bitter. As I glance anxiously around at the assembled crowd, I catch sight of Elena. Her mouth is open. She's stunned—horrified even, and I can't help a small but intense feeling of satisfaction to see her dumbstruck. What the hell is she doing here, anyway?

Carrick and Grace interrupt my uncharitable thoughts, and soon I am being hugged and kissed and passed around by all the Greys.

'Oh, Ana—I am so delighted you're going to be family,' Grace gushes. 'The change in Christian . . . He's . . . happy. I am so thankful to you.' I blush, embarrassed by her exuberance but secretly delighted, too.

'Where is the ring?' exclaims Mia as she embraces me.

'Um . . .' *A ring! Jeez*. I hadn't even thought about a ring. I glance up at Christian.

'We're going to choose one together.' Christian glowers at her.

'Oh, don't look at me like that, Grey!' she scolds him, then wraps her arms around him. 'I'm so thrilled for you, Christian,' she says. She's the only person I know who is not intimidated by the Grey glower. It has me quailing . . . Well, it certainly used to.

'When will you get married? Have you set a date?' She beams up at Christian.

He shakes his head, his exasperation palpable. 'No idea, and no we haven't. Ana and I need to discuss all that,' he says irritably.

'I hope you have a big wedding—here,' she beams enthusiastically, ignoring his caustic tone.

'We'll probably fly to Vegas tomorrow,' he growls at her, and he's rewarded with a full-on Mia Grey pouty grimace. Rolling his eyes, he turns to Elliot, who gives him his second bear hug in as many days.

'Way to go, bro.' He claps Christian's back.

The response from the room is overwhelming, and it's a few minutes before I find myself back beside Christian with Dr. Flynn. Elena seems to have disappeared, and Gretchen is sullenly refilling champagne glasses.

Beside Dr. Flynn is a striking young woman with long, dark, almost black hair, impressive cleavage, and lovely hazel eyes.

'Christian,' says Flynn, holding out his hand. Christian shakes it gladly.

'John. Rhian.' He kisses the dark-haired woman on her cheek. She's petite and pretty.

'Glad you're still with us, Christian. My life would be most dull—and penurious—without you.'

Christian smirks.

'John!' Rhian scolds, much to Christian's amusement.

'Rhian, this is Anastasia, my fiancée. Ana, this is John's wife.'

'Delighted to meet the woman who has finally captured Christian's heart.' Rhian smiles kindly at me.

'Thank you,' I mutter, embarrassed again.

'That was one googly you bowled there, Christian,' Dr. Flynn shakes his head in amused disbelief. Christian frowns at him.

'John—you and your cricket metaphors.' Rhian rolls her eyes. 'Congratulations to the pair of you and happy birthday, Christian. What a wonderful birthday present.' She smiles broadly at me.

I had no idea Dr. Flynn would be here, or Elena. It's a shock, and I rack my brains to see if I have anything to ask him, but a birthday party hardly seems the appropriate venue for a psychiatric consultation.

For a few minutes we make small talk. Rhian is a stay-at-home mom with two young boys. I deduce that she is the reason Dr. Flynn practices in the United States.

'She's good, Christian, responding well to treatment. Another couple of weeks and we can consider an outpatient program.' Dr. Flynn's and Christian's voices are low, but I can't help listening in, rather rudely tuning out Rhian.

'So it's all playdates and diapers right now . . .'

'That must take up your time.' I flush, turning my attention back to Rhian, who laughs sweetly. I know Christian and Flynn are discussing Leila.

'Ask her something for me,' Christian murmurs.

'So, what do you do, Anastasia?'

'Ana, please. I work in publishing.'

Christian and Dr. Flynn lower their voices further; it's so frustrating. But they stop when we're joined by the two women I didn't recognize earlier—Ros and the bubbly blonde whom Christian introduces as her partner, Gwen.

Ros is charming, and I soon discover they live almost opposite Escala. She is full of praise for Christian's piloting skills. It was her first time in *Charlie Tango*, and she says she wouldn't hesitate to go again. She's one of the few women I've met who isn't dazzled by him . . . well, the reason is obvious.

Gwen is giggly with a wry sense of humor, and Christian seems extraordinarily at ease with both of them. He knows them well. They don't discuss work, but I can tell that Ros is one smart woman who can easily keep up with him. She also has a great, throaty, too-many-cigarettes laugh.

Grace interrupts our leisurely conversation to inform everyone that dinner is being served buffet-style in the Grey kitchen. Slowly the guests make their way toward the back of the house.

Mia collars me in the hallway. In her pale pink, frothy babydoll dress and killer heels, she towers over me like a Christmas tree fairy. She's holding two cocktail glasses.

'Ana,' she hisses conspiratorially. I glance up at Christian, who releases me with a best-of-luck-I-find-her-impossible-to-deal-with-too look, and I sneak into the dining room with her.

'Here,' she says mischievously. 'This is one of my dad's special lemon martinis—much nicer than champagne.' She hands me a glass and watches anxiously while I take a tentative sip.

'Hmm . . . delicious. But strong.' What does she want? Is she trying to get me drunk?

'Ana, I need some advice. And I can't ask Lily—she's so judgmental about everything.' Mia rolls her eyes then grins at me. 'She is so jealous of you. I think she was hoping one day that she and Christian might get together.' Mia bursts out laughing at the absurdity, and I quail inside.

This is something I will have to contend with for a long time—other women wanting my man. I push the unwelcome thought out of my head and distract myself with the matter in hand. I take another sip of my martini.

'I'll try and help. Fire away.'

'As you know, Ethan and I met recently, thanks to you.' She beams at me.

'Yes.' Where the hell is she going with this?

'Ana—he doesn't want to date me.' She pouts.

'Oh.' I blink at her, stunned, and I think, *Maybe*

618

he's just not that into you.

'Look, that sounded all wrong. He doesn't want to date because his sister is going out with my brother. You know—he thinks it's all kind of incestuous. But I know he likes me. What can I do?'

'Oh, I see,' I mutter, trying to buy myself some time. What can I say? 'Can you agree to be friends and give it some time? I mean you've only just met him.'

She cocks her eyebrow.

'Look, I know I've only really just met Christian but . . .' I frown, not sure what I want to say. 'Mia, this is something you and Ethan have to work out together. I would try the friendship route.'

Mia grins.

'You've learned that look from Christian.'

I flush. 'If you want advice, ask Kate. She may have some insight as to how her brother feels.'

'You think?' Mia asks.

'Yes.' I smile encouragingly.

'Cool. Thanks, Ana.' She gives me another hug and scuttles excitedly—and impressively, given her high heels—to the door, no doubt off to bother Kate. I take another sip of my martini, and I'm about to follow her when I am stopped in my tracks.

Elena breezes into the room, her face taut, set in grim, angry determination. She closes the door quietly behind her and scowls at me.

Oh, crap.

'Ana,' she sneers.

I summon all my self-possession, slightly fuzzy from two glasses of champagne and the lethal cocktail I hold in my hand. I think the blood has drained from my face, but I marshal both my subconscious and my inner goddess in order to

619

appear as calm and as unflappable as I can.

'Elena.' My voice is small, but steady—despite my dry mouth. Why does this woman freak me out so much? And what does she want now?

'I would offer you my heartfelt congratulations, but I think that would be inappropriate.' Her piercing cold blue eyes stare frostily into mine, filled with loathing.

'I neither need nor want your congratulations, Elena. I'm surprised and disappointed to see you here.'

She arches an eyebrow. I think she's impressed.

'I wouldn't have thought of you as a worthy adversary, Anastasia. But you surprise me at every turn.'

'I haven't thought of you at all,' I lie, coolly. Christian would be proud. 'Now if you'll excuse me, I have much better things to do than waste my time with you.'

'Not so fast, missy,' she hisses, leaning against the door, effectively blocking it. 'What on earth do you think you're doing, consenting to marry Christian? If you think for one minute you can make him happy, you're very much mistaken.'

'What I'm consenting to do with Christian is none of your concern.' I smile with sarcastic sweetness. She ignores me.

'He has needs—needs you cannot possibly begin to satisfy,' she gloats.

'What do you know of his needs?' I snarl. My sense of indignation flares brightly, burning inside me as adrenaline surges through my body. How dare this fucking bitch preach to me? 'You're nothing but a sick child molester, and if it were up to me, I'd toss you into the seventh circle of hell and walk away smiling. Now get out of my way—or do I have to make you?'

'You're making a big mistake here, lady.' She shakes a long, skinny, finely manicured finger at me. 'How dare you judge our lifestyle? You know nothing, and you have no idea what you're getting yourself into. And if you think he's going to be happy with a mousy little gold digger like you . . .'

That's it! I throw the rest of my lemon martini in her face, drenching her.

'Don't you dare tell me what I'm getting myself into!' I shout at her. 'When will you learn? It's none of your goddamned business!'

She gapes at me, horror struck, wiping the sticky drink off her face. I think she's about to lunge at me, but she's suddenly shunted forward as the door opens.

Christian is standing in the doorway. It takes him a nanosecond to assess the situation—me ashen and shaking, her soaked and livid. His lovely face darkens and contorts with anger as he comes to stand between us.

'What the fuck are you doing, Elena?' he says, his voice glacial and laced with menace.

She blinks up at him. 'She's not right for you, Christian,' she whispers.

'What?' he shouts, startling both of us. I can't see his face but his whole body has tensed, and he radiates animosity.

'How the fuck do you know what's right for me?'

'You have needs, Christian,' she says her voice softer.

'I've told you before—this is none of your fucking business,' he roars. Oh crap—Very Angry Christian has reared his not-so-ugly head. People

621

are going to hear.

'What is this?' He pauses, glaring at her. 'Do you think it's you? You? You think you're right for me?' His voice is softer but drips contempt, and suddenly I don't want to be here. I don't want to witness this intimate encounter. I'm intruding. But I'm stuck—my limbs unwilling to move.

Elena swallows and seems to draw herself upright. Her stance changes subtly, becoming more commanding, and she steps toward him.

'I was the best thing that ever happened to you,' she hisses arrogantly at him. 'Look at you now. One of the richest, most successful entrepreneurs in the United States—controlled, driven—you need nothing. You are master of your universe.'

He steps back as if he's been struck and gapes at her in outraged disbelief.

'You loved it, Christian, don't try and kid yourself. You were on the road to self-destruction, and I saved you from that, saved you from a life behind bars. Believe me, baby, that's where you would have ended up. I taught you everything you know, everything you need.'

Christian blanches, staring at her in horror. When he speaks, his voice is low and incredulous.

'You taught me how to fuck, Elena. But it's empty, like you. No wonder Linc left.'

Bile rises in my mouth. I should not be here. But I'm frozen to the spot, morbidly fascinated as they eviscerate each other.

'You never once held me,' Christian whispers. 'You never once said you loved me.'

She narrows her eyes. 'Love is for fools, Christian.'

'Get out of my house.' Grace's implacable,

furious voice startles us. Three heads swing rapidly to where Grace stands on the threshold of the room. She is glaring at Elena, who pales beneath her Saint-Tropez tan.

Time seems suspended as we collectively take a deep gasping breath, and Grace stalks deliberately into the room. Her eyes blaze with fury, never once leaving Elena, until she stands before her. Elena's eyes widen in alarm, and Grace slaps her hard across the face, the sound of the impact resounding off the walls of the dining room.

'Take your filthy paws off my son, you whore, and get out of my house—now!' she hisses through gritted teeth.

Elena clutches her reddening cheek and stares in horror for a moment, shocked and blinking at Grace. Then she hurries from the room, not bothering to close the door behind her.

Grace turns slowly to face Christian and a tense silence settles like a thick blanket over us as Christian and Grace stare at each other. After a beat, Grace speaks.

'Ana, before I hand him over to you, would you mind giving me a minute or two alone with my son?' Her voice is quiet, husky, but oh-so-strong.

'Of course,' I whisper, and exit as quickly as I can, glancing anxiously over my shoulder. But neither of them looks at me as I leave. They continue to stare at each other, their unspoken communication blaringly loud.

In the hallway I am momentarily lost. My heart pounds and my blood races through my veins . . . I feel panicked and out of my depth. Holy fuck, that was heavy and now Grace knows. I can't think what she's going to say to Christian, and I know it's wrong, but I lean against the door trying to listen.

'How long, Christian?' Grace's voice is soft. I can barely hear her.

I cannot hear his reply.

'How old were you?' Her voice is more insistent. 'Tell me. How old were you when this all started?' Again I can't hear Christian.

'Everything okay, Ana?' Ros interrupts me.

'Yes. Fine. Thank you. I . . .'

Ros smiles. 'I'm just going to get my purse. I need a cigarette.'

For a brief moment, I contemplate joining her.

'I'm off to the bathroom.' I need to gather my wits and my thoughts, to process what I've just witnessed and heard. Upstairs seems the safest place to be on my own. I watch Ros stroll into the drawing room, and I bolt two stairs at a time to the second floor, then up to the third. There's only one place I want to be.

I open the door to Christian's childhood bedroom and shut it behind me, taking a huge gulping breath. Heading for his bed, I flop onto it and stare at the plain white ceiling.

Holy cow. That has to be, without doubt, one of the most excruciating confrontations I've ever had to endure, and now I feel numb. My fiancé and his ex-lover—no would-be bride should have to see that. Having said that, part of me is glad she's revealed her true self, and that I was there to bear witness.

My thoughts turn to Grace. Poor Grace, to hear all that. I clutch one of Christian's pillows. She'll have overheard that Christian and Elena had an affair—but not the nature of it. Thank heavens. I groan.

What am I doing? Perhaps the evil witch had a point.

No, I refuse to believe that. She's so cold and cruel. I shake my head. She's wrong. I am right for Christian. I am what he needs. And in a moment of stunning clarity, I don't question *how* he's lived his life until recently—but *why*. His reasons for doing what he's done to countless girls—I don't even want to know how many. The how isn't wrong. They were all adults. They were all—how did Flynn put it?—in safe, sane, consensual relationships. It's the why. The why was wrong. The why was from his place of darkness.

I close my eyes and drape my arm over them. But now he's moved on, left it behind, and we are both in the light. I'm dazzled by him, and he by me. We can guide each other. A thought occurs to me. *Shit!* A gnawing, insidious thought and I'm in the one place where I can lay this ghost to rest. I sit up. Yes, I must do this.

Shakily I get to my feet, kick off my shoes, walk over to his desk, and examine the bulletin board above it. The photos of young Christian are all still there—more poignant than ever, as I think of the spectacle I've just witnessed between him and Mrs. Robinson. And there in the corner is the small black-and-white photo—his mother, the crack whore.

I switch on the desk lamp and focus the light on her picture. I don't even know her name. She looks so much like him, but younger and sadder, and all I feel, looking at her sorrowful face, is compassion. I try to see the similarities between her face and mine. I squint at the picture, getting really, really close, and see none. Except maybe our hair, but I think hers is lighter than mine. I don't look like her at all. It's a relief.

My subconscious tuts at me, arms crossed, glaring over her half-moon glasses. *Why are you torturing yourself? You've said yes. You've made your bed.* I purse my lips at her. Yes I have, gladly so. I want to lie in that bed with Christian for the rest of my life. My inner goddess, sitting in the lotus position, smiles serenely. Yes. I've made the right decision.

I must find him—Christian will be worried. I have no idea how long I've been in his room; he'll think that I've fled. I roll my eyes as I contemplate his overreaction. I hope that he and Grace have finished. I shudder to think what else she might have said to him.

I meet Christian as he climbs the stairs to the second floor, looking for me. His face is strained and weary—not the carefree Fifty I arrived with. As I stand on the landing, he stops on the top stair so that we are eye to eye.

'Hi,' he says cautiously.

'Hi,' I answer warily.

'I was worried—'

'I know,' I interrupt him. 'I'm sorry—I couldn't face the festivities. I just had to get away, you know. To think.' Reaching up, I caress his face. He closes his eyes and leans his face into my hand.

'And you thought you'd do that in my room?'

'Yes.'

He reaches for my hand and pulls me into an embrace, and I go willingly into his arms, my favorite place in the whole world. He smells of fresh laundry, body wash, and Christian—the most calming and arousing scent on the planet. He

626

inhales with his nose in my hair.

'I'm sorry you had to endure all that.'

'It's not your fault, Christian. Why was she here?' He gazes down at me, and his mouth curls apologetically.

'She's a family friend.'

I try not to react. 'Not anymore. How's your mom?'

'Mom is pretty fucking mad at me right now. I'm really glad you're here, and that we're in the middle of a party. Otherwise I might be breathing my last.'

'That bad, huh?'

He nods, his eyes serious, and I sense his bewilderment at her reaction.

'Can you blame her?' My voice is quiet, cajoling.

He hugs me tightly and he seems uncertain, processing his thoughts.

Finally he answers. 'No.'

Whoa! Breakthrough. 'Can we sit?' I ask.

'Sure. Here?'

I nod and we both sit at the top of the stairs.

'So, how do you feel?' I ask, anxiously clutching his hand and gazing at his sad, serious face.

He sighs.

'I feel liberated.' He shrugs, then beams—a glorious, carefree Christian smile, and the weariness and strain present moments ago have vanished.

'Really?' I beam back. Wow, I'd crawl over broken glass for that smile.

'Our business relationship is over. Done.'

I frown at him. 'Will you liquidate the salon business?'

He snorts. 'I'm not that vindictive, Anastasia,' he admonishes me. 'No. I'll gift them to her. I'll talk to my lawyer Monday. I owe her that much.'

I arch an eyebrow at him. 'No more Mrs. Robinson?' His mouth twists in amusement and he shakes his head.

'Gone.'

I grin.

'I'm sorry you lost a friend.'

He shrugs then smirks. 'Are you?'

'No,' I confess, flushing.

'Come.' He stands and offers me his hand. 'Let's join the party in our honor. I might even get drunk.'

'Do you get drunk?' I ask as I take his hand.

'Not since I was a wild teenager.' We walk down the stairs.

'Have you eaten?' he asks.

Oh, crap.

'No.'

'Well you should. From the look and smell of Elena, that was one of my father's lethal cocktails you threw on her.' He gazes at me, trying and failing to keep the amusement off his face.

'Christian, I—'

He holds up his hand.

'No arguing, Anastasia. If you're going to drink—and toss alcohol on my exes—you need to eat. It's rule number one. I believe we've already had that discussion after our first night together.'

Oh yes. The Heathman.

Back in the hallway, he pauses to caress my face, his fingers skimming my jaw.

'I lay awake for hours and watched you sleep,' he murmurs. 'I might have loved you even then.'

Oh.

He leans down and kisses me softly, and I melt everywhere, all the tension of the last hour or so seeping languidly from my body.

'Eat,' he whispers.

'Okay,' I acquiesce because right now I'd probably do anything for him. Taking my hand, he leads me toward the kitchen where the party is in full swing.

*   *   *

'Good night, John, Rhian.'

'Congratulations again, Ana. You two will be just fine.' Dr. Flynn smiles kindly at us, standing arm in arm in the hallway as he and Rhian take their leave.

'Good night.'

Christian closes the door and shakes his head. He gazes down at me, his eyes suddenly bright with excitement.

What's this?

'Just the family left. I think my mother has had too much to drink.' Grace is singing karaoke on some game console in the family room. Kate and Mia are giving her a run for her money.

'Do you blame her?' I smirk at him, trying to keep the atmosphere between us light. I succeed.

'Are you smirking at me, Miss Steele?'

'I am.'

'It's been quite a day.'

'Christian, recently, every day with you has been quite a day.' My voice is sardonic.

He shakes his head. 'Fair point well made, Miss Steele. Come—I want to show you something.' Taking my hand, he leads me through the house to the kitchen where Carrick, Ethan, and Elliot are talking Mariners, drinking the last of the cocktails, and eating leftovers.

'Off for a stroll?' Elliot teases suggestively as we make our way through the French doors. Christian ignores him. Carrick frowns at Elliot, shaking his head in a silent rebuke.

As we make our way up the steps to the lawn, I take off my shoes. The half moon shines brightly over the bay. It's brilliant, casting everything in myriad shades of gray as the lights of Seattle twinkle in the distance. The lights of the boathouse are on, a soft glowing beacon in the cool cast of the moon.

'Christian, I'd like to go to church tomorrow.'

'Oh?'

'I prayed you'd come back alive and you did. It's the least I could do.'

'Okay.'

We wander hand in hand in a relaxed silence for a few moments. Then something occurs to me.

'Where are you going to put the photos José took of me?'

'I thought we might put them in the new house.'

'You bought it?'

He stops to stare at me, and his voice full of concern. 'Yes. I thought you liked it.'

'I do. When did you buy it?'

'Yesterday morning. Now we need to decide what to do with it,' he murmurs, relieved.

'Don't knock it down. Please. It's such a lovely house. It just needs some tender loving care.'

Christian glances at me and smiles. 'Okay. I'll talk to Elliot. He knows a good architect; she did some work on my place in Aspen. He can do the remodeling.'

I snort, suddenly remembering the last time we crossed the lawn under the moonlight to the boathouse. Oh, perhaps that's what we're going to do now. I grin.

'What?'

'I remember the last time you took me to the boathouse.'

Christian chuckles quietly. 'Oh, that was fun. In fact . . .' He suddenly stops and scoops me over his shoulder, and I squeal, though we don't have far to go.

'You were really angry, if I remember correctly,' I gasp.

'Anastasia, I'm always really angry.'

'No, you're not.'

He swats my behind as he stops outside the wooden door. He slides me down his body back to the ground and takes my head in his hands.

'No, not anymore.' Leaning down, he kisses me, hard. When he pulls away, I'm breathless and desire is racing around my body.

He gazes down at me, and in the glow of the strip of light coming from inside the boathouse, I can see he's anxious. My anxious man, not a white knight or a dark knight, but a man—a beautiful, not-quite-so-fucked-up man—whom I love. I reach up and caress his face, running my fingers through his sideburns and along his jaw to his chin, then let my index finger touch his lips. He relaxes.

'I've something to show you in here,' he murmurs and opens the door.

The harsh light of the fluorescents illuminates the impressive motor launch in the dock, bobbing gently on the dark water. There's a rowboat beside it.

'Come.' Christian takes my hand and leads me up the wooden stairs. Opening the door at the top, he steps aside to let me in.

My mouth drops to the floor. The attic is unrecognizable. The room is filled with flowers . . . there are flowers everywhere. Someone has created a magical bower of beautiful wild meadow flowers mixed with glowing Christmas lights and miniature lanterns that glow soft and pale all around the room.

My face whips around to meet his, and he's gazing at me, his expression unreadable. He shrugs.

'You wanted hearts and flowers,' he murmurs.

I blink at him, not quite believing what I'm seeing.

'You have my heart.' And he waves toward the room.

'And here are the flowers,' I whisper, completing his sentence. 'Christian, it's lovely.' I can't think of what else to say. My heart is in my mouth as tears prick my eyes.

Tugging my hand, he pulls me into the room, and before I know it, he's sinking to one knee in front of me. *Holy hell . . . I did not expect this!* I stop breathing.

From his inside jacket pocket he produces a ring and gazes up at me, his eyes bright gray and raw, full of emotion.

'Anastasia Steele. I love you. I want to love, cherish, and protect you for the rest of my life. Be mine. Always. Share my life with me. Marry me.'

I blink down at him as my tears fall. My Fifty, my man. I love him so, and all I can say as the tidal wave of emotion hits me is, 'Yes.'

He grins, relieved, and slowly slides the ring on my finger. It's beautiful, an oval diamond in a platinum ring. *Whoa—it's big . . .* Big, yet simple and stunning in its simplicity.

'Oh, Christian,' I sob, suddenly overwhelmed with joy, and I join him on my knees, my fingers fisting in his hair as I kiss him, kiss him with all my heart and soul. I kiss this beautiful man, who loves me as I love him; and he wraps his arms around me, his hands moving to my hair, his mouth on mine. I know deep down I will always be his, and he will always be mine. We've come so far together, we have so far to go, but we are made for each other. We are meant to be.

~ § ~   ~ § ~   ~ § ~

The cigarette end glows brightly in the darkness as he takes a deep pull. He blows the smoke out in a long exhale, finishing with two smoke rings that dissolve in front of him, pale and ghostly in the moonlight. He shifts in his seat, bored, and takes a quick shot of cheap bourbon from a bottle wrapped in shabby brown paper before resting it back between his thighs.

He can't believe he's still on the trail. His mouth twists in a sardonic sneer. The helicopter had been a rash and bold move. One of the most exhilarating things he'd ever done in his life. But to no avail. He rolls his eyes ironically. *Who would have thought the son of a bitch could actually fly the fucker?*

He snorts.

They have underestimated him. If Grey thought for one minute he'd go whimpering quietly into the dusk, that prick didn't know jack shit.

It had been the same all his life. People constantly underestimating him—just a man who reads books. Fuck that! A man with a photographic memory who reads books. Oh, the things he's learned, the things he knows. He snorts again. *Yeah, about you, Grey. The things I know about you.*

Not bad for a kid from the gutter end of Detroit.

Not bad for the kid who won a scholarship to Princeton.

Not bad for the kid who worked his ass off through college and got into publishing.

And now all of that's fucked, fucked because of Grey and his little bitch. He scowls at the house as if it represents everything he despises. But there's nothing doing. The only drama had been the stacked, blonde broad in black, teetering down the driveway in tears before she climbed into the white CLK and fucked off.

He chuckles mirthlessly, then winces. Fuck, his ribs. Still sore from the swift kicking Grey's henchman delivered.

He replays the scene in his mind. *'You fucking touch Miss Steele again, I'll fucking kill you.'*

That motherfucker will get it good, too. Yeah— get what's coming to him.

He settles back in his seat. *Looks like it's going to be a long night.* He'll stay, watch, and wait. He takes another drag off his Marlboro Red. His chance will come. His chance will come soon.

19.99